Terrance Glasscock

The Soulfast Reprisal

Published by Glorybound Publishing, Charleston, South Carolina
1st Ed
Published in the United States of America
ISBN 978-1-60789-383-7 1-60789-383-5
Library of Congress Cataloging-in-Publication data is available on file.
Glasscock, Terrance 1948-

The Soulfast Reprisal/Terrance Glasscock
Includes biographical reference.

1. Fiction 2. Historical Fiction

I. Title

www.terranceglasscockbooks.com
www.gloryboundpublishing.com

The Soulfast Reprisal

TERRANCE GLASSCOCK

Glorybound Publishing
Charleston, South Carolina USA
2026

The Soulfast Trilogy

Book series by
Terrance Glasscock

The Soulfast *– First of the Soulfast Trilogy*

The Soulfast follows two modern-day lovers on a daring quest to recover an ancient pagan relic rumored to wield the power to rewrite history. This artifact, a ring, holds the promise of reversing time and fulfilling a forbidden love denied nine centuries ago. Their journey takes them from the vibrant streets of Brahmin Boston to the hallowed halls of Oxford, through Jerusalem's sacred heart, and into the shadowy labyrinths of Cairo. Every step closer to the relic, they encounter escalating danger, pursued by relentless enemies determined to stop them. The lovers' fate is ultimately decided in the snow-draped, ancient forests of Wales, where the forces of nature herself decide their fate. Rich with vivid historical detail and unrelenting suspense, *The Soulfast* explores the timeless power of love and the extraordinary lengths to which people will go to protect it. Ultimately, it reveals how Nature's mystic aim may deny her own inviolate laws to shape our destiny.

The Soulfast: Book of Choices *– Tristan and Sabina*

The second installment of *The Soulfast Trilogy* delves into the story of Tristan and Sabina, set against the backdrop of 12th-century England. As promised, Nature reunites the devoted couple, granting them the chance to share a full life. However, the Mother of Creation entrusts them with a vital mission—one that holds the key to England's very survival.

She grants them a remarkable gift: a book from the future—*The Book of Choices*. This mysterious tome is adorned with strange symbols, hieroglyphs, morphemes, and an indecipherable language, delivering cryptic messages about pivotal decisions that must be made. Yet it offers no hint as to who will make these choices or what consequences will follow from each path.

As the couple examines the mysterious volume, Sabina suddenly finds herself able to decipher the first page—the first Choice, although the rest remain shrouded in mystery. But they soon discover that as each

Choice is made, the next page—the next Choice, unveils itself to her.

The Choices grow increasingly significant with each new revelation, carrying far-reaching consequences. It quickly becomes evident that these decisions will shape the very course of English history. Tristan and Sabina must race against time to interpret each Choice and identify the individual destined to make it. Failure would mean the loss of England's independence and its very identity.

***The Soulfast Reprisal**: Simon and Sabrina*

Catherine, once the radiant fiancée of Simon, a globally renowned scholar of ancient mythology, lost everything to her own greed and jealousy. Their engagement collapsed after her betrayal, and fate completed her undoing when the Soulfast ritual reunited Simon with Sabrina, the woman destined to be his true soulmate. As Simon's life flourished with love and purpose, Catherine's unraveled. Stripped of her prestigious position at the Museum of Fine Arts in Boston, she was left disgraced, isolated, and consumed by a quiet, corrosive resentment.

Now, she wants revenge.

In a chilling act of calculated malice, Catherine kidnaps Sabina, the five-year-old daughter of Simon and Sabrina's closest friends, Drew and Lauren, and vanishes with her to a remote and nearly inaccessible island in the South Atlantic, home to only a handful of inhabitants. From this distant refuge, she delivers her ultimatum: Simon must destroy his own legacy.

Her demands are as ruthless as they are precise. He must leave his teaching position, publicly denounce his groundbreaking research as plagiarism, surrender the prestigious Wolfson Prize awarded to him, and stand by as his reputation collapses before the world.

Each demand arrives with a cryptic clue, a breadcrumb pointing toward Catherine's hidden location. With every message, the pressure mounts, forcing Simon to confront an impossible choice between the truth that defines him and the life of an innocent child.

In the end, the question is not only how far Catherine will go, but how much Simon is willing to sacrifice to stop her.

Dedication

To my beloved grandchildren

—Austin, Jaden, Lily, Ady, and Gabi—

You are the brightest chapters of my life.

This book is for you, written with pride, with joy,

and with a love that only grows stronger with time.

Dedication

[illegible]

Prologue

Wales — The Night of the Winter Solstice

The trees parted to reveal a broad, circular clearing, a perfect circle in the forest's heart. The ground, level but thickly covered in shimmering snow, lay undisturbed by wind or movement. All was still save for the crackling and hissing of a bonfire roaring in the center. Soft, intricate snowflakes floated from the sky, drifting gently like spirits seeking rest. Beyond the edge of the clearing, the distant murmur of a mountain stream could be heard, flowing steadily toward the valley below.

Simon and Sabrina stood side by side, their backs warmed by the fire as they faced Emryn. The others gathered quietly to the side, observing. Lauren stood just behind Sabrina, like a bridesmaid at a wedding, while Drew mirrored her, standing behind Simon. Although neither participated in the ceremony, Emryn had allowed them to witness the sacred moment.

Before beginning, Emryn's gaze settled on the couple. "Before we proceed, I must ask," he said, his voice rich and deep with the weight of the occasion. "Are you both unwavering in your covenant to bind your souls in eternal love until time surrenders all claims to the future?"

Their response was immediate, a unified "Yes."

Emryn nodded, his eyes, a striking blue, glinting in the firelight. "You are both children of Nature," he began, his tone somber and deliberate. "As such, you are connected by invisible bonds to the Unknown Power that governs all. The vows you intend to exchange on this most sacred night must not be spoken lightly." He paused, looking each of them in the eye to ensure they understood the weight of his words.

"The Soulfast is Nature's most hallowed ritual. It may only be invoked under the rarest and most extraordinary circumstances. By seeking this union, you call upon Nature herself to intervene, to set aside her unyielding order."

"Before we begin, I must ask you to remove your clothing. Nothing made by the hands of man may separate you."

They had never seen each other's bodies but obeyed without hesitation. Lauren and Drew accepted the clothing and left their side. The raging fire radiated a golden glow onto their bodies.

Sabrina's hair flared with gilded brilliance. Her petite body confirmed the perfection her clothed form had promised. Her elegant breasts, full for her stature, stood firm and alert, her red nipples challenging each snowflake privileged to fall upon them. Her tiny waist sloped into an inverted valentine in the back. The airy cornsilk between her legs already glistened with tiny beads of passion.

Simon stood rigid, his body fit and youthful. The rippling firelight caressed the definition of his able physique. His manhood pulsed as he gazed at the naked perfection before him. But even when confronted with Sabrina's flawless form, her sparkling eyes arrested him more. He searched their depths for immortality. Would he someday plunge into them and never surface?

Emryn let the silence settle, letting the gravity of what they were about to undertake sink in fully. The stillness, broken only by the fire and the stream, magnified the moment's significance.

Emryn spoke once more, his voice steady and soft. "Please, kneel before the fire and face each other."

They obeyed without hesitation.

"Now, take each other's hands as a tender expression of your love," he instructed.

The tears they had held back until now began to flow. Their lips trembled, and with tears tracing paths down their cheeks, they gently clasped each other's hands.

Emryn's voice echoed with reverence. "The invocation of the Soulfast knows neither beginning nor end. It was born with time itself and shall depart only when time abandons humanity. Be aware: the Soulfast is to be invoked. Let none here stand against their will. To enter this covenant with even the slightest shadow of doubt will bring eternal sorrow."

Then, as occurred nearly a thousand years before, Emeryn invoked earth, fire, wind, and water to witness the Soulfast.

Snow continued to fall gently onto their naked bodies as if blessing their union.

Malek emerged silently from the shadows, holding a white leather pouch fastened with delicate gold threads. Handing it to Emryn, he stepped back. Emryn untied the pouch and let two simple gold rings drop into his palm.

Sabrina's gaze lingered on the rings, noting their plainness. They were not hers. Emryn smiled knowingly.

"There are only two rings, dear one," he explained. "Nature guides them through the ages, as she guides us all. When they find their chosen souls, they are remade."

Resting the rings in his palm, he continued. "These are the first rings, Nature's own. They hold a power lost to humankind, woven from ageless wisdom. It is the power to grant a Soulfast, binding two souls eternally in the endless circle of time."

He placed a ring into each of their hands. "Beloved ones, with the exchange of these sacred orbits, your souls shall transcend your earthly years. Your essence will not die but live in the hearts of two others."

"In this way, the Soulfast binds your love to the rhythm of time," Emryn continued, his voice calm yet reverent. "When you exchange these sacred rings, your souls will embark on a journey that transcends your mortal lives. Separated by this act, your souls will wander through time and space, carrying the grief of separation, until they reunite once more when time relents. In that moment, the love that was once denied to you will bloom anew in the hearts of others, just as you now complete the promise that Tristan and Sabina could not."

Emryn paused for a breath, letting the words settle before continuing. "When these sacred rings are exchanged by another pair of lovers, Nature's covenant will be fulfilled. Your souls will finally find their union, and your lives will be renewed. This is Nature's vow to you, sealed by the promises you make tonight. Beyond this, no mortal can know. The mystery of the Soulfast is hidden in the endless enigma of time."

As Simon absorbed these words, a strange sense of familiarity washed over him, as though Emryn had spoken them before, even though the last Soulfast had been invoked nearly a thousand years ago.

"Beloved ones," Emryn's voice grew heavy, "you must now remember the great sacrifice that comes with Nature's promise. Only through unwavering vows of body and spirit will your souls endure beyond this life. Should either of you falter, the Soulfast will be shattered, and your love will be lost for all eternity."

The weight of his words deepened further. "You must never look upon each other again. Even the briefest accidental glance will destroy the bond. Nature will test you relentlessly. Even now, her storm stirs, trying to prevent your parting. But if either of you sees the other after leaving this sacred place, all will be lost."

Tears shone in Emryn's eyes as he asked, "Do you accept this fate freely?"

They both nodded, their voices lost to the gravity of the moment.

"Simon," Emryn said softly, "place Nature's most sacred ring on Sabrina's hand and declare your devotion."

With trembling hands, Simon slid the ring onto Sabrina's finger.

"Simon, do you come before Nature's altar of your own free will to bind your timeless soul to Sabrina, declaring her as your one true and eternal love, pledging your soul to hers for all time?"

"I do," Simon said, his voice unwavering despite the emotion he felt.

"Sabrina," Emryn continued, "place Nature's talisman on Simon's hand and declare your devotion."

Sabrina, her hands shaking slightly, placed the ring on Simon's finger.

“Sabrina, do you come before Nature’s altar of your own free will to bind your timeless soul to Simon, declaring him your true and eternal love and pledging your soul to his for all time?”

“I do,” Sabrina whispered, her voice filled with quiet resolve.

Emryn raised his hands skyward. “May Nature bind your souls together for all eternity.”

As the final words left his lips, the rings ignited in cold, white flames, a radiant star-fire glowing around the sacred bands, Nature’s promise etched into the smooth gold.

“Quod non erat, fit,” Emryn translated, his voice filled with wonder. “That which was not, now becomes. May your souls find joy in future hearts. Now, rise, beloved ones, and share one last embrace—a kiss to seal the bond that will outlast your lives. After this, you must part.”

They rose, their hearts breaking as they embraced one final time, tears blending sorrow with hope.

“Goodbye, my love,” Simon choked out, his voice raw with emotion.

Sabrina smiled softly through her tears. “I’ll find you in the next life,” she whispered.

Then they turned away. Lauren gently guided Sabrina toward Daffodil, where her new garments awaited, while Drew led Simon into the forest.

The Soulfast was complete.

Chapter One

Nature's Promise Kept

Emryn still stood by the fire, his hands folded into his sleeves, motionless as a carved figure set there long before memory. The flames licked upward in restless tongues of amber and blue, snapping softly as sap pockets surrendered with tiny sighs. Sparks broke free and rose, brief and defiant, only to be swallowed by the Stygian sky, a sky so deep and lightless it seemed less an absence of stars than a deliberate erasure of them.

The night pressed close. It smelled of ash and cold earth, of old stone and older secrets. Somewhere beyond the fire's reach, the darkness held its breath.

Then a breeze came, not sudden, but purposeful, as if summoned. It slid through the clearing and worried the edges of the blaze, coaxing the flames into brighter agitation. The fire responded eagerly, flaring and showering incandescent embers upward. They spiraled like living things, a brief constellation of fireflies tracing impossible arcs before vanishing into nothing.

At that, Emryn's head lifted, almost imperceptibly, the movement so slight it might have been mistaken for a trick of the light. His eyes followed the sparks, not with wonder but with recognition, as though they confirmed something he had already known. The fire reflected in his gaze, multiplying itself there, lending his expression a depth that did not belong to the present moment.

A whisper of a smile crossed his face quickly, restrained, and profoundly out of place in the surrounding gloom. It was not a smile of joy, nor even of satisfaction, but of acknowledgment.

The kind shared between old adversaries, or older friends. The kind that suggests patience rewarded, or a long calculation quietly reaching its final term.

The breeze passed. The fire settled back into its steady rhythm. The sky resumed its mute indifference.

Emryn did not move again, but the stillness around him had changed. The night seemed less empty now, as though it had taken note of him at last, and was waiting.

Eustace and Sir Roger stood shoulder to shoulder before the fire, their silhouettes rigid and dark against the trembling light. Neither spoke. Each man stared into the blaze as though it might offer absolution.

Emryn still stood as he had before, hands folded into his sleeves, his posture unaltered. Yet Malek's unease grew. There was a difference, a misalignment between what his eyes reported and what his instincts insisted upon. The firelight touched Emryn differently now, lingering where it had once passed, as though reluctant to leave him. Shadows bent at unfamiliar angles. The space around him felt… attentive.

And yet.

They all sensed a change, undeniable and unsettling, like the moment before a storm when the world pauses and listens to itself. They could not fathom its source, only its presence. Reason offered no purchase. There was no sound, no gesture, no spoken word to anchor the feeling.

The fire cracked sharply, sending a brief scatter of sparks upward.

Their eyes lingered on Emryn. Whatever had shifted had not done so loudly. It had arrived quietly, respectfully even, as though aware it was being observed.

With a sudden, piercing scream that shattered the stillness, Sabrina burst from the vehicle and ran headlong into the clearing. Her boots struck the ground unevenly, her breath coming in ragged gasps, but she did not slow. The fire drew her like a lodestone. She reached it and stopped abruptly, as though an invisible wall had risen before her. Tears streamed freely down her face, unchecked and shining in the firelight, her hands trembling at her sides.

Eustace stiffened at the sound of her cry. His head snapped up, grief momentarily displaced by alarm. He turned just in time to see her reach the fire, and something in his expression broke, an old, protective instinct flaring to life. He took a half-step forward, then stopped himself, as though unsure whether to intervene or bear witness. His mouth opened, but no words came. Whatever this moment was, it did not belong to him.

Sir Roger reacted more slowly, but no less profoundly. His shoulders sagged, the rigid formality draining from him as recognition dawned. He removed his gloves with deliberate care, clutching them tightly in one hand, as if grounding himself against the surge of emotion. His eyes glistened openly now. He did not look at Sabrina at first, but at the fire, as though bracing himself for what must follow. When he finally turned toward her, his face carried a deep, aching sorrow, tinged with helpless resignation. This, he knew, could not be undone.

Lauren followed close behind Sabrina, her voice raw with panic as she ran after her.
"No, Sabrina! No!" she cried. "You cannot look at him!"

The words echoed across the clearing, sharp and desperate. Eustace flinched at them. Sir Roger closed his eyes briefly, as though he already understood their terrible weight.

Sabrina spun around, tears blurring her vision, her face flushed with grief and fierce resolve.
"But I can, Ell," she said, her voice breaking but unyielding. "I can!"

Lauren reached her then and wrapped her arms around her tightly, holding her as though she might vanish if loosened even for a moment. Sabrina collapsed into the embrace, sobbing openly now. Lauren's own breath shuddered as she fought to remain steady, to be the one who did not fall apart.

Over Sabrina's shoulder, Lauren lifted her eyes toward Emryn. They were wide and pleading, stripped of anger or defiance; only a desperate appeal remained. A silent request for mercy. For restraint. For anything that might spare them what was clearly unfolding.

Drew followed her gaze. His jaw clenched hard, the muscles standing out beneath his skin. He felt suddenly furious, not with

Emryn, but with fate itself for allowing such cruelty to wear the mask of inevitability. His fists curled at his sides, nails biting into his palms.

Emryn's smile widened.

It was neither cruel nor mocking. It was something far more puzzling: a smile of fulfillment. Of satisfaction long delayed and now fully realized. Joy flickered in his eyes, warm and unguarded, as though this reunion, this agony, completed a design only he had ever understood.

Drew's breath caught in his chest. "God help us," he murmured, barely audible.

Lauren clutched Sabrina tighter, but her gaze never left Emryn.

And in the firelight, with joy burning as fiercely as the flames themselves, Emryn stood triumphant, as though the night had finally given him exactly what it owed.

Simon had made a headlong rush back to the fire. The fire cast long, wavering shadows across the thawed ground, its heat having carved a raw, steaming circle in the snow. And then Simon saw her.

Sabrina stood there, alive, breathing, joyful.

The sight terrified him.

"No… please no," he cried, the words tumbling out like a reflex learned from loss. His head bowed, shoulders shaking, as if his body still remembered a world where miracles did not happen.

Sabrina turned at the sound of his voice.

The instant she saw him, something bright and tender lit her face. She didn't hesitate. She ran to him, boots splashing through melted snow and mud. She reached him just as he swayed, and her momentum carried them both down onto the wet brown grass beside the fire. The cold soaked through their clothes instantly, but neither noticed.

She gathered his face in her hands, laughing softly through tears that shimmered in the firelight.

"It's okay," she said gently, her voice steady and bright. "It's really okay."

Her voice was calm, astonishingly calm, like someone who had crossed a great distance and finally arrived. She kissed his brow, his cheek, the corner of his mouth, grounding him in small, undeniable proofs of her presence.

She pressed her forehead to his, smiling through the tears. "We made it," she whispered. "It's over. Nature kept her promise."

"Someone…in the future…?" Simon's voice faded.

"Yes, darling. It is done. We are back."

"But what happened?" Simon stunned.

"We'll never know, dear. It doesn't matter."

She held his face firmly now, forcing his eyes to meet hers. "The Soulfast," she said, "It worked. We're back."

At the sound of those words, the fire answered.

The flames surged upward in a final, triumphant spiral, flinging a thousand glowing embers into the night. The clearing glowed, briefly and brilliantly, as if the world itself were bearing witness.

Simon stood frozen for a heartbeat, unable to breathe. Then he looked into Sabrina's eyes and saw it, joy, unmistakable and complete. Not relief. Not disbelief. Joy.

Lauren stood nearby, her hands pressed to her chest, tears still falling, but now she was smiling openly, the tension finally gone.

The fire again burned gently. The night felt open again.

And in the quiet clearing, beneath a sky no longer empty, joy settled in, simple, steady, and real.

For a long while, no one spoke.

The fire burned low, its earlier brilliance settling into a steady, golden glow. The last of the embers drifted upward in slow, unhurried spirals, fading gently into the night. The air had softened. Even the cold seemed to hold its distance, as though unwilling to disturb what had taken root there.

Simon and Sabrina remained close, their foreheads touching, their laughter now quiet, shared in small, private breaths. Around them, the others stood in a loose circle, no longer bound by fear or urgency, but by something calmer, something understood without needing to be said.

Lauren wiped her cheeks and let out a long, steady breath. When she looked again, it was not to search for danger, but to take it all in. She ran to Drew, throwing her arms around him. The tears of joy began once more.

And through it all, Emryn remained by the fire.

He had not moved, nor needed to. The flames cast a softer light across his face, tracing the lines of it with a warmth that had not been there before. His hands were still folded into his sleeves, his posture unchanged, but there was no longer any distance in him.

His eyes moved slowly across the clearing, taking in each of them, Simon and Sabrina, still wrapped in one another; Eustace, finally unguarded; Sir Roger, quietly astonished; Lauren, no longer afraid; Drew still stunned.

Emryn lingered there, not as an observer, but as someone witnessing the completion of something deeply known. His smile widened then.

It carried none of the earlier mystery, none of the unsettling certainty that had once set him apart. There was joy in it. There was peace.

Emryn inclined his head slightly, not toward any one person, but toward the moment itself, as though acknowledging it. As though giving thanks. Then he lifted his gaze briefly to the sky. It was still dark, still vast, but no longer empty. The stars had appeared, faint but steady, holding their place above the clearing.

And in that quiet, where nothing more was required, and nothing more need be remade, the Soulfast promise had been kept.

For the first time in a thousand years, nothing more was needed.

Chapter Two

Five Years Later

Morning came gently to Simon and Sabrina, as if the world itself had learned, at long last, to accept their presence.

The light arrived first, tentative and respectful, slipping through the tall windows of Simon's old house in Concord. It did not blaze or demand attention. It lingered at the edges, pale and patient, laying long, honey-colored bands across the hardwood floor and the rumpled sheets as though it were blessing each thing it touched.

A few miles away, the city of glass was already alive. Traffic murmured in distant arteries. Horns stitched impatience into the air. Somewhere, a delivery truck groaned into place. Somewhere else, a siren sang briefly and vanished. That was Boston.

But that life felt far away, muted by miles and meaning. Here, inside the room, there was only breath and warmth and the quiet miracle of stillness.

They slept as people do only when they no longer fear waking alone. Simon lay on his back, one arm curved instinctively around Sabrina's shoulders, his hand resting where her arm met her collarbone. She was half-draped across his chest, her weight familiar, anchoring. Her golden hair spilled across his skin like sunlight given form. One leg was tangled loosely with his. Her fingers traced slow, absent shapes against him, circles, lines, little hesitations, as though she were drawing a map she already knew by heart but loved to revisit.

There was no urgency in the movement. No hunger that needed satisfying. This was intimacy after survival. Closeness stripped of desperation. Happiness, they had learned, did not announce itself loudly. It settled in. It exhaled. It stayed.

"For the record," Simon murmured, eyes still closed, his voice thick with sleep and contentment, "this is officially my favorite gift from nature."

Sabrina smiled against his chest.

"Mmm," she said. "You mean the one with central heating and a coffee maker?"

"Don't diminish the poetry," he replied as a smile lit up his face.

Sabrina laughed softly, unguarded. "You say that every morning," she said.

"And I mean it every morning," he said. "Consistency is the soul of contentment."

She lifted her head and propped her chin on his chest, studying his face. The faint lines were earned honestly. The calm behind his eyes. The way his expression still softened when he noticed her looking.

"What are you thinking?" she asked.

"That we have beaten the odds," he said.

"Statistically or emotionally?"

"Yes."

She smiled.

"Also," he went on, "that if I move even one inch, I'll regret it for the rest of the day."

"You're allowed to move," she said. "I won't vanish."

"I know," he said quietly. "That's the miracle."

Her expression shifted, just slightly. Not sadness. Not fear. Something gentler. Something like recognition.

She lay her head back down.

"I have rounds in an hour," she said at last.

There was no complaint in her voice. Just acknowledgment, like naming the weather. Simon sighed theatrically and tightened his arm around her.

"The children of the city call," he intoned solemnly, "and you must answer."

"They always do."

"And you always will."

"Yes," she said simply.

After a pause, she added, "You don't resent that, do you?"

He opened one eye.

"Resent that you save lives before breakfast?"

"Before coffee," she corrected.

"Heroic," he said. "Dangerous. Slightly unhinged. No, I do not resent it."

"Good," she said. "Because I'd ignore you."

"I know," he said proudly.

The walk-in clinic adjacent to Children's Hospital had become her axis, the place around which her days now turned. Modest in size, almost deliberately so, it occupied a low, unassuming building just off the main campus. No grand signage. No marble floors. No donor names etched in glass.

There was no billing office. No insurance desks barricaded with forms and fine print. No subtle architecture designed to discourage the poor. Just doctors and nurses…helping children.

Word of the new clinic had spread with the quiet velocity of truth. Pediatricians volunteered hours between hospital shifts. Retired nurses returned part-time, sleeves rolled up, grateful for purpose. Social workers drifted in and never quite left.

Parents arrived exhausted and wary, braced for refusal or judgment. They left lighter. Sometimes crying. Sometimes smiling. Always changed.

Sabrina would move through the clinic like someone who had finally stepped into her true shape. She knelt to the children's eye level. She spoke softly to frightened parents. She remembered names. Allergies. Siblings. Stories.

She never succumbed to exhaustion. But this wasn't heroism. It wasn't martyrdom. It was devotion. The steady, daily choice to show up and stay present.

ϒ ϒ ϒ

Simon, for his part, had returned to Phillips Academy as if no time had been lost. The classrooms were the same. Tall windows. Desks worn smooth by generations of restless hands.

But his lectures now carried new gravity. His pauses were longer. His questions sharper and more generous. He listened differently to answers. To silences. To the hesitations that students didn't yet know how to voice.

They noticed.

"Dr. Sterling," a student had once said, "why do myths always end badly?"

"They don't," Simon replied. "They end honestly."

He taught mythology. Students learned not by memorizing knowledge, but by using their imagination.

ϒ ϒ ϒ

Hanging at the Museum of Fine Arts, framed and protected, the painting had become quietly famous. Not flashy. Not sensational. Visitors simply stopped longer than expected.

Critics wrote of its emotional density. Both its sorrow and its hope. They still talked about the scandal, but no one knew the whole story. Only fragments. Hints. Speculation.

Simon and Sabrina had agreed that this was as it should be. Some truths were not meant to be fully explained.

On weekends, they sometimes went to see it together. They never stood too close. Never spoke while looking at it. It was their legacy.

"Still there," Simon would say.

“Still breathing,” Sabrina would answer.

ϒ ϒ ϒ

That morning, Sabrina finally slipped out of bed. Simon watched her dress, efficient, unselfconscious, radiant in motion with glistening blond hair. He too rose to dress.

“You’re staring,” she said, tugging on her sweater.

“Documenting,” he replied.

“For what?”

“For when I’m old and annoying.”

“You’re already annoying.”

“But comfortingly so.” He winked

She leaned down and kissed his forehead.

As she gathered her bag, he reached for her hand. Held it. Just a second longer than necessary.

“Come home early tonight,” he said quietly.

She looked at him, really looked. Warm. Certain.

“Always.”

“Liar.”

When the door closed behind her, Simon prepared to go on his morning run. Summer in New England was a wonderful time to make your own breeze.

ϒ ϒ ϒ

Cherry still lived in Morgantown. With a new doctor, young, earnest, and perpetually on the edge of being overwhelmed, she now ran the Mite-Y children's free clinic with brisk confidence and an efficiency that surprised even herself.

“I don’t know how I became management,” she had once told

Sabrina over the phone, half-laughing. "But apparently… I did."

The last five years had been kind to Cherry. Her red hair was still brilliant, catching the light wherever she went, and she was noticeably slimmer, stronger somehow, as if purpose itself had reshaped her. Her skirts were still short, her heels still high. She still hadn't settled on a boyfriend, though there was certainly no shortage of applicants, and she seemed in no particular hurry to do so.

Sabrina's father, Robert, had finally retired for good. He'd been replaced by two young doctors, Bethany and Jacob, both fresh out of residency and still learning the art of calm under pressure. Sandy, the longtime PA, was still there too, steady as ever. But Cherry was the administrator now, the quiet center of gravity. No one underestimated her anymore.

Under Cheri's watch, the Morgantown clinic didn't merely survive. It thrived.

That evening, Cherry sat in her usual booth at the Mountain Mama bar, nursing a drink and watching the familiar ebb and flow of customers. George "Bear" Carter had owned the place for over twenty years, and in all that time, it had never once required a police visit. Despite its popularity, and perhaps because of it, the bar had developed its own unspoken code of tolerance and vigilance. Students mixed with professors. Mechanics laughed with lawyers. Bikers shared stools with poets. It was a rare crossroads of lives. And though it was best known as a haven for "Bears", the affectionate term for big, bearded gay men, it welcomed everyone who respected the room.

"How are things, Teddy?" Cherry asked, using the nickname she'd bestowed years ago.

Bear grinned. "Couldn't be better, Cherry Blossom. Business is booming, and Tiny's got himself a new boy toy."

She laughed softly. "Good for Tiny."

"And you?" Bear asked. "Still ruling the medical world with an iron stiletto?"

"With lots of caffeine," she said.

Bear nodded approvingly. "You heard from Sabrina lately?"

"She's busy as usual," Cherry replied. "That new clinic of hers is overflowing with wee tots. She barely sleeps."

He smiled. "Figures. And that whole painting business… finally settled?"

"Seems to have," Cherry said, after a moment. "Life's been quieter."

They sat in companionable silence for a few beats, the hum of conversation and soft music wrapping around them.

"Well," Cherry finally said, sliding out of the booth, "I'd better head home before tomorrow starts yelling at me."

She tugged her miniskirt down just a touch, respectable, but not surrendering any ground, and slung her purse over her shoulder. Her heels clicked sharply against the floor as she crossed the room, a confident rhythm, familiar and unmistakably hers.

Bear watched her go, smiling.

ϒ ϒ ϒ

Founded in 1096, the University of Oxford stands as the oldest university in the English-speaking world. By the early thirteenth century, it had already become Britain's leading center of learning, a magnet for restless minds and dangerous ideas, for young scholars who arrived burdened with questions and left armed with convictions. Within its ancient walls, ambition and inquiry learned to live side by side, sometimes as partners, sometimes as rivals.

Its stones remember Latin prayers whispered in echoing chapels and midnight debates carried out in drafty corridors. They remember candlelit lectures and fragile manuscripts borne through rain and doubt, clutched to chests as if they were sacred relics. They remember generations of scholars who believed knowledge was not decoration, not ornament for polite society, but power, something to be tested, challenged, defended, and earned through struggle.

Within this long tradition of intellectual gravity, two professors of English history stood as modern exemplars of Oxford's enduring excellence. Sir Roger Abelard and Professor Eustace Fairfax still held sway as prominent stars in the university's scholarly heavens, respected, admired, and occasionally feared for the sharpness of their minds. Heroes of the Soulfast saga, they remained closely connected to every member of the small circle that comprised the company of people who experienced it.

Now, each seated in their familiar wood-paneled rooms, surrounded by towering shelves and the quiet authority of centuries, they enjoyed a rare moment of calm. Dust motes drifted lazily in shafts of afternoon light. Papers lay neatly arranged. Teacups cooled beside open books.

For the moment, all seemed still.

Chapter Three

The Vanishing

Drew Idle had been born with the sort of advantages that usually guaranteed an effortless life: movie-star looks, a vast family trust fund, and a mind sharp enough to cut glass. By the time he graduated from Harvard, he had already acquired a reputation as one of the most gifted students in his class, and one of the most incorrigible. He and Simon had been inseparable there, known as much for their elaborate pranks as for their flawless academic records. Professors alternated between exasperation and admiration. No one doubted they would go far. Few imagined how far.

After several years of world travel, trying to find himself, and then returning to Harvard for his law degree, Drew settled in Washington, D.C., to begin his career.

Within a decade, he was regarded as one of the capital's finest attorneys, brilliant in court, disarmingly charming in negotiation, and relentlessly ethical in a profession not always known for restraint. He could have made millions defending corporations or lobbying Congress. Instead, he chose a narrower, more different road.

He chose Lauren.

Lauren Idle was petite, dark-haired, and breathtakingly beautiful in a way that seemed almost unfair. Years earlier, she had won Pennsylvania's Miss America competition, where judges had quickly learned that her intelligence outshone even her smile. She possessed a quiet intensity, a way of listening that made people feel truly seen.

She and Drew had shared something no one else quite understood, the mystery of the great adventure that had bound them to Simon and Sabrina, an experience that had altered all their lives in ways still unfolding. It was the invisible thread beneath their marriage, their work, their choices. It reminded them daily that life was fragile and that meaning was earned.

After their wedding, Lauren enrolled at Georgetown Law, balancing casebooks with late nights and, eventually, a new baby. She graduated at the top of her class. Together, she and Drew founded their own practice, a modest firm on K Street that would quietly and steadily grow into something far more important than either of them had planned.

Idle & Idle, Attorneys at Law.

They specialized in immigration. Not corporate visas, not celebrity green cards, but for desperate individuals seeking asylum.

They represented people who arrived with nothing but battered documents, trembling hands, and stories too painful to tell all at once. They fought for families fleeing war, persecution, famine, and political prisons. They learned the geography of suffering by heart. Syria. Honduras. Myanmar. Eritrea. Venezuela. Ukraine. Places that appeared nightly on the news and daily in their waiting room.

They worked longer hours than most of their peers and earned far less. Of course, with Drew's wealth, that made no difference to them.

But their greatest joy was not found in courtrooms or legal briefs.

It slept in the small bedroom of their Kalorama Heights mansion, surrounded by stuffed animals and half-finished coloring books.

Sabina.

At five years old, Sabina Idle was already becoming unmistakably beautiful, inheriting her mother's dark eyes and her father's mischievous grin. She was precocious without being pretentious, curious without being reckless, serious about her dolls and wildly imaginative about everything else. She asked questions that made adults pause. She told stories that wandered gloriously off course. She believed fiercely in fairness.

In the fall, she would begin kindergarten. She spoke of it as if preparing for an expedition. Backpacks were examined daily.

Shoes were tried on and discarded. Crayons were carefully sorted. She practiced writing her name with solemn concentration, tongue between her teeth.

Drew and Lauren watched all of this with quiet wonder. Nothing in law school had prepared them for how much they would love being parents.

This morning, the Idle law office was already overflowing.

The narrow lobby on K Street buzzed with anxious voices and whispered translations. Children clung to their parents. Folders were clutched like life preservers. Phones vibrated with bad news from distant borders. A television in the corner murmured about new executive orders, tightened regulations, and suspended programs.

Immigration had become terrifying under the current federal administration. Rules shifted weekly. Protections vanished overnight. Judges were reassigned. Deadlines shortened. Appeals denied without explanation. Families who had lived peacefully in America for years now feared sudden removal. People slept with packed bags by their doors.

Drew stood at the reception desk, loosening his tie, scanning the day's schedule. It was already full. Lauren emerged from her office carrying three files, her expression calm but focused.

"Two emergency hearings," she said softly. "One detention case. And the Rahimi family just arrived."

Drew nodded.

"Okay," he replied. "Let's get to work."

And together, once again, they stepped into the quiet storm, armed with law books, stubborn hope, and the unshakable belief that every story deserved to be heard.

ϒ ϒ ϒ

It was nearly one o'clock by the time the conference with the Rahimi finally ended.

The narrow office felt drained of air and energy, as though the arguments, affidavits, and whispered calculations had consumed everything usable, leaving only fatigue behind. Papers lay scattered across the table like fallen leaves after a storm. Coffee cups stood abandoned, their contents long gone cold.

Drew closed his folder with deliberate care and leaned forward, his voice steady, measured, and reassuring.

"Mister Rahimi," he said gently, "we will represent you at the hearing. Please don't worry. We will get this straightened out."

Across from him, Rahimi sat rigid, hands clasped so tightly his knuckles had gone pale. His wife was still in custody at the Immigration and Customs Enforcement office, locked behind fluorescent corridors and bureaucratic indifference. Every minute apart from her felt like another small tearing.

Drew met his eyes.

"This will be a fight," he continued. "But we're ready for it."

Lauren, standing beside him, nodded once, sharp, decisive. And Amad Rahimi believed them. Drew was relentless when justice demanded it. And Lauren, when lives were on the line, was merciless. They rose, gathering their things.

"Dotty," Drew said, glancing at his watch, "we'll grab a quick lunch around the corner. Be back in half an hour."

Dorothy Johnson, their office manager, looked up from her desk, glasses perched low on her nose. She smiled and waved them off with practiced affection.

"Take some time for a change," she said lightly. "You've earned it."

They didn't take time. They never did.

Twenty minutes later, they pushed back through the downstairs door, minds already racing ahead to motions and deadlines and emergency filings. Lunch had been eaten standing up, barely tasted. Work waited.

Dorothy was halfway down the stairwell, purse slipping from her shoulder, her face pale and strained. When she saw them, she froze, then bolted toward them.

"Oh, thank God," she cried. "You have to go. Both of you. Right now!"

Her voice cracked.

Drew stopped short.

Lauren's breath caught.

"What's wrong?" Drew demanded.

"What happened?" Lauren asked, already moving toward her.

Dotty grabbed the railing to steady herself.

"Sabina is missing," she said. "Your nanny can't find her. She's looked everywhere. Everywhere."

The words struck like a physical blow. Lauren felt it first. The world seemed to tilt. Her stomach hollowed. Her ears rang. For a moment, she couldn't breathe.

"Call the police," she said, her voice urgent and emotional. "Call them now. We're on our way."

"They're already there," Dorothy said. "They're there now."

Lauren lifted her head slowly.

"At the house?" she asked.

Her voice had gone cold. Flat. Dangerously controlled.

"Yes," Dotty whispered. "At your house."

Silence fell between them. Drew's hand closed around Lauren's without thinking. Somewhere inside her, fear turned into fire. And they were already moving.

ϒ ϒ ϒ

They reached their house in record time.

Drew turned into their neighborhood, tires humming against familiar pavement, already scanning the street ahead. As they approached the cul-de-sac, both of them instinctively leaned forward.

Patrol cars blocked the entrance. Yellow tape stretched across the mouth of the circle like a warning line drawn through their lives. Blue and red lights pulsed silently against tidy houses and summer-green trees, transforming their quiet street into something unrecognizable.

Drew hit the brakes and stopped short of the barricade. An officer stepped away from his cruiser and walked toward them, one hand resting near his radio.

Drew rolled down the window and leaned out.

"We're the parents," he shouted. "She's our daughter."

His voice cracked despite his effort to control it.

The officer nodded, calm and professional, but did not relent.

"I understand, sir," he said evenly. "I just need to see some identification, please."

Drew's jaw tightened. But before he could speak again, Lauren reached across and placed her hand gently on his arm.

"They're being careful, D," she murmured. "It's a good thing."

Her voice was soft, but firm enough to anchor him. He exhaled sharply and pulled out his wallet.

Once the officer examined his license, he stepped back and raised his hand. He signaled toward several officers clustered in their driveway. One of them immediately broke away and hurried into the house.

The yellow tape was lifted. They drove slowly now, past flashing lights and unfamiliar faces, until they reached their own driveway. Their home looked the same. And yet, nothing about it did.

Before they had even fully parked, a woman stepped out through the front door and walked toward them with confident purpose. She was a Black woman in her early forties, composed, alert, wearing a tailored dress and, of all things, high heels on the uneven pavement. Neither of them noticed. They barely noticed anything.

"Mr. and Mrs. Idle," she said, extending a hand. "I'm Detective Captain Annette Ramsey. Please, let's go inside."

Her voice was calm, practiced, steady enough to hold panic at bay. They followed her without a word. Inside, the house felt wrong. Too quiet. Too crowded.

They passed through the living room, past unfamiliar officers and scattered notebooks, and into the library. Anna sat on the couch, folded inward, shoulders shaking as she cried. Two detectives stood nearby, their expressions serious but gentle.

They turned as Drew and Lauren entered.

"Dawson," one said, offering his hand.

"Jameson," said the other.

Drew shook automatically. Lauren barely registered it.

Anna looked up. The moment she saw them, she broke.

She stood abruptly and rushed forward, collapsing into Lauren's arms.

"I'm so sorry," she sobbed. "I'm so, so sorry."

Lauren held her tightly, one arm around her shoulders, the other steadying her trembling back.

Drew stepped closer. "What happened?" he asked.

His voice was urgent, clipped, controlled by sheer will.

"Tell us what happened."

Anna tried to speak, but her words tangled in tears.

"She was there," she gasped. "Then she… she wasn't. She was gone. Gone." Her breath hitched. "Oh God, I'm so sorry. I just, "

Her knees buckled.

One of the detectives rushed forward and helped guide her back onto the couch.

Detective Ramsey stepped closer.

"Mr. and Mrs. Idle," she began carefully, "it appears that your daughter, "

"Sabina," Lauren said immediately.

"Yes," Ramsey nodded. "Sabina was riding her bicycle around the cul-de-sac, as she usually does. Miss Grey went inside to prepare her lunch, as usual. She was gone for approximately fifteen minutes. When she returned, Sabina was no longer outside."

"I ran everywhere," Anna blurted, lifting her head. "I ran to the end of the street. I ran down every block. I called her name. She was just… gone."

Her voice broke again.

Lauren turned to Ramsey, her eyes sharp despite the fear burning beneath them.

"What about her bicycle?"

"The bike was found in your front yard," Ramsey replied. "Lying on its side. As if she had just dropped it."

Lauren closed her eyes briefly. Then opened them.

"No one heard anything?" Drew asked.

"We've canvassed the closest neighbors so far," Detective Dawson replied. "No one reported hearing a struggle, a scream, or anything unusual."

Jameson added, "Uniformed officers are going door to door now. We're also requesting access to security footage from nearby homes."

"What about our camera?"

"We just reviewed it. Someone spray-painted it earlier this morning. It shows nothing. I'm sorry." Captain Ramsey said.

Lauren and Drew cringed, then moved together and sat beside Anna, one on each side. Without speaking, they formed a small, fragile circle. Three hearts breaking.

Detective Ramsey sat forward in her chair, her notebook balanced neatly on her knee. She did not open it yet. Instead, she studied Drew and Lauren for several seconds, as if weighing not just their words, but their silences.

"Mr. and Mrs. Idle," she said at last, her voice calm and deliberate, "do you know of anyone who might have a motive for kidnapping Sabina?"

The question seemed to drain the air from the room. Drew's face went still. Not cold. Not angry. Just empty, like a door closing. He shook his head once.

"No," he said. "No one."

Ramsey nodded, but did not move on.

"Anything connected to your work?" she asked. "A client who felt betrayed? Someone who thought you didn't do enough? Someone who blamed you for an outcome?"

Drew leaned back slightly, folding his arms.

"Not really," he replied. "We help people. That's what we do. We don't prosecute. We don't testify. We don't put anyone in prison. Most of our clients leave better off than when they came in."

Lauren shifted beside him.

"I don't think it's revenge," she said quietly. "At least, no, it can't be." She hesitated, then added, "But my husband does have… substantial wealth…quite substantial actually."

She hated how calculated it sounded.

Ramsey's expression remained neutral.

"I see. Money is always the first assumption," she said. "But ransom cases are far rarer than people think. Banks flag large transfers. Phones are traceable. Even criminals know that collecting money is harder than it used to be."

She paused.

"Still," she continued, "when nothing else fits, we have to consider it."

She opened her notebook gently.

"There is another category," she said, more slowly now. "Personal motivation."

Drew stiffened.

"Are you certain," Ramsey asked, "that neither of you has ever seriously angered someone? Someone who felt exposed. Humiliated. Ruined. Someone who never moved on."

The room went quiet. A clock ticked faintly on the wall. Then, almost simultaneously, Drew and Lauren turned to face each other. Their eyes met. For a moment, neither spoke. Lauren's lips parted, then closed again. Finally, she took a breath.

"There is… one person," she admitted. "But it was five years ago. It feels like another lifetime." She shook her head. "I honestly can't believe she would do this. Not to a child."

Ramsey's gaze sharpened slightly.

“The Boston scandal?” she asked.

Lauren looked at Drew. Ramsey obviously knew about it. Drew looked down at the carpet.

“Yes,” he said quietly.

“I hate even thinking it,” he continued. “We didn’t intend to destroy her. We told the truth. That’s all. But… the fallout was brutal.”

“ Her name is Catherine Lodge. She lost everything,” Lauren said. “Her career. Her reputation. Most of her friends. She became… invisible.”

“And she never forgave us,” Drew added.

Ramsey wrote a few lines in her notebook.

“When was your last contact with her?” she asked.

“A letter,” Lauren said. “About four years ago. Maybe five. It was… angry. Rambling. Accusatory. But it wasn’t to us. It was to Simon Sterling.”

“And since then?” Ramsey pressed.

“Nothing,” Lauren replied. “No calls. No emails. No sightings.”

Ramsey considered this.

“Sometimes,” she said quietly, “people don’t disappear. They just wait.”

Lauren’s hands trembled slightly. Drew noticed and took one of them in his.

“We need to make a phone call,” he said.

He looked at her, and she understood immediately.

“Yes,” she said. “We should. Right now.”

Ramsey rose smoothly to her feet.

“To Mr. Sterling?

Drew nodded.

“I agree,” she said. “If Catherine is involved, any delay helps her. If she isn’t, your call may still give us valuable information.”

She gestured toward the hallway.

"Please let me know as soon as you finish your call."

Drew nodded. Lauren stood, still holding his hand. Together, they left the study and walked down the corridor toward their bedroom, toward privacy, toward fear, toward help.

Chapter Four

The Arc of Reprisal

Simon sat alone in his Concord study, though alone was never quite the right word for that room.

The walls were lined floor to ceiling with books—history, theology, archaeology, philosophy, and more. Volumes were stacked two deep in places where scholarship had outrun shelving. Between them, as if history itself had seeped out of the pages and taken form, were objects: a chipped Greek oil lamp; a Roman bronze fibula; a small Egyptian ushabti no taller than a thumb; a medieval iron key mounted in shadowed velvet. Civilizations watched him while he worked.

The late afternoon light filtered through the tall windows, catching the glass cases and casting faint reflections of relics across the hardwood floor. Simon leaned back in his leather chair, reading a passage on ritual symbolism, pencil resting against his lip.

His cell phone chimed.

He glanced at it absently, expecting a student or perhaps Sabrina. Instead, he saw Drew's name.

Simon smiled and answered immediately.
"Hey, D., you calling from jail again? Need bail money?"

Silence.

Then Drew's voice, thin, trembling. "Prof, I need your help. We need your help."

Simon sat upright at once. The room seemed to contract.

"Drew. What's wrong?"

A breath. Then, steadier, as if forcing himself into coherence: "Sabina has been abducted. Someone took her."

The words struck like a physical blow. Simon felt the air leave his lungs.

"D… explain. When? How? Where? Tell me what you know."

"From home. From the front yard. A couple of hours ago. Ell and I were at work. She was there with her nanny." His voice was tightening, moving from panic toward grim resolve. "She was just riding her bike around the circle. Then she was gone."

Simon stood, pacing instinctively. "The police?"

"They're here. Detectives. They don't know much yet."

In the silence that followed, Simon's eyes drifted unconsciously to the medieval key on his desk. He had once lectured on how doors, literal and symbolic, were the most vulnerable thresholds in human architecture. Safety was always an illusion at the threshold.

"Prof," Drew said carefully, "I need to ask you something… rather unpleasant."

"Of course."

"The police are looking for a motive. They don't think ransom is likely. They say it's rare now, too hard to collect."

Simon stopped pacing.

"Okay… then what could it be?"

There was a pause long enough to become an answer.

"They say maybe… revenge."

The word hung between them like smoke.

Simon closed his eyes for several long moments.

"Oh, God. Surely not. She wouldn't really harm anyone. And she isn't angry at you. She's angry at us." His voice lowered. "I just can't believe she would do something like this."

Drew did not respond. His silence was heavier than denial.

Simon's jaw tightened. "D, I'll call Sabrina. We'll be there on the next flight."

"Ell is calling her now. Just let us know your arrival time."

"Hold together, D," Simon said quietly, though his own pulse was racing. "We'll get her back. We will."

He ended the call.

For several seconds, Simon stood in the center of the study, surrounded by centuries of human triumph and cruelty, faith and conquest. History offered no comfort. It only reminded him that evil was never obsolete.

He moved.

ϒ ϒ ϒ

Simon was in the bedroom packing when the front door slammed below.

"Simon!"

Sabrina's voice echoed through the house, sharp, breathless, breaking.

He turned just as she rushed into the bedroom, still in her clinic coat, her golden hair loose from its tie, eyes wide with shock.

They collided in an embrace so fierce it nearly knocked them off balance.

He felt her shaking.

She pulled back, pushing tears from her face with impatient hands. "Tell me. What did Drew say?"

Simon guided her gently to the edge of the bed. They sat, knees touching, hands still clasped.

"Here's what I know," he began, repeating the details: front yard, nanny, police, uncertainty.

"I know," she said quietly. "Ell called me between patients. I left in the middle of an exam." Her voice faltered. "Simon, she was just playing outside. She's five."

"I know."

They sat in silence, the enormity of it pressing in.

Finally, Simon stood. “We have a flight in ninety minutes. I’ve pulled the suitcases out.”

Sabrina nodded. She rose mechanically, moving toward the closet.

They packed without speaking at first.

Drawers opened and shut. Hangers slid along rods. The zipper of a suitcase rasped like something tearing. Simon folded shirts with excessive precision, as if order could be imposed through fabric.

Sabrina stopped suddenly, holding one of Sabina’s small sweaters in her hands. It had been left there after a weekend visit. Pink. Soft. Tiny.

She pressed it to her face.

Simon crossed the room in two steps and wrapped his arms around her from behind.

“We’re going to get her back,” he whispered into her hair.

“You don’t know that.”

“No,” he admitted. “But we’re going to act as if we do.”

She turned to face him. “Do you really think it’s, you know…her?”

He hesitated only a fraction of a second. “I don’t know.”

“But you think it’s possible.”

“Yes.”

Sabrina looked away, jaw tightening. “Five years.”

“I know.”

“Five years of silence. Of thinking that chapter was closed.”

Simon’s voice hardened. “Some chapters don’t close. They wait.”

Sabrina moved to the dresser and resumed packing, her motions quicker now, more purposeful.

“If it is reprisal,” she said quietly, “then this is about us. Not Drew. Not Ell.”

“Yes.”

“And Sabina is just… leverage.”

The word shattered in her mouth.

Simon zipped his suitcase shut. “If that’s true, then whoever did this wants our attention. And they’ll get it,” Sabrina said.

Her phone buzzed in her hand.

She looked down.

Ell.

She answered immediately. “Ell?”

Simon could hear only fragments, Lauren’s voice strained, fighting tears.

“…police are canvassing… neighbor’s camera… dark SUV… no plate…”

Sabrina’s face drained of color.

“We’re on our way,” she said firmly. “We land in three hours. I’ll text you the flight information.”

She ended the call and looked at Simon.

“They found camera footage from a neighbor. It’s grainy. A dark SUV. No plates.”

Simon’s mind was already assembling patterns. “Professional.”

“Yes.”

“Which argues against emotional impulse.”

“Or suggests planning.”

They stood in the middle of the room, two scholars accustomed to analyzing history, motive, narrative, and now thrust into the center of one.

Sabrina reached for his hand.

“Simon… if this is about what we did…”

He squeezed her fingers.

“Then we will face it,” he said. “But we will not let this little girl pay for it.”

Forty minutes later, the house was dark.

As Simon locked the front door, he glanced back through the glass at the hallway beyond, at the quiet stillness of their life suspended mid-breath.

For a fleeting second, he felt something older than fear.

History did not simply sit in glass cases.

It could haunt you.

He turned the key.

They walked to the car without another word.

ϒ ϒ ϒ

Kalorama Heights was consistently ranked among the most exclusive neighborhoods in Washington, D.C. Tucked into the northwest quadrant, it possessed a hidden, insulated quality, tree-lined streets, towering historic mansions, and an almost eerie sense of privacy. Diplomats, politicians, and industrial magnates favored it precisely because it felt worlds away from the chaos of downtown, even though it was only minutes from the White House.

Some called it the Beverly Hills of Washington.

Drew guided the car through the ornate arched entrance and into the four-car garage at the rear of the property. Police vehicles lined the street outside, their presence anything but discreet. Officers waved them through without question.

Inside, the house was unusually quiet.

When they reached the large study, Detective Captain Annette Ramsey rose from her chair to greet them. Two other detectives were setting up electronic monitoring equipment connected to the landline, devices that could also be linked to mobile phones.

"It was kind of you to come so quickly, Mr. and Mrs. Sterling," Ramsey said, extending her hand.

"We wouldn't be anywhere else," Sabrina replied.

"Please," Simon added, "tell us what you know."

They took their seats. Ramsey folded her hands and began.

"There has been no ransom call. No note. No digital contact of any kind." She paused. "That doesn't surprise us. Kidnappings like this are extremely rare now, especially in the United States."

She glanced briefly at Simon.

"However, we are aware of thc Boston incident and the MFA scandal. We cannot ignore them as possible motives."

Silence settled over the room.

"I'd like to hear your thoughts," Ramsey continued. "Do you believe that incident could be connected to this?"

Simon leaned forward.

"Catherine Lodge is an angry, wounded person," he said carefully. "We all know that. And she has the resources to make something like this happen. Connections. Money. Lots of money and connections."

He hesitated.

"Frankly, I can imagine her wanting revenge. But on me. On Sabrina. Not… this."

"Would you say it's impossible?" Ramsey asked. "That she could be responsible?"

Simon glanced at Sabrina.

Before he could answer, she spoke.

"I think she is fully capable of it," Sabrina said. Her voice was steady. "I have no doubt."

"I think she might be capable," Simon added quietly.

"For now," Ramsey said, "let's treat it as a working scenario. If Catherine were involved, what would you expect her next move to be?"

Simon answered first.

"She's brilliant. Strategic. She plans everything three steps ahead. She has wealth and reach, far beyond the U.S. Her contacts are international."

He looked down briefly.

"And she's had five years to think about this…to plan it."

Ramsey nodded, listening.

"I'm surprised," Simon went on, "that she would involve Sabina. It's symbolic, yes. But she's a child. That would have given the old Catherine pause."

Ramsey leaned in slightly. "From your perspective, what would she be capable of? Where Sabina's safety is concerned?"

Simon exhaled.

"I thought I knew," he said. "But now I'm not sure.

Sabrina stiffened and looked at Simon.

"Do you think she would hurt the girl?"

Ell and Sabrina exchanged a look.

"I don't think so," Simon answered.

"I don't entirely agree," Sabrina said.

"Me either," Ell added softly.

Simon turned to them.

"She's manipulative. Calculating. Yes. But she's also deeply insecure. She understands vulnerability. I just don't think…" Simon's voice faded

He met Ramsey's eyes.

"I just don't want to believe she could hurt Sabina."

Ramsey studied him for a moment.

"And if you're wrong?" she asked gently.

Simon didn't answer immediately.

When he did, his voice was barely above a whisper.

"Then we're all in more trouble than I want to imagine."

The room fell silent again, filled only by the faint hum of electronic equipment and the distant sounds of police radios outside.

Somewhere, not far away and yet impossibly distant, a young girl was terrified.

And every person in that room felt it.

"Okay, let's take this one step further," Ramsey said, breaking the silence. Her voice was calm, deliberate, the voice of someone used to walking people through worst-case scenarios. "What will her demands be? What will her payback likely consist of?"

No one answered at first.

The question hung in the air, heavy and ominous. Each of them seemed to turn inward, testing possibilities, discarding them, circling back to darker ones.

Drew shifted in his chair. When he finally spoke, his voice was low but steady.

"She wants revenge on Simon," he said. "That's the core of it. I agree with Simon, her threats won't focus on Sabina's safety. They'll focus on reprisal. On control. The real target will be Simon. Every demand will be made of him."

For once, no one argued.

Heads nodded slowly around the room.

Ramsey folded her arms. "What about asking for money?" she asked. "Ransom."

Simon shook his head immediately. "No. That wouldn't satisfy her."

"I agree," Sabina said quietly. Her hands were clenched in her lap. "She won't want money. She doesn't need it. She'll want a sacrifice. Something that hurts. Something that lasts." She looked at Simon. "She wants her pound of flesh."

Ramsey's brow furrowed. "Then what? What kind of sacrifice?"

Silence again.

Simon leaned forward, resting his elbows on his knees. He stared at the floor for a long moment before answering.

"I honestly don't know," he said. "But I know this much: it won't be simple. And it won't be minor." He looked up, his eyes dark with certainty. "She was humiliated. Publicly. She lost her position, her standing, her credibility, and her reputation. Everything she valued."

He exhaled slowly.

No one spoke.

The implication was ominous.

With the conversation no longer focused on her, Lauren's composure finally broke. Her shoulders began to shake. She covered her mouth, but the sob slipped through anyway.

Sabrina moved instantly to her side, wrapping her arms around her. Tears streamed down Sabrina's face as well, silent and unrestrained.

"It's my fault," Lauren whispered. "It's all my fault…I should have been here."

"No," Sabrina said firmly, holding her closer. "None of this is your fault. None of it."

Simon watched them for a moment, then straightened, forcing himself back into command.

"We can't think of ourselves as powerless," he said, turning to Drew and Ramsey. "We're not."

He looked directly at Drew.

"We have two brilliant minds who are personally invested in this. They won't treat this as an abstract problem. They'll live it." A faint, determined smile touched his lips. "Sir Roger and Fairfax will be our braintrust."

Drew nodded. "Absolutely."

"I'll contact them tonight," Simon continued. "By email. I want them thinking about this before Catherine even makes her first move."

Ramsey made a note on her pad.

"There's something else," Simon added. "A name you should have."

Ramsey looked up. "Go ahead."

"Chester Morris," Simon said. "Principal at International Inquiry Agents in New York. I doubt he's involved directly, but he knows Catherine's darker side better than almost anyone. He's worked for her many times. If she's planning something intricate, he may recognize the pattern."

Ramsey closed her notebook. "We'll reach out first thing."

She stood, straightening her jacket.

"I'm heading out for the night. Dawson and Jameson will remain until their replacements arrive. We'll monitor all communications, email, phone, everything. Any attempt to contact you, directly or indirectly, we'll see it."

She met Drew's eyes.

"We'll connect again in the morning."

"Thank you," Drew said quietly.

Ramsey nodded once and moved toward the door.

After she left, the house seemed suddenly too quiet.

Drew sat beside Lauren and pulled her into his arms.

Simon took Sabrina's hand.

Outside, the night pressed against the windows.

None of them expected sleep.

It would be a endless night.

Chapter Five

Where All Paths Narrow

Sir Roger's rooms in Balliol College were most reliably described as Dickensian, as though some Victorian scholar had stepped out briefly for tea and simply never returned. The ceilings were high and intricately molded, their pale ornamentation softened by decades of lamplight and pipe smoke. Floor-to-ceiling shelves lined nearly every wall, bowed slightly under the weight of countless volumes, leather-bound classics, fading journals, cracked-spine monographs, and marginally annotated proofs of forgotten arguments.

Dark oak tables occupied the center and corners of the rooms, their surfaces scarred with the small histories of academic life: ink stains, faint burns from careless candles, grooves worn by restless fingers tracing invisible patterns during long debates. Side-chairs stood at measured intervals, as if placed according to some unwritten geometry of scholarship, each positioned for contemplation rather than comfort. The floors, covered in Oriental rugs on polished wood, absorbed sound, giving the rooms a permanent hush, broken only by turning pages or the soft creak of leather.

The sitting room itself seemed designed less for hospitality than for custody. It felt like a place where documents were summoned, examined, judged, and archived, rather than where guests were entertained. Papers lay in careful stacks, manuscripts were pinned with precise clips, and folders occupied their own quiet territories on every available surface.

To one side, a deep, narrow closet held Sir Roger's ceremonial robes, hung with almost religious care. The heavy fabrics, crimson, black, and gold-threaded, rested in solemn rows, awaiting only the most formal occasions, like vestments prepared for rare rites.

Four overstuffed leather chairs formed a loose square near the hearth, their cracked arms and softened cushions bearing witness to decades of intellectual combat. They were chairs meant for endurance rather than elegance, built for long arguments that stretched into thc night, for thoughtful silences between carefully chosen words, for conversations in which ideas were dismantled and rebuilt with patient rigor. One could imagine generations of scholars sitting there, leaning forward, gesturing with pens and pipes, defending theories, surrendering them, and departing wiser, or at least more stubborn, than when they arrived.

In these rooms, scholarship did not merely reside. It lingered, accumulated, and quietly ruled.

Sir Roger sat cross-legged in one of the cushioned leather chairs, his posture relaxed in a way only long familiarity with comfort could produce. White-haired and slender, he possessed the refined spareness of a man who had spent a lifetime in libraries and lecture halls rather than gyms and drawing rooms. His hair was snowy and meticulously groomed, brushed back from a high, thoughtful brow, giving him the faintly ethereal look of a benevolent scholar who might at any moment drift into abstraction.

He was dressed impeccably, as always. His black suitcoat hung neatly over the back of a nearby chair, aligned with almost military precision. Beneath it, he wore a high-collared, starched white shirt, crisp enough to suggest that wrinkles were a personal affront. From his collar fell a blue silk tie, knotted with understated elegance, neither ostentatious nor careless, perfectly Roger.

Sir Roger was one of Oxford's most revered dons, a living institution within an institution. Well past the age when most of his contemporaries had retired to memoirs and garden walks, he continued to teach advanced courses in the History of Great Britain. His lectures were famously demanding, dense with nuance, contradiction, and inconvenient truths. Yet he was loved by his students, not in spite of this rigor, but because of it. He demanded their best and gave them his own in return.

Across from him sat Professor Eustace Fairfax.

At first glance, the two men might easily have been mistaken for brothers. They shared the same narrow frames, the same high foreheads, the same weathered faces shaped by decades of intellectual labor. Both had the pale complexion of men who preferred parchment to sunlight. Both wore their age with stubborn defiance.

But that was where the resemblance ended.

Where Roger radiated calm precision, Eustace projected restless volatility. His hair, though just as white, was perpetually untidy, as though he had lost an argument with his comb decades earlier and never forgiven it. His jacket hung crookedly, one sleeve always seeming longer than the other. His spectacles slid perpetually down his nose, giving him a perpetually irritated expression, even when silent.

Fairfax was every bit as accomplished as his old friend, perhaps more so in raw intellect, but his temperament made him infamous. Brilliant, caustic, and relentlessly demanding, he had reduced generations of graduate students to nervous exhaustion. They referred to him, only half in jest, as "Unfairfax," a nickname born of merciless grading, impossible expectations, and tutorials that felt more like cross-examinations.

Despite this, or perhaps because of it, the two men had been inseparable since their first day at Oxford more than sixty years earlier. They had debated, competed, collaborated, and occasionally nearly come to blows over footnotes and interpretations. Their friendship had survived wars, marriages, funerals, scandals, and academic feuds. It was as indestructible as it was improbable.

"Damnation!" Eustace exploded suddenly, slapping his hand against the arm of his chair. "I knew we hadn't heard the last from that witch…woman."

Roger raised an eyebrow. "You knew nothing of the kind, you old goat."

"Pshaw!" Eustace snapped, turning his head sharply away in irritation. "So tell me this, Sir High-and-Mighty, why aren't we in Boston right now?"

Roger folded his hands loosely over his knee. "Aside from the fact that authorities probably wouldn't allow you in," he replied mildly, "we are not searchers. We are analysts. We can help best from here."

"Then why aren't we?" Eustace blurted.

Roger sighed and shook his head. "Quit complaining. You know as well as I do that we need data. Our job is to help unravel any mysteries contained in the demands she will make. We are supposed to be brilliant, remember?"

"Ha!" Eustace snorted. "You never were brilliant! You never studied. No one bloody well knows where you'd be without me!"

Roger's mouth curved into an unrepentant grin. "Entirely lost, no doubt."

He leaned forward slightly. "All right. What can we surmise with only the past knowledge we possess of Catherine?"

Eustace pushed himself up from his chair and began pacing the rug in tight, agitated loops. He had always thought better on his feet, as if movement coaxed coherence from chaos. His hands clasped behind his back, then released, then clasped again.

"Manipulative," he muttered. "Morally questionable. Devious. Ruthless when cornered."

"Smart," Roger added calmly. "Exceptionally well-educated. A world traveler. And not only beautiful, but persuasive."

"And rich," Eustace snapped over his shoulder.

Roger nodded. "Yes. And wealthy. Which brings us to the important question." He paused. "What does she know best?"

Eustace stopped pacing abruptly. He stood still for a moment, staring at the far wall as though consulting an invisible archive.

Then he turned.

"Art," he said flatly. "Art history. Museums."

He looked back at Roger, eyes narrowing.

"And everything that hides inside them."

"Yes," Roger said at last, his voice measured and thoughtful. "I think we can rely on the probability that she will use that knowledge and those connections in whatever plot she is constructing. Museums, private collections, curators, benefactors, and invisible networks of influence. She understands how those worlds operate." He paused, then added quietly, "Though I confess, I have no idea how she intends to weave them together this time."

Eustace grunted in response, neither agreeing nor disagreeing.

He returned slowly to his chair, lowering himself into it with a faint sigh of protest from both leather and joints. The two men sat in silence, facing one another across the small space, surrounded by centuries of accumulated scholarship. The ticking of a distant clock marked the passing seconds. Somewhere in the corridor outside, footsteps echoed and faded. A radiator clicked faintly, as if uncertain whether it ought to join the conversation.

For several minutes, neither spoke.

Roger studied his old friend from behind half-lowered lids. Eustace's face, usually animated by irritation or sarcasm, was now set in a rare stillness. His eyes were distant, fixed on nothing in particular. Roger knew that look well. It meant Eustace was thinking not merely with his intellect, but with memory.

Roger hesitated.

At last, he cleared his throat softly.

"You know who defeated her before," he said, keeping his tone deliberately flat, almost casual, as though mentioning the weather.

The effect was immediate.

Eustace stiffened. His gaze snapped to Roger's face for a brief moment, searching, sharp and thoughtful, before drifting downward to the floor. One hand tightened on the armrest.

"Yes," he said quietly. "I know." He swallowed. Then his voice hardened. "But how in God's name would he be of any use now?"

Roger shrugged, a small, noncommittal gesture. "I didn't say he would be," he replied. "Only that he exists. And we have no idea what he can do."

He kept his eyes on Eustace, refusing to let the subject dissolve into evasion.

The silence returned, heavier this time.

Eustace stared at the rug, its faded pattern blurring beneath his unfocused gaze. Old images stirred behind his eyes, lectures long past, arguments forgotten by everyone else, a younger man's confidence, choices made too quickly, regrets never spoken aloud.

He exhaled slowly.

Finally, he spoke.

"I'll think about it," he muttered.

It was not a promise.

But for Eustace Fairfax, it was close enough.

Roger allowed himself a small, satisfied smile.

Not triumphant. Not relieved.

Just quietly hopeful.

He leaned back into his chair, folded his hands once more, and waited.

ϒ ϒ ϒ

Catherine had planned for years. In truth, she had planned *everything*. It had taken her nearly three years to conceive the architecture of her scheme, its motives, its risks, its contingencies, and another two to bring every moving part into quiet, obedient alignment. Nothing had been left to chance. Not the timing. Not the location. Not even the way the wind moved across the island in the late afternoon.

The island was perfect.

Tiny, pristine, and temperate, it rose from the ocean like a forgotten Eden, volcanic slopes softened by green pastures, cloud-wreathed peaks guarding a ring of humble cottages and narrow roads. There were fewer than three hundred residents, most of them descended from the same handful of families, bound together by generations of isolation and mutual dependence. They farmed the rich black soil, tended cattle and potatoes, and lived by rhythms older than satellites and stock markets.

To Catherine, it was invisible.

Remote well beyond inconvenience. Protected by distance. Wrapped by the ocean.

It had taken her more than a year of negotiations, letters, inspections, and carefully staged patience to persuade the authorities to permit her construction. Every application had been flawless. Every environmental study was immaculate. Every concern was met with calm, courteous reassurance. She never hurried them. She never pressured. She simply waited, smiling, until resistance softened into approval.

She promised restraint.

A modest footprint. Sustainable materials. Minimal disruption.

She promised commitment.

Two years only, she said. No more. After that, the property would be donated outright to the government, transformed into a permanent residence for the Royal Governor, a gift to the island's future.

And she promised generosity.

Before the first foundation was poured, she had already funded repairs to the school roof. New computers appeared in classrooms. Scholarships quietly materialized. The medical clinic received upgraded equipment. The harbor gained improved lighting. Community halls were refurbished. No announcement was ever made. No plaque bore her name.

The gratitude arrived anyway.

By the time construction began, she was no longer "the American investor." She was simply Catherine.

The house itself rose slowly, deliberately, as though it had grown from the land rather than been imposed upon it. Elegant but understated. Stone and glass. Wide windows facing the sea. Terraces sheltered from prevailing winds. Solar arrays disguised as architectural flourishes. Rainwater systems are hidden beneath manicured gardens.

It was beautiful without being ostentatious.

Impressive without being provocative.

Inside, every room had been designed with precision: sightlines, acoustics, privacy, security. No contractor ever saw the complete plans. No single person understood the whole structure. That, too, had been intentional.

The locals accepted her presence easily.

She attended church. She volunteered at festivals. She hosted small dinners and listened far more than she spoke. She learned names, remembered birthdays, and asked after relatives. She laughed easily. She dressed simply. She never displayed impatience.

She was generous. Warm. Disarmingly ordinary, though she looked anything but.

Not at all what they had expected from a wealthy American.

To them, she was a benefactor who had chosen their forgotten island out of kindness and curiosity. A woman seeking solitude. A temporary resident who would leave behind something lasting.

To Catherine, it was all exactly as planned. Every smile. Every donation. Every promise.

Every stone had been laid in place.

Chapter Six

The Gathering

Along the Charles River, the college rowing teams continued to practice even though school was out, Harvard, B.U., B.C., U.Mass. The sky hung low and gray, pressing softly against brick buildings and hospital towers, as if the city itself were holding its breath. Traffic murmured along Memorial Drive, distant and impersonal, while inside a quiet Lexington home, two women sat in the middle of a storm no weather could touch.

Sedi Monroe and Sabrina had been best friends for nearly twenty years.

They had met during their first brutal months at Harvard Medical School, two exhausted, overworked students sharing late-night coffee, stolen sandwiches, and whispered fears in fluorescent-lit corridors. Friendship had come quickly and without negotiation. Sedi, brilliant and fearless, had admired Sabrina's calm intelligence. Sabrina, thoughtful and grounded, had leaned on Sedi's fire when her own confidence wavered.

Sedi had been compared to a light-skinned Iman: tall, graceful, statuesque. She had modeled all through school to help with her finances. Sabrina was the petite, golden-blonde counterpoint. She was just as beautiful, but in an entirely different way. They were often referred to as Ebony and Ivory after the song.

After graduation, their paths had diverged but never separated.

Sedi had stayed in Boston, rising steadily through the ranks at Boston Children's Hospital, becoming known for her surgical precision and her uncompromising advocacy for her patients. Sabrina had gone south, opening her clinic in Morgantown, building a life rooted in service and quiet resilience.

Nonetheless, they spoke every week. They trusted each other completely. And now, for the first time in years, neither knew what to say.

Sabrina sat rigidly on the edge of the sofa, her hands folded in her lap, her eyes unfocused. She looked as though she might leave at any moment or collapse.

Sedi paced.

Back and forth. Across the Persian rug. Past the tall windows. Around the antique writing desk.

Her long strides were sharp and angry, her movements clipped and restless. Normally graceful, she now moved like a caged animal. Her beautiful face, usually composed and thoughtful, was transformed by fury.

"I'll kill the bitch," she snapped suddenly. "I'll find her and strangle her face-to-face."

Sabrina did not flinch.

"That doesn't help, Sedi," she answered quietly.

Her voice was steady, but only because she was forcing it to be.

Sedi stopped mid-stride. She closed her eyes. Breathed in. Held it. Let it out slowly. Then she crossed the room and dropped onto the sofa beside her friend, elbows on her knees, head in her hands.

"I know," she said softly. "I'm sorry…"

She hesitated, then lifted her head.

"But I'll do it. Someday."

A thin smile flickered and vanished.

"What's the plan, Sabrina? What role do I have?" Her voice sharpened again. "I have to have one."

Sabrina shook her head.

"I don't know. I really don't."

For a moment, Sedi stared at the far wall, her jaw tightening.

Then something changed.

The anger drained from her face, replaced by something harder, colder. Her expression settled into the familiar look her residents feared and respected: focused, analytical, relentless.

She stood. Crossed to the antique desk against the wall. Opened a drawer.

Removed a yellow legal pad and a fountain pen. Returned to the sofa.

"All right," she said.

She flipped open the pad.

"First question. What do you think her plan is?"

"We aren't certain it's Catherine," Sabrina replied.

Sedi looked up sharply.

"Don't be stupid. Of course it's her."

She began writing.

"But what does she want? It can't be money. She's rich."

"Yes," Sabrina said quietly. "Everyone agrees with that. It's vengeance."

Sedi nodded once.

"Undoubtedly. It may be Drew and Ell's child, but the reprisal is aimed at you and Simon."

"Again, everyone agrees," Sabrina said.

Sedi scribbled.

"You said this happened five days ago?"

"Yes."

"And no demands yet?"

"None."

Sedi's pen paused.

"Why do you think there's been no contact?" she asked.

"We don't know."

They fell silent.

The only sound was the faint ticking of a mantel clock and the distant rush of traffic.

Sabrina stared at the floor.

Sedi stared at the page.

Then, suddenly, Sedi's head snapped up.

"Travel time."

Sabrina blinked.

"What?"

"Travel time," Sedi repeated. "She has to get little Sabina to wherever she's going to hold her."

Sabrina straightened.

"Brilliant," she whispered. "Yes. That could be it."

"Catherine won't make contact until she's settled," Sedi continued, already writing again. "Until she knows everything is secure."

She tapped the page.

"The delay will tell us something. How long it takes her to reach out will tell us how far she's gone. How isolated the location is."

They sat with that. Letting it settle. Letting hope and fear intertwine.

"Okay," Sedi said finally. "Next question. Who knows about this?"

"The D.C. police," Sabrina replied.

She paused.

"Oh. And Sir Roger and Fairfax."

Sedi raised an eyebrow.

"No one else?"

"No."

"Well," Sedi said, "that's the whole gang. Except for…"

She hesitated.

“Morgantown. Cheri.”

Sabrina sighed.

“Yes. But if I tell Cheri, she’ll be here before her plane lands. She’s…quite a force.”

Sedi smiled despite herself.

“Yes.”

Then she leaned back.

“You know, for over four hundred years, Scotsmen have been at the front of the British line in every war.”

Sabrina looked at her.

“The fearless find a way forward.”

Sabrina smiled faintly.

“Besides,” Sedi added, “Cheri will never forgive you if you leave her out of this.”

“That’s true,” Sabrina admitted.

“I’ll contact her.”

“Today?” Sedi asked.

Then, with the ghost of her old humor returning,

“Yes, today, Mother.”

Sedi laughed softly.

And for the first time since arriving back in Boston, Sabrina felt something loosen inside her chest. Not relief. Not peace. But resolve.

They were no longer helpless. They were planning. They were fighting back. And Catherine, wherever she was, would soon discover that she had not just kidnapped a child; she had stirred a hornet's nest. And when you kick a hornet’s nest, it the hornets that decide when things are over.

It felt as though they had declared war.

Not with speeches or banners, not with threats or grand gestures, but with resolve. With sharpened minds and hardened hearts. With the quiet understanding that fear would no longer be allowed to dictate their next move.

Now, that waiting was over. They were no longer reacting. They were preparing. She felt the thought crystallize inside her, clear and undeniable.

They all needed to meet. All of them. Immediately.

"Sedi, let's go."

Sabrina stood so abruptly that the sofa cushions barely had time to recover their shape.

Sedi looked up in surprise.

"We aren't finished."

Sabrina turned back to her, her eyes bright with urgency.

"No," she said. "But we need to be together to figure things out."

She took a breath, steadying herself.

She moved toward the door.

"Let's go back to our house in Concord. Simon is there, but Drew and Ell are at their home in D.C. They are staying close to home waiting for a call…some contact."

Her voice strengthened as she spoke.

She reached for her keys.

"We need to sit in the same room and look each other in the eye."

Sedi rose slowly, understanding dawning.

"And make a war plan," she said.

"Yes," Sabrina answered.

ϒ ϒ ϒ

As usual, Cheri Stevens was a sight to behold.

Over the past five years, she had slimmed down in all the right places and remained prominent in the right places, giving her an enviable feminine form that seemed sculpted by equal parts discipline and defiance. Her face had narrowed into something almost cinematic, high cheekbones, sharp lines, eyes that could soften into kindness or harden into steel in the span of a breath. And her fiery red hair still served as both an enchantment and a warning, a living flame that announced her presence long before she spoke a word.

This morning, it blazed even brighter.

Cheri hurried across the narrow street, barely waiting for traffic. Her stilettos clicked furiously against the pavement, echoing like gunshots in the quiet mid-morning stillness. If her hair wasn't enough of a warning, her orange-red dress, short, tight, and unapologetic, might as well have been a flare shot into the sky.

Her jaw was clenched. Her eyes shot laser beams. Her lips had nearly vanished, pulled into a razor-thin line of fury and fear.

She didn't slow.

She reached the curb, grabbed the brass handle, and threw open the door to the Mountain Mama Bar.

"Teddy!" she yelled.

The door slammed against the wall behind her, sending a hollow boom through the room.

The Mountain Mama had seen many years. It had been standing on that corner since before most of its patrons had been born, and it wore its age like a badge of honor.

But since George "Bear" Carter purchased it twenty years ago, it had been transformed into a clean and polished place. The oak floor was once scuffed and darkened by spilled beer, cigarette ash from long-ago smoking days, and the boots of miners, mechanics, and drifters who had passed through over the long past decades. Now it was polished and clean. The walls were paneled in knotty pine, stained a dark honey color.

A jukebox in the corner hummed quietly to itself, resting between jobs like a tired old storyteller.

Mounted above the bar was a massive black-and-white photograph of the town's first coal crew, stern men staring out from another century.

Mountain Mama smelled of beer, lemon cleaner, old wood, and comfort.

At this early hour, the place was nearly empty.

Two long- retired miners sat at the far end, nursing coffees and arguing quietly about football. A delivery driver leaned at the bar, scrolling his phone. Otherwise, the Mountain Mama was in its daytime slumber.

That slumber ended the moment Cheri walked in. “Teddy,” she screamed again.

George “Bear” Carter rushed from the back room.

He had never heard Cheri scream like that.

Bear was six-foot-six and built like a misplaced refrigerator, broad shoulders, thick arms, barrel chest. Years earlier, he had been a linebacker before a knee injury and a love of beer redirected his life. Now he owned the Mountain Mama and guarded it like a den. “The Mama” was an institution in Morgantown. Though the Mountain Mama was best known as a haven for “Bears”, it welcomed everyone who respected the room.

He crossed the room in long, thunderous strides.

Even “Tiny,” the bartender, moved quickly.

Tiny was nearly as tall as Bear but carried at least another hundred pounds, most of it in his chest and shoulders. His hands looked like they had been carved from butcher blocks. He had been polishing a glass when Cheri shouted; he dropped it without hesitation and hurried over.

“Cheri, what’s wrong, girl?” Bear’s deep voice burst out, equal parts concern and command.

She stood there, breathing hard, chest rising and falling, eyes blazing.

Noticing Tiny, Cheri snapped, “Bring me a Nate’s, Tiny.”

Tiny didn’t ask questions. He turned and lumbered back behind the bar.

Nate’s Nut Brown Ale, brewed just outside town, was practically a civic religion. Ordering it was less a request than a declaration of belonging.

Bear gently guided Cheri toward her favorite booth.

It sat in the corner beneath a framed photograph of a long-closed dance hall from a century earlier. This corner was hers.

He slid in across from her.

Cheri sat heavily, as though her legs had finally given out. She pressed her palms flat on the table and took several deep breaths.

Bear reached across and covered one of her hands with his massive own, nearly swallowing it.

"Talk to me," he said.

His voice was low now. Steady. After several breaths, Cheri finally found her voice.

"You know Sabrina…"

"I love Sabrina," Bear interrupted. "Did something happen to her?"

"Shut up and listen," Cheri snapped.

Bear immediately closed his mouth.

She swallowed.

"I know you are not aware of what went on five years ago. And kindly did not ask."

"None of my business," Bear said quietly.

Tiny arrived and set the beer in front of her with care, as if placing something fragile.

Cold condensation already beaded down the glass.

He lingered.

"The bar, Tiny," Bear said gently, nodding.

Tiny hesitated, then retreated, though his ears remained fully engaged.

Cheri lifted the beer and took a long drink. Too long. She set it down slowly.

"It's a long story," she said. "And I can't tell you all of it."

She stared into the amber liquid.

"But Sabrina and Simon have close friends in D.C., Drew and Lauren."

Bear nodded.

"They had a little girl nearly five years ago. Named her Sabina. After Sabrina."

She looked up now, hcr eyes dark and steady.

"The little girl has been kidnapped."

The words fell into the room like stones dropped into deep water.

Bear's fingers tightened around hers, too tight, before he realized it and forced himself to loosen his grip. For a few seconds, no one spoke. The air seemed to thicken.

Somewhere in the corner, the jukebox clicked softly as if considering another song. Outside, a truck rumbled past on the street, its tires hissing over the pavement. The ordinary sounds of the world suddenly felt far away.

Tiny, who had been pretending very badly not to listen, suddenly slammed his fist onto the bar. The crack of it snapped through the room like a pistol shot.

"Tell me what I can do," Bear growled. "I'll find them, and I'll kill them."

His voice was low, rough, and dangerous.

Cheri turned toward him slowly.

"You wouldn't be fast enough, Teddy," she said flatly. "I'd get there first."

For a moment, Bear stared at her. Then, despite everything, he snorted.

"Yeah," he said, shaking his head. "Yeah, you probably would."

He leaned forward again, elbows on his knees.

"Well… what's the plan? Because whatever it is, I'm in."

Some of the hard fury drained from Cheri's face, leaving something closer to exhaustion. She looked suddenly older, as if the anger had been the only thing holding her upright.

"Nothing yet," she said quietly. "I just need a friend."

She lifted her glass and took another slow sip.

"There is nothing I can do right now. Sabrina is asking me to stay put… but be ready to help the moment she calls. That's it." She shook her head, her jaw tightening again. "It's infuriating."

Bear leaned back and crossed his massive arms across his chest, the chair creaking beneath him.

"Can't we do something?" he asked.

Cheri frowned and shook her head.

"Not yet."

Bear studied her for a moment, then nodded slowly.

"Well," he said, "when the time comes… You won't be alone."

He grinned faintly.

"When you need me, I'll be there. I'll bring so many bears with me, you'll think you're in Yellowstone Park."

Cheri blinked, then laughed, a short, surprised burst that broke the tension in the room for the first time since she had spoken.

For a moment, at least, the weight lifted.

Chapter Seven

The Sanctuary

The long, sleek yacht slid toward the concrete pier with the unhurried confidence of something that knew it was being watched. It did not merely approach the harbor; it entered it, parting the water with a deliberate grace that felt almost ceremonial. The hull cut cleanly through the low Atlantic swell, leaving behind a widening fan of white froth that dissolved into the deeper green of the sea. The yacht was equipped with sails and engines so it could travel long distances without refueling. Today, its engines were purring.

The ocean itself seemed intent on admiring the vessel. The water that afternoon was not the hard blue of postcards but a layered, living green, emerald where the sun struck it full, jade where it deepened, and nearly obsidian in the troughs between rolling swells. Light shattered across its surface in fragments, scattering silver flecks that winked and vanished with each breath of wind. The tide moved with slow authority, lifting and lowering the yacht as though testing its balance, acknowledging its presence.

The yacht's lines were impossibly smooth, sweeping in a single, uninterrupted arc from the razor-sharp bow to the gently tapered stern. Nearly one hundred feet in length, it seemed longer because nothing about it was abrupt. There were no harsh angles, no utilitarian protrusions. Even the tinted windows curved in harmony with the hull, dark and reflective, giving no hint of the life within. Stainless steel railings traced the perimeter in slender, polished ribbons, catching the sun and casting thin shards of light across the deck.

But it was the color that transformed admiration into fascination.

Painted in a soft pastel mint green, the vessel appeared less constructed than composed, as if it had risen organically from the sea itself. Against the water's shifting shades, the yacht did not contrast; it conversed. The hull echoed the ocean's lighter tones, while darker green accents traced its contours, emphasizing its length and motion even while it idled. When a swell lifted it, the mint surface mirrored the water beneath, blurring the boundary between craft and sea. It seemed, at moments, as though the yacht were carved from the ocean and temporarily shaped into form.

Above, the sky stretched in pale blue expanses streaked with gauzy clouds, and the scent of salt hung thick in the air. Gulls wheeled and cried overhead, their shadows skimming across the deck before darting away. The faint thrum of twin engines reverberated through the pier, a restrained purr rather than a roar, power disciplined by elegance.

As it drew alongside the concrete pier, ropes were cast with effortless precision. The yacht settled into place with a gentle sigh of displaced water, rocking once, twice, then growing still. Even moored, it possessed movement, the ocean continuing to breathe beneath it.

Catherine had chosen the color with calculated audacity. The pastel mint green did not merely complement the sea; it heightened her own presence. When she stood at the rail, her flagrant red hair, brilliant and unapologetic, flared like a signal fire against the softened green. Sea and vessel formed a cool, fluid canvas upon which she was the deliberate stroke of flame. The yacht was not just transportation. It was theater. It was statement. It was an extension of Catherine.

And as the sun slid lower and burnished the water, the mint hull absorbed the changing light, shifting subtly in tone, as if aware that it carried not just wealth, but intention.

White-uniformed sailors moved with ceremonial precision, their caps bright beneath the pale southern light, as they extended the railed boarding plank from the yacht to the pier. The polished wood settled into place with a muted thud, and two of the men stepped forward, gloved hands ready, steadying the descent as though royalty were about to pass.

Catherine emerged first.

She paused only a moment at the top of the gangway, the wind catching the hem of her tailored coat and pressing it against the elegant lines of her body. She was as sleek as the yacht behind her, long, sculpted, and engineered for attention. There was nothing hurried in her movement. She did not walk so much as glide, each step deliberate, balanced, assured. Her dark glasses concealed her eyes, but nothing about her suggested concealment. She was accustomed to being seen. And she loved it.

In her hand, she held that of a small, dark-haired girl, perhaps five or six. The child's coat was buttoned to her chin, her free hand clutching a woolen cap she had refused to wear. She walked obediently at Catherine's side, matching her pace without complaint, her large eyes absorbing the strange harbor, the black volcanic rock, the low gray sky pressing down on sea and land alike.

The sailors inclined their heads as the pair passed. Catherine acknowledged them with the faintest nod, gracious but economical. She neither lingered nor spoke.

At the edge of the pier, a pure white Jeep waited, improbably pristine against the rugged backdrop of the island. Its tires were lightly dusted with fine ash-colored grit, but the body shone like porcelain. A driver, tall and silent, stepped forward and opened the rear door.

A gust of wind swept in from the Atlantic, sharp and bracing. June here marked the first month of winter, and the air carried a damp chill that slid easily beneath fabric and into bone. Catherine did not shiver. The child did, almost imperceptibly.

Beyond them, rising from the island's center, the great barren peak loomed, dark, volcanic, and austere. It stood without its winter crown for now, its summit still free of snow, though the clouds gathered around it as if considering the transformation to come. The mountain appeared watchful, ancient, and indifferent, as though measuring the newcomers and withholding judgment.

Catherine glanced once toward the peak before stepping into the Jeep. The girl followed, climbing carefully onto the seat. The door closed with a solid, final sound.

Moments later, the vehicle pulled away from the pier, its white frame diminishing against the vastness of rock, sea, and sky, carrying with it a woman who had planned every detail, and a child who had no idea she was part of something far larger than the cold wind of a southern winter.

The Jeep moved slowly through the tiny settlement, its tires humming over the narrow paved road that stitched together the island's modest homes. The town was little more than a cluster of whitewashed cottages, low stone walls, and wind-bent shrubs clinging stubbornly to volcanic soil. Smoke curled from a few chimneys, dissolving quickly into the cold June air. Islanders paused in their quiet routines to watch the vehicle pass. News traveled quickly here. A white Jeep climbing toward the mountain was not an ordinary sight, but they all knew who it was.

The road soon left the village behind and began its ascent along the foot of the island's defining peak. The mountain rose abruptly from the earth, dark and immense, its slopes carved by time and weather into severe lines of rock and hardened ash. The Jeep leaned into its climb, winding through deliberate switchbacks cut into the mountainside. With each turn, the view widened, first the town, then the harbor, then the endless sweep of steel-gray Atlantic stretching toward the horizon.

Sabina pressed her face lightly to the window, watching the world fall away beneath them.

At last, the large house came into view.

It stood three stories high, commanding yet refined, its silhouette echoing the angular thrust of the mountain behind it. The architect had not tried to compete with nature but to converse with it. The rooflines rose in sharp, elegant pitches that mirrored the steep incline of the peak. Expansive windows faced the sea, their glass catching the pale winter light like sheets of ice. The façade, a subtle shade of dusty green, shifted subtly with the changing sky, sometimes silver, sometimes pearl, sometimes nearly white against the volcanic stone.

The Jeep glided through wrought-iron gates that opened soundlessly, then curved around a crescent drive paved in dark basalt. Low lanterns lined the arc of the driveway, their flames steady despite the wind. Manicured hedges, an improbable achievement on such rugged ground, outlined the approach, and beyond them, terraces descended in precise geometric tiers.

The vehicle came to a gentle stop before a wide cascade of marble steps that fanned outward from the entrance like a ceremonial invitation. The marble, pale and veined, stood in striking contrast to the black earth from which the mountain rose. Above the steps, tall double doors of carved oak framed the entry, their panels etched with understated classical motifs. Two servants waited at the base of the staircase.

They were dressed in dark green livery trimmed with subtle gold braid, their posture impeccable, hands folded neatly before them. The color was deliberate, rich against the residence's muted shade, regal against the barren landscape. They bowed slightly as a footman stepped forward to open the passenger door.

Catherine emerged first, composed as ever, her coat settling around her like a mantle. Sabina followed, quieter now, her dark eyes sweeping upward along the height of the house. The wind tugged at her hair, but she stood still.

The servants moved with quiet efficiency, offering gloved hands. Catherine and Sabina were gently assisted up the broad marble steps, their footsteps echoing softly against the stone. The climb felt ceremonial, each step lifting them farther from the world below.

At the top, the wide double doors were opened inward.

Warm light spilled out into the cool mountain air.

ϒ ϒ ϒ

The June afternoon sun filtered through the tall, multi-paned windows of Simon and Sabrina’s library. It turned the room into a cathedral of amber light. The glass, imperfect, faintly wavy, fractured the brightness into prisms that scattered across leather-bound volumes and polished wood. Bronze antiquities caught fire where the light struck them: an Egyptian ushabti, a Roman oil lamp, and a medieval astrolabe resting beneath its glass dome. The room smelled faintly of lemon oil and old paper, a fragrance of permanence and thought.

Sedi sat elegantly at one end of the long couch, her legs crossed with unconscious precision. She wore a finely knitted dress in her favorite shade, soft beige, nearly the color of sand at dusk. The fabric traced her form without clinging, as though it understood its assignment: to suggest, never to boast. Slender and ravishing, she had once financed her way through college and medical school by modeling. It could have become a lucrative career; agencies had courted her relentlessly. But Sedi and Sabrina shared a deeper allegiance, to children, to medicine, to purpose over applause.

Photographers had often compared Sedi to Iman, with the same regal poise and luminous presence, but with a warm caramel complexion that seemed to drink in light and give it back, enriched. Even now, in a private library among friends, she appeared as though she might be called to a runway at any moment. Yet beneath the immaculate exterior lived a mind as disciplined as it was brilliant.

Sabrina sat at the other end of the couch, sunlight striking her golden hair until it gleamed like spun honey. She wore a white peasant blouse and faded blue jeans, her uniform of comfort. Unlike Sedi, she dressed for ease rather than spectacle. Still, there was no mistaking her natural beauty; when required, she could transform herself into something arresting. But in her own home, among books and battle plans, she preferred simplicity.

Simon entered carrying a polished silver tray. On it rested a crystal pitcher of freshly squeezed lemonade beaded with condensation, and three heavy, cut-glass tumblers that caught the light like small chandeliers.

"Best to stay sober today, I figured," he said lightly, though his eyes betrayed the strain beneath the humor.

"Thank you, Simon. I agree," Sedi replied.

"Are we ready to Zoom with Drew and Ell?" Sabrina asked, pouring the pale gold liquid into the glasses. Ice clinked softly.

"Yes. They're waiting for us," Simon said, positioning himself between the two women so all three would be visible to the camera.

The screen flickered to life. Drew appeared first, composed but weary, his jaw tight. Lauren sat beside him, her face pale with worry.

"Hello, Sedi. It's good to see you again," Lauren said, forcing a fragile smile.

"Yes," Drew added. "And we're grateful for your help. The more minds at work here, the better."

"First, any new information?" Simon asked, leaning forward slightly.

Drew shook his head. "Nothing. The police have repeatedly canvassed the neighborhood. No usable private camera footage. No unfamiliar vehicles logged. We're at a standstill until she makes contact."

"I'm going crazy," Ell whispered, her voice trembling. "Why doesn't she contact us?"

"The police are cautious about naming Catherine outright," Drew continued, "but privately they admit she's the most likely suspect. What they can't explain is the delay."

A silence fell, thick, airless.

"Do you think…" Ell swallowed. "Is it possible she intends never to give Sabina back?"

"No," Simon said immediately, his tone firm. "I can't believe so. She wants me. Sabina is just her leverage. There will be a demand. And it will be for Sabrina or me."

"But then why is she waiting?" Drew pressed.

Sabrina glanced toward Sedi. "Sedi has a theory. And I think it's a good one."

Sedi leaned forward, elbows resting lightly on her knees. Her composure shifted from elegance to analysis.

"I don't believe she's stalling," Sedi began. "I believe the delay is logistical. Catherine is meticulous. She would never initiate her plan until every variable was controlled. That suggests distance, significant distance."

"Go on," Drew said quietly.

"She's chosen a remote location," Sedi continued. "Not simply far, but difficult to access. Somewhere that requires layered travel, perhaps multiple modes of transportation. A place insulated by geography. Ocean. Mountain territories. Jungles. Somewhere she can establish security before making her move."

The idea hung in the air.

"Genius," Drew breathed, a spark of energy returning to his face. Lauren nodded slowly, hope and dread mingling in her eyes.

"It's been five days," Sedi went on. "In theory, you can reach almost anywhere in the world in much less time than that. Which means the obstacle isn't pure distance. It's accessibility."

"And control," Simon added, thinking aloud. "She would want a place where she can control communications, limit surveillance, and anticipate response time."

"Exactly," Sedi said. "This isn't a delay for intimidation. It's preparation."

The room, both rooms, fell silent again, but it was a different silence now. Not helplessness. Calculation.

"And if that's true," Drew said slowly, leaning back in his chair as the weight of the idea settled over him, "then wherever she is… it's somewhere chosen long ago."

Simon's gaze hardened, the lightness gone from his features. A faint muscle tightened along his jaw.

"Yes," he said evenly. "Which implies she's been planning this for years. Not months. Years."

The word seemed to echo.

"And that means her demands will not be impulsive," Drew continued. "They will have been contemplated, refined, rehearsed. And they will be severe." He paused. "I'm afraid of what that might look like."

"But how will she make her demands?" Sabrina asked, frowning slightly. "Electronic communication is difficult to conceal for long. The authorities will monitor everything: emails, texts, and encrypted apps. And Catherine isn't a cyber expert."

"No," Drew agreed, "but she could hire someone who is."

Simon shook his head immediately. "Yes, she could. But I don't think so. That isn't her style." His tone sharpened with certainty. "Catherine will not outsource the heart of her revenge. She'll design the communication herself. It will be theatrical. Personal. Controlled."

“What does that mean?” Sabrina pressed.

Simon exhaled slowly, searching for words. “I don’t know exactly. But I expect something… elegant. Frustratingly deliberate. Perhaps layered. Something that unfolds in stages rather than explodes all at once.” He gave a tight half-smile.

“Elegant?” Sabrina repeated, incredulous.

“Yes. Beautifully constructed. Painfully slow. Something that forces us to participate in a game, her game.” He paused. “She won’t simply send a ransom note.”

“She could wait forever,” Ell said softly, her voice barely steady. “She has Sabina.”

“No,” Simon replied quietly but firmly. “She won’t wait forever. She’s disciplined, yes, but she’s also driven by fierce emotion. Her humiliation has been fermenting for too long. This is not only a strategy. It’s a catharsis.” He leaned forward, elbows on his knees. “She will begin as soon as she is secure in her sanctuary.”

The word hung in the air, sanctuary. It sounded almost sacred, though everyone knew it would be anything but.

“Accepting Sedi’s theory about distance, and I think she’s correct,” Simon continued, “I would estimate we hear from her within the next forty-eight hours. With her resources, there is no place on earth she cannot reach within a week. And once she is in position, she won’t delay the opening act.”

Drew nodded slowly. “So we brace ourselves.”

“Yes,” Simon said. His voice lowered, steady and resolute. “Because when she moves, it will be complicated, calculated, and designed to unnerve us at every step.”

“Just one more thought,” Sedi interjected, leaning forward as if afraid the idea might evaporate if she did not speak it quickly. “Wasn’t there a detective that Catherine used to help find the ring?”

Simon straightened in his chair, the fatigue momentarily stripped from his face. “Yes. Yes, there was. Of course there was.” He pressed his fingers to his lips, searching. “What was his name?”

“Chester Morris,” Luaren said without hesitation. Her memory for details was rarely wrong. "I contacted him for her. He was based in New York." She narrowed her eyes slightly, assembling the rest. "International Inquiry Agents. IIA. That was the firm."

Simon's expression hardened. "IIA," he repeated quietly. "If Catherine needed something found, or someone, she would call them."

Sedi's jaw tightened. "And if she's orchestrating all of this, she wouldn't leave the investigative side to chance."

"We need to contact him," Simon said firmly. "If he's not directly involved, he may know something. And if he is involved…" He let the sentence hang.

Drew glanced toward the door, instinctively cautious. "Should we tell the police?"

"Not yet," Simon replied after a measured pause. His voice had shifted, calmer now, more deliberate. "If Morris is connected, he'll go quiet the moment law enforcement breathes down his neck. Drew, I think you and I need to pay Mr. Morris a visit first. Quietly."

Ell nodded slowly. "If he's innocent, we lose nothing. If he isn't, we may learn more from surprise than from procedure."

Silence settled over the room again, but this time it was different. Not the hollow stillness of confusion or fear, but something sharper. Focused. Anticipatory.

For the first time since Sabina's disappearance, they were not merely reacting.

They were about to make a move.

Chapter Eight

The First Alliance

The offices of International Inquiry Agents occupied three full floors of the Empire State Building, that limestone-and-steel cathedral to commerce that had defined the Manhattan skyline since the depths of the Great Depression. The agency itself had been founded in 1911, when New York still measured its ambition in brownstone blocks and harbor tonnage, and it had taken rooms in the building as one of its earliest tenants when construction was completed in April 1931. While the world staggered under economic collapse, the firm planted its flag high above Fifth Avenue, declaring, quietly but confidently, that information, properly gathered and discreetly used, would always be valuable.

Time had only widened its reach. What began as a discreet investigative bureau serving industrialists and foreign consulates had grown into a global intelligence consultancy, with offices in London, Paris, Rome, and Singapore. Their brass plaque was modest, almost self-effacing. Its influence was not.

Simon and Drew sat quietly in the reception lobby on the 80th floor, suspended between earth and sky. The elevator ride had been swift and nearly soundless, the kind that unsettled the stomach just enough to remind one how far above the pavement one now stood. When the doors opened, they stepped into an atmosphere that felt at once modern and reverent.

The lobby was a studied homage to the firm's origins. Rich walnut paneling lined the walls, polished to a muted glow. The wood bore subtle vertical inlays of brushed nickel, a quiet nod to the Art Deco geometry that had dominated the building's original design. Black-and-white photographs, sepia originals carefully restored, depicted the firm's early days: stern-faced men in three-piece suits; a 1917 telegram room humming with wires and codebooks; a 1930s conference table surrounded by cigar smoke and war maps.

The reception desk was a single, sweeping curve of dark walnut, its surface unmarred, its edges razor-clean. Behind it sat a young woman with her dark hair in a bob. She wore a dark blue conservative dress. Her expression was composed and attentive, as though nothing in the world could surprise her.

But it was the windows that commanded attention.

Floor-to-ceiling panes of reinforced glass wrapped the outer wall, revealing Manhattan in all its restless grandeur. From eighty stories up, the city's noise dissolved into abstraction. Yellow taxis became threads of motion; pedestrians, mere flecks crossing the chessboard of intersections. The Hudson lay to the west, steel-gray and dignified, catching the late light in fractured shards. To the south, Lower Manhattan bristled with towers, symbols of finance, law, and ambition, each vying for prominence. Even from this height, the city seemed not still but coiled, as if preparing for its next transaction, its next conquest.

From this height, the city's unparalleled commercial power was visible in steel and glass. But within these three floors, power took another form, less visible, more precise. Information. Leverage. Timing.

Simon leaned back slightly in his chair, hands folded, his gaze drifting from the skyline to the historical photographs. Drew sat forward, elbows resting on his knees, studying the room with a strategist's eye. The setting was not ostentatious; it was deliberate. It conveyed longevity, discretion, and power without theatrical flourish.

The young woman rose gracefully from behind the polished walnut reception desk and crossed the lobby with quiet efficiency. Her heels made a soft, measured rhythm against the marble floor.

"Mr. Sterling. Mr. Idle," she said, her voice professional but not unfriendly. "Mr. Morris is free now. Please follow me."

Simon and Drew stood simultaneously.

They followed the receptionist down a corridor that seemed to stretch longer than it truly was, its thick carpeting absorbing every sound. A few more recent color photographs hinted at modern operations: Singapore's skyline at dusk, Rome's terracotta rooftops, London's gray silhouette beneath a brooding sky.

The receptionist stopped before a set of red mahogany double doors. She knocked once, opened them, and stepped aside.

"Gentlemen."

Chester Morris was already standing.

He was a man in his fifties, solidly built, silver at the temples but thick-haired, with the alert eyes of someone who rarely missed nuance. His suit was tailored and conservative, charcoal with a faint pinstripe. No flashy watch, nothing that drew attention.

"Gentlemen," he said with a faint smile, extending his hand first to Simon, then to Drew. "Should I have you checked for firearms?" he quipped lightly.

Simon's lips curved in response. "Time heals all wounds. Or almost, I suppose."

Morris chuckled. "Almost." He gestured toward the seating area. "Please, have a seat."

The office was a prestigious corner suite. Windows wrapped two full walls, offering an elevated view of Manhattan's restless geometry. Morris remained behind his desk for the moment while Simon and Drew settled into the side chairs opposite him.

"Your call," Morris began, folding his hands lightly, "was rather cryptic. Of course, we're accustomed to initial contacts being… enigmatic. However, given our history, albeit on opposite sides of a rather unpleasant matter, I must assume this is somehow related."

"It is," Simon replied evenly. "And I think it's best that I be direct, to save us all some time."

"By all means. Bluntness is efficient."

Simon did not hesitate. "First, I need to know if you are, let's say, currently involved with Catherine's activities in any capacity."

Morris did not flinch. "Understandable question." His tone lost its levity. "I am not. I have had no contact with her since the…episode… five years ago. I don't even know where she is."

"Good," Drew said quietly. "You've just answered our second question."

Morris's expression sharpened. "Then this is serious."

"It is," Simon said. "We suspect Catherine of a crime. A serious one. Law enforcement is actively trying to locate her."

Morris leaned back slightly. "How serious, if I may ask?"

Drew's voice carried none of Simon's philosophical cadence. It was direct, stripped down to the bone.

"She is the prime suspect in the abduction of my five-year-old daughter."

The words seemed to alter the air in the room.

For several long seconds, no one moved.

"Kidnapping?" Morris leaned forward abruptly, forearms on the desk. He searched their faces. "You said, suspect. You don't know with certainty?"

Simon answered, his tone measured but edged with steel. "If I wake to a bright sun and find the ground covered in snow, I may not have seen it fall, but I am certain it snowed during the night."

Morris nodded slowly. "Understood." He shifted his gaze to Drew. "You've had no ransom demand?"

"Not yet," Drew replied. "But we believe one is imminent."

Morris rose from behind his desk.

"Come over here, gentlemen," he said. "Let's not conduct this conversation across a barricade."

He moved toward a sitting area along the windows, a deep brown leather couch, two matching chairs, and a low glass table between them. The skyline stretched behind it like a silent audience.

Simon and Drew sat on the couch. Morris dragged one of the leather chairs closer, reducing the physical and psychological distance between them.

Simon leaned forward, elbows on his knees.

"Mr. Morris, "

"Chet," he interrupted gently. "Please. Let's dispense with formality."

"Chet," Simon continued, "the authorities believe, and we agree, that this is not financially motivated. It has been nearly a week with no demand."

"Then it's not about money," Morris said immediately. "Seven days is too long. If it were ransom-driven, you'd have heard within forty-eight hours."

"Exactly," Drew said.

"Given the history," Simon added, "we believe Catherine orchestrated this. Not for profit. For revenge."

Morris's jaw tightened slightly. He scratched his chin, thinking.

"I can see that premise," he admitted. "It does not require much extrapolation. But what is her objective?"

Simone's voice entered the space quietly but firmly. "Her hatred is directed at me. She believes I destroyed her career and reputation. She would see the most effective way to control me as targeting someone I care about."

Morris studied him carefully. "And she chose the child."

"Yes," Drew said.

Another silence followed, this one heavier.

After a moment, Morris exhaled slowly. "If I were conducting this investigation independently, I would likely reach the same conclusion. It aligns with her psychological profile."

He stood and walked toward the window, hands in his pockets, looking down eighty floors at the moving threads of traffic.

"But why the delay?" he said aloud. "Why no communication? Catherine was never impulsive. She was methodical. Theatrics mattered to her. But she was not a patient person."

"That troubled us as well," Drew replied. "We believe she may have chosen a remote location to stay. Somewhere distant. Perhaps even isolated enough that communication itself required staging."

Simon added, "It may have taken time to reach her location before initiating the next phase."

Morris turned back toward them. "Remote," he repeated thoughtfully. "She did always prefer dramatic geography."

He resumed his seat, leaning forward now.

"This is not merely unacceptable," he said, his voice low and firm. "It is outrageous. I will say this clearly: I have had no contact with Catherine. If she is responsible, she is acting entirely independently of this firm."

He looked from Simon to Drew.

"But if she is the perpetrator, IIA will assist you."

Drew's eyes narrowed slightly. "In what capacity?"

"In every capacity available to us," Morris replied without hesitation. "We have offices in London, Paris, Rome, and Singapore. We maintain relationships in places you would not expect. We have access to transportation records, maritime movements, private aviation logs, offshore registries, and information streams not immediately accessible to law enforcement."

Simon studied him. "Why help us?"

Morris did not answer immediately.

"Because," he said at last, "five years ago, despite being on opposing sides, I respected how you conducted yourself. And because of whatever our past disagreements, abducting a child crosses a line no professional should ever tolerate."

He paused.

"Once you confirm definitively that it is Catherine, notify me immediately. In the meantime, I will begin reviewing her old contact network, friends, former associates, and financial conduits. Catherine never did anything without leaving her fingerprints. We may know best where to look."

The skyline behind him shimmered in the summer light.

Simon nodded slowly. "We believe we'll hear from her within forty-eight hours."

Morris's expression hardened.

"Then we had better be ready when she makes contact.

ϒ ϒ ϒ

It was unusually warm for winter. The air had risen to nearly seventy degrees, ten degrees above the island's most mild seasonal norm. The breeze drifting in from the sea carried no bite, only the soft scent of salt and distant greenery. Outside, the sky stretched in an unbroken sweep of blue, the kind of polished brilliance that made the ocean shimmer like hammered glass.

Sunlight poured generously through the crystal-cut windows of the fashionable bedroom, fracturing into prisms along the polished floor. The room itself had been arranged with calculated tenderness. It was clearly designed for a young girl, yet not merely furnished, but curated.

A canopied bed dominated one wall, draped in sea-green and white linen that fell in soft folds to the floor. The canopy fabric moved gently in the warm breeze, giving the illusion of sails breathing in the harbor. The carpet beneath was plush and pale, matching the green accents woven subtly into its pattern. A white-painted toy chest lay against the far wall, its brass hinges polished to a gleam. A small writing desk stood beneath the window, neatly arranged with colored pencils, a watercolor set, and thick drawing paper. Even the drapes echoed the color scheme, white with embroidered sea-green vines climbing their length.

Catherine entered the room quietly, carrying a white box tied with a wide green bow. The ribbon caught the sunlight, glowing faintly as she crossed the floor.

"Sabina," she said warmly. "Look what your mother and father sent you."

The beautiful dark-haired little girl looked up from her coloring book. She was charming, with large eyes and soft curls falling against her cheeks, but the innocence had been dimmed by confusion. The page before her was only half-colored. Her small fingers tightened slightly around the crayon.

She did not smile.

"Why haven't they come?" she asked in a voice that tried very hard not to tremble.

Catherine lowered the box onto a low table beside the bed and knelt gracefully so that she was nearly at eye level.

"They will come, sweetheart," she said softly. "I promise you. This is just a little vacation for you. A surprise adventure. They had to finish something important first. But they'll be here very soon." She tilted her head slightly. "In the meantime, they wanted you to have something special."

Sabina hesitated.

Children understand tone long before they understand circumstance. Her eyes searched Catherine's face, looking for something that would confirm the promise.

Catherine smiled, calculated, patient.

"Go on," she said gently. "Open it."

Sabina slid off the bed and walked slowly toward the white box. Each step was careful, uncertain. She stopped beside it and glanced up once more at Catherine, as if asking silent permission. Then she reached for the lid and lifted it.

Inside, a white fluffball shifted.

A tiny yip escaped the box, high and hopeful. Two bright black eyes blinked up at her. A small black nose sniffed furiously, and the little creature attempted to scramble upward, its miniature paws slipping against the smooth interior.

Sabina gasped.

The fear evaporated from her face in an instant, replaced by astonished delight.

"It's a puppy!" she cried, her voice lifting into laughter for the first time in days.

She reached into the box and carefully lifted the tiny white bundle into her arms. The puppy was impossibly soft, warm, and wriggling, its heart fluttering rapidly against her chest. It licked her chin with a tiny pink tongue.

"For me?" she shouted, her voice echoing lightly in the bright room. "To keep?"

"Yes," Catherine replied smoothly, rising to her feet. "Of course. Your parents wanted you to have a playmate while you waited for them. Someone to keep you company."

Sabina buried her face into the puppy's fur, giggling as it squirmed.

"She's so little!" she exclaimed. "She's like a cloud!"

"Do you wish to name her?" Catherine asked.

Sabina grew suddenly thoughtful, cradling the pup carefully. She examined the tiny ears, the soft belly, the perfect little nose. She thought for some time.

"I think her name should be Sugar," she decided. "Because she's white and so sweet."

Catherine smiled.

"Perfect," she said. "Sugar it is."

The sunlight shifted slightly, glinting off the crystal edges of the windowpanes. Outside, the ocean breeze stirred the tall grasses beyond the terrace. Somewhere in the distance, seabirds called.

"Why don't we take Sugar outside?" Catherine suggested lightly. "Let her see her new home."

Sabina jumped to her feet immediately, the hesitation of moments earlier forgotten.

"Come on, Sugar!" she laughed, turning toward the door.

"Wait," Catherine said gently. "Put her down. Let's see if she will follow you."

Sabina knelt and placed the tiny white pup onto the polished floor.

For a second, Sugar stood uncertainly, her small paws splayed slightly as she oriented herself. Then she looked up at Sabina, gave a determined little yip, and trotted forward, tail wagging furiously, following the child toward the hallway.

Sabina squealed with delight as the puppy bounded after her, sliding slightly on the smooth surface before regaining her footing.

From the bedroom door, Catherine watched them go down the hall.

Her smile remained.

But her eyes were distant, calculating.

Outside, the warm winter sun shone over the island, bright and deceptive.

Chapter Nine

Where the Game Begins

Sedi stood on her front porch, holding the elegant ivory envelope she had just removed from the delivery package. The paper was thick, expensive, stationery meant to be noticed. Even before opening it, she could feel the quiet arrogance of it in her hands.

A handsome young African-American man stood beside her on the walkway. His delivery van idled at the curb, its engine humming softly beneath the rustle of the early morning breeze. The sign painted neatly along the side read *Boston Express Dispatch*. It was a local courier service, efficient, reliable, and well-known. Nothing about it suggested international intrigue or calculated menace.

Across the quiet Lexington street, the branches of old maples shifted gently, their shadows sliding across the brick walkways and brownstone facades. Sedi reached out suddenly and caught the young man's sleeve just as he turned to leave.

She silently read the address written in graceful looping script across the front of the envelope.

To My Marvelous Friend, Lesedi

The words seemed overplayed. Sedi's expression hardened.

She looked back at the package cover to double-check the sender. The name stared up at her in stark simplicity.

Catherine Lodge.

For a moment, the world seemed to narrow to the single line of ink. Then Sedi lifted her eyes slowly.

"Sir, was this hand-delivered to your office?"

The man paused, mildly puzzled, and tapped the face of his electronic notebook. The small screen reflected faintly in his glasses as he studied the delivery record.

"It doesn't say, ma'am," he replied after a moment. "It was left at our Tremont office downtown at 8:37 this morning. Whoever brought it in paid cash for the service."

Sedi's mind moved quickly now, too quickly for comfort. Cash. No sender information. Local courier. Deliberate.

"I'm afraid you are going to be delayed, uh… what's your name, please?"

The young man straightened slightly, surprised by the sudden seriousness in her tone.

"Arthur Samuels, ma'am," he said, offering a polite smile.

"Arthur," Sedi said calmly, though the tension in her voice was unmistakable, "you should contact your supervisor and tell them that you are indefinitely delayed."

Arthur frowned. He shifted his weight awkwardly, glancing back toward his van.

"I'm sorry, ma'am, I really need to go. I've got a full route today. Timing is important in this business, I'm afraid."

Sedi looked him straight in the eye.

Her gaze was steady, clinical, almost surgical.

"I understand," she said quietly, "but you have unwittingly just been made a party to a felony."

Arthur blinked.

For a moment, he simply stared at her, unsure he had heard correctly.

"What? How?" he exclaimed. "Oh, my God."

"You need to call your supervisor and tell him exactly where you are," Sedi said, already moving toward the door. "And that the Boston police will want to speak with you shortly, and your supervisor, I'm sure."

Arthur stood frozen for half a second. Then the reality of the situation seemed to settle over him all at once.

"Yes, ma'am," he said quickly, fumbling for his phone.

Sedi pulled open the front door of her house.

"Come inside," she said. "This is going to take some time."

Arthur retrieved his phone from his jacket and followed her in, the quiet suburban afternoon suddenly feeling far less ordinary than it had just moments before.

ϒ ϒ ϒ

Sedi's study had never felt so crowded.

Normally, it was a quiet, thoughtful room, Sedi's sanctuary of medical books and study, but now it held far more tension than scholarship.

Two Boston Police detectives occupied straight-backed chairs that had been pulled from the dining room. Their posture was stiff, their notebooks balanced on their knees. Both men wore the tired, methodical expressions of officers who had long ago learned patience in the face of chaos.

Sedi sat opposite them in a luxurious leather chair that belonged more naturally in a gentleman's club than a crime scene. Normally composed and elegant, she now leaned forward with restless agitation. Her fingers tapped lightly against the armrest, a small but constant rhythm betraying the fury simmering beneath her calm exterior.

Simon and Sabrina shared the couch beneath the tall window. Simon's normally impeccable composure had begun to fray. His hands were clasped tightly together, knuckles pale. Sabrina sat very still beside him, her posture rigid, her eyes fixed on the envelope lying on the desk as if sheer concentration might force its contents to reveal themselves.

On the large computer screen in front of them, Drew and Lauren appeared from D.C., their faces framed in the glow of their own home lighting. The connection was clear, but the distance felt enormous. Drew leaned forward toward the camera, elbows on his knees, while

Lauren hovered beside him, her expression tight with worry. Even through the screen, their anxiety filled the room.

In the corner of Sedi's study, beside an antique walnut table that she had once purchased in London, two CSI investigators were finishing their meticulous work. Their black equipment cases lay open on the floor, revealing brushes, powders, plastic bags, and sealed evidence envelopes. One investigator carefully photographed the envelope under angled light, while the other completed a final DNA swab along the edge of the paper.

For three hours, the house had been transformed into a laboratory. Fingerprints had been dusted and lifted. Fibers had been inspected. The paper had been photographed, measured, and sealed. Every inch of the envelope and the letter inside had been scrutinized. And still no one had been allowed to read the message.

The delay had stretched the group's nerves nearly to the breaking point. Finally, Simon could endure no more.

"May we read the damn thing now?" he blurted.

His voice cracked through the room like a snapped branch. The frustration in it surprised even him. Everyone looked up. Even the CSI technicians paused.

The lead detective, a middle-aged man with thinning brown hair and a patient, deliberate manner, slowly rose from his chair. His name was Detective Michael Taylor, a veteran of the Boston Police Department with twenty-five years of experience and the calm demeanor of someone who had seen every variety of human ugliness.

He understood impatience. But procedure was procedure.

Taylor crossed the room and spoke quietly with the technicians. The three of them leaned over the evidence table for a brief exchange of low voices. One of the technicians nodded and sealed a small plastic bag before placing it into a larger evidence container.

A few more quiet words passed between them. Then Taylor picked up a plastic bag containing the letter. For the first time since it had arrived that morning, the message was no longer under forensic custody. Taylor returned to his chair and extended the clear evidence bag toward Simon.

“Thank you for your patience, sir,” he said calmly. “You may look at it now.”

Simon reached for it immediately. But Sabrina’s hand intercepted the motion.

With quick determination, she took the plastic-covered letter and laid it carefully across her lap. The room fell silent as paper crackled softly between her fingers.

Across the room, Drew and Lauren leaned forward toward the screen, as though proximity alone might bring them closer to the moment.

Even the detectives seemed to lean slightly toward her.

Sabrina cleared her throat.

Her voice was steady, but everyone could hear the tension beneath it.

She began to read.

How are you, my brilliant, beautiful, and deceitful mahogany friend, Sedi?

Please give my regards to the others who are undoubtedly with you at present. Oh well... why don’t I simply address you all?

I’m certain law enforcement has already scoured this note with everything but a Brillo pad. It will do them no good. I readily admit who I am and what I’ve done.

That isn’t your problem, is it?

Where’s Waldo?

Although I must say, I am considerably smarter than Waldo... and heaven knows infinitely more beautiful.

Sabrina paused briefly, her jaw tightening before she continued.

Yes, sweet little Sabina is with me.

Believe me when I say she is well cared for. A bit confused, naturally, but relatively happy. She awaits her parents with great anticipation.

She believes they are away on a long trip and is staying with “Aunti Catherine.”

Simon closed his eyes for a moment.

Across the screen, Lauren pressed a hand to her mouth.

Sabrina continued.

Her life is brightened somewhat by her new puppy, which she has undoubtedly named by now.

Oh yes... Mommy and Daddy, let the tears flow. They will do you no good.

The words seemed to chill the room.

Sabrina read on.

Every one of you conspired to ruin my life.

And every one of you will pay.

Mommy and Daddy are distraught? Good.

But the greatest evil among you is my fiancé.

Oh, I'm sorry.

My EX FIANCÉ!

Simon's eyes opened slowly.

The detectives exchanged a quick glance.

Sabrina continued.

Simon, my dear. You will pay.

Oh, you will pay.

When I am through with you, no one will believe in the goodie-two-shoes Simon. They will see you exactly as I do.

A failure.

A wicked deceiver.

Sabrina's voice grew quieter as she read the next lines.

So... what comes next?

Prepare yourselves for a long and incredibly stressful journey.

And Simon... prepare to destroy your reputation.

Oh, how delicious this will be.

A heavy silence settled in the study.

Even Detective Taylor leaned forward slightly.

Sabrina continued.

Five days from today, yes, I know exactly what day it is, you must be in Paris.

I have reserved two rooms for my sorrowful couples at the Georges V Hotel. They are prepaid. I am no cheapskate.

A courier will bring my next message to you there.

Drew whispered under his breath.

"My God…"

Sabrina read the final lines.

For Simon and Drew, and their annoying Shakespeare quotations:

"The world's mine oyster, which I with sword will open."

The Merry Wives of Windsor

But of course, you arrogant fools already knew from whence it comes.

Adieu!

Sabrina slowly lowered the plastic-wrapped letter.

No one spoke.

For several long seconds, the only sound in the room was the faint hum of the computer connection.

Then Detective Taylor quietly said,

"Well… that certainly clears a few things up."

But Simon wasn't listening.

He had taken the letter and stared at it as if it were something alive.

And somewhere in the back of his mind, a terrible realization began to form.

Catherine would be ruthless.

ϒ ϒ ϒ

It was ten o'clock in the evening when Drew and Lauren finally arrived. Their jet had landed an hour earlier at Hanscom Field, the small but efficient executive airport just five miles from Simon and Sabrina's historic home in Concord. The drive from the airfield had been quiet and tense, the autumn night wrapped in the cool stillness of rural Massachusetts. The old colonial houses along the road glowed softly with porch lights, but the peaceful scenery felt strangely detached from the turmoil that had descended upon them all.

Sedi had joined them again, and the five of them sat together in Simon's study.

Sedi sat in one of the deep leather chairs near the hearth. Simon occupied his usual chair beside the desk. Drew and Lauren sat close together on the couch, Lauren leaning slightly against her husband as though the physical contact might keep her from collapsing. Sabrina stood for a moment near the fireplace before finally sitting beside them.

On the low table between them lay a single sheet of paper.

The copy of Catherine's letter.

The Boston police had taken the original as evidence and stored it in their downtown locker, but they had graciously left the group with a carefully photographed copy. But the result had not helped.

They had read the message several times.

Each reading seemed only to make the situation darker and more ominous.

No one spoke for a moment. The room carried the heavy silence of people trying to summon courage they were not certain they possessed.

Finally, Sedi broke the quiet.

"So you're prepared to leave for Paris?"

Her voice was calm, but the strain beneath it was unmistakable.

Everyone nodded.

Simon glanced around the room slowly, as if committing the moment to memory.

"Yes," he said quietly. "We're all packed."

"We're prepared for a long journey. Who knows how long we will be gone?" Lauren added.

Her voice trembled slightly. The past hour had not been kind to her composure. Thin streaks of tears marked her cheeks, evidence of several emotional collapses she had tried unsuccessfully to hide. Her eyes were red but determined.

"God only knows where we'll be going," she continued softly. Sabrina reached across the table and gently took Lauren's hand.

"We'll find her," she said. "I promise you. Sabina will come home."

Lauren nodded, though the gesture carried more hope than certainty.

Sedi leaned forward slightly.

"I called the George V to confirm that they have your reservation," Sedi said. "They do. Your rooms are prepaid for the next two weeks."

The mention of the famous Paris hotel made the situation feel even more surreal.

Two weeks.

It sounded like an eternity.

Drew leaned back and exhaled slowly, rubbing his face with both hands.

"Okay," he said after a moment. "We need to toughen up."

He looked around the room at the others.

"I am confident sweet Sabina is safe."

The words hung in the air as though everyone was afraid to challenge them.

"Oddly enough," he continued, "I feel…relieved."

Simon raised an eyebrow.

Drew shrugged.

"Think about it. We can eliminate any other possibility that might be more concerning. We know who did this. We know it's Catherine."

He shook his head grimly.

"That's not good, but at least we know who we're dealing with."

Simon nodded slowly.

"That's true, Drew," he said. "And I'm glad to learn that the burden will be placed on me."

He spoke without self-pity, simply stating what had become increasingly clear to them all.

Lauren's composure finally cracked again.

"I'm so sorry, Simon," she whispered.

Her voice broke.

"I can't tell you how much I appreciate your sacrifice. God… I don't want this to be your burden alone."

Simon looked at her with gentle sympathy.

"Let's not start that," he said calmly.

He leaned back slightly in his chair, fingers steepled.

"We are dealing with an unbalanced mind. Catherine has spent years convincing herself that I am responsible for every failure in her life."

His voice remained measured, but his eyes carried a deeper tension.

"In her mind, I am the villain of her story."

He sighed quietly.

"And if she believes that… then there is no other way but to pay her price."

Sedi studied him for a moment.

"Are you flying to Paris right away?" she asked.

Simon shook his head.

"No."

He glanced toward Drew.

"We'll leave in the morning, but we're going to Oxford first."

Sedi looked surprised.

"Oxford?"

"Yes," Simon said. "We need to meet with Sir Roger and Eustace."

Even in the middle of a crisis, the names carried a certain weight.

"They feel ownership in this situation," Simon continued. "And frankly, we need as much intellectual firepower as we can get."

He tapped the letter on the table.

"Catherine's plan will not be simple. She is theatrical by nature. Whatever she demands of me, it will be elaborate."

Sabrina nodded.

"And humiliating," she added quietly.

Simon gave a faint smile.

"Yes. That too."

He leaned forward slightly.

"She will demand things of me, certainly. But our real challenge is figuring out where she is hiding. As quickly as possible."

Silence returned to the room.

"That means analyzing every word she sends," Simon continued. "Every clue, every hint, every mistake."

"I still don't understand why she sent the first message to me," Sedi said.

Simon shook his head.

"She just needed to vent her hatred for you as well."

Sabrina sighed.

"That's Catherine," Sedi said. "Vindictiveness has always been her hobby."

She folded her arms thoughtfully.

"Well," she continued, "I'll stay here and wait for more communication. I'll coordinate with Boston police and the authorities in Washington."

Simon nodded approvingly.

Sedi looked around the room.

"What else can I do?"

Simon thought for a moment.

"First thing in the morning, contact Chester Morris in New York. I'll leave you his information."

"The detective?" Sedi asked.

"Yes."

Simon nodded.

"Bring him up to date and make sure he has all of our phone numbers."

"There isn't much he can act on yet," Simon continued, "but he already agreed that Catherine was likely involved. Once we confirm it, he'll bring his entire apparatus into motion."

Sedi gave a firm nod.

"I'll take care of it first thing."

Simon turned toward Drew.

"What did you set as wheels-up time?"

Drew straightened slightly.

"The pilots have already filed the flight plan," he said. "Estimated departure is eight o'clock tomorrow morning."

"What are we flying in?" Sabrina asked.

Drew shrugged casually.

"It's a new Gulfstream 650."

Simon raised an eyebrow.

"You bought a Gulfstream?"

Drew laughed.

"No. I didn't buy it."

He paused.

"I leased it."

Then he added with a slight grin,

"With the option to purchase."

Lauren rolled her eyes faintly.

Drew spread his hands.

"Who knows. Maybe I will."

He leaned forward.

"I have it for as long as we need it. No time limit."

Sabrina smiled faintly.

"It's good to have friends who are obscenely rich."

Drew chuckled darkly.

"Heck," he said, "I'd buy a B-52 if it would help get Sabina back."

The joke landed softly but carried an unmistakable edge of truth.

No one doubted he meant it.

For several minutes, the room fell silent again. The fire crackled softly in the grate.

Each of them sat with their own thoughts, imagining the unknown journey ahead.

Finally, Sedi stood.

"I should head home," she said. "I'll start making calls in the morning."

They all rose with her.

Simon walked her to the door, and the cold night air slipped briefly into the house before the door closed again behind her.

When he returned to the study, the others were still standing near the table, the letter lying between them like a challenge.

No one spoke.

They all understood.

The terrifying game had begun.

Chapter Ten

A War of Wits

Oxford, England, is filled with so much history that a visitor might feel less like an observer and more like a participant in a living reenactment. The city seems suspended between centuries. Elegant church towers pierce the sky above narrow lanes worn smooth by the passage of countless generations. Medieval stone colleges, cloistered courtyards, and ivy-draped walls stand shoulder to shoulder with quiet gardens and ancient libraries whose shelves hold the thoughts of nearly a millennium. It is a place where the past does not merely linger; it breathes.

Everywhere one turns, there are reminders that Oxford has been a crucible of ideas for almost a thousand years. Scholars once walked these same cobbled streets debating theology, philosophy, science, and politics by candlelight. The city grew not around a single campus but around dozens of independent colleges, each a small intellectual kingdom unto itself.

Oxford University is the oldest university in the English-speaking world and among the most respected centers of learning. Monarchs have consulted its minds. Revolutions have been debated in its lecture halls. Empires have been imagined here and dismantled here as well.

The River Thames, which the locals call the Isis as it winds through the city, flows slowly between the meadows and college walls. In Oxford, it seems reluctant to hurry, as though even the river understands that time itself moves differently in this place. Punts drift lazily along its surface, guided by students who laugh and argue while gliding past ancient boathouses and quiet gardens.

Within this ancient world, Sir Roger Abelard and Professor Eustace Fairfax had long stood as towering figures. For more than sixty years, the two men had taught history at Oxford, guiding generations of students through the labyrinth of the past. Their names were known in academic circles across Europe and America, their lectures quoted, their books studied with reverence. They were, in many ways, the embodiment of Oxford's intellectual tradition: brilliant, argumentative, and utterly devoted to the pursuit of truth.

Age had bent their shoulders slightly and slowed their steps, but their minds remained sharp as ever. Their friendship, forged over decades of scholarship and debate, was legendary. They disagreed constantly, argued fiercely, and mocked each other mercilessly, yet their loyalty was unshakeable.

Simon had once been among their students. Years earlier, he had arrived at Oxford as a young scholar searching for answers to questions that few historians even dared to ask. Under the demanding tutelage of Sir Roger, Simon had completed his doctorate, earning admiration for his extraordinary insight and relentless curiosity. Later, on his own, he had achieved international recognition, culminating in the prestigious Wolfson Prize for historical scholarship, an honor awarded only to the most significant contributions to the field.

But Simon's achievements extended far beyond academia.

Five years earlier, with the guidance and support of Roger and Eustace, he had played a central role in fulfilling the mysterious Soulfast prophecy. This event had pushed the boundaries of both history and understanding. What had begun as an obscure historical puzzle had evolved into something far stranger and more profound. The experience had been mystical, transcendent, and deeply unsettling. It had changed the course of history, and every one of them knew it.

Now those same individuals sat together again in Sir Roger's rooms at the college.

The room itself was quintessentially Oxford. Dark wooden shelves climbed toward the high ceiling, sagging slightly beneath the weight of centuries-old books. A small ornamental fire crackled in the hearth, casting a warm glow across the worn Persian rug that lay at the center of the room. It was summer, but it was always cold in the old chambers.

Simon, Drew, Sabrina, and Lauren sat heavily in the deep leather chairs arranged around the sitting area. Their journey and the weight of recent events had left them visibly exhausted. The tension in the room was thick enough to feel.

Sir Roger sat among them, calm but watchful.

Professor Eustace Fairfax, however, was pacing.

He had been pacing for nearly ten minutes, moving slowly back and forth across the rug while rereading Catherine's message for what must have been the twentieth time. The letter hung loosely in his hand as he muttered half-formed thoughts to himself.

"Will you sit down!" Sir Roger finally snapped.

Eustace ignored him.

Roger leaned forward in irritation.

"You know this rug has to be replaced every fifty years," he continued dryly. "At the rate you're marching across it, you'll have it worn through by next term."

Eustace stopped mid-stride and glared at him.

"Oh shut up, your majesty."

The insult hung in the air with practiced familiarity.

Roger had been knighted years earlier for his contributions to historical scholarship, an honor he wore with mild embarrassment. Eustace, however, had been offered the same recognition decades ago and had famously declined it. He considered the entire system of titles to be pompous and unnecessary.

He never missed an opportunity to remind Roger of it.

"I see no clues here," Eustace continued irritably, waving the letter. "It's purposely disambiguous, crafted to say something plainly, bluntly."

He dropped the message onto a nearby table and collapsed into a chair.

"But I suppose we might start with the obvious question," he added. "Why Paris?"

The others exchanged glances.

Roger leaned back thoughtfully.

"Before we chase that question," he said slowly, "let's begin with the conclusions you've already reached, particularly your theory about the delay in notification."

Eustace grunted in acknowledgment.

"I think you are correct about that."

Simon nodded.

"So we're unanimous on that point."

Drew leaned forward.

"Yes, but Paris. That's the puzzle. Why bring us there? Is she planning to make her demands in Paris?"

"Perhaps," Roger replied. "But the real question is simpler. Why compel someone to be in a particular place at a particular time?"

Sabrina spoke quietly.

"There are only a few reasons. You either have to do something… or meet someone."

"It won't be to meet her," Lauren said immediately. "That much is obvious."

"No," Simon agreed. "But we know she will give us instructions for whatever comes next."

Drew spread his hands.

"She could do that anywhere. So why Paris?"

Eustace rose again and resumed pacing.

"Because," he said slowly, "aside from the pleasure of inconveniencing you, I suspect there is something she wants you to see."

The room fell quiet.

"Something," he continued, "that can only be seen in Paris."

Sabrina frowned.

"A historic site?"

Roger smiled faintly.

"I think the old goat may be right… for once."

Eustace snorted but continued pacing.

"There could be something there she attaches meaning to," Roger went on. "Something symbolic. Something personal."

He turned to Simon.

"Is there any place in Paris that holds special significance between you and Catherine?"

Simon shook his head.

"Not really. I don't think that's it."

He paused, thinking.

"But the idea that she wants to show us something… that makes sense."

Eustace finally stopped pacing and exhaled heavily.

"Speculating at this point is useless," he said.

He picked up the message again and stared at it thoughtfully.

"But allow me one more thought."

Everyone looked up.

"Her goal," Eustace said quietly, "is to destroy Simon."

The bluntness of the statement hung in the room.

"Her demands will not be trivial."

He stepped toward the center of the room.

"But I suspect something more."

They waited.

"She intends to wage a war of wits with us."

Roger nodded slowly.

"She has had five years to plan," he said. "Five years to think through every detail."

"And she's clever," Eustace added.

"And manipulative."

Roger sighed.

Drew rose and walked toward the window.

"That's exactly her style," he said. "She'll scatter clues and red herrings everywhere. From here on out, nothing will be straightforward."

Roger nodded again.

"Which means we must examine every communication for hidden meaning."

Simon extended his hand.

"Let me see the message again."

Drew retrieved it and handed it over.

Simon studied the words carefully.

"Could there be a code hidden in this?"

The others leaned closer.

Sabrina frowned.

"That doesn't really sound like something she would do."

"Oh yes, it does," Lauren said quietly. "If she needed help, she would find the very best people available to help her."

Simon looked up.

"It doesn't appear structured," Drew said. "No obvious pattern."

Roger sighed.

"This is beyond our expertise."

He folded his hands.

"We need help."

Eustace grunted.

"I know exactly who we need."

Roger raised an eyebrow.

"Someone in mathematics?"

"Bollocks!" Eustace snapped. "Too slow. I said I know who we need, and he isn't on any faculty."

The group stared at him expectantly.

"We need Loki."

Roger blinked.

"The Norse god of chaos?"

"Close," Eustace said.

"There is a shadowy figure on the dark web who calls himself Loki. He's one of the greatest hackers alive. No one knows who he is. No one has ever caught him."

"Is he dangerous?" Sabrina asked.

"No," Eustace said thoughtfully. "He's not malicious. Just a trickster."

Simon nodded slowly.

"And you think he might help us?"

"If we can find him," Eustace replied.

"I believe I know where to start."

Simon looked around the room.

"Okay. Agreed."

Roger stood.

"I think it is time you all return to your hotel."

He glanced at the clock.

"We will meet again in the morning. Tomorrow, there will be three days left before you must be in Paris."

One by one, they gathered their coats and left the room.

When the door finally closed behind them, Roger turned back toward Eustace.

"Sit a moment longer, my friend."

Eustace obeyed without question.

Roger's voice softened.

"Speaking of gods…"

Eustace groaned.

"Don't say it."

"I told you, I fail to see how he could help us."

Roger leaned back in his chair.

"Who knows what he is capable of?"

"All we know," he continued quietly, "is that he can do things no one else can."

"Things beyond understanding."

They sat in silence for several minutes.

Finally, Eustace sighed deeply.

"We'll see."

"When the time comes," he said, "we'll cross that Rubicon."

Roger nodded slowly.

They sat without speaking.

ϒ ϒ ϒ

Sedi sat on the long cream-colored couch beside her daughter, Clarice. The late afternoon light filtered softly through the tall windows, casting gentle amber patterns across the hardwood floor and the quiet room.

Clarice was eight years old and already a striking young reflection of her mother. She was tall for her age, with a naturally straight posture and a deep caramel complexion that glowed warmly in the sunlight. Her features were finely cut, elegant and thoughtful, suggesting a seriousness beyond her years. Her thick curls were pulled loosely into a ribbon at the back of her head, though several rebellious strands had already escaped and framed her face.

She sat sideways on the couch with her legs tucked neatly beneath her, completely absorbed in the book resting in her lap. It was a novel, one normally assigned to children three or four grade levels older.

Clarice turned each page slowly and carefully, occasionally pausing to consider a sentence before moving forward. Her lips moved slightly as she read, whispering the words to herself in concentration.

Every so often, she glanced up toward her mother, not because she needed anything, but simply for reassurance. Sedi would smile faintly, and Clarice would return to her book, content.

Sedi, however, was not content.

She sat at the far end of the couch, her body angled slightly toward the small desk where her computer screen glowed. With one hand, she casually thumbed through a glossy fashion magazine, stopping occasionally on an advertisement or photograph, though she barely registered what she was looking at. Her attention was divided. Most of it rested on the quiet rhythm of the security camera recordings that played silently on the computer screen.

She wasn't paranoid. In fact, Sedi prided herself on being one of the most rational people she knew. Years of navigating difficult medical situations had trained her mind to remain calm, analytical, and controlled.

But the circumstances had changed.

Lauren's daughter had been taken.

The thought arrived again, like a cold hand closing around her chest.

She glanced toward Clarice.

Her treasure.

The most precious thing in her life.

Every time she imagined what Lauren must be feeling, the helplessness, the fear, the constant dread, Sedi felt a slow-burning anger begin to grow inside her. Not panic. Not fear.

Anger.

She forced her mind back to the screen.

The small suburban street where their house stood was in a quiet, prosperous neighborhood, where most of the homes were large but modestly elegant, tasteful rather than ostentatious. Their street itself was only three blocks long, running between two much busier thoroughfares.

Technically, it was a residential street. In practice, it functioned as a shortcut.

Drivers who knew the area often cut through to avoid the traffic lights at either end of the neighborhood. As a result, cars passed by frequently throughout the day. Nothing alarming. Nothing unusual. Just the normal hum of suburban movement.

Their house sat almost exactly in the middle of the street. It was nestled among a small copse of massive oak trees whose branches stretched wide across the property, their leaves forming a natural canopy overhead. In the summer, the shade was deep and cool. In the fall, the yard filled with rust-colored leaves.

But the front lawn itself was open and expansive, an uninterrupted sweep of grass stretching from the porch to the street. It was beautiful. And very visible.

Not that they had planned it that way, but the house's position had created a small technological advantage. Their door camera had a wide-angle lens, and because of the open lawn and the angle of the street, it recorded almost everything that passed in front of the house: cars, pedestrians, delivery trucks, and even dogs being walked along the sidewalk.

Sedi often joked that the camera gave them better surveillance of the neighborhood than the Lexington police.

She paused while flipping through the magazine. A Cartier advertisement filled the page, diamonds arranged in an impossibly elegant necklace. She glanced at it absently.

Then something moved on the screen. Her eyes snapped up instantly. A black van rolled slowly past the house. Too slowly. Her instincts reacted before her mind fully processed what she was seeing. The magazine slid off her lap and fell soundlessly onto the rug. Sedi leaned forward and clicked the replay control.

The video rewound several seconds. She watched carefully this time. The van appeared again, entering the frame from the far end of the street. It was an older model, dark, almost matte black, with tinted windows that reflected the sunlight just enough to obscure the interior.

It crept along the road at a speed far below the normal flow of neighborhood traffic. Ten miles per hour at most. Maybe less.

Sedi narrowed her eyes. Two silhouettes were visible in the front seats. She paused the recording. Then advanced it frame by frame. The driver became slightly clearer. A man. Dark sunglasses. Thick beard.

His head turned slightly as the van passed the house. He was looking directly at it.

Sedi's jaw tightened. She advanced another frame. The passenger seat. A woman. Or at least she believed it was a woman. The figure was smaller and slimmer than the driver, but the lighting and reflections made it difficult to see clearly. No visible features. No clear hair color. Nothing distinctive. But the posture was unmistakable. She too was staring at the house. Not glancing. Studying.

The van continued past and disappeared from view. Sedi looked at the timestamp. Midmorning. Two days ago. Her fingers moved quickly across the keyboard now. She rewound the footage and began scanning through the midmorning recordings for each of the previous days. Minutes passed. Clarice turned another page quietly.

Sedi continued reviewing the footage with increasing focus. Then. There. Four days earlier. The same van. The same slow crawl down the street. The same two figures in the front seats. Watching the house.

She leaned back slowly in her chair. Her face hardened. It was not the expression of a frightened mother. It was something far colder—controlled anger.

This might mean nothing. It could be a contractor lost in the neighborhood. A delivery vehicle. A couple searching for an address.

But given what had happened to Lauren's daughter…

Coincidences suddenly felt very unlikely.

Sedi folded her arms and stared at the frozen image on the screen. She should call the police. That was the obvious answer. But the more she thought about it, the less useful that solution appeared.

What would they do? A black van driving slowly through a residential street was not a crime. Even if the police took the report seriously, they could do little more than note it. They could not station a patrol car outside the house. They could not provide protection.

And protection was exactly what she needed.

Sedi and her husband both worked long hours, often six days a week. His medical practice demanded it, and her hospital responsibilities rarely allowed her to leave early. Their schedules overlapped in frustrating ways.

Clarice spent much of the day with their nanny. A wonderful woman. Responsible. Trustworthy. But Lauren and Drew had trusted their arrangements, too. And look what had happened.

Sedi glanced again at her daughter. Clarice was still reading peacefully, completely unaware of the tension quietly forming around her. The sight sent a surge of fierce protectiveness through Sedi's chest.

She would not allow anything to happen to her child.

Not now.

Not ever.

Which meant the solution could not wait.

The police might eventually become involved, but she needed something immediate. Something effective. Someone.

Her mind began turning rapidly now, assembling possibilities, calculating risks. She needed a new layer of protection. And she needed it today.

Chapter Eleven

The Gathering Force

Sedi sat nervously on the front porch of her home, wrapped in a quiet that felt almost unnatural given the storm of anxiety inside her. It was a bright, mild morning in Lexington, the kind of spring day that normally invited calm reflection. Sunlight filtered through the tall oaks that lined the street, scattering soft shadows across the brick walkway and the wide green lawn that stretched to the curb.

A thin curl of steam rose from the dark roast coffee in her mug, drifting slowly into the cool morning air. The neighborhood was waking gently. Birds hopped along the branches above her, chirping and darting from tree to tree as if celebrating the arrival of the day. Somewhere down the block, a dog barked lazily, and a distant lawn mower hummed to life.

To anyone passing by, the scene would have appeared peaceful, almost idyllic.

But Sedi felt none of it.

Her eyes remained fixed on the tablet resting beside her chair, its screen displaying footage recorded by the security cameras mounted along the front of the house. She had already reviewed the recordings from the night before three separate times. Each viewing left her both relieved and unsettled.

Relieved because the black van had not appeared again.

Unsettled because she could not convince herself that it would not return.

Her mind kept circling the same thought. Sabina had been abducted. Whoever had done it was capable of planning, surveillance, and patience. That meant the van might not have been a coincidence at all. And if someone truly was watching the house, Clarice might be in danger as well.

That thought alone was enough to keep Sedi's stomach clenched in a tight knot.

She had already cancelled her shift at the hospital. The decision had been easy. Her husband had an early surgical procedure to conduct that morning and could not postpone it, which meant the responsibility of staying home had naturally fallen to her.

Inside the house, Erin, their nanny, was keeping Clarice occupied with breakfast and cartoons in the family room. Clarice had asked why she wasn't going to school today, and Sedi had offered a vague explanation about a "family day." The girl had accepted the answer with the easy trust of childhood.

Sedi knew she could not keep her home forever. Eventually, life would have to return to normal.

But not today.

The police had been helpful, though their options were limited. Lexington patrol units had agreed to drive by the house roughly once an hour, keeping a quiet eye on the neighborhood. Unfortunately, without a license plate or identifying details on the van, there was little more they could do.

Sedi lifted the mug to her lips and took another slow sip of coffee, letting the warmth settle her nerves, at least temporarily.

Then she reached for her phone.

It was seven o'clock in Lexington. That meant it was noon in England.

Her thumb hovered over the screen for only a moment before pressing the number assigned to the first slot on her speed dial. She held the phone to her ear and listened as the call connected.

Across the Atlantic, Sabrina and Lauren sat at a small wooden table just inside the pale blue double doors of a venerable Oxford establishment known simply as *The Grand Cafe*.

The café carried a quiet pride in its history. Established in 1650, it was widely considered the first coffeehouse in England, a place where scholars, merchants, and philosophers once gathered to debate politics and ideas over steaming cups of imported coffee.

Centuries later, the room still held that atmosphere of thoughtful conversation.

Tall windows allowed pale midday light to spill across the polished wooden floors. Shelves lined the walls, filled with old books and porcelain teapots, while the faint aroma of roasted coffee beans and baked pastries drifted through the air.

Before the women sat a modest luncheon: two cups of tea and a small plate of pastries that neither had eaten much of.

They spoke quietly, almost in whispers.

The weight of the situation had settled heavily over them.

Simon and Drew were meeting with the two professor friends on the university campus, men who might help them locate a mysterious figure rumored to be one of the most skilled hackers operating on the dark web. The hope was slim, but it was something.

For the moment, however, the women had retreated to the café to gather their strength.

Sabrina's phone chimed softly against the tabletop.

She glanced down at the screen and immediately recognized the caller.

"Sedi?"

She answered without hesitation.

"Yes, girl," Sedi said, her voice carrying a mixture of fatigue and forced calm. "How are you? Is there anything new since yesterday?"

Sabrina sighed quietly.

"No… nothing new." She glanced across the table at Lauren before continuing. "Lauren and I are sitting in a coffee shop having lunch. Simon and Drew are meeting with the professors on campus. They're trying to track down a computer hacker, some fellow who apparently rules half the dark web."

"I guess we're all doing what we can," Sedi replied softly.

There was a pause.

A longer one than Sabrina liked.

"Sedi?" she said carefully. "What is it?"

Sedi inhaled slowly.

"Sabrina… I hate to bring this up. I don't want to burden you with anything else right now."

Sabrina straightened slightly in her chair.

"What is it? Is something wrong? Has something happened?"

"I'm not sure there *is* anything wrong," Sedi said cautiously. "Not exactly. But a dark van has driven by our house at least three times that we know of. We caught it on the door camera."

Sabrina's voice sharpened immediately.

"You think your house is being watched? Does it look like the same SUV that was outside Lauren's place in D.C.?"

"I don't know," Sedi admitted. "I'm trying not to jump to conclusions, but I can't help it. I'm worried… actually, I'm a little frantic."

"Have you called the police?"

"Yes. They've been helpful. They're even coordinating with the D.C. police to compare notes."

"Good. That's exactly what you should do." Sabrina's tone hardened with resolve. "What about Clarice?"

"That's the other problem," Sedi said quietly. "Erin is here with her, but I'm trying to find someone else who can help keep an eye on things when I have to leave the house."

Sabrina didn't hesitate.

"Sedi, listen to me," she said firmly. "I'm going to get you some reliable help. You remember Cheri, my friend from Morgantown?"

Sedi smiled faintly.

"Oh yes, I remember Cheri."

"Well, I'm calling her right now. She's been asking how she can help ever since this whole mess started. This is exactly the sort of thing she'd be perfect for."

"That would mean a lot to me."

"Oh, believe me," Sabrina added with a small laugh, "Cheri doesn't take prisoners. Though I may ask her to leave her guns at home. She won't be able to bring them on the plane anyway."

Sedi laughed softly for the first time that morning.

"I feel better already. Thank you, girl."

"And you keep me updated on anything you see," Sabrina said. "Anything at all."

"I will."

"Stay safe."

"You too."

The call ended.

Sabrina set the phone down and immediately explained the situation to Lauren.

The two women reached across the table and clasped hands.

"I'll take care of this," Sabrina said, picking up the phone once more as determination replaced the worry in her eyes.

Then she began dialing Cheri.

ϒ ϒ ϒ

Once again, Simon and Drew sat in Sir Roger's rooms with Roger and Eustace. The familiar study, lined from floor to ceiling with centuries of accumulated scholarship, felt unusually tense. The old leather chairs, the towering bookcases, and the faint scent of polished oak and pipe tobacco had long been a sanctuary for quiet academic debate. Today, however, the atmosphere was different. Urgency had crept into the room.

This time, another person was present.

She was a young woman who was obviously an Oxford student. She wore the mandatory white blouse, a black ribbon bow tie, a black skirt, and black shoes. Her short black, sleeveless "commoner's gown" hung loosely over her attire. Large black-rimmed glasses completed her appearance, giving her an air of quiet intelligence that seemed entirely appropriate within those ancient walls.

"Please relax, Chelsea," Roger reassured her gently, gesturing toward a chair. "We really appreciate your willingness to help."

"Yes, professor," Chelsea replied.

She was not timid. On the contrary, her posture and voice were confident and clear. Yet she is clearly an introvert, the kind of student who fills their day in the Bodleian Library. The result was a careful politeness rather than nervousness.

Roger folded his hands thoughtfully.

"We have explained the dreadful reason for asking for your assistance," he continued.

"Yes, professor."

"I wish to make it clear that we are asking only for electronic contact with Loki. In no way are we attempting to learn his identity. We simply need help and believe that he might provide it."

"I understand."

There was a short hesitation as Chelsea appeared to gather her thoughts. Her eyes drifted briefly to the tall windows where pale afternoon light filtered through the old glass.

"Well, girl, can you help us or not?" Eustace barked in his usual gruff fashion, leaning forward impatiently.

Chelsea did not seem the slightest bit intimidated.

Instead, she adjusted her glasses and regarded the four men calmly.

"First," she said, "how much do you know about what people call the dark web?"

All four men glanced at each other.

"You should assume that we know nothing," Roger replied kindly.

Chelsea sighed softly, though not disrespectfully, as if preparing to explain something very basic.

"The dark web is often confused with the deep web," she began. "The deep web is simply the part of the internet that isn't indexed by search engines. Private databases, academic archives, subscription sites, things you can't find through Google."

She paused briefly to be sure they were following.

"The dark web, however, is different. It's made up of websites known as darknet sites. These are accessible only through special networks built specifically for that purpose. In other words, you can't simply type in an address and go there. You need the tools and connections to access it."

Simon gave a small shrug.

"We wouldn't even know how to search for it anyway."

Chelsea nodded.

"Well, beyond that, there is something referred to as the black web," she continued. "That's an entirely different level. No one enters the black web without an invitation. Access is tightly controlled and always requires multiple layers of verification."

She looked at them carefully.

"You follow?"

"We aren't ignoramuses, girl!" Eustace snapped, clearly irritated by the experience of being instructed on a subject he knew absolutely nothing about.

Chelsea ignored him and continued without missing a beat.

"The black web is where Loki lives," she said. "I don't have direct access to it. But I do know someone who does. He can connect with Loki, and he will do so for me."

Drew leaned forward immediately.

"Perfect. How quickly can you do this?"

"Today," Chelsea said casually. "My friend can send a message right now. But there's a complication."

She raised one finger.

"No one knows where Loki actually lives. We don't know which country or time zone he's in, or when he checks his messages. He might respond in minutes, or it could take hours."

Simon exchanged a quick glance with Drew.

"Please do this as soon as possible," Simon said. "This is a desperate situation."

Chelsea nodded.

"What exactly do you wish to tell Loki?"

"We want to know if he can help with some cryptology," Simon explained. "Specifically, we are looking for a hidden code."

Chelsea tilted her head thoughtfully.

"Interesting," she said. "That might actually appeal to him. Loki enjoys puzzles, particularly impossible ones."

After a silent moment, she rose from her chair.

"I'll contact my friend immediately. Give me a few hours."

She paused at the door and looked back.

"Do you want me to call you when I receive a reply, regardless of what time it is?"

"Definitely," Roger said firmly.

Chelsea nodded once more, then walked to the door and stepped quietly into the corridor.

The door closed behind her with a soft click.

For several seconds, none of the men spoke. The old room seemed suddenly very quiet.

"Good Lord," Eustace muttered at last. "When did the world become so complicated?"

ϒ ϒ ϒ

Cheri sat in her usual place in the Mountain Mama bar, the same booth she had claimed for years. The place smelled faintly of beer, wood smoke, and fried onions, and the jukebox in the corner hummed softly beneath the low conversations of the afternoon regulars.

But Cheri wasn't listening to any of it.

Anger flashed from her eyes. Somehow, even her red hair seemed to flare with it, catching the light above the bar like a warning signal.

Across from her sat Bear.

The big man filled the chair like a tree that had grown there naturally. His massive hands rested calmly on the table, though his eyes watched her carefully. Anyone who knew Cheri understood that when her temper sparked like this, something serious had happened.

Bear leaned back slightly.

"So, this friend of Sabina's…"

"Her best friend," Cheri interrupted sharply.

Bear nodded slowly.

"…has a small daughter and thinks she may be in danger from the same people who took the little girl."

"As I said," Cheri continued, her voice tight with frustration, "they've spotted a black van watching her house on several occasions. Just driving past. Two people inside."

Bear's brow lowered slightly. He had heard enough stories in his life to know when something didn't feel right.

"And you're sure about this?"

"Sure enough," Cheri replied. "They've seen it more than once."

Bear rubbed his beard thoughtfully.

"So," he said after a moment, "you're flying there to watch after the girl?"

"Clarice."

"What?"

"Her name is Clarice," Cheri said firmly. "Eight years old."

For a moment, the big man said nothing.

“Anyway,” Cheri went on, softening slightly, “I don’t think the clinic is in any danger. But I’d like you to keep an eye on things here while I’m gone.”

Bear’s expression changed instantly.

His face became stone cold.

“No.”

Cheri blinked in surprise. For a moment, she didn’t quite process the answer.

Her brow wrinkled, but she remained silent.

“No, Cheri blossom,” Bear continued calmly. “I’m going with you.”

He leaned forward slightly.

“Not just me either. A few of my friends will be coming too.”

Cheri opened her mouth.

“Bear—”

“Don’t bother arguing,” Bear interrupted, raising one hand gently but firmly. “You already know how that conversation ends.”

Cheri studied him for a long moment.

Then, unexpectedly, she smiled.

“Okay,” she said. “My flight leaves at two. I’ll see if I can get you on it.”

Bear chuckled and pulled out his phone.

“We won’t need a plane.”

He squinted at the screen for a moment.

“Says here it’s about nine hours riding time from here to Lexington.”

He looked up with a grin.

“We’ll make it in seven.”

Cheri tilted her head.

“Riding time?”

Bear smiled wider.

“Motorcycles are hard to catch.”

He slid the phone back into his pocket.

“We’ll leave this morning,” he added casually. “Say around ten o’clock. We may even beat you there.”

Cheri leaned across the table and kissed him lightly on the cheek.

For the first time since hearing about the black van, the tightness in her chest eased slightly.

Help was on the way.

Chapter Twelve

War on Many Fronts

Sedi met Cheri at the front door.

The redhead stood framed by the morning light, elegant and a bit provocative. She wore a short black skirt, high heels, and a fitted jacket that seemed somehow both stylish and practical. Her bright copper hair caught the sunlight, and her confident smile carried the easy warmth of someone who had already decided that everything would be all right.

Sedi did not even attempt composure. The moment the door opened, she stepped forward and embraced her.

"Oh, thank you so much, Cheri," she whispered, emotion breaking through as a few tears slipped down her cheeks.

Cheri hugged her firmly, patting her shoulder with easy reassurance.

"Psh," she said lightly. "I'm delighted to be here. Honestly, I was going a bit mad not being able to help."

Sedi laughed softly through the tears.

"Your room is ready. I hope you'll be comfortable."

Cheri waved the suggestion away with theatrical indifference.

"I would sleep in the backyard if necessary. We'll worry about the room later. Let's talk."

Sedi smiled despite herself.

"I love that about you, so damn direct and focused."

She led Cheri down the hallway and into her study, a quiet room lined with bookshelves and soft afternoon light. The two women settled into chairs opposite one another.

Cheri immediately leaned forward, her tone shifting to business.

"Bring me up to date. Any more sightings last night or today?"

"No, thank goodness," Sedi replied. "But I had two additional cameras installed this morning. They're hidden in the bushes out by the street. If that van comes back, I'm hoping to get a license number."

"Good thinking," Cheri nodded approvingly. "So, how do you want to handle this? What should I be doing?"

"There really isn't much you can do directly," Sedi admitted. "I have to keep my hospital schedule. Erin, our nanny, is here during the day, but I would feel much better knowing you were here as well."

"No problem," Cheri said instantly. "I'm a hawk… with very sharp talons."

Sedi allowed herself a faint smile.

"There is still the matter of Clarice going to school. I hate to ask this of you, but I would be enormously relieved if you could spend the next few days sitting outside the school. Just watching to see if the van appears."

Cheri shrugged casually.

"Done. Hell, I'll sit in her classroom if you want."

"There's no need for that," Sedi laughed softly. "It's just the transfer time that worries me. Erin always picks her up right on time, but that moment between the door and the car…"

Cheri nodded thoughtfully.

"I understand."

Then she added, almost casually,

"I'll explain in a moment, but I assure you, every place your daughter goes, she will be protected."

Sedi looked puzzled by the comment but decided not to press the matter yet.

"Now," Cheri said brightly, shifting gears. "May I meet your daughter? What's her name?"

"Clarice."

Cheri's face lit up.

"Beautiful name! Is she named for, "

"Yes," Sedi laughed. "When I was a child, I was absolutely enchanted with the *Rudolph the Red-Nosed Reindeer* cartoon. I especially loved the little doe named Clarice. That's where the name comes from."

"That's wonderful," Cheri laughed. "I loved that show too. I still watch it every year."

"We do too. I'll get her."

Sedi rose and stepped into the hallway. A moment later, she returned with a young girl who so strongly resembled her mother that it was almost startling.

Clarice was tall for her eight years, with the same rich caramel complexion and delicate features. Her curious eyes immediately settled on Cheri.

After the introductions, Cheri reached for her carry-on bag.

"Well now," she said conspiratorially. "I brought you something, Clarice. I hope you don't already have one."

She opened the bag and produced a box. Carefully lifting the lid, she removed a large, clear plastic board with a small power cord attached, followed by several brightly colored pens.

"This," Cheri said, "is a light drawing board. You can draw pictures in different colors, and they glow when you turn it on."

Clarice's eyes widened with delight as she carefully took hold of the board.

"Oh, Cheri," Sedi said in amazement. "You have no idea. She's been begging me for one of those for months. I kept telling her she had to wait for her birthday."

Clarice was nearly glowing.

"May I?" she asked, turning politely toward her mother.

"Yes, of course, darling," Sedi said warmly. "Take it to Erin. She'll help you set it up."

Clarice dashed from the room, arms full of her new treasure.

A deep rumbling sound suddenly rolled through the quiet neighborhood.

Sedi jumped to her feet, alarm flashing across her face.

Cheri simply smiled.

"That," she said, rising calmly, "is what I was just going to tell you about."

She walked toward the front door.

"The cavalry has arrived. Let's go take a look."

Outside, four large motorcycles were parked neatly in the driveway. Beside each one stood a massive man dressed in black leather. All wore full beards, yet despite their intimidating size, they appeared immaculately groomed.

The largest of the men stepped forward and approached the porch.

"Sedi," Cheri said warmly, "this is my dear friend George Carter. Most people know him as Bear."

Bear extended a large hand and shook Sedi's gently.

"I apologize for the clatter, ma'am," he said politely. "We'll have the bikes out of here in a few minutes."

Sedi looked from one enormous biker to another, her earlier alarm quickly fading into curiosity.

Cheri stepped beside her.

"Let me explain. Bear and his friends are here to help. They'll keep a twenty-four-hour watch on the house and on the school. Clarice will never be alone."

Sedi blinked in surprise.

"And the best part," Cheri added, "is that no one will notice. I know these men very well. They're remarkable people. And despite the appearance… quite kind and caring."

Bear nodded calmly.

“Yes, ma’am. You’ll seldom see us, and you’ll never hear us. But we’ll always be nearby. We’ll find that van and whoever’s inside it.”

“You can count on that,” Cheri added.

Sedi exhaled slowly, overwhelmed but grateful.

“I don’t know what to say. I’m grateful, more than you know. But… where arc you staying?”

Bear gave a reassuring smile.

“No worries there. We’ll take care of that ourselves. Just know we’ll be watching, quietly.”

Cheri turned toward him.

“Bear, could you introduce our friends?”

“Certainly.”

He gestured toward each man in turn.

“The one with the red beard is Griz… short for Grizzly.”

Griz smiled broadly and gave a friendly nod.

“The one in the cowboy hat is Timber.”

Timber tipped the brim politely.

“Ma’am.”

“And the little one is Tink.”

Tink was “little” only in comparison to the others. He stood at least six feet two. He smiled shyly and even blushed slightly.

“Tink,” Cheri added with a laugh, “is short for Tinkerbell.”

Sedi blinked, then burst into laughter.

“You see,” Cheri explained casually, “they’re all gay.”

Still smiling, Sedi nodded warmly.

“Well then, welcome to all of you. I’m sorry if I seemed startled at first. I am truly grateful.”

“Our pleasure, ma’am,” Bear said respectfully.

He stepped back toward the motorcycles.

"We'll be moving out now. Two of us will sit at the ends of your street until our night shift replaces them. I'm heading to the police department to introduce ourselves. You may receive a call for verification."

Sedi simply shook her head in quiet disbelief as the men mounted their bikes.

How things had changed in twenty-four hours.

ϒ ϒ ϒ

It was nearly midnight when Chelsea returned to Sir Roger's chambers. Oxford had grown quiet by then. The ancient quadrangles lay beneath a thin mist, and the old stones of the college seemed to absorb the dim glow of the scattered lanterns that lined the narrow pathways. The hour suited the mood of the gathering perfectly.

Inside the chambers, the atmosphere had not improved since the previous evening.

This time, both Sabina and Lauren had joined the others. None of them had slept properly since the ordeal had begun. Sleep came only in brief, fractured stretches, an hour or two perhaps, sometimes less, interrupted by anxious thoughts and restless pacing. The exhaustion had settled into their faces like a permanent shadow. In such circumstances, meeting late into the night hardly mattered. Time itself had lost any ordinary rhythm.

When Chelsea entered, her presence seemed almost mechanical against the weary tension in the room.

Roger rose immediately and offered brief introductions. Sabrina stood beside Lauren near the fireplace, both women composed but visibly drained. Chelsea acknowledged them with a short, respectful inclination of her head.

Though she was not someone given to emotional display, she spoke quietly.

"I am sorry for what has happened to you," Chelsea said.

The words were delivered without flourish, but they were sincere. Sabina and Lauren received them with polite nods. Their eyes remained dry. The grief and fear they carried had moved well beyond tears.

Chelsea did not linger on sentiment. She turned her attention back to the scholars gathered around the long oak table.

Roger, who had been waiting impatiently since she arrived, leaned forward.

"You have something, I hope."

"I do."

Her expression, as always, was completely neutral, almost mask-like. No excitement, no triumph, no anxiety. Merely information waiting to be delivered.

"We were fortunate," she continued. "Loki was available immediately. There have been several exchanges over the past few hours."

The name hung in the room like a whispered rumor.

"Loki expressed interest. However, before committing himself to anything further, he conducted his own research."

She glanced around the table.

"On each of you."

Several eyebrows lifted.

"He probably knows more about you than you would prefer."

That produced a few uneasy glances between the professors. Eustace rubbed the bridge of his nose while Roger gave a soft, resigned sigh.

"Needless to say," Chelsea continued, "he was fascinated by your… uh…previous story."

The slight pause before the word story carried meaning.

The Soulfast affair was not entirely unknown to the outside world. Bits and fragments had escaped into obscure academic circles and internet forums over the years, rumors, speculation, and half-truths. None of it formed a coherent narrative, but in the strange ecosystem of the internet, fragments had a habit of growing into elaborate theories.

Apparently, Loki had taken notice.

"He has tentatively agreed to an…interaction."

Chelsea paused.

The room leaned forward.

"But," she continued calmly, "he has done so under two conditions."

The tension sharpened immediately.

"First," she said, "he wishes to know about what he refers to as the 'inscrutable interstice' in the story."

For several seconds, there was silence.

Even among the formidable intellects gathered there, the phrase produced more confusion than recognition.

Brows furrowed. Simon tilted his head slightly. Sabina looked toward Roger.

Finally, Eustace broke the silence with a dismissive grunt.

"Mysterious gap."

Chelsea remained expressionless.

Sir Roger slowly turned toward his old colleague.

"You know what he means, don't you?"

Eustace glared at him.

"Of course I know what he means, you old fool."

The irritation in his voice carried the comfortable hostility of a friendship that had lasted more than half a century.

He leaned back heavily in his chair, staring at the ceiling as if calculating something unpleasant.

"Damnation," he muttered.

A long pause followed.

"I will have to ask permission."

Everyone in the room understood what he meant.

Eustace scratched his chin thoughtfully.

"Not that it will do this Loki any good," he added with a cynical snort. "Unless he fancies a rather long trek through the forest."

No one asked further questions.

Chelsea gave a small nod and continued.

"The second condition is simpler."

That seemed unlikely, given the first.

"He wishes you to solve what he described as an 'infantile riddle.'"

Eustace waved his hand impatiently.

"Go on."

Chelsea recited it without emphasis.

"Explain how you can take *one* away from *eleven* and get *ten*, and take *one* away from *nine* and also get *ten*."

The sentence hung in the air.

Several seconds passed.

Then several more.

Despite the formidable concentration of intellect in the room, two of Oxford's most celebrated historians, a prize-winning scholar, and several minds accustomed to unraveling philosophical puzzles, not one of them spoke.

Simon frowned slightly.

Roger blinked.

Sabrina tilted her head.

Even Eustace looked irritated rather than enlightened.

Finally, Chelsea reached into her coat pocket and placed a small card on the table.

"You have my number," she said calmly. "You may contact me at any hour."

She gave a brief nod to the room, turned, and walked toward the door.

Her stiff, deliberate movements were odd; she never swung her arms when she walked.

Within seconds, she had disappeared down the corridor, leaving the group behind in silence.

Roger stared at the closed door for a moment.

Then he slowly turned back toward the others.

“Well,” he said quietly.

“Apparently, we have homework. And we must do this quickly.”

ꝎꝎꝎ

Sabina raced along the wide stretch of beach, her laughter carried away by the steady whisper of the surf. Little Sugar chased after her with determined enthusiasm, the tiny dog’s paws kicking up small sprays of sand as she struggled to keep pace. Every few moments, Sabina would glance back, squeal with delight, and dash forward again, sending Sugar into another burst of heroic pursuit. The little dog answered with occasional high-pitched yips, as if announcing to the entire shoreline that this was the most important race in the world.

Sabina’s clothes fluttered lightly in the ocean breeze, a crisp white blouse tucked into a soft brown skirt, with a small suede jacket buttoned neatly at the front. It was the sort of outfit one might expect for an afternoon walk in a village garden rather than a romp along the sand. Catherine, however, would accept nothing less than perfection. Even a captive child, in her mind, must appear immaculate.

Not far away, Danielle sat quietly on the cool sand with her legs folded beneath her. The young nanny had abandoned any attempt to keep Sabina tidy. She simply watched the child run back and forth across the shore, laughing now and then at the determined little dog galloping behind her. Every so often, Sabina would run toward her, breathless and hopeful.

“Danielle! Can I go in the water now? Just a little bit?”

Danielle would glance automatically toward the house, though she already knew the answer.

“I’m afraid not, sweetheart.”

Sabina would drop her shoulders, sigh dramatically, then race away with Sugar bounding after her.

It was too cool for swimming, despite Sabina's persistent pleas. The air was unusually mild for the season, nearly seventy degrees, but the Atlantic was another matter entirely. The water lay dark and restless beyond the surf line, its temperature far colder than the deceptive warmth of the afternoon sun. Catherine had forbidden it completely. No risks. Not a fall, not a fever, not even the smallest chance that anything might happen to Sabina.

High above the beach, Catherine stood alone on one of the house's wide sundecks. From there she could see everything: the bright line of the surf, the gulls circling lazily in the wind, the child racing along the sand, and the patient nanny keeping watch nearby.

For a brief moment, as Sabina's laughter drifted up to her, the corners of Catherine's mouth began to lift. The smile appeared almost involuntarily, as if it had escaped from some long-forgotten part of her.

But just as quickly, she forced it away.

Her face hardened again into the severe composure she had worn for years.

Five years of torture had taught her many things. One of them was how to bury joy so deeply that it could not betray her.

Still, as she stood there watching the child run along the beach, a faint brightness flickered somewhere behind her eyes.

Her joy was coming.

In fact, it was very nearly here.

Chapter Thirteen

One Riddle Solved

It was six o'clock in the morning, and everyone was exhausted.

Lauren and Sabrina were curled up asleep together on the long leather couch, each wrapped in a blanket someone had thoughtfully draped over them hours earlier. Sabrina's head rested on Lauren's shoulder, and neither had stirred for nearly an hour.

Simon sat slumped in the overstuffed chair by the fireplace, drifting in and out of sleep. Every few minutes, his head dipped forward before he jerked awake again.

Drew and Sir Roger sat side by side near the large desk, surrounded by a battlefield of scribbled notes, torn scraps of paper, and several empty coffee cups. Pencils rolled across the clutter whenever someone bumped the desk.

Eustace, meanwhile, had resumed pacing. He had been pacing for hours. The old wooden floor creaked beneath his steps like a metronome measuring his irritation.

Finally, he stopped, turning sharply toward the others.

"How the bloody hell," he demanded, "can you take one from eleven and get ten, yet also take one from nine and get ten?"

Everyone ignored him.

Drew rubbed his eyes.

"We've tried every mathematical base from two to ten," he said wearily. "Binary, ternary, quaternary… all the way through decimal. Nothing works."

Simon muttered from his chair without opening his eyes.

"You skipped base three point seven."

Drew glanced over.

"That isn't a real base."

Simon opened one eye.

"Not with that attitude."

Eustace groaned and resumed pacing.

Sir Roger leaned back in his chair and glanced at the clock.

"Do you think Nathaniel might be awake yet?" he asked cautiously.

Eustace stopped dead in the middle of the room.

He turned slowly.

"You think," he said in a dangerously calm voice, "that I am going to call that twit, Nathaniel Almany, and admit that we could not solve a child's riddle?"

Roger raised his hands mildly.

"I'm merely suggesting the possibility."

"I will not!" Eustace barked.

Simon chuckled quietly.

Roger sighed and rubbed his temples.

"Eustace, the others leave for Paris this afternoon," he said patiently. "They need to be there to receive instructions from Catherine."

"That damn witch," Eustace muttered darkly.

Roger continued.

"We do not have to solve the riddle before they leave. But it would be rather unfortunate if we fell behind simply because we could not decipher the first message."

Drew added quietly,

"Assuming there even *is* anything to decipher."

Silence settled over the room.

Simon straightened in his chair, now fully awake.

"Well," he said, stretching his arms above his head, "I've tried everything I know."

Eustace glared at him.

"Have you tried thinking?"

Simon grinned.

"I even tried praying."

Drew looked over at him.

"To whom exactly, my irreverent friend? Surely not the Almighty."

Simon shook his head.

"No. I started with Loki. It seemed appropriate."

Drew chuckled.

"And?"

"No response. So then I tried Mercury."

"The Roman messenger?" Roger asked.

"Yes. Trickster, traveler, patron saint of thieves and liars," Simon said thoughtfully. "He seemed like the sort who might appreciate riddles."

Drew leaned back in his chair dramatically.

"*Fly like chidden Mercury from Jove,*" he declaimed, raising one arm toward the ceiling.

Simon pointed at him immediately.

"Troilus."

Drew nodded.

"*Troilus and Cressida,* Act Four."

Roger groaned softly.

"Oh no. Not this again."

Simon grinned wickedly.

"You started it."

The two men stared at each other.

The two men continued firing quotes back and forth like dueling pistols.

Sir Roger shook his head.

"This ridiculous game again."

Eustace pointed angrily toward the couch where the two sleeping women lay.

"If they wake up and hear this nonsense… "

"They loathe the game," Roger said.

"Exactly."

Drew continued triumphantly.

Eventually, the energy drained out of the room again.

The clock ticked loudly on the wall.

Even Eustace gave up pacing and collapsed into a chair.

Everyone sat in silence.

Finally, Eustace spoke.

"Look up Nathan's number, I suppose."

Roger nodded reluctantly.

Nathaniel Almany was not exactly a friend.

More of an acquaintance.

He was the head of the mathematics department at Magdalen College, a brilliant man with a reputation for solving mathematical problems that baffled others.

Calling him would be embarrassing.

But he would know the answer.

Roger reached for his phone.

Simon suddenly bolted upright.

"Wait!"

Everyone looked up.

Simon stood quickly and began pacing.

Not Eustace's angry pacing.

This was different.

Faster.

More focused.

His eyes were bright.

"What?" Roger asked.

Simon muttered to himself.

"Mercury…"

He snapped his fingers.

"Rome…"

Drew sat forward instantly.

He knew that tone.

Simon spun around.

"Mercury was Roman."

"Yes…" Roger said cautiously.

Simon pointed toward the desk.

"The numbers!"

Drew's eyes widened.

"Oh, my God."

He grabbed a scrap of paper and began scribbling.

"Roman numerals!"

Simon laughed.

"Exactly!"

Drew wrote quickly while speaking aloud.

"Eleven is XI."

He circled it.

"And nine is IX."

He wrote the second number beside it.

"Now watch this…"

He crossed out the I in XI.

"That leaves X."

Then he crossed out the I in IX.

"That also leaves X."

He held up the paper.

"Ten!"

For a moment, the room was silent.

Then Eustace exploded out of his chair.

"Of course!"

Roger jumped up as well.

"Roman numerals!"

Simon laughed triumphantly.

"I knew Mercury would come through eventually."

Even Drew stood up, grinning.

And suddenly the entire room erupted.

Eustace clapped Roger on the back.

Roger grabbed Drew's shoulders.

Simon spun around in a ridiculous little victory dance.

For several joyful seconds, the exhausted scholars bounced around the room like schoolboys who had just solved the world's greatest puzzle.

Lauren stirred slightly on the couch.

Sabrina opened one eye.

"What are they doing?" she whispered sleepily.

Lauren glanced over at the celebrating men.

She closed her eyes again.

"They figured something out."

Sabrina nodded.

"That explains the madness."

And both women went right back to sleep.

ϒ ϒ ϒ

It was just after seven o'clock when Chelsea returned to the room.

The early morning light now streamed through the tall windows, casting long pale beams across the cluttered study. The battlefield of papers still covered Roger's desk, scribbled calculations, abandoned theories, and the victorious scrap that now held the Roman numeral solution.

Lauren and Sabrina had already left to pack for their flight to Paris. Their absence made the room feel oddly lonelier, though the men remained gathered around the desk, looking equally tired and satisfied.

Chelsea stepped inside, adjusting her glasses.

"You wanted to see me?"

Eustace gestured toward the desk.

"Yes. We have solved the riddle."

Chelsea's eyebrows lifted slightly.

"Oh?"

Simon leaned forward with renewed enthusiasm.

"It's Roman numerals. The numbers in the riddle are XI and IX. Remove the 'I' from each, and you are left with X, ten in both cases."

Chelsea nodded slowly, her expression thoughtful.

"Yes," she said after a moment. "That works perfectly."

She covered her mouth as a yawn slipped out.

None of them blamed her.

Everyone in the room looked equally exhausted.

"We need you to tell Loki to use Roman numerals," Eustace said firmly. "He'll understand immediately. It solves his riddle."

Chelsea nodded again.

"Yes, I see."

She pulled a small notebook from her bag and jotted something down.

"And tell him," Eustace continued, "that the mysterious gap will be explained to him… and only him."

Chelsea paused, pen hovering above the page.

"Understood."

She looked up.

"What message would you like me to send him?"

Simon stepped forward and retrieved a copy of Catherine's letter from the desk.

"Send him this."

Chelsea accepted the paper and briefly glanced it over.

Simon continued.

"Tell him we are unsure whether there is any hidden message inside it. There may not be. But we would like him to examine it carefully to see if he can find any pattern or anomaly that might indicate something."

Chelsea nodded.

"Yes, of course."

Drew added from behind Simon,

"And tell him there will be additional messages coming. Some may contain hidden meaning, even if there is no formal cipher involved. We would appreciate any thoughts or observations he might have."

Chelsea scribbled a few more notes.

"Will do."

She closed the notebook and slipped it back into her bag.

"Anything else?"

Roger smiled kindly.

"No, that's all. But thank you very much, Chelsea. We are extremely grateful."

Chelsea gave a small nod.

"I'll get back to you as soon as I hear from him," she said in her usual calm, matter-of-fact tone.

The latch clicked softly behind her as she stepped into the quiet hallway.

Her footsteps faded slowly as she padded down the corridor.

Inside the study, the tension finally broke.

Eustace exhaled a long breath of relief and gathered his coat and papers.

"Well," he announced, "I am going to find a bed and attempt something resembling sleep."

He headed for the door.

"I've been awake for nearly thirty hours."

Roger chuckled.

"An excellent plan."

Eustace paused at the doorway and looked back.

"Try not to solve any more riddles without me."

Then he disappeared down the hall.

The remaining men sank back into their chairs.

Roger turned toward Drew and Simon.

"You leave this afternoon, don't you?" he asked. "What time is your flight?"

Drew exchanged a glance with Simon and then gave Roger a slightly sheepish grin.

"Whenever we manage to get ourselves ready."

Roger looked puzzled.

Drew shrugged casually.

"We have our own plane."

Roger blinked once.

Then he laughed.

"Of course you do. I'd forgotten."

Simon stretched his arms above his head.

"When do you expect your next contact?" Roger asked.

Drew shrugged.

"She told us to be in Paris by tomorrow," Simon said. "So I imagine we'll hear something from her then."

Roger leaned back in his chair.

"And what do you suppose she'll ask you to do next?"

Simon smiled tiredly.

"Absolutely no idea."

He rubbed his eyes.

"Heaven only knows what she has planned."

For a moment, the room was quiet again.

Then Drew leaned back and sighed contentedly.

"Well… at least we can get some sleep tonight."

Roger nodded. "Me too."

ϒ ϒ ϒ

Chester Morris sat at the head of the long walnut conference table, his hands folded calmly in front of him.

The conference room occupied the entire corner of the upper floor, and the tall windows offered a sweeping panorama of the New York skyline. Morning light reflected off the glass towers across the avenue, and far below, the traffic crawled through Manhattan like a restless river of metal.

Inside the room, however, the mood was considerably heavier.

A young assistant moved quietly around the table, refilling coffee cups. She paused briefly beside Chester before topping off the mugs of the others seated there.

Three people faced him, two men and one woman, each watching him with varying degrees of curiosity and concern.

The conversation resumed as soon as the coffee pot was set down.

"So," one of the men said slowly, leaning back in his chair, "this Catherine Lodge has kidnapped a child."

He tapped his fingers lightly on the table.

"And we know this for certain?"

Chester nodded.

"I was just getting to that."

He opened the leather portfolio in front of him and withdrew several photocopies of a handwritten letter.

Without ceremony, he passed them down the table.

"Take a minute and read this," he said. "It confirms that she is responsible."

The papers circulated.

For several moments, the only sound in the room was the soft rustle of pages.

One man leaned closer to the document, squinting slightly.

Another shook his head slowly as he read.

Then someone gave a low whistle.

"Good Lord."

Another voice followed.

"Dear God…"

The woman at the table lowered the paper carefully, her expression tightening as she absorbed the contents.

One by one, the copies were placed back on the table.

Chester waited until everyone had finished.

Then he spoke again.

"Our assignment," he said calmly, "is to find her."

He paused.

"It sounds simple when stated that way."

A faint, humorless smile crossed his face.

"But I suspect it will prove to be quite difficult."

He tapped the letter with a finger.

"This is a very clever woman."

The woman seated near the end of the table leaned forward slightly.

"What's her motive?"

Chester leaned back in his chair.

"I'm sure most of you remember the incident five years ago," he said. "The matter involving the purloined painting."

Several heads nodded immediately.

"That scandal made the front pages on three continents," one of the men said.

"Yes," Chester replied quietly. "It did."

He cleared his throat.

"Unfortunately… we were unknowingly on the wrong side of that affair."

More nods.

One man muttered,

"That was an unpleasant week."

Chester continued.

"It would appear that Miss Lodge has not forgotten the episode. This is her way of seeking revenge against those who ruined her reputation."

The room fell silent for a moment.

Finally, one of the men broke the pause.

"Alright," he said, leaning forward. "Where do we begin, chief?"

Chester steepled his fingers.

"We will be receiving additional messages from her."

Several eyebrows rose.

"She intends to communicate with us?"

"Not us but to our client," Chester replied calmly. "But the messages will almost certainly conceal her real intentions."

He gestured toward the letter.

"They may, however, provide small clues. Patterns. References. Anything that might suggest where she is operating from."

One of the men lifted the letter again and scanned it.

"I don't see anything here that would hint at a location."

"I agree," Chester said.

"Nevertheless, there is work we can begin immediately."

He opened his portfolio again.

"I know who her friends are."

He glanced around the table.

"Or at least who they used to be."

Another man nodded thoughtfully.

"Start with the social circle."

"Exactly."

Chester continued.

"They likely will not know where she is now. But they will know her habits."

He began counting off points with his fingers.

"Places she liked to visit."

"Cities she favored."

"Associates."

"Interests."

"Old patterns of behavior."

He closed the folder.

"And sometimes those small details lead to very large discoveries."

One of the men straightened in his chair.

"Alright then," he said. "Let's get moving."

He gestured toward the portfolio.

"I assume you'll be assigning each of us contacts."

"Yes," Chester said.

He withdrew several sheets of paper and passed them around the table.

"I've prepared a list for each of you."

The pages moved from hand to hand. Each was headed with the name of one of the agents present.

"I'll be traveling to Europe, first London, then perhaps Paris."

"God, I hate England," he added.

A few chuckles sounded around the table.

"They drive on the wrong side of the damn road," he continued indignantly. "No civilized country should tolerate that kind of chaos."

Now the entire table laughed. The mood lightened for a moment. But only for a moment.

Chester tapped the letter once more.

"Ladies and gentlemen," he said quietly, "let's remember why we're here."

The room settled again.

"A child has been taken."

His voice remained calm.

"Our task is to find Catherine Lodge."

He paused.

"And bring this matter to an end."

Silence filled the room.

Then chairs began to slide back as the team prepared to go to work.

Chapter Fourteen

The Paris Summons

The Hotel George V in Paris is among the city's most celebrated luxury hotels, long admired for its elegance, history, and impeccable service. Situated just off the Champs-Élysées, on the prestigious Avenue George V, the hotel stands in the heart of one of Paris's most refined neighborhoods, surrounded by grand boutiques, elegant cafés, and the quiet hum of one of the world's most beautiful cities.

Opened in 1928, the hotel was named, somewhat unexpectedly for a Parisian landmark, after King George V of the United Kingdom, reflecting the large number of wealthy British and American travelers who flocked to Paris during the golden age of transatlantic travel. Built in the fashionable Art Deco style of the era, the George V quickly established itself as a sanctuary of refined luxury, attracting aristocrats, film stars, financiers, and dignitaries from around the world.

The two suites reserved for Simon and Sabrina and for Drew and Lauren were located side by side on an upper floor of the hotel, their tall windows offering a breathtaking view of the Eiffel Tower rising above the Paris skyline. By day, the famous iron lattice shimmered in the distance; by night, it sparkled like a constellation against the dark sky.

Both suites were exquisitely appointed, embodying the quiet opulence for which the George V is renowned. Polished marble floors, delicate crystal chandeliers, and finely carved antique furnishings created an atmosphere of timeless French elegance. Rich fabrics, soft lighting, and carefully arranged décor gave the rooms the feeling of a private Parisian residence rather than a hotel. Every detail, from the silk draperies to the fresh flowers arranged with effortless grace, spoke of understated luxury and the enduring tradition of hospitality that has defined the George V for nearly a century.

The flight from Oxford to Paris had taken barely an hour, yet it felt far longer. Exhaustion clung to them all, the kind that settles into the bones after days of tension and sleepless nights. Despite their fatigue, none of them had managed to sleep on the plane. Their minds refused to quiet themselves; every thought seemed to circle inevitably back to Sabina, to Catherine, and to the unknown game that awaited them.

But once they arrived at the hotel and were shown to their suites, the strain finally claimed them. It was midday when they collapsed onto the beds, and within minutes all four had surrendered to a deep, dreamless sleep that lasted several hours.

Now it was eight o'clock in the evening, and the friends sat together in the elegant dining room of *L'Orangerie*, the two-star Michelin restaurant at the hotel. The softly lit room glowed with understated luxury, white tablecloths, polished silver, and delicate crystal glasses catching the warm light. Beyond the tall windows, the lights of Paris shimmered gently in the night.

They had briefly considered dining at the hotel's famous three-star Michelin restaurant, *Le Cinq*, but ultimately decided against it. The women, despite their natural elegance, were convinced they had not packed clothing suitable for such rarified formality. Their dresses were tasteful and refined, but in their minds they fell short of the level demanded by Le Cinq.

Judging by the subtle glances from nearby tables, however, it seemed that the assessment was entirely mistaken. They could have dined anywhere in Paris.

"God, it's nice to feel like a whole person again," Lauren sighed, leaning back slightly in her chair. "Just for a few hours, I want to pretend things are normal."

Sabrina lifted her glass and took a thoughtful sip of wine. A small smile touched her lips.

"You deserve a little normalcy, Ell," she said gently. "Tomorrow morning, we climb back onto the roller coaster."

Simon raised his wineglass.

"I propose a temporary treaty," he said. "Tonight, we avoid serious discussion. No theories, no strategizing, no catastrophizing. Let's take a vacation from angst."

They all lifted their glasses in agreement, and the crystal chimed softly as they toasted.

Drew pursed his lips thoughtfully.

"Nonetheless," he said after a moment, "purely out of curiosity, any guesses about tomorrow?"

Simon frowned but said nothing.

Lauren waved the question away with a small shrug.

"I think we've speculated as much as we possibly can," she said. "At this point, we'll simply have to wait and see."

Simon leaned forward slightly, his fingers loosely clasped.

"Well, Paris has always been Catherine's favorite city. She adores it here. Because of that, one might conclude she's here herself." He paused. "But I doubt it."

Sabrina shook her head immediately.

"Not likely," she said. "As much as she would enjoy watching us squirm in person, she wouldn't risk being apprehended. No chance."

"I agree," Lauren added. "But she may very well have sent someone else to meet us."

"Yes," Sabrina said. "Though that could have been arranged anywhere in the world. Catherine would enjoy forcing us to travel for it. Elegant inconvenience is very much her style."

The others nodded. They all knew Catherine well enough to recognize that phrase as perfectly descriptive.

Simon swirled the wine in his glass, studying it as though it might reveal something.

"I still suspect something more elaborate than a simple meeting," he said slowly. "Catherine treats Paris almost like her hometown. She knows the city intimately, its museums, its back streets, its hidden corners. I suspect there's something here she wants us to see."

Drew tilted his head thoughtfully.

"This is starting to feel like an old-fashioned scavenger hunt."

Sabrina's eyes lit slightly.

"Now that you mention it, I think you might be right. Perhaps she'll have us collecting objects or visiting locations, each one revealing a new clue."

"Possibly," Lauren said. "But clues leading to what?"

"Sabina's location," Sabrina answered quietly.

The sound of her daughter's name hung heavily in the air.

Lauren's expression faltered, the fragile calm she had maintained all evening beginning to crack. Her eyes filled suddenly, and she lowered her gaze toward the table.

"I'm sorry, Ell," Sabrina said softly, reaching across the table to take her hand.

For a moment, no one spoke. The muted murmur of the restaurant filled the silence as Lauren fought to regain control.

Finally, she drew a slow breath and nodded faintly.

Simon spoke carefully.

"If this truly is a scavenger hunt," he said, "you can be certain there will be false trails, clever red herrings scattered throughout. Catherine is many things, but subtle she is not. She will enjoy drawing this out."

He paused before continuing.

"I believe she will return Sabina eventually. But not before she extracts her pound of flesh from us…or just me."

Lauren looked up sharply. The meaning of his words struck her instantly, and her expression changed from sorrow to sudden understanding.

"Oh, Simon…" she said quietly. "I'm so sorry."

He looked at her, puzzled.

"All this time I've been thinking only about Sabina," she continued. "I never stopped to remember her true intention. She isn't just tormenting us… She's trying to destroy you."

Realization spread across the table.

"Oh my God," Lauren whispered. "She's going to make demands of you. Terrible demands."

Sabrina closed her eyes briefly and took a slow breath.

Drew looked directly at Simon.

"Simon, I'm sorry," he said. "I've been completely focused on Sabina, too. I never meant to ignore what this will mean for you."

Simon shrugged lightly, though the gesture carried a trace of resignation.

"It will be what it will be," he said calmly. "I'll do what I must. And yes… I fully expect the opening salvo to come tomorrow."

Sabrina exhaled softly.

"Well," she said with a faint smile, "I suppose we failed rather spectacularly in our pledge for the evening."

Drew chuckled quietly.

"I'm not sure any of us are capable of ignoring the nightmare we're in."

The tension gradually softened again as the meal continued. They spoke of other things, old travels, amusing memories, small stories from happier years. It was not exactly a normal conversation, but it was close enough.

And for a few hours, in the warm glow of a Parisian dining room, they allowed themselves the fragile illusion of ordinary life.

ϒ ϒ ϒ

All four friends gathered in Simon and Sabrina's suite midmorning. Sunlight streamed through the tall windows overlooking the elegant avenue below, casting warm reflections across the polished parquet floors. The room itself was a study in quiet opulence, cream-colored silk walls, gilded moldings, and a pair of tall French doors that opened to a small balcony where the faint sounds of Paris drifted upward:

distant traffic, a passing scooter, and the occasional murmur of voices from the street cafés already filling for the late morning.

Breakfast had been arranged with the effortless precision for which the hotel was famous. Croissants were plentiful and perfectly assorted on a polished silver salver, some plain and buttery, others filled with almond cream or chocolate. Their delicate flakes scattered like confetti across a linen napkin beneath them. A gold coffee urn stood proudly on the Louis XIV refectory table along one wall, steam rising gently from its spout. Beside it stood a tall matching creamer and a small bowl of sugar cubes. The rich aroma of freshly ground coffee mingled with the buttery scent of pastry, creating a small island of comfort amid the tension that hung over the room.

Everyone had taken care with their appearance. Paris demanded it.

Rather than the ultra-casual American style that would have seemed jarringly out of place, the women had chosen modest yet unmistakably fashionable attire. Sabrina wore a light yellow A-line dress that moved gracefully when she walked. Around her neck hung the elegant strand of pearls that Sedi had insisted she purchase five years earlier during a spontaneous shopping excursion in London. Sabrina had protested at the time that they were extravagant. Now she wore them often, and the soft luster of the pearls complemented her perfectly.

Lauren had chosen a midi dress in creamy beige that was understated but elegant, its tailored cut flattering without calling attention to itself. Her jewelry was subdued, a delicate bracelet and a pair of small gold earrings that caught the light when she turned her head. Both women wore kitten heels, a practical compromise between fashion and the miles of walking Paris would inevitably demand.

The men had adopted the relaxed European look with equal care. Simon and Drew wore loose, well-cut trousers in neutral tones paired with white dress shirts and unstructured sports coats. Neither wore a tie. The look suggested ease rather than formality, but the quality of the fabrics and the quiet precision of the tailoring made their affluence unmistakable. It was the sort of elegance that did not announce itself loudly but could not be mistaken.

Yet despite the beauty of the room, the food, and the city beyond the windows, an undercurrent of impatience hung in the air.

“We wait and wait,” Sabrina sighed, leaning back in her chair and stirring her coffee absentmindedly.

Lauren glanced toward the window as if the streets themselves might offer an answer. “We need Professor Fairfax here to do some pacing for us,” she quipped.

Drew chuckled softly. “Yeah. I have a feeling we’re going to be doing quite a bit of pacing of our own today.”

Simon took another sip of coffee, savoring the warmth. “At least I feel better rested than I have in days,” he said. “Yesterday I thought I might collapse from exhaustion.”

For a moment, they simply sat there, listening to the quiet ticking of the ornate mantel clock.

Then the doorbell to the suite rang.

The sound startled them all, freezing everyone in place for a brief, electric second.

Chairs turned almost in unison as Simon rose and walked toward the door. The others watched him cross the room, their anticipation suddenly thick enough to feel.

Simon opened the door.

In the hallway stood a rather short man, immaculately dressed in the hotel’s livery: a dark coat, brass buttons polished to a mirror shine, and white gloves that seemed almost ceremonial. He held a single envelope delicately between two fingers.

“Monsieur, if you please,” he said politely.

His English was flawless, though softened by a distinct Parisian accent.

He extended the envelope to Simon with a small, respectful bow.

“This was just left for you at the desk. You instructed us to bring any message to you immediately. Here it is.”

He smiled with professional warmth.

“Thank you, Henri,” Simon said, glancing at the nametag pinned neatly to the man’s jacket. “May I ask if you saw who left the envelope?”

"I did indeed, sir." Henri tilted his head thoughtfully. "It was a boy, sir. How do you say…" He paused, searching for the correct word. "Teenager? Yes. A boy."

Drew hurried to the doorway, already pulling a bill from his wallet. He handed Henri a fifty-euro note.

"Merci, Henri," Drew said, pronouncing the name carefully in French.

Henri's smile widened slightly.

"Merci beaucoup, Monsieur." He bowed once more and disappeared quietly down the corridor.

Simon closed the door.

Behind him, Sabrina and Lauren were already on their feet, their composure giving way to curiosity and anxiety.

"Well?" Lauren said.

Simon tore open the envelope.

Inside was a single slip of fine note paper, thick, expensive stationery, folded once with precise care.

He unfolded it slowly and read aloud.

"Louvre pyramid. Noon. Man in a yellow hat."

Silence followed.

"That's it?" Lauren asked, her voice edged with disbelief. "That's all?"

Sabrina stepped forward and gently took the note from Simon's hand. She read it silently, her eyes scanning the brief message as if it might somehow grow longer under closer inspection.

Then she nodded.

"That's all."

Simon returned to his chair and leaned back, forcing himself to relax.

"Okay," he said calmly. "Let's all breathe for a moment. Our greatest asset over the next few weeks is patience. We should have anticipated that Catherine would play on our anxiety. This is just a passive-aggressive way of doing it."

Drew checked his watch.

"It's about a ten-minute taxi ride to the Louvre," he said thoughtfully. "But we should probably arrive half an hour early."

He shrugged.

"Though my guess is that no matter how early we are, her instructions to the messenger are exact. Whoever this is will just let us stand there until noon."

Sabrina frowned slightly.

"You understand the yellow hat?"

They all paused.

Lauren sighed.

"Curious George," she said. "The man in the yellow hat."

Simon rubbed his forehead.

"Right," he muttered. "And we're the trained monkeys."

A faint laugh passed through the room, but it carried little humor.

One by one, they sank back into their chairs again.

The pastries remained untouched.

Outside the windows, Paris carried on with its effortless elegance.

Inside the suite, however, time seemed suddenly to move at half speed.

The next hour was going to pass very slowly indeed.

Chapter Fifteen

The Paris Clue

Rain pelted the tall windows that overlooked the Atlantic, each gust driving the drops against the glass with a sharp, impatient rattle. Sheets of water blurred the horizon until the boundary between sea and sky dissolved into a single brooding mass of gray. The ocean had turned an ominous, storm-dark gree, its surface churning and twisting like a living thing in fury. Waves rose high and collapsed violently against the rocky shoreline below, exploding into white plumes of foam that were immediately torn apart by the wind. It seemed as though the sea itself resented the island's stubborn existence, as if the ancient waters were attempting, once again, to reclaim the land that had risen defiantly from its depths.

At the island's center, the long-dormant volcano watched the chaos in silent indifference. Its dark slopes, softened by centuries of vegetation, rose steadily above the storm like an ancient monarch unmoved by the tantrums of lesser forces. The volcano had endured tempests far more savage than this one. It had known fire, earthquakes, and the violent birth of the island itself. Compared to those memories, the raging sea and screaming wind were little more than a passing irritation.

Perched along the cliffs, the mansion seemed equally unimpressed by the assault. Though newly built, it carried itself with the dignity of something far older. The structure had been designed with deliberate grandeur, thick stone walls, sweeping terraces, and tall, narrow windows framed in polished limestone. Every line of the architecture suggested confidence. The house stood firm against the gale as though it were a noblewoman standing in a stiff wind, chin lifted slightly, her expression conveying polite disdain for the weather's theatrics. The storm battered the cliffs, clawed at the gardens, and hurled itself against the walls, yet the mansion remained immovable, its lights glowing steadily through the rain like calm eyes watching the turmoil outside.

Inside, the Emerald Room offered a world entirely removed from the fury beyond the glass. The chamber was warmed by a steady fire that crackled and sighed within the hearth, its golden light flickering across the room in soft, dancing patterns. True to the room's name, the fireplace itself was carved from a single massive jade boulder, polished until its deep green surface glowed with subtle variations of color, dark forest hues blending into lighter translucent veins. The stone caught the firelight beautifully, giving the impression that the hearth itself held an inner life.

The floor was a flawless expanse of white marble, cool and luminous beneath the fire's glow. It was so perfectly polished that it reflected the light like a still pool of water. Catherine had refused to cover even a portion of it with rugs, insisting that nothing should interrupt the purity of the stone. The marble seemed to agree, presenting itself with a quiet, stubborn elegance that demanded to be seen.

The walls were painted a delicate sea green, a color that echoed the surrounding ocean yet softened its wildness into something serene. Large windows allowed the storm's dim light to mingle with the warm firelight, creating a gentle contrast between the raging world outside and the cultivated calm within. The furnishings followed the same restrained palette, chairs upholstered in pale ivory silk, long sofas in muted jade velvet, and delicate side tables crafted from polished white wood. Every piece seemed carefully chosen to harmonize with the room's tranquil character.

The effect was one of deliberate serenity. Outside, the Atlantic roared with ancient anger, wind shrieked through the cliffs, and rain lashed the island without mercy. But inside the Emerald Room, the air was warm, the light soft, and the quiet confidence of wealth and design created a sanctuary that felt utterly untouched by the storm.

Catherine sat alone, her long legs stretched languidly along the length of the silk-covered chaise lounge, the posture of a woman entirely at ease in her solitude. The chaise itself curved elegantly beneath her, its pale green silk catching the glow of the fire and reflecting it in soft, rippling highlights that seemed almost liquid in their movement.

Beside her, on a small white lacquer table, rested a crystal carafe. It was half-filled with an expensive tawny port, whose deep red-amber color glowed richly in the firelight. The cut facets of the crystal caught the dancing flames and shattered them into tiny fragments of light that scattered across the marble floor like droplets of liquid gold. Each flicker of the fire sent new patterns gliding slowly across the polished surface, as though the room itself were breathing.

Catherine held the delicate stem of her glass between two fingers, the cool crystal contrasting with the warmth of the room. She lifted it lazily from time to time, allowing the port to roll slowly against the sides of the bowl before bringing it to her lips. The wine was smooth and heavy, carrying the deep sweetness of dried figs and dark cherries, and she allowed it to linger on her tongue before swallowing.

The warmth of the room wrapped around her like an embrace. Firelight moved across her skin in slow, flickering strokes, highlighting the subtle contours of her form. Her dark hair spilled loosely over one shoulder, catching faint glints of copper where the flames touched it.

Holding the tiny crystal glass of port loosely in one hand, Catherine let her gaze drift to the small clock resting on the table beside the carafe. It was an exquisite little thing, fashioned entirely from glass, its delicate mechanism visible through the clear casing. The slender hands moved with quiet precision, marking the passing seconds with an almost hypnotic inevitability.

She watched it patiently, her eyes fixed upon the thin, minute hand as it crept forward. The fire crackled softly behind her, and the distant roar of the storm pressed faintly against the windows, but Catherine seemed to hear none of it. Her attention remained entirely on the clock.

At last, the minute hand slid forward and settled precisely at twelve.

The moment it did, Catherine lifted the glass slightly and took a slow sip of the port, savoring its sweetness. Then a smile spread across her face, slow, deliberate, and unmistakably malicious. The expression transformed her features, soft elegance giving way to something colder, something sharpened by anticipation.

She lowered the glass again, her eyes still fixed on the clock.

"It begins," she murmured quietly to herself.

ϒϒϒ

The great glass pyramid of the Louvre shimmered in the warm Parisian sunlight like a jewel set into the heart of the city. Its geometric planes reflected the blue of the sky and the steady movement of tourists crossing the vast courtyard. Behind it stretched the immense wings of the Louvre itself, mile after mile of pale stone façades, arcades, and slate roofs that seemed more like a city devoted entirely to art and history than a single building.

Few visitors standing in the courtyard realized that this elegant palace had once been something far more severe. In the twelfth century, it had been a fortress guarding the western edge of medieval Paris. Nearly four hundred years later, in 1546, King Francis I ordered the old fortress demolished and began transforming the site into a royal residence worthy of the French crown. For more than a century, the Louvre served as the seat of French royalty, until 1682, when Louis XIV, seeking greater grandeur and distance from Paris's politics, moved the court permanently to Versailles.

Over the centuries, the palace evolved into something even greater. Its halls became repositories of human creativity, housing works gathered from across Europe and beyond. Today, the Louvre is often regarded as the finest art museum in the world, a vast cathedral of culture where centuries of human genius hang quietly upon its walls.

At the entrance beneath the glass pyramid, four Americans stood among the milling crowd.

Simon, Sabrina, Drew, and Lauren tried to appear like ordinary tourists, but the tension in their posture betrayed them. A long line of visitors snaked across the courtyard toward the entrance. Languages from every corner of the world floated through the warm air, French, German, Italian, Mandarin, English, blending into a constant murmur of anticipation.

Each of them checked their phones repeatedly. They had been told precisely when to be there.

Seconds ticked past.

Simon glanced once more at the time and lowered his phone.

"Okay," he said quietly. "Now."

Almost on cue, a tall man strode toward them up the stone steps. What made him instantly noticeable was the bright yellow cowboy hat perched confidently atop his head. It was a thoroughly un-Parisian outfit that drew curious glances from passing tourists.

The man stopped before them.

"Shall we go?" he said simply.

His voice carried a crisp English accent.

Drew folded his arms, studying him.

"Yes," he said slowly. "But first, who are you, and what can you tell us about all this?"

The man smiled politely but offered no answer. Instead, he tilted his head slightly, as though asking again whether they were prepared to follow.

Simon looked at him for a long moment, then gave a resigned sigh.

"Right then," he muttered. "Here we go. *Lay on, Macduff...*"

Drew finished the quotation automatically.

"*...and damned be him that first cries, 'Hold, enough.'*"

Sabrina groaned.

Lauren was less restrained.

"Stop it!" she snapped.

Without another word, Yellow Hat turned and began walking toward the entrance. The group followed.

To their mild astonishment, he guided them directly to the front of the long queue. A uniformed attendant at the barrier recognized him immediately. The two exchanged a brief nod, and the rope was lifted.

Moments later, they descended beneath the pyramid into the museum.

Inside, the vast corridors of the Louvre buzzed with movement. Streams of visitors flowed through the halls like currents in a river. The smell of polished stone and old wood lingered faintly in the cool air.

Along the walls hung paintings worth fortunes beyond measure.

Here and there, young art students sat on folding stools, their canvases propped before them. With intense concentration, they copied the masters, brushstrokes careful and deliberate, as though participating in a centuries-old ritual.

Their guide moved confidently through the maze.

Up staircases.

Through vaulted galleries.

Past rooms filled with sculptures, tapestries, and gilded frames.

To the untrained eye, the route seemed almost impossibly complex, yet Yellow Hat never hesitated. His stride remained steady, purposeful, as if he had walked this path many times before.

No one in the group spoke.

Eventually, they reached a gallery marked *Denon Wing*.

From there, they moved on to the section devoted to Italian painting. Finally, the guide stopped before a doorway labeled *Room 710* and stepped inside.

The gallery was hushed and elegant. The walls glowed softly beneath carefully angled lighting, each painting suspended in its own halo of illumination.

Their guide led them across the room and stopped before a particular canvas.

He pointed.

"She wishes you to view this work of art," he said.

That was all.

The painting before them was a dramatic Renaissance masterpiece by *Titian*.

The large oil canvas depicted the solemn procession carrying the body of Christ to the tomb. Figures clustered around the lifeless form, disciples bowed with grief, their faces etched with anguish. Mary Magdalene knelt in despair, her posture twisted with sorrow. The Virgin Mary, overcome with mourning, was supported by those beside her.

The scene was heavy with emotion, each face illuminated by Titian's masterful use of light and shadow. The entire composition seemed to pulse with human vulnerability, love, loss, and devotion captured in paint nearly five hundred years earlier.

For several moments, the four Americans simply stared.

None of them possessed any serious knowledge of art.

Of course, Catherine did. Before all of this madness, she had been a curator of European Art at the Museum of Fine Arts in Boston.

Eventually, the group exchanged puzzled looks.

"What are we supposed to make of this?" Drew muttered.

Simon turned toward their guide.

"Sir… do you know what we're meant to look for here?"

"I'm sorry, sir," the man replied calmly. "I have no idea. I was simply instructed to bring you here and show you this painting, and another located in the Musée d'Orsay."

Sabrina folded her arms.

"You were more than *instructed*, I suspect," she said sharply. "You were paid."

The man smiled again.

"Yes. Quite handsomely."

"Do you know who paid you?"

"I haven't the slightest idea."

The group turned back toward the painting.

If there was a message hidden there, it was not obvious.

They moved closer, examining the details. Drew photographed the work from several angles. Simon stepped back and captured the entire canvas. Lauren photographed the placard beneath the frame.

Le Transport du Christ vers le tombeau

They took pictures up close… and at a distance… carefully documenting every detail.

Yet nothing revealed itself.

After nearly half an hour of fruitless examination, Drew rubbed his forehead.

"How exactly do you analyze something when you don't even know what you're looking for?"

No one answered.

Finally, Simon sighed and turned back to their guide.

"You mentioned another painting… at the Musée d'Orsay?"

"Indeed," Yellow Hat said. "A car is waiting."

ϒ ϒ ϒ

The Musée d'Orsay stood across from the Seine in a magnificent former railway station whose soaring iron arches and tall windows flooded the interior with light. Inside, the atmosphere felt entirely different from the Louvre, less ancient, more vibrant, filled with the color and movement of nineteenth-century art.

Again, their guide moved with quiet efficiency. Through halls filled with Monet, Degas, and Van Gogh. Up a staircase. Across a long gallery.

Until at last they arrived at *Room 30*.

At the center of the room hung a painting instantly recognizable to even the most casual observer.

Renoir's Bal du moulin de la Galette.

The canvas shimmered with life.

Sunlight filtered through the trees onto a lively crowd gathered at the famous dance garden in Montmartre. Men and women laughed, talked, drank wine, and danced beneath the soft Parisian afternoon light. Renoir's loose brushstrokes captured the energy of a Sunday gathering where working-class Parisians came to escape the demands of the week.

The scene felt joyful, almost musical.

It could not have been more different from Titian's solemn procession.

The four Americans stared at it in silence.

Yes, it was beautiful.

Yes, it was famous.

But what possible message could be hidden in a crowd of Parisians dancing and drinking?

This painting had been created more than four hundred years after the first. The connection between them was completely unclear.

They no longer bothered questioning Yellow Hat. It was obvious he knew nothing beyond his instructions.

Once again, they photographed everything. Up close. From across the room. The title. The figures. The surrounding wall.

When they finally finished, Simon turned toward the guide.

"Is there anything else?"

"Yes," the man replied. "I was asked to inform you that you will receive another message at your hotel tomorrow."

"That's it?" Drew asked incredulously.

"Yes, sir. That is all."

Drew exhaled sharply.

"You've been a tremendous help," he said with heavy sarcasm.

The guide merely tipped the brim of his ridiculous yellow hat.

As they walked out into the fading Parisian evening, one thing was certain.

Their night would be spent studying photographs of two masterpieces, Titian and Renoir, searching desperately for meaning.

And they still had absolutely no idea what they were looking for.

Chapter Sixteen

Paris Deliberations

Back in the quiet luxury of their hotel suite, all four gathered around the small dining table as though preparing for an examination they had not studied for. The curtains had been drawn against the Paris night, and the soft golden light from the lamps cast warm pools across the room. On the table sat coffee, untouched wine, and four mobile phones, each filled with images of the two paintings they had spent the day photographing from every conceivable angle.

No one spoke at first.

Simon leaned forward with his elbows on the table, swiping slowly through the images on his phone. Drew sat beside him, brow furrowed, jaw clenched in concentration. Across from them, Sabrina and Lauren had each spread their own devices before them, enlarging details, comparing shots, and occasionally exchanging glances that were part frustration, part exhaustion.

It felt absurd.

Four intelligent adults, sitting in one of the finest hotels in Paris, studying photographs of masterpieces as if they were cryptograms left by a mad genius.

And perhaps they were.

"Well," Simon said at last, rubbing his face, "we must assume she did not go to this much trouble merely to improve our appreciation of Western art."

Lauren let out a weary breath that was almost a laugh.

"No, though if this is all a bizarre attempt to make us cultured, I'd prefer a guided tour and a glass of champagne."

Sabrina did not smile. Her eyes remained fixed on one of the photographs of the Titian.

"Catherine never does anything without purpose," she said quietly. "If she sent us to those paintings, there is a reason. The difficulty is that we are trying to enter the mind of someone who is brilliant, theatrical, vindictive, and probably enjoying every second of this."

"That narrows it down nicely," Drew muttered.

Simon enlarged the image of Titian's *Transport of Christ to the Tomb* until the faces of the mourners filled his screen.

"Let's begin with the obvious. The first painting is death, grief, burial, and mourning. A procession. Loss."

"And the second is life," Lauren said, lifting her eyes from Renoir's *Bal du moulin de la Galette*. "Movement, society, pleasure, noise, people enjoying themselves. The two paintings are almost opposites."

"Exactly," Simon said. "So perhaps the contrast is the point."

Drew shook his head.

"Maybe. But contrast alone is too vague. Catherine would want something more precise than that. She wants us to see something specific."

He reached for his phone and pulled up the photograph he had taken of the placard beneath the Titian.

"Look at the dates. Titian, early sixteenth century. Renoir, late nineteenth century. Hundreds of years apart. Different styles, different countries, different moods, different everything."

"Except that she chose both," Sabrina said.

That quiet statement settled over the room.

They all knew it was true. The only true link between the paintings was Catherine.

Lauren enlarged a wide photograph of the Renoir and studied the crowd clustered beneath the dancing light.

"What if it isn't the whole painting?" she said. "What if it's some detail in each? A face, a gesture, the placement of figures, a color, something hidden in plain sight?"

For the next several minutes, they began working more methodically.

Simon compared close-ups of the Titian figures, identifying each posture. Drew studied the arrangement of bodies within the frame. Sabrina made notes on hotel stationery, listing everything they knew: burial, sorrow, Christ, followers, tomb, procession. Lauren did the same for the Renoir: dance, crowd, leisure, Paris, movement, Sunday, pleasure.

The room grew quieter still.

From somewhere below came the faint hum of Paris traffic, softened by height and distance.

At length, Drew sat back and let out an irritated sigh.

"Here's the problem. Every symbol leads to twenty interpretations. Death and life. Mourning and celebration. Silence and noise. Religion and society. Sixteenth century and nineteenth century. Italy and France. Sacred and secular. We could sit here until morning inventing meanings."

Sabrina looked up sharply.

"Then perhaps we should ask what Catherine would find amusing."

That shifted the energy in the room.

Simon turned toward her.

"Go on."

"She knows we are not art historians," Sabrina said. "She knows this would be maddening. So perhaps the message is not subtle in an academic sense. Perhaps it is personal. Something she expects us to connect because of her, not because of art history."

Lauren nodded slowly.

"She used to be a curator. This is her language."

"Yes," Sabrina said. "And she is using it the way another person might use riddles or codes."

Simon stood and began pacing, something Lauren had apparently inherited from Professor Fairfax in her teasing earlier. He stopped behind his chair and stared down at the photographs spread across the table.

"Then let's think as she might think," he said. "What would appeal to Catherine? Drama. Symbolism. Grand themes. She would want the selections to feel elegant and intelligent. Something that says: *I am still the smartest person in the room.*"

"That certainly sounds like her," Drew said dryly.

Simon pointed to the Titian image.

"The carrying of Christ to the tomb. A body being borne away. Something precious lost, removed, taken."

Lauren's eyes shifted almost involuntarily to Sabrina.

Sabina.

The child.

The abduction.

The air in the room changed.

Drew leaned forward at once.

"You think that painting represents Sabina?"

"I don't know," Simon said. "But I think Catherine may want us thinking in terms of removal, grief, a stolen beloved figure surrounded by helpless mourners."

Sabrina's face had gone still.

"And the Renoir?" she asked.

No one answered immediately.

They all turned to the bright, bustling image of *Bal du moulin de la Galette*. It seemed almost mocking now in its gaiety.

Lauren studied it for a long moment.

"A public place," she said at last. "Crowds. Noise. So many people that one person can disappear inside them."

Drew's expression sharpened.

"A crowd as concealment."

"Yes," Lauren said, warming to the idea. "The first painting shows the taking away. The second suggests where someone might vanish, in the middle of life, of movement, of distraction."

Simon nodded slowly.

"From grief to camouflage."

Sabrina frowned.

"That is clever. Too clever, perhaps. It feels possible, but not certain."

Drew swiped back to a closer photograph of the Renoir placard.

"Could the titles matter? Maybe not just the images."

Simon looked at his own image files.

"*Le Transport du Christ vers le tombeau.* The Transport of Christ to the Tomb."

"Transport," Lauren repeated softly. "Movement."

"And *Bal du moulin de la Galette,*" Drew said. "A dance at the Moulin de la Galette. A location. A gathering. An event."

Sabrina's eyes flickered.

"Transport… and destination?"

Simon looked up at once.

"Or transport and crowd."

"Or taking and hiding," Lauren said.

Drew pushed back in his chair and stood, too restless now to remain seated. He crossed to the window, parted the curtain slightly, and looked out over Paris glowing beneath the night.

"I hate this," he said. "Because every interpretation sounds plausible for about thirty seconds, and then it dissolves."

"That may be exactly the point," Sabrina replied. "She wants us uncertain. Uncertainty is power."

Simon sat again, this time more heavily.

"All right. Let's not chase abstractions alone. What facts do we have? Catherine arranged access to both museums. She hired a courier-guide. She wanted us to see these specific paintings in sequence. She told us nothing. Then she promised another message tomorrow."

Lauren's eyes narrowed.

"In sequence," she said.

The others looked at her.

"In sequence matters. First Titian, then Renoir. First sorrow, then society. First removal, then crowd. First tomb, then dance. The order is intentional."

Drew turned back from the window.

"So the message progresses."

"Yes," Lauren said. "It isn't simply that the two paintings are linked. It's that one follows the other."

Sabrina slowly laid down her pen.

"Taken… then hidden among many."

Simon nodded.

"Or death… then resurrection into another world."

Drew grimaced.

"Let's hope not literally."

For a moment, no one spoke. The possibility hung there, uninvited and chilling.

Sabrina broke the silence.

"She wants us working," she said. "She wants us anxious, tired, and off balance. Whatever conclusion we reach tonight may not solve the puzzle completely. It may only prepare us for the next clue."

"That," Lauren said, "is the first thing anyone has said tonight that sounds unquestionably true."

The tension eased just enough for Simon to give the faintest smile.

Still, they kept working.

They compared individual figures in Titian's mournful procession with clusters in Renoir's festive crowd, wondering whether number or placement mattered. They zoomed in on hands, faces, shadows, bits of landscape, scraps of color. They considered whether the clue might lie in the plaques, the dates, the artists' nationalities, or even the rooms in which the paintings hung.

At one point, Drew proposed that Catherine might be spelling out some historical sequence known only to art scholars.

At another, Lauren wondered whether the clue might involve religion yielding to modernity, sacred grief swallowed by worldly pleasure.

Simon briefly pursued the notion that the paintings represented emotional states Catherine wished to impose upon them, despair followed by confusion in a crowd of false leads.

And Sabrina, more than once, returned to the same dark intuition: that Catherine had chosen these works not merely for symbolism, but for emotional effect. She wanted them to feel loss. She wanted them to imagine a beloved figure carried away beyond their reach. She wanted them to understand helplessness.

By midnight, the table was covered in notes.

Arrows connected words like *transport*, *burial*, *crowd*, *Paris*, *concealment*, *movement*, and *destination*. Several theories had been proposed, challenged, reshaped, and abandoned. Coffee had replaced wine entirely.

At last, Lauren leaned back and closed her eyes for a moment.

"So," she said tiredly, "our best conclusion is that Catherine may be telling us Sabina has been taken and hidden among many people, or transported to some place of public life, or symbolically buried and disguised, or possibly that she simply enjoys tormenting us with Titian and Renoir."

Simon finally set his phone down and leaned back in his chair, rubbing his eyes as though trying to clear them of the endless details they had been staring at.

"I think all we're doing at this point is confusing ourselves," he said. "We've been circling the same possibilities for an hour now, and every theory sounds convincing for about thirty seconds before it collapses under its own weight."

He gestured toward the photographs glowing on the table.

"It is entirely possible that there is less here than meets the eye. We're assuming there must be layers upon layers of meaning because Catherine sent us to see them. But that may be exactly the trap she wants us to fall into."

Lauren tilted her head slightly. "You think we're overthinking it?"

"I think we may be doing exactly what she expected," Simon replied. "Analyzing every brushstroke, every face in the crowd, every title and date as if this were some elaborate academic puzzle."

He tapped the image of the Titian painting with one finger.

"This is the opening salvo. The first move in a much longer game. She isn't going to reveal anything substantial this early. Not Catherine. That would spoil her fun."

Drew gave a dry chuckle.

"That certainly sounds like her."

Simon nodded.

"She wants us unsettled. Curious. A little desperate. These paintings might not contain the answer at all, only the suggestion that a game is underway. Something to get our attention and keep us chasing the next clue."

Sabrina folded her arms, looking thoughtfully at the two paintings side by side on the table.

"So you're saying this is just the prologue," she said quietly.

"Exactly," Simon replied. "The curtain rising. She's letting us know she's in control of the stage… but the real performance hasn't begun yet."

"Okay," he said, his voice calm but decisive. "In any case, our next step is fairly obvious. We send these photographs and a summary of our thoughts to Sir Roger and Fairfax. They'll pass everything along to Loki. If anyone might see something in all of this that we're missing, it's probably him."

Drew gave a faint, tired grin. "Yes, well… if anyone possesses a mind sufficiently convoluted to decipher Catherine's games, Loki would certainly qualify."

Simon allowed himself a brief smile.

"Exactly. Forward every photograph you have to me, every angle, every close-up, everything. I'll organize them and write a summary of what we've discussed tonight. Then I'll send the whole package off to Oxford."

He gathered his phone and began stacking the scattered notes on the table.

"After that," he added firmly, "everyone goes to bed. We've stared at these things long enough for one night, and fatigue isn't going to make us any smarter."

Sabrina nodded slowly.

"And tomorrow," Lauren said quietly.

"Yes," Simon replied. "Tomorrow we receive the next message."

"For tonight," he said, "that will have to be enough."

Chapter Seventeen

The First Ultimatum

Luxury rarely loses its charm, but when one is forced to sit still while waiting for something that feels almost life-or-death, even the most exquisite surroundings begin to fade into the background. Anticipation dulls the glitter of chandeliers and robs silk upholstery of its comfort.

Once again, the four friends had gathered for breakfast in Simon and Sabrina's suite at the Hôtel George V. Morning sunlight filtered through the tall French windows, illuminating the elegant room in soft gold. The view beyond showed Paris waking slowly, distant traffic murmuring along the avenues, and the faint outline of the Eiffel Tower rising through a pale morning haze.

Spread across the polished table was a breakfast that might have delighted royalty. A silver tray held flaky croissants whose buttery layers shattered delicately at the slightest touch. Beside them were glossy pain aux raisins, spiraled with custard and plump raisins; golden chaussons aux pommes, their pastry shells hiding fragrant apple filling; and a bowl of airy sugar-dusted chouquettes, light little cream puffs that seemed almost too delicate to exist.

The two men approached the display with enthusiasm bordering on reverence. Drew had already claimed a second pastry before Simon finished his first croissant. The women were more restrained. Sabrina and Lauren sipped tea from thin porcelain cups and allowed themselves only a single croissant each, nibbling politely while the men made noticeable progress through the buffet.

Between bites, Simon brought them up to date.

"Early this morning, Sir Roger and Professor Fairfax confirmed they received our photographs and the summary I sent," he said, brushing a few crumbs from his fingers. "They admitted they're having exactly the same trouble we are; nothing in the images makes obvious sense. They've forwarded everything to Loki, but they have no idea when he might respond."

Drew shrugged without slowing his assault on a pain aux raisins.

"Simon," Lauren asked thoughtfully, "what do you expect this morning?"

Simon leaned back slightly in his chair, considering.

"Well, if we're thinking about this as a sequence of moves, I suspect this will be the first shoe to drop. Her first true demand."

"And it won't be a comfortable shoe," Drew muttered.

Sabrina smiled gently and covered his hand with hers.

"It's all right, darling. We'll get through it."

The clock on the mantel ticked steadily. Conversation faded. One by one they glanced toward it.

Ten o'clock.

That was exactly the time the previous message arrived.

Without anyone commenting, the room grew quiet. The sounds of Paris drifted faintly through the windows, the distant rumble of traffic, a faint siren somewhere across the city, but inside the suite, the air felt thick with waiting.

Two minutes passed.

Then there came a polite knock on the door.

Simon rose immediately and opened it. Standing in the hallway once again was Henri, the hotel's impeccably composed concierge. He held a small envelope delicately between his fingers.

"Monsieur, another message has been delivered," he said with a small bow.

"Once again, Henri," Simon asked, "did you see who delivered it?"

"Mais oui, monsieur. This time it was a woman."

Drew stepped beside Simon.

"Can you describe her, Henri?"

"I can do so," Henri replied. "But anticipating your interest, I also spoke with her."

At this, Sabrina and Lauren quickly rose from the table and joined them near the door.

"Wonderful. Please come in, Henri," Simon said.

Henri stepped two paces into the suite but stopped respectfully near the entrance, as though unwilling to intrude too far into the private space of his guests.

"What did you learn, Henri?" Drew asked.

"The woman was perhaps just past thirty, attractive, well-dressed, but not extravagantly so. A pleasant dress, dark hair."

The group exchanged glances.

"When I asked whether she would mind telling me why she was delivering the letter," Henri continued, "she was not at all secretive. She said she and her husband were visiting Paris for the first time. The concierge at their hotel asked them if they would kindly deliver the letter because he could not leave his desk."

Henri lifted one shoulder slightly.

"He told them it must be delivered precisely at ten o'clock. He also gave them five hundred euros, which he said had been provided by the gentleman who left the envelope with him."

Henri hesitated politely.

"I'm afraid that is all I was able to learn, monsieur."

"Well done, Henri," Simon said sincerely. "Did she mention which hotel they were staying in?"

"Yes, monsieur. I asked. They are staying at the Hotel Relais du Louvre, not far from here."

"Did you happen to ask her name?" Simon continued.

"Yes indeed. Her name was Denise Thompson."

"This is all quite helpful, Henri. Thank you," Simon said, reaching toward his wallet.

Drew interrupted him, producing a thick stack of euro notes and pressing it into Henri's hand.

"I believe you should receive at least as much as the delivery woman did, Henri. There are seven hundred euros there."

Henri's eyes widened.

"Oh, merci! Thank you very much, monsieur!" he exclaimed, trying to conceal his delight with meticulous manners.

After a few more grateful bows, Henri departed down the hallway.

The door closed.

For a moment, no one spoke.

Finally, the four of them returned to the table. The pastries now seemed strangely unimportant.

Simon held the luxurious envelope in both hands. For a moment, he simply stared at it, as though it might explode.

Then he broke the seal.

He did not read it silently first. Instead, with the solemnity of a man delivering a verdict in a murder trial, he began to read the letter aloud.

"How are you, my lovelies?

With nearly a thousand IQ points among you, particularly when one includes the illustrious Oxford contingent, I can only assume your collective brilliance is already circling my modest little "hideout." Truly, the thought comforts me. One hates to construct an elaborate game only to discover the participants are dull.

Yes, Simon... I was always far too forthcoming with you. That was my error, wasn't it? I mistook curiosity for kindness, intellect for character. You listened so attentively. You asked such clever questions. How flattering it all seemed at the time. Of course, now I realize you were simply collecting ammunition.

Still, if you find yourselves struggling, as brilliant minds sometimes do when their pride is wounded, I might be persuaded to provide another clue to where Sabina and I are vacationing.

But the next clue will cost you. Dearly.

You humiliated me. Not privately, not discreetly, but magnificently. Publicly. Methodically. My carefully cultivated reputation was stripped away in a matter of hours. You watched while the whispering began. You stood comfortably while the polite academic smiles sharpened into knives.

Do you remember, Simon? The silence? The way the eyes in that hall turned toward me, not with curiosity, but with that particular academic delight reserved for someone else's downfall?

Of course not. You weren't there for me. I remember.

Every detail.

And so it is only fitting that repayment be made in the same currency I was forced to spend.

Your reputation.

You should be proud of me, really. Observe the discipline. Not a single word in ALL CAPS. Not even the vulgar indulgence of an exclamation point. One must maintain standards. Rage, after all, is such an inelegant emotion when poorly dressed.

Besides, theatrics are unnecessary.

My joy will come soon enough.

And you, my brilliant friends, will provide it.

Now, to ease your minds: sweet little Sabina is doing wonderfully. She has proven to be quite charming company. The mountain air agrees with her beautifully. She runs about in the sunlight, chattering endlessly, asking questions that only children think to ask. The sort of innocent curiosity that scholars often lose somewhere between tenure committees and conference panels. But she seems to be a little sleepy lately. Wink.

The mountains are particularly lovely this time of year. Cool mornings, golden afternoons, quiet forests stretching for miles. One can disappear rather comfortably here. One can think. Reflect. Plan.

You should join us.

If you can find the way.

Oh, I know what you're imagining, that I am laughing as I write this. And you would be correct, though not in any crude or theatrical sense. Nothing so vulgar as a villain's cackle. No.

Picture instead a quiet, ladylike amusement. A soft smile behind a glass of wine while watching a play whose ending you already know.

And what an entertaining play this is becoming.

Now then… where was I?

Ah yes.

It is time for you to leave the paradise of Paris and return to the dreary, practical world of the United States. Your first real test awaits you at home.

A simple task, really.

To receive the next clue, Simon, you must begin preparing for a new career.

Or perhaps retirement.

You must leave your position at Phillips.

Resign.

Immediately.

Do not misunderstand me; I am not yet asking you to invent a scandal or fabricate a humiliating explanation for your departure. That particular pleasure can wait. Consider this merely… the opening move.

For now, you will simply resign.

Quietly.

Abruptly.

Without explanation.

Walk away from your sacred post. Leave your colleagues puzzled. Leave the committees whispering. Leave the ambitious younger scholars calculating who will inherit your office, your grants, your carefully curated prestige.

Let the scholarly vipers speculate. That will be quite enjoyable enough.

Academics can be such fearsome creatures when confronted with a mystery. Their imaginations will do far more damage than any story you could invent.

I'm sure they will be kind.

Or perhaps not.

You see, Simon, reputation is such a delicate thing. It takes decades to build and only moments to unravel. You taught me that lesson rather effectively.

Now it is your turn to experience it.

I will know when you have done as I ask.

And when I know...

Then, and only then, will you receive the next clue.

Until that moment, my dear geniuses, you remain exactly where I wish you to be:

Confused. Frustrated. And very afraid.

Ciao."

Everyone's face was downcast except Simon's. He looked at them all. Without raising her face, Lauren was the first to speak.

"Simon, there are no words..."

"No, Lauren, actually, this is better than I expected."

Sabrina stood, walked to Simon's chair, and put her arms around him. A tear ran down one of her cheeks. "We'll get through this, Darling," she whispered.

Drew slammed his hand on the table, causing the remaining pastries to jump. He stood and walked to the center of the room, then turned.

"Catherine thinks this is revenge. She thinks this is pain. It isn't. She's just throwing fuel on a dangerous fire." He began nodding his head

"She wants humiliation. She wants us to feel helpless. That's the currency she trades in."

Drew's jaw tightened slightly, though his voice never rose.

"But she's forgotten something very important."

He looked at Simon and the others.

"Revenge only works when the other side is afraid of you."

A faint smile crossed his face.

"And I'm not afraid of Catherine Lodge."

He hesitated, internalizing his fury.

"But the moment she touched Sabina… she made a deadly mistake."

His voice dropped lower.

"When we find her, and we will, Catherine is going to learn something about revenge that she clearly never understood."

He paused.

"Real revenge doesn't come with riddles."

He turned back toward them.

"It comes with consequences."

The others were just short of stunned. Drew was the most easygoing person any of them knew, a man who met life's frustrations with a shrug and a crooked smile. Even Simon, who had been his closest friend since they were teenagers, could hardly remember seeing him genuinely angry. Yet now the easygoing charm was gone. Something harder had taken its place.

Lauren, on the other hand, was visibly seething. If Drew's anger simmered like a banked fire, hers flashed openly. Her eyes fixed on the note in Drew's hand, and the look she cast toward the room suggested that if Catherine Lodge were to walk through the door at that moment, she might not leave it alive.

For several seconds, no one spoke.

Simon finally moved.

He crossed the room slowly, as though approaching a wounded animal that might bolt or strike. When he reached Drew, he studied his friend's face. The anger was there, unmistakable, but it was tightly contained, pressed down beneath years of discipline and self-control.

Simon spoke quietly.

"Drew, Catherine will answer for this."

Drew's jaw tightened, the muscles along his cheek flexing.

"As God is my witness, she will."

Simon nodded slightly. "She will. I give you my word. But revenge can wait," Simon continued gently. "Sabina cannot."

Drew slowly let out a breath.

The anger did not vanish, but it settled, like a storm withdrawing temporarily beyond the horizon.

"Yes. Of course you're right," he said at last, his voice low and controlled.

Simon allowed himself the smallest nod.

ϒ ϒ ϒ

It was midday in Lexington when the sky suddenly opened and unleashed a pounding deluge on the busy streets. Rain hammered rooftops, bounced off windshields, and turned the asphalt slick and shining beneath the gray light.

The black van turned onto Sedi's street, its tires hissing on the wet pavement as it proceeded slowly past her house. It had entered from the end where Timber was keeping watch.

The giant biker stepped out from the shelter of a nearby porch and walked calmly toward his motorcycle. Rain rolled off the brim of his cowboy hat as he swung a leg over the seat. He pulled out his phone and pressed a single button.

"It's coming, Bear," he said quietly. "I'll lag behind."

A brief crackle came through the earpiece.

"Copy," Bear replied. Nothing more.

The black van rolled slowly down the quiet street, its darkened windows reflecting rows of tidy houses and carefully trimmed lawns.

The vehicle moved with the lazy patience of someone who had nowhere urgent to be, but the pauses at each corner lasted just a bit too long, the speed just a bit too deliberate.

Well behind it, the low thunder of a motorcycle drifted through the warm morning air.

Bear was at the other end of the street. He leaned forward slightly over the wide handlebars of his Harley, the massive bike already rumbling beneath him like a restrained animal. His broad shoulders filled his worn leather jacket, the wind tugging at the gray strands of his beard beneath the helmet.

As the van passed him, he pulled his bike in beside Timber, who was on a sleek black Ducati, the machine lighter, quicker, and far more agile. Timber's eyes remained fixed ahead, calm and calculating behind the dark visor.

"That's them," Timber said through the helmet headset.

Bear didn't answer immediately. He watched the van's movements for another moment, studying the way it slowed as it left Sedi's street.

"No doubt about it," Bear finally replied. "Same van Cheri described."

The van drifted past the corner again without turning.

"They're watching the house," Timber muttered.

"Not for much longer."

Bear twisted the throttle.

The Harley's engine roared.

Both motorcycles surged forward, closing the gap with startling speed.

Inside the van, the driver noticed almost instantly.

"Motorcycles," the man said sharply.

The woman in the passenger seat turned in her seat and looked through the rear window.

Two bikes were bearing down on them fast.

"They're coming up quick."

The driver's hands tightened on the steering wheel.

"Damn it."

He stomped the accelerator.

The van lunged forward, its engine whining as it shot down the street and swung hard onto Richmond Road.

"Well," Timber said calmly, "there we go."

Bear grinned beneath his helmet.

"About time."

The bikes followed, engines howling as they darted through morning traffic. Lexington's calm suburban rhythm was shattered instantly as the van barreled down the road.

The van blasted through a yellow light.

Bear and Timber followed without hesitation.

A sedan screeched to a halt sideways in the intersection, its driver leaning on the horn.

"Careful!" Timber said.

Bear laughed. "You're the careful one."

The van swerved violently between lanes, cutting across traffic before darting onto a side street lined with small brick houses and parked cars.

"Trying to lose us," Timber said.

"Not happening."

Bear leaned his big Harley hard into the turn, the foot peg scraping the pavement with a burst of sparks as the bike roared down the narrower street.

Ahead of them, the van fishtailed as it accelerated again.

Inside, the woman twisted around once more.

"They're still there!"

"Of course they are," the driver snapped. "Hang on."

He jerked the wheel and swung the van through a crowded shopping plaza parking lot.

"Stupid move," Timber muttered into the headset. "Lots of obstacles."

The van shot between parked cars, tires squealing.

Pedestrians jumped aside, shouting as the vehicle tore across the lot.

Bear thundered in behind it, the Harley's exhaust echoing off storefront windows.

"Bear," Timber said sharply, "don't kill anyone."

"Not planning to."

Timber zigzagged through the traffic more precisely, the Ducati weaving through narrow gaps that the Harley barely fit through.

The van blasted out the far exit of the plaza and screeched onto a narrow service road behind the buildings.

For a moment, the road was empty.

Then the driver slammed the brakes.

The van skidded sideways with a scream of rubber.

"What the, " Bear started.

The side door flew open before the van had even fully stopped.

A man and a woman leapt out.

Both wore dark clothing and baseball caps pulled low. The man hit the ground running. The woman followed instantly.

"Foot bail!" Timber shouted.

The pair sprinted toward a row of trees and apartment buildings behind the service road.

Bear skidded his Harley sideways, gravel spraying as the big bike slid to a stop. He was off it before the engine even died.

"Stop!" he roared.

Timber had already dropped his Ducati and was sprinting across the grass.

They chased the fleeing figures between two apartment buildings.

The suspects ran fast.

Very fast.

“Split them!” Bear shouted.

But the runners had planned their escape well.

Behind the buildings, the narrow walkway exploded into a maze of small paths, laundry lines, fences, and backyards.

The man vaulted a low fence and disappeared behind a garage.

The woman cut left toward a narrow alley.

Timber chased her, boots pounding on the pavement.

“Stop!” he shouted.

She didn’t slow.

She reached a chain-link fence where a section had been cut open. Without breaking stride, she ducked through it and vanished into the neighborhood beyond.

Timber reached the fence seconds later.

Gone.

Across the alley, Bear emerged from another passage, breathing hard.

“You get him?”

Timber shook his head.

“Lost her at the fence.”

Bear looked through the opening in the chain link. Beyond it stretched a quiet neighborhood of backyards, sheds, and winding alleys, perfect terrain to disappear in seconds.

“Damn it.”

Behind them, the abandoned van sat crooked in the service road, engine still idling, one door hanging open.

Bear slowly turned back toward it.

“Well,” he said grimly, “they didn’t get away with everything.”

Timber followed his gaze.

The van.

Still running.

Still full of whatever secrets they had brought with them.

"Let's see what they left us," Timber said.

Chapter Eighteen

The Opening Gambit

The offices of the International Inquiry Agency in London occupied one of the most discreetly prestigious addresses in the world. Their headquarters were nestled quietly among the embassies and diplomatic residences of Kensington Palace Gardens, a wide, tree-lined avenue just west of Hyde Park. In diplomatic circles, the street was often referred to as "Billionaire's Row," though the name hardly captured the gravity of the place. It was not merely wealth that resided there; it was power, influence, and the careful choreography of international politics.

Tall iron gates guarded nearly every property along the avenue. Behind them stood immense nineteenth-century mansions, each set well back from the street and partially hidden by old English oaks and meticulously maintained gardens. Security cameras watched silently from stone pillars. Armed guards in dark coats often stood near the entrances, their presence subtle but unmistakable.

The agency occupied a suite of offices within the imposing mansion at 18 Kensington Palace Gardens, a stately building that had once belonged to the Rothschild family during the height of their financial empire. The structure still carried the quiet grandeur of that era, high stone façades, tall arched windows, and an entrance framed by carved columns that had seen more than a century of discreet arrivals.

Just down the street, the Russian Embassy stood behind its formidable gates at numbers 6 and 7, a compound that seemed perpetually under the watch of both the British security services and curious journalists hoping for the faintest hint of intrigue. Farther along the avenue, Number 11 served as the official residence of the French Ambassador, a role it had maintained since the end of the Second World War. Diplomats, intelligence officers, and the occasional discreet limousine were common sights along the quiet boulevard.

To an ordinary passerby, the International Inquiry Agency might have appeared to be just another quiet diplomatic office tucked among the embassies. The brass plaque beside the door was modest, almost understated.

Inside, however, the atmosphere was very different.

The agency's London clientele rarely consisted of private individuals. Their clients were far more likely to be governments, ministries, and intelligence services, countries that preferred their inquiries conducted by someone who officially did not exist in the matter. Disputes between states, delicate investigations, the quiet recovery of stolen artifacts, discreet intelligence gathering, these were the sorts of matters that arrived at their door.

Most of the agency's work was secretive, and a great deal of it was highly classified. Files were stored in vaults rather than cabinets. Conversations were conducted in rooms carefully shielded from electronic surveillance. Visitors were admitted by appointment only and rarely announced their true purpose aloud.

In Kensington Palace Gardens, that kind of discretion was not unusual. On that quiet London street, discretion was simply the price of doing business.

Chester Morris sat comfortably in an impeccably furnished office, the sort of room that quietly announced both proparity and authority without the slightest need to boast. At one end of the spacious chamber, several large, deep-brown leather chairs were arranged in a conversational circle around a low mahogany table polished to a mirror finish. A long Chesterfield-style couch completed the grouping, its cushions worn just enough to suggest that important discussions had been held there for many years.

The tall windows along the far wall rose nearly to the ceiling, their panes divided by slender wooden mullions that looked out over the dignified greenery of Kensington Palace Gardens. Long silk draperies, a rich cream color with faint gold thread woven into the fabric, framed the windows. They were gathered back neatly with heavy braided cords tipped with gold tassels, allowing pale London sunlight to spill into the room. The light glinted softly off polished wood, crystal decanters, and framed oil portraits that lined the walls.

Across from Chester sat a distinguished gray-haired man whose appearance left absolutely no doubt that he was British in the most traditional sense of the word. His hair was neatly parted and brushed back, his posture upright without appearing rigid. His suit was perfectly tailored, the fabric dark and understated, with a crisp white shirt and a discreetly patterned tie. His manner carried the subtle confidence of someone accustomed to authority and long experience.

The expression on his face possessed that classic "stiff upper lip" composure, though his eyes betrayed a sharp intelligence and a quietly mischievous sense of humor.

He chatted casually with Chester as though the two men had been sharing offices and stories for decades, which, judging by their ease with one another, might very well have been true.

"So, Chet," the man said pleasantly, leaning back slightly in his chair, "what brings one of our distinguished senior partners all the way to our tiny outpost?"

Chet laughed easily, the deep, relaxed laugh of someone perfectly comfortable wherever he happened to be.

"Harold," he began, glancing around the room with theatrical sympathy, "I felt so sorry for you, here in this penurious backwater, that I thought I should come personally and lift your spirits."

"How kind of you, Chet." Harold smiled broadly, the corners of his eyes crinkling.

"Just to show you the depth of my concern for you," Chet continued, reaching down beside his chair, "I've brought you a bottle of W. L. Weller nineteen-year-old bourbon."

Harold's chin dropped in genuine astonishment.

"My God, man!" he exclaimed. "What a gift! You're not asking for my beautiful firstborn daughter, are you?"

"Like she would leave her husband for an old guy like me," Chet replied dryly. "Isn't he a duke or something?"

"Something," Harold answered with a knowing smile.

Chet leaned back comfortably in his chair.

"And I promise," he added with mock solemnity, "to keep your well-guarded secret of preferring expensive Kentucky bourbon over the angelic amber of your neighboring Scots."

Harold chuckled quietly, shaking his head.

"Careful, Chet. If word of that ever reached Edinburgh, I'd be permanently banned north of the border."

"So, my friend, what is so urgent?" Harold continued, settling deeper into his chair and folding his hands with the calm patience of a man accustomed to hearing difficult matters.

"I am dealing with a sensitive issue. And, I think you can help."

Harold then looked at Chet, a faint hint of amusement touching his expression.

"As you know, 'sensitive' is what we do best here, my friend."

Chet smiled slightly. "And that is precisely why I want this office handling it. I'll be leading the investigation overall, but I may have to travel. Either way, I'll be in constant contact."

Chet opened the file he had brought with him and began a careful, thorough explanation. He walked Harold through the five-year history that had led to the present crisis, outlining the events that had slowly built toward the current situation. He described the abduction, its calculated nature, and the growing evidence pointing to Catherine.

At several points, Chet added details, filling in Catherine's past, her temperament, her intelligence, and the motivations driving her actions. His description made clear that this was no impulsive criminal but a patient and highly capable adversary.

He also explained the victims: Drew and Lauren, and their close friends, Simon and Sabrina. Their backgrounds, their resources, and the complex network of relationships surrounding them were carefully laid out.

Finally, Chet leaned forward slightly, his tone firm.

"Our objective is simple, Harold. We find Catherine. Nothing more, nothing less. The New York office will handle our U.S. contacts and resources. You must coordinate everything here in Europe."

He nodded toward the file resting on Harold's desk.

"Harold, I'm hoping some of your more… discreet diplomatic resources might be of assistance. This is the complete file."

Harold listened without interruption, his expression thoughtful as he slowly closed the folder.

"I understand, Chet," he said after a moment. "You say this is high priority?"

Chet gave a short nod.

"The highest, Harold."

ϒ ϒ ϒ

The windows were open in Simon and Sabrina's library, allowing the cool morning air to drift inside. Outside, it was raining, not a violent storm, just a soft, steady rain that soaked the gardens and darkened the stone terrace. The rhythmic patter against the leaves created a quiet, almost reflective mood inside the room.

Sedi and Cheri had joined the other four around the long library table. The room, normally a place of quiet study and comfortable conversation, now carried a faint tension. Sedi held the morning's copy of the *Boston Globe*, its pages slightly creased from having already been passed from hand to hand several times. The "Education" section lay open across the table, the headline circled in ink.

She read it aloud once more, though everyone already knew every word.

Prestigious Scholar Leaves Phillips

Dr. Simon Sterling, a highly regarded teacher at Phillips Academy, has left his post without explanation.

His international reputation as a renowned scholar makes the sudden resignation all the more surprising. Dr. Sterling submitted his resignation yesterday without comment. Officials at the school declined to elaborate on the circumstances.

Phillips Academy, founded in 1778, remains one of the most distinguished preparatory schools in the world. Dr. Sterling, frequently courted by the faculties of Harvard, Yale, Princeton, and other Ivy League universities, had long chosen instead to devote his career to shaping the minds of younger students.

The Globe is seeking further clarification regarding the circumstances of his departure and hopes to have more information by tomorrow's edition.

Sedi lowered the newspaper slowly.

The quiet rain continued outside, but inside the library, the article's meaning hung heavily in the air. Everyone understood what it was.

"Before anyone says anything more, let's not turn this into a wake," Simon said firmly, lifting a hand as if to halt the gathering gloom that had settled over the room. "The first payment has been made. That's all that matters."

"As you wish, my friend," Drew sighed, though the weight behind the words was impossible to hide.

Cheri leaned forward in her chair, impatience flickering across her face. "So what the hell happens next?" she asked, barely restraining herself.

Simon shrugged slightly.

"We wait again," Lauren said quietly.

"It's her move," Sabrina added.

"Yes," Sedi said thoughtfully. "And she won't be in any hurry, I'd guess. She wants to let us all suffer a bit. She's waited five years already. A few more days will mean nothing to her."

Simon rose from his chair and walked to the open windows. Outside, the property's giant trees glistened as droplets slipped from their leaves onto the wet ground below. A few birds hopped along the branches, happily bathing in the rain, oblivious to human troubles.

He watched them for a moment before turning back to the others.

"Well," he said calmly, "this is the opening gambit. We have made the move she demanded of us. We may still be in check, but the game is far from over."

He gestured toward the newspaper lying on the table.

"So let's begin by discarding that paper. We look forward now, not backward."

His voice was steady, and the room seemed to take strength from it.

"Yes," Sabrina said, her expression firming with resolve. "Sabina is our focus. She is our only concern. Whatever troubles we face personally are of no consequence compared to her."

Drew nodded and then turned toward Sedi.

"Sedi, I was shocked, and frankly furious, to hear about your stalker. Where do we stand with that?"

Sedi offered a reassuring smile.

"Thank you, Drew. Well, thanks to Cheri and her… army, I believe we may have frightened them away, at least for the time being. The police traced the van to a used car dealer in New Hampshire. The buyer paid cash and very clearly used false identification."

She paused, glancing toward Cheri.

"The boys, Bear and company, managed to get a quick but reasonably clear look at the two stalkers before they ran. They've been circulating through bars in the surrounding towns… anywhere that sort might drift through."

Drew turned to Cheri. "Thank you, Cheri. This is incredibly generous of you and your friends."

Cheri waved the gratitude away with a casual flick of her hand.

"We'll find them," she said confidently. "I promise you that. What I can't promise is what they'll look like when we finally hand them over to the police."

Sabrina grinned.

"Fortunately, Bear is in charge. He knows where to draw the line."

Cheri frowned slightly, though a hint of reluctant amusement tugged at the corner of her mouth.

Simon returned to his chair and settled back, the tension in his shoulders easing just slightly.

"I'm hoping we hear something from Oxford today," he said. After a moment, he added, "Or rather, from Loki."

He glanced down at his watch and tapped the crystal lightly with his finger.

"It's two o'clock here," he continued. "Which means it's six in the evening in Oxford. That seems as good a reason as any to operate on their schedule."

He looked around the room at the others, offering a faint, encouraging smile.

"So, I suggest we switch to Oxford time and serve some refreshment."

Chapter Nineteen

The Architect of Consequence

Roger and Fairfax sat once again at their usual table in the Grand Café. They had managed, with the subtle cunning of men who had been frequenting the establishment for decades, to secure a small corner table tucked behind one of the café's enormous marble pillars. The pillar itself had likely been there since the Norman Conquest, or so Fairfax insisted, and served as both architectural support and a convenient shield from the occasional draft that wandered in whenever the door opened.

The rest of the café was an agreeable symphony of dark wood: the counter polished to a warm sheen, the small round tables worn smooth by generations of elbows and teacups, and the chairs that creaked with the dignified complaint of furniture that had witnessed far too many academic arguments. Brass lamps glowed softly against the wood-paneled walls, and the faint aroma of coffee, butter, and baked sugar hovered in the air like a permanent resident. The place had history in its bones. You could practically hear the ghosts of Victorian scholars debating empire and pudding.

Fairfax, however, had no interest in historical ambiance.

"It's just stupid!" he announced loudly, stabbing a finger toward the wall. "What's the bloody purpose?"

Sir Roger sighed the sigh of a man who had heard this speech so often that he could probably deliver it himself in three languages and two dialects.

"Do we have to go through this again, Eustace?" he asked patiently.

“You can’t answer, can you?” Fairfax demanded triumphantly. “Neither can they!”

He swept his arm dramatically toward the staff behind the counter, nearly upsetting a sugar bowl in the process. The young barista glanced up with mild interest, as though observing a particularly familiar species of bird.

Actually, it wouldn’t be lunch at the Grand with Professor Fairfax without this outburst. He had been performing it, with only minor variations in phrasing, for nearly fifteen years. The regular patrons had come to regard it as part of the café’s atmosphere, rather like the espresso machine or the slightly crooked painting of the Thames on the far wall.

A pair of graduate students at the next table discreetly checked their watches.

Right on schedule.

“Just look at the stupid sign!” Fairfax continued, pointing again.

He read it aloud with theatrical outrage.

“Hours: Monday–Thursday, nine a.m. to six-thirty p.m. Friday–Sunday, nine a.m. to seven p.m.”

He leaned back in his chair, glaring at Roger as if he had personally authored the policy.

“Half an hour! Half an hour! Why? What is the possible civilizational purpose of thirty additional minutes of pastry access on weekends? It’s vacuous!”

Roger chuckled quietly into his teacup.

“This is not the heart of civilization, Eustace. It’s a café.”

“But it’s irrational!”

“Most things are.”

“That is not an argument!”

Roger took a calm sip of tea.

“It’s an observation.”

At that moment, the young server arrived, carrying their usual order:

a pot of Earl Grey, two delicate porcelain cups, and a pair of small cakes that appeared to have been engineered with more precision than most Oxford dissertations.

She placed them down gently.

"It's good to see you again, professors," she said with a warm smile.

Fairfax pointed accusingly at the sign.

"Miss, perhaps you can explain something to me."

Roger closed his eyes briefly.

The girl did not even hesitate.

"No, Professor Fairfax," she said cheerfully. "I cannot explain the extra half hour on weekends."

Fairfax froze.

Roger nearly laughed.

The server straightened, clearly enjoying herself.

"But," she added sweetly, "the manager says if we removed it, you would have nothing to complain about, and the café would lose a great deal of atmosphere."

The nearby tables erupted in quiet chuckles.

Fairfax blinked at her.

Roger raised his cup in salute.

"See?" he said. "You're part of the décor."

Fairfax stared at the cake in front of him, then muttered darkly,

"I refuse to believe a pastry shop has institutionalized me."

"Let's focus on our business, shall we?" Roger began, setting his teacup down with the deliberate calm of a man attempting to restore order to a room that had recently hosted a minor philosophical riot.

Fairfax, known to his friends as Eustace when he was not in the middle of an argument with furniture, signage, or the general structure of the universe, grunted his approval and reached for the small silver pitcher of cream. He poured it into his tea with the careful attention of a chemist conducting a volatile experiment.

"We've not heard back from Loki, and it's been four days," Roger continued.

"Yes, I know," Eustace replied, stirring his tea slowly. "But we've not had any additional information to send him. One cannot very well prod the oracle without offering something new for him to chew on."

Roger leaned back slightly in his chair.

"Yes, I suppose I'm impatient. Probably more due to our lack of production than his."

Eustace nodded, though his expression suggested that impatience was a condition he considered both natural and underappreciated.

"Well, the Fellowship is back in the States waiting for the next strike on the anvil," he said.

The term had become a sort of shorthand between them. As students at Oxford decades earlier, both Roger and Eustace had at least brushed shoulders, figuratively, if not academically, with two of the university's most famous literary figures: *J.R.R. Tolkien* and *C.S. Lewis*. Tolkien, of course, had written *The Lord of the Rings*, including *The Fellowship of the Ring*. At the same time, Lewis had produced *The Chronicles of Narnia*, which had kept generations of children happily distracted from their homework.

Eustace, who possessed a fondness for literary nicknames and an equally profound aversion to unnecessary syllables, had taken to calling Simon, Sabrina, Drew, and Lauren "the Fellowship." It spared him from repeating all four names every five minutes, and it lent their present predicament a suitably epic tone. However, Roger privately suspected Tolkien had envisioned fewer croissants and considerably more swords.

"It bothers me not to be doing anything," Roger said thoughtfully. "I dislike waiting."

Eustace snorted softly. "Oh, you think I'm the one of us blessed with patience? I'm no Job, you know."

Roger smiled. "No, you're definitely not Job. If anything, you're more like Moses, specifically the moment he threw the commandments off the mountain."

Eustace grunted again, which in his case was as close to laughter as most people ever witnessed.

"Well," he said, cutting into his cake with the grim determination of a man attacking an enemy fortification, "at any rate, perhaps we should speak to Chelsea again."

Roger nodded slowly.

"It will probably be a waste of time," Eustace added, pausing to examine his fork as if considering whether cake might hold the answers Loki had failed to provide. "But I suppose it won't hurt anything."

Roger lifted his cup.

"Precisely. Sometimes investigation advances not because one expects success, but because doing nothing is intolerable."

Eustace raised an eyebrow.

"You realize that is the academic equivalent of pacing."

"Yes," Roger replied calmly. "But pacing with tea feels far more dignified."

ϒ ϒ ϒ

It was raining. The island seemed to draw winter storms the way a magnet draws iron filings. Dark clouds gathered over the South Atlantic with relentless regularity, and the wind carried the heavy scent of salt and seaweed across the low dunes. At times, the ocean looked almost black beneath the thick sky, its waves rolling in with a cold fury that made it difficult to believe this was the same ocean that, in summer, glittered beneath bright sun and gentle breezes. The South Atlantic, Sabina had learned, could be every bit as treacherous as its northern cousin. Ships had been lost here, fishermen had vanished, and the sea often seemed to roar with an ancient, restless impatience.

The rain struck the tall windows of the mansion in steady, insistent sheets. The sound filled the rooms with a constant whispering percussion, punctuated now and then by the low groan of wind moving around the corners of the house. On days like this, the fireplace was not merely decorative. Though the temperature rarely dropped to the bitter extremes of the northern continents, the damp chill of the ocean had a way of creeping through the bones. The stone hearth glowed with a lively fire, its flames casting warm amber light across the polished floors and high ceilings.

Sabina sat curled in one of the deep chairs near the hearth, a blanket loosely around her shoulders. Sugar lay stretched beside her, chin resting on Sabina's foot, ears occasionally twitching at the sound of thunder rolling somewhere far out over the water. Neither of them liked being trapped indoors. Sugar would glance hopefully toward the tall glass doors every few minutes, as though expecting the rain to vanish suddenly. Sabina understood the feeling all too well. There was something about the island that made confinement feel heavier than usual. Like today, Sabina's only distraction, other than playing with Sugar, was Danielle reading to her.

But there was no real alternative. The rain showed no sign of letting up, and the wind had grown strong enough to send fine sprays of sand skittering across the beach like ghostly veils. Even on days when Sabina was allowed outside, there was rarely much to occupy her time. The island was beautiful in its stark way, but it was also painfully limited.

Sometimes she and Danielle would walk the narrow road that led into the tiny town. It was hardly more than a scattering of buildings gathered around a gravel square. A small gas station doubled as a general store, its faded wooden sign creaking in the wind. Inside, shelves held canned goods, fishing gear, and the few necessities the island's residents required. Next to it stood a modest post office, little more than a square building with a single counter and rows of brass boxes that had likely served the same families for generations.

Only about 250 people lived on the island. It was a place where everyone knew everyone else, where news traveled quickly, and where needs were simple because few people had the means, or the desire, for anything more elaborate. Money was scarce, but so were ambitions beyond the rhythms of sea and weather.

Against this modest backdrop, Catherine's mansion seemed almost unreal.

The manor house rose above the shore like something transported from another world. Built of pale green stone and long expanses of glass, it stood with a quiet arrogance against the gray horizon. Its tall windows faced the sea, and its wide terraces overlooked the restless surf. At night, its lights could be seen from nearly anywhere on the island, glowing like a distant ship anchored permanently on the shore.

It was the only truly remarkable man-made structure anywhere on the island.

The mansion had only been permitted because Catherine had agreed to certain conditions. The town council, cautious but practical, had insisted on a rather unusual arrangement. Someday, no one knew precisely when, the property would pass into the town's ownership. That had been the price Catherine paid for permission to build something so grand on such a humble island.

To their credit, the council had also been wise enough to require the establishment of a maintenance trust. Even the most magnificent house quickly becomes a ruin if no one can afford to care for it, and the island's residents knew perfectly well that such a building would be far beyond their modest means to maintain.

Catherine had agreed without hesitation.

Indeed, she had been astonishingly generous. For some reason, this island was critical to her.

The trust fund she established was large enough to ensure the preservation of the mansion for generations. When the day came that the house belonged to the town, the people of the island would inherit not only the building itself, but the resources required to keep it standing proudly against the sea.

Many of the islanders regarded the arrangement as a remarkable stroke of good fortune. They spoke of the future with a kind of quiet pride, imagining the great house as a museum, a retreat, or perhaps even a small resort that might bring visitors, and much-needed income, to their isolated community.

To them, Catherine had seemed almost like a benefactor.

Catherine was curled comfortably on the long couch nearest the fire, the flames dancing warmly in the stone hearth beside her. She had chosen that particular seat for its perfect balance of heat and light.

The fire threw a soft golden glow across the room, illuminating the polished wood floor and the deep burgundy rug that stretched beneath the furniture. Outside, the storm continued its relentless assault on the island, but inside the mansion, there was warmth, elegance, and quiet control.

She had prepared for this place with meticulous foresight. Long before construction had even been completed, Catherine had arranged for shipments of seasoned hardwood to be delivered to the island. It had amused her to discover that no proper trees grew here. The land supported only stubborn tangles of scrub brush, wind-bent grasses, and the occasional stunted shrub clinging to the sandy soil. There were no forests, no towering oaks, no maples to harvest for winter fuel. Firewood was not something the island could provide for itself.

But Catherine believed in comforts, especially those denied by circumstance. And so, a barge arrived during the construction months, carrying neatly stacked cords of oak and maple from the mainland. Now, in a small outbuilding behind the house, thousands of split logs rested in perfect rows beneath a cedar roof, enough to keep the fireplaces of the mansion burning warmly for years.

The fire beside her burned bright and steady, the wood popping softly as sap pockets burst in the heat. Catherine found the sound soothing. Fire had always fascinated her. There was something hypnotic about watching flame consume wood, slowly transforming it into glowing embers and soft gray ash. Creation and destruction were in perfect balance.

She lifted her coffee cup, delicate white porcelain edged in a thin line of gold, and took a slow sip. The coffee was strong and rich, exactly as she preferred it. Even the china had been chosen carefully, part of a small but exquisite collection she had acquired in London years earlier. Catherine had always believed that the small rituals of life deserved elegance.

Balanced easily across her lap was her electronic tablet, its soft glow illuminating her face in the dim morning light. The storm outside had darkened the sky enough that the room remained comfortably shadowed, the firelight and the screen combining to cast shifting reflections across her features.

Most striking were her eyes.

The pale green of polished emeralds seemed to capture the light and hold it there. At the moment, they reflected the tablet's pale screen as she read.

And reread.

And reread.

She had already gone through the article half a dozen times that morning—perhaps more. The headline from the *Boston Globe* sat proudly at the top of the page, the bold letters announcing precisely the sort of public humiliation she had hoped for. Simon had resigned.

Each time she read it, her smile deepened.

At first, the expression had been subtle, just the faint upward curve of lips that were already naturally expressive. But with each reading, the satisfaction grew. Her eyes seemed to smile as much as her mouth, bright with a private amusement that no one else in the room could understand.

She set the cup carefully into the delicate saucer on the small marble table beside the couch and leaned back slightly, allowing the tablet to rest lightly against her knees.

The piece had been written with just enough journalistic restraint to appear responsible, but the implications were deliciously destructive. The public adored scandals, especially when they involved respected people who had previously seemed untouchable. And now the seeds of suspicion had been planted.

Exactly as she intended.

Her smile broadened further as she imagined the reactions spreading outward, readers forwarding the article, commentators speculating, acquaintances whispering to one another with raised eyebrows. Reputations were fragile things. It did not take much to fracture them.

At last, Catherine lowered the tablet slightly and savored the moment.

Then the smile broke into laughter.

There was no wildness in it at all.

It was simply joyful.

A warm, delighted sound that rose naturally from her chest as she leaned back against the couch cushions, her head tipping slightly toward the firelight. The laughter carried through the quiet room, like that of someone who had just heard the most pleasing news imaginable.

When it faded, she exhaled slowly and picked up the tablet once more.

Her emerald eyes gleamed.

"Oh, Simon," she murmured softly to the empty room.

"You have no idea how entertaining this is going to become. So my next arrow should arrive tomorrow."

Chapter Twenty

Fear Without Substance

Three large men stood in the parking lot of the *Never To Late* bar in Waltham, appearing as nothing more than casual patrons enjoying the mild evening air. They leaned against a battered pickup truck and a pair of motorcycles, talking idly about nothing in particular. Their voices were low, relaxed, the easy banter of men with time on their hands. To anyone passing by, they were just three friends killing a few minutes before heading inside.

But their eyes never strayed far from the couple seated at one of the outdoor tables.

The outdoor dining area itself was hardly elaborate. A narrow slice of pavement wedged between two aging brick buildings had been converted into a makeshift patio. A line of large potted plants, half-hearted attempts at greenery, separated it from the parking lot. The tables were nothing more than heavy wooden picnic benches, each shaded by a large yellow umbrella that flapped lazily whenever a breeze slipped down the narrow corridor. String lights hung overhead, casting an amber glare over the diners.

The smell of grilled meat, garlic, and hops drifted through the air.

The *Too Late* had become something of a local curiosity. Though it looked like a typical small-town bar from the outside, it had quietly developed a reputation among regulars for its unexpectedly good food and its unusually diverse collection of beers and mixed drinks. People came from neighboring towns, Lexington, Arlington, Belmont, and occasionally even Boston, to sit beneath the umbrellas, drink craft beer, and enjoy the sort of meals one normally expected to find in far more expensive establishments.

Tonight, the place was moderately busy.

The couple under observation sat near the far end of the patio. They looked young, mid-twenties perhaps. The man was thin with messy hair and a beard. His girlfriend was petite and cheerful. Her blond ponytail bobbed while she talked animatedly, waving a French fry for emphasis. They looked entirely at ease with the world.

Which was precisely why the three men in the parking lot were slightly unsure that they had the right people.

Bear, Timber, Grizz, and Tink had spent the better part of three days searching bars and restaurants in towns surrounding Lexington. Arlington and Waltham had been the primary targets. The police had provided them with an electronic rendering of the two individuals they described from inside the black van, the same van that had crept slowly down Sedi's quiet street days earlier.

The rendering was decent but not perfect. Enough to give a general idea of the faces they were hunting. Enough to start conversations. Enough to make bartenders and waitresses think.

The search had been tedious. One bar after another. Quiet questions. Casual glances. Tips left on counters, along with photographs on phone screens.

Nothing. Until late that afternoon.

The proprietor of *Too Late* had merely glance the digital image on Timber's phone before nodding.

"Oh yeah… they come in here."

That was the moment the long, frustrating search had finally produced something useful. Now the three men waited in the parking lot.

Timber stood with his arms crossed, his towering frame partially blocking the light spilling from the bar's entrance. At six foot five and built like a wood chipper, he was not a man who blended easily into crowds. Tonight, he wore a faded leather jacket and jeans that had clearly seen years of road dust. His thick beard caught the glow of the streetlamp above him.

Grizz leaned against the hood of the pickup, chewing thoughtfully on a toothpick. His nickname had not been given lightly. The man was enormous, with wide shoulders, a barrel chest, and arms that looked carved from stone. His dark beard made him appear even more intimidating than he actually was.

Tink, the smallest of the three but still an imposing figure, stood slightly apart, pretending to scroll through his phone while keeping the couple in his peripheral vision.

All three men spoke quietly.

"So," Grizz muttered, glancing toward the patio, "those are our people?"

Timber shook his head slowly.

"Not a chance."

"Why not?"

Timber tilted his head toward the patio.

"Watch them."

The young man had just dropped his fork. He fumbled awkwardly beneath the table, trying to retrieve it, while his girlfriend laughed and offered entirely unhelpful suggestions.

Grizz watched for a moment.

Then another.

Then he chuckled softly.

"Yeah… maybe."

Timber nodded.

Tink just shrugged his shoulders.

They had already spoken at length with the proprietor, a tall, thin, cheerful man called Sticks who seemed to know most of his customers by name. The conversation had been friendly, relaxed, and aided by Timber's generous purchase of a bottle of bourbon for the house.

Sticks had studied the images again, then waved a hand dismissively toward the patio.

"Those two?" he had said. "Nah. Nice kids, but not exactly criminal masterminds."

"Why's that?" Grizz had asked.

Luis had laughed.

"Because last week they asked me where the bathroom was… twice"

Timber had raised an eyebrow.

"Twice?"

Luis nodded solemnly.

"Yep."

He leaned closer and lowered his voice conspiratorially.

"They were standing ten feet from the door."

The three men had exchanged glances.

Sticks had shrugged.

"In my professional opinion, gentlemen… those two couldn't stalk celery."

So the conclusion had become obvious.

They had finally found the faces from the van. They may be the two they were looking for, but they were not criminals.

For the moment, however, the three men remained where they were.

Because Bear and Cheri were on their way. They'd figure it out.

Cheri had insisted, firmly, that she would lead the confrontation.

No one had argued with her.

Even Bear hadn't tried.

The distant rumble of an approaching motorcycle rolled down the street.

Timber glanced toward the sound.

"They're here."

Grizz pushed himself off the pickup hood.

Tink slipped his phone into his pocket.

The motorcycle's headlight entered the parking lot, engine growling softly as it rolled to a stop beside the others.

Cheri dismounted from the back first. Unaccustomed to wearing pants, she nearly fell. Then Bear swung off, removing his helmet with slow deliberation.

Cheri pulled off her helmet and shook out her bright red hair, her eyes already locked on the patio.

Timber nodded toward the couple.

"That's them."

Cheri studied them carefully.

The young man was now attempting, unsuccessfully, to open a stubborn ketchup bottle while his girlfriend offered entirely contradictory instructions.

Cheri watched for a long moment.

Then she sighed.

"Well," she said calmly, "this should be interesting."

ϒ ϒ ϒ

"DHL?" Drew asked. "It came by DHL?"

Simon held the new letter in his left hand as he rubbed his forehead with his right.

"Just a DHL delivery driver. That's all. And his hat was red and orange, not yellow," Simon smiled.

Both Sabrina and Lauren frowned at Simon's attempt at humor.

"Okay, let us hear it, Prof," Drew said.

They were in Concord again. They had to be there. Simon and Sabrina's house was the only place they could expect the messages to arrive. Drew and Lauren had been staying in the large, comfortable guest room ever since their return from Europe.

The delivery arrived early in the morning. They all sat in the country kitchen's dining area. The men wore shorts and T-shirts, while the women were a bit more fashionable in silk pajamas.

"I'll read it, but it looks like we will be leaving for New York this afternoon. Drew, you should contact the pilots to get the Gulfstream ready." With that, Simon started reading.

Dearest Simon,

I was so terribly sorry to learn that you have lost your job. Truly. One hates to hear of such unfortunate setbacks among acquaintances. That must have been painful for you, professionally, personally, perhaps even spiritually. After all, a man's reputation is such a delicate thing, isn't it? One little crack and the entire façade begins to crumble.

Please know that I am simply heartbroken for you.

You can imagine how utterly devastated I was when the news reached me. I nearly dropped my wine glass. For a moment, I thought I might even faint from the shock of it all. But then I remembered something rather important, and my grief quickly gave way to a... different emotion.

Memory.

Do you remember the last day I walked out of the MFA? Of course you do. It was a lovely afternoon, if I recall correctly. The sun was shining, the museum steps looked exactly as they always had, and yet somehow everything had changed. My career, so carefully built, so passionately pursued, ended with the quiet closing of a door behind me.

You remember that, don't you?

Oh... right.

You weren't there.

But then again, Simon, in a way, you were there. Weren't you? In fact, one might say you played a rather central role in that particular moment of my life. It is remarkable how thoroughly people can still shape events despite their absence.

You see, you made it happen.

Still, I suppose we must all accept the consequences of our actions. It is one of those dreary little truths that adults are expected to acknowledge from time to time. Cause and effect. Action and response. A sort of moral bookkeeping, if you will.

Excuse me for a moment while I dab away these tears.

There now.

Funny how tears can turn into smiles so quickly.

Now then... let me think. What comes next? Ah yes. Another pleasant little excursion. A cultural outing, if you like. You always did enjoy museums, Simon. Or perhaps I should say you enjoyed the places where my career flourished. The halls where my name once meant something. The galleries where I was welcomed, respected, and even admired.

Yes... museums.

Let's visit one again.

This time we shall make it a short trip: New York. A city of culture, reputation, and opportunity. I believe you know it well. So many wonderful institutions there, each one full of priceless objects, delicate histories, and reputations that can rise or fall depending on who whispers what in the right ear.

Let's say tomorrow afternoon, the Metropolitan Museum. Two o'clock should do nicely. The light is lovely on the steps at that hour.

You will recognize the meeting point immediately. A man will be waiting on the front steps for you. A very distinctive fellow. He will be wearing a fashionable yellow hat.

You remember the yellow hat, don't you?

Well... actually, it isn't the same man.

But it is the same hat.

I do so hope punctuality remains one of your virtues, Simon. It would be terribly disappointing if you kept my associate waiting.

And you wouldn't want to disappoint me again.

Now would you?

Do try not to be late.

Simon let the letter slip from his fingers onto the table as if it weighed nothing at all. The thin sheet of paper landed beside his coffee cup with a faint whisper against the polished wood. He leaned back in his chair and calmly took another sip, his expression composed, almost detached, as though the venom dripping from Catherine's words had been nothing more than a mildly irritating business memo.

Across the table, the reaction could not have been more different.

Sabrina let out a sharp, angry groan and slammed her fist against the tabletop. The cups rattled, and a spoon jumped against a saucer with a small metallic clatter. Her jaw tightened, and the color in her cheeks deepened as she stared at the letter as though it might burst into flames.

Lauren's eyes, meanwhile, burned with something far colder and far more dangerous than Sabrina's anger. They blazed with an icy fury that seemed to rise from somewhere deep within her. She said nothing for several seconds, but the tightening of her shoulders and the rigid stillness of her posture made it perfectly clear what thoughts were passing through her mind.

Finally, she spoke, the words tumbling out before restraint could catch them.

"I won't deprive my sweet Sabina of her mother by killing that woman and going to prison," Lauren blurted, her voice sharp with barely restrained rage. "But I swear to God that is the only thing that will stop me from doing it."

The room fell silent for a moment.

Drew, who had been leaning against the counter with his arms folded, pushed himself upright and walked slowly toward the table. His expression was thoughtful rather than angry, but there was an unmistakable hardness behind his eyes.

"Don't worry, Precious," he said calmly, laying a reassuring hand on Lauren's shoulder. "Her destiny is far more painful than death."

The quiet certainty in his voice sent a chill through the room.

Sabina leaned forward, elbows on the table, her fingers pressed against her temples as she struggled to keep her voice steady.

"So," she said at last, gesturing toward the letter with a bitter flick of her hand, "another visit to admire paintings that won't mean a thing to us. Another stage for her little performance." She shook her head in frustration. "She is getting exactly what she wants. Every moment of this."

Her voice dropped lower, tightening with emotion.

"She keeps us angry and anxious…confused and frustrated…and terrified at the same time. It's like she's pulling invisible strings. God only knows what her next demand will be."

Simon reached over and placed an arm around her shoulders, drawing her gently toward him. His hand rested reassuringly on her upper arm.

"Right always defeats wrong," he said quietly.

Sabina turned slightly to look at him, searching his face.

Simon gave a faint, tired smile.

"It's just frustrating how long it takes sometimes."

Drew exhaled slowly and rubbed the back of his neck before straightening. The moment for anger had passed. Action was required now.

"Well," he said, glancing around the room at the others, "our charming friend has spoken."

He pulled his phone from his pocket and tapped the screen.

"I'll call the airport. Let's leave this afternoon."

Sabrina pushed back her chair and stood, her expression already shifting from anger to determined efficiency.

"I'll get us into the Pierre for the night," she said. "If we're going to dance to Catherine's tune, we may as well stay somewhere civilized."

Drew gave a faint smile.

"Practical as always."

The group began to move, chairs scraping softly across the floor as they stood. No one spoke again. Each of them carried the same silent understanding.

The game had moved to another board.

Within minutes, the room was empty. One by one, they retreated to their rooms to pack, make calls, and prepare for the next move in Catherine's cruel and carefully orchestrated game.

On the table, the letter remained where Simon had dropped it, the elegant handwriting almost cheerful in its malice. Besides, the coffee in Simon's cup had gone cold.

ɤ ɤ ɤ

Sedi sat rigidly in the small living room, perched on the very edge of her chair as if she might spring to her feet at any moment. Across from her sat Cheri and Bear. The afternoon light filtered softly through the tall windows, but the calmness of the room did nothing to ease the tension that had settled over the three of them.

Cheri had just begun to speak.

Bear, in contrast to the nervous energy filling the room, appeared entirely at ease. He lounged comfortably in the chair opposite Sedi, his long legs stretched out in front of him, one heavy boot resting on the other. His massive shoulders seemed to sink into the cushions as if he were relaxing after a long day rather than delivering the results of a serious investigation.

Cheri, however, looked more irritated than relaxed. Her eyes flicked briefly toward Bear before she turned back to Sedi.

"Well," she began, tilting her head slightly to one side, "we have great news… and we have annoying news."

Sedi leaned forward even further, her fingers gripping the arms of the chair. The only thing that mattered to her was her daughter's safety. For the past several days, she had lived in a constant state of dread, imagining every possible danger that might be stalking Clarice.

"Just tell me," she said quietly.

Cheri didn't hesitate.

"Sedi, Clarice is in no danger. None at all. We found the stalkers, if you can even call them that."

Bear let out a low chuckle that ended in a snort of amusement.

"The people in the van," Cheri continued, "are absolutely nothing to worry about. They were paid to drive past your house from time to time. That's it. Just cruise by slowly so it looked like they were keeping an eye on the place."

She shook her head in disbelief.

"They didn't even know why."

"What?" Sedi's face twisted into complete confusion. The tension that had been tightening inside her for days suddenly had nowhere to go.

Bear shook his head slowly, still faintly amused, and Cheri continued.

"They were approached by a man who gave them the van and offered them a thousand dollars to drive by your house at least once a week for three weeks. Nothing more complicated than that."

She paused, trying to keep the irritation out of her voice.

"The man's name is Oliver. Nice enough fellow, apparently. Skinny. Short. Very short, in fact. The police said he had to put a thick cushion on the driver's seat just to see comfortably over the steering wheel."

Bear grinned.

"And Petunia…"

"Petunia?" Sedi blinked, unsure she had heard correctly.

"Yes," Cheri replied, holding up her hands in surrender. "Petunia. Honest to God. I doubt she can even spell it, but that's her name. She wasn't even involved in the arrangement. She was just riding along in the van."

Sedi stared at her for a moment, struggling to process the absurdity of it.

"I can't believe this," she muttered. Color began creeping into her cheeks, the fear she had carried for days rapidly transforming into anger.

“We found them and turned them over to the police,” Cheri said. “But there really isn’t anything to charge them with. They thought it was some sort of harmless prank arranged by a friend. They had no idea they were scaring anyone.”

Sedi rose from her chair and walked slowly across the room, her arms folded tightly across her chest. She stopped beside the window and stared out into the quiet street.

“So Catherine was just amusing herself,” she said bitterly. “Getting her thrill by terrifying my daughter and me.”

She turned back toward them, her eyes blazing.

“God, I hate that woman.”

“It certainly appears that way,” Bear said calmly, speaking for the first time since the explanation began.

Sedi shook her head, trying to steady herself.

“So all of this… all this fear…” She exhaled sharply. “It was just a red mackerel,” said Cheri.

“Herring,” Bear corrected mildly.

She waved a dismissive hand.

“Whatever.”

“Well, the boys are leaving this afternoon,” Cheri said. “And I’ll get a flight tomorrow.”

Sedi walked back toward them and stopped in front of the two chairs.

“I thank you both so much,” she said sincerely. “All of you. This was completely unnecessary, and yet you did so much for us. I don’t know how I could possibly repay you.”

Bear pushed himself up from the chair with easy strength and gave a broad grin.

“Nah,” he said. “We were long overdue for a road trip anyway. And honestly…”

His grin widened.

“…we enjoyed the excitement while it lasted.”

He stepped forward and wrapped Sedi in a warm, reassuring hug.

A few minutes later, they said their goodbyes at the door.

When the house finally fell quiet again, Sedi stood alone in the living room, shaking her head slowly.

All that fear.

All that worry.

And it had been nothing more than a red "mackerel" all along.

She finally allowed herself to laugh.

Chapter Twenty-one

A Puzzle Without Meaning

The approach to the Metropolitan Museum of Art feels less like arriving at a building and more like ascending into history itself. A grand sweep of wide stone steps rises from Fifth Avenue, drawing visitors upward in a slow procession. At the top, towering arched doorways, framed by massive Corinthian columns, stand open like a ceremonial threshold. The façade, both elegant and imposing, suggests permanence, as if the stories housed within have always been waiting. Street noise fades with each step, giving way to a quiet anticipation. Crossing inside, the vast Great Hall unfolds, light-filled, echoing, and alive with movement, welcoming you into a world where centuries meet under one roof.

The car eased to the curb along Fifth Avenue, and for a moment none of them moved. The great façade of the Metropolitan Museum of Art loomed above them, its long flight of stone steps rising like an invitation, or a challenge.

Simon stepped out first, his eyes already searching. Sabrina followed, her hand brushing his sleeve as if to anchor herself to something real. Drew closed the door with deliberate calm, while Lauren lingered a half-step behind, taking in the scale of the place, the weight of it.

"Quite a meeting spot," Drew muttered, glancing up.

"Oh, this was Catherine's dream. This is where she thought she'd end up," Simon replied

The steps were alive with motion, tourists, students, and a scattering of locals pausing in the late afternoon light. But even among the shifting crowd, Simon saw him immediately.

At the very top of the stone staircase, just beneath the shadow of the great arches, stood a man who did not belong.

He wore a yellow cowboy hat.

It was not subtle. It was not fashionable. It was, in fact, absurd against the classical dignity of the museum. And yet, there he stood, perfectly still, as if he had been placed there with intention. The hat caught the sunlight, a bright, unmistakable marker in a sea of muted colors.

Sabrina saw him next. Her breath caught.
"That's him," she said quietly.

Lauren narrowed her eyes. "He's not even trying to blend in."

"No," Simon replied, his voice low. "He wants us to spot him immediately."

Drew exhaled through his nose, half amused, half wary. "Well… that's consistent."

They began to climb.

Each step felt heavier than the last, not from the incline, but from the awareness of being watched. The city noise dulled behind them, replaced by something tighter, more focused. The man in the yellow hat did not move. He simply waited.

Halfway up, Sabrina slipped her hand into Simon's. He didn't look at her, but his grip tightened in response.

At the top, the crowd thinned, as if unconsciously giving space. The man tilted his head slightly as they approached, a faint smile touching the edge of his mouth, not warm, not welcoming, but knowing.

"Simon," he said, as if greeting an old acquaintance.

The name landed with quiet precision.

The man in the yellow hat did not offer his hand. He simply regarded Simon with a calm, almost practiced ease, as though he had been standing there his entire life waiting for this exact moment.

"Simon," he said again, with a slight nod. "I'm sure you and your friends know why I'm here."

Simon held his gaze. "We have a pretty good idea."

Drew shifted his weight, folding his arms. "We tend not to get invited to places like this for casual conversation."

Sabrina stepped forward just slightly. "Do you know Catherine?"

The man's expression didn't change. Not a flicker. Not a pause.

"Catherine who?" he replied evenly.

Lauren frowned. "That's either very good acting or very bad timing."

The man gave a faint shrug. "I don't deal in names. I deal in instructions." He adjusted the brim of his yellow hat. "I've been paid to escort you. Nothing more."

"Escort us where?" Simon asked.

"To see two paintings."

There was a brief silence. It wasn't confusion, it was calculation.

Drew let out a short breath. "Of course."

The man turned without another word. "If you'll follow me."

They exchanged glances, a quick, unspoken agreement, and then fell in behind him.

Inside, the vastness of the Metropolitan Museum of Art swallowed them whole. Their footsteps echoed faintly against marble floors as they moved through the Great Hall and into a series of corridors that seemed to stretch endlessly in every direction.

The man walked with quiet confidence, never hesitating, never checking a sign. He moved as though he knew the museum intimately, or as though he had been told exactly where to go.

"Do you even know what we're looking for?" Lauren asked.

"I know what I was told," he replied without turning. "You'll see what you're meant to see."

"That's reassuring," Drew muttered.

They passed through galleries filled with centuries, armor, portraits, fragments of civilizations long gone, yet none of it seemed to touch the man in the yellow hat. He remained focused, a guide without curiosity.

Finally, they turned into a quieter wing. The lighting softened. The air felt different, more intimate, more deliberate.

"Department of Modern and Contemporary Art," Sabrina read softly from a nearby plaque.

The man slowed, then stopped.

He turned to them for the first time since they'd entered.

"This is the first."

He gestured toward a painting on the wall.

"Still Life with Brass Candlestick."

Simon stepped closer, his eyes narrowing slightly as he studied it.

Drew leaned in beside him. "A still life?"

Lauren tilted her head. "Once again, I don't understand."

Sabrina said nothing. She simply stared.

Behind them, the man in the yellow hat watched in silence, as if his task was already half complete, and the rest no longer concerned him.

Drew leaned in, close enough to study the brushwork, then straightened and read the placard aloud with a tone that hovered somewhere between curiosity and irritation.

"*Still Life with Brass Candlestick.* By John Stuart Ingle." He paused, then looked over his shoulder. "Who the hell is, or was, he?"

Simon stepped beside him, hands tucked casually into his coat pockets, though his eyes were anything but casual. "I've heard of John Stuart Mill," he said, glancing at the frame, "but not Ingle."

Sabrina shifted her weight and looked to Lauren, offering a small, resigned shrug. Lauren returned it, her brow furrowed, already searching for meaning where none seemed obvious.

Drew turned back to the man in the yellow hat, impatience creeping in. "All right. What's this about? Who was this guy?"

The man didn't hesitate. He simply lifted one shoulder. "I have no idea."

Lauren's head snapped slightly in his direction. "That's not an answer," she said sharply. "What *do* you know?"

The man smiled, a mild, almost pleasant expression that somehow made it worse, and gave the same small shrug. He said nothing more.

The silence pressed in.

Sabrina exhaled, long and controlled, as if forcing frustration out of her system. "Fine," she said at last. "Then let's do what we came to do. Let's get our pictures."

Phones appeared in their hands almost in unison.

Simon took a direct shot of the painting, then stepped to the side for another angle. Drew crouched slightly, tilting his camera as though perspective might reveal something hidden. Lauren photographed the placard first, then widened her scope to capture the frame, the spacing, and the adjacent works. Sabrina moved closer, focusing on detail, the candlestick, the subtle gradations of light, the quiet composition that seemed too deliberate to be accidental.

"Everything," Lauren said. "Get everything in the room."

They did. Every painting, every label, every inch of wall that might matter.

When they regrouped, the painting seemed unchanged, stubbornly ordinary.

Lauren lowered her phone and shook her head. "I think this is just a ploy to aggravate us. The proverbial chasing of wild geese."

Drew let out a soft breath and gave a crooked smile. "Maybe. But there's a purpose. There's always a purpose." He glanced again at the painting, frustration edging his voice. "We just haven't caught on yet. Damn it."

Simon, who had been standing slightly apart, studying the piece with a distant focus, suddenly stepped back. He straightened, lifted his chin just enough to suggest performance, and with quiet drama declared,

"*Now is the winter of our discontent,*
Made glorious summer by this sun of York."

Drew turned toward him, already opening his mouth to explain, but

Sabrina beat him to it. She spun on Simon, her expression tight, her patience finally spent. Her delicate hand curled into a small, determined fist.

"I swear to God," she said, her voice low and precise, "if you utter one more Shakespeare quote, I will punch you in the nose."

For a moment, Simon simply blinked.

Drew froze, caught somewhere between surprise and laughter.

Then Lauren, who had been tense, analytical, and quietly burdened for what felt like weeks, broke. "If she doesn't, I will."

Simon raised his hands slightly in surrender. "Noted."

Drew shook his head, grinning now. "Well, that answers that."

Sabrina held her glare for a second longer… then, despite herself, the corner of her mouth betrayed her.

Behind them, the man in the yellow hat watched it all unfold, silent and unmoved, his faint smile unchanged, as though he knew something they did not, and was content to let them find it the hard way.

The corridors of the Metropolitan Museum of Art seemed to stretch longer this time, quieter somehow, as though the museum itself were drawing them inward. The man walked with the same unbroken certainty, no hesitation, no glance at a map, until he slowed before a smaller, more intimate gallery.

"Robert Lehman Collection," Lauren read softly. "Room 825."

The man stepped aside and gestured toward the wall. "Here."

Simon's eyes lifted first, and this time there was no confusion in his expression, only recognition.

"Seurat," he said.

Before them hung *Study for A Sunday on La Grande Jatte*, a preparatory work, but unmistakable in its composition. The figures, the stillness, the peculiar balance of order and quiet tension, it was all there, even in its unfinished state.

Drew let out a low whistle. "Well… at least now we're dealing with someone we've actually heard of."

Sabrina stepped closer, her voice softer now. "Not just heard of. Admired."

Lauren nodded. "Pointillism. Structure. Precision. Everything is placed exactly where it belongs."

Simon studied the painting in silence, his gaze moving slowly across it, as if searching for something beneath the obvious.

"And yet," Drew added, folding his arms, "we're still no closer to knowing why we're here."

"Agreed," Lauren said. "This isn't random. It can't be. But what are we supposed to learn from this?"

No one answered.

Sabrina sighed again, though less sharply this time. "All right. Same as before."

Phones came out once more.

They photographed the painting carefully, wide shots, close details, angles that captured texture and light. Lauren took images of the placard and the surrounding works.

When they finished, the silence returned.

Drew turned, once again, to the man in the yellow hat. "All right. Enough of this. What do you know about these paintings? Why these two?"

The man met his gaze calmly. "I've told you what I know."

"That's not an answer," Lauren pressed.

"It's the only one you're getting."

Sabrina crossed her arms. "You don't find it odd? Two paintings. No explanation. No context."

The man shrugged lightly. "I was paid by an anonymous source to bring you here, to show you these works… and to say no more."

Simon's eyes narrowed slightly. "Anonymous."

"Yes."

Drew gave a short, humorless laugh. "Of course."

Lauren shook her head. "So we're supposed to what, decode art now? Is that the game?"

The man didn't respond.

He simply stood there, hands relaxed at his sides, the yellow hat catching the soft gallery light, as if he were nothing more than a marker, a fixed point in a puzzle they had yet to understand.

Simon looked back at the Seurat, his voice quieter now. "Two paintings," he said. "Both deliberate."

Sabrina followed his gaze. "Then the meaning is deliberate too."

Drew exhaled slowly. "Which means we're missing something."

Lauren nodded. "Something obvious."

No one spoke after that.

Because whatever it was… it was right in front of them.

ϒ ϒ ϒ

They settled into their seats with the quiet efficiency of people too occupied to notice comfort, yet grateful for it all the same. The spacious cabin hummed with a low, steady vibration as the plane lifted from New York, banking gently north toward Hanscom Field near Concord. Outside, the city fell away quickly, steel and glass dissolving into a patchwork of gray sky and distant coastline.

It was, as Drew had noted, barely an hour's flight.

And yet, it felt longer.

No one spoke at first.

Sabrina leaned back, eyes closed but not asleep, her thoughts clearly elsewhere. Lauren sat by the window, watching the clouds pass beneath them, her reflection faintly visible in the glass. Drew flipped idly through the photographs on his phone, stopping now and then to zoom in, searching, always searching.

Simon, seated across from them, opened his laptop.

If there was an answer to be found, it would not come from silence alone.

He began composing an email.

To: Sir Roger, Professor Fairfax

Subject: Met – Paintings

Gentlemen,

We have completed the meeting in New York.

As expected, it was neither straightforward nor informative, at least not in any obvious sense.

We were led by an intermediary (identity unknown, likely uninformed) to two works at the Metropolitan Museum of Art. The first: Still Life with Brass Candlestick, attributed to John Stuart Ingle. An obscure name, none of us recognized him, and initial impressions suggest that may be intentional.

The second: a study by Georges Seurat for A Sunday on La Grande Jatte, located in the Robert Lehman Collection. This, at least, is a work of recognized importance.

We have photographed both extensively, along with surrounding works and placards, which I have attached here.

At present, we remain uncertain as to the purpose or meaning behind this exercise. There is no accompanying message, no stated demand, only implication.

We assume this is not random. What would be the point?

If Loki can make any progress using these photos, we would welcome it now.

We must now sit idle, awaiting Catherine's next move.

Regards, Simon

He read it once more, then hit send.

Drew glanced over. "Anything enlightening?"

Simon closed the laptop. "No. But they needed to know where we are."

Lauren turned from the window. "And where is that, exactly?"

Simon gave a faint, humorless smile. "Somewhere between confusion and uncertainty."

Sabrina opened her eyes. "That's not helpful."

"It's accurate."

A quiet moment passed.

Drew leaned back, exhaling slowly. "So… we wait for Loki to work whatever magic Loki works."

"For now," Simon said.

Lauren folded her arms. "I don't think Catherine is going to make this easy for us."

"No," Simon agreed. "She won't."

Sabrina looked at him directly. "You said we would wait for her next demand."

"We will," Simon replied. "But I don't think it will take long."

Drew nodded. "And when she does, it'll be worse."

There was no argument.

Lauren spoke more softly now. "It already cost you your job."

Simon's expression didn't change, but something in his eyes tightened, just briefly. "Yes."

Sabrina watched him, then said quietly, "That wasn't nothing."

"No," he said again. "It wasn't."

The cabin fell silent once more, but it was a different silence now, less uncertain, more resolved.

Lauren turned back to the window, though she wasn't watching the clouds anymore. "Then we should expect something… more punishing."

Sabrina's voice was steady. "And more personal."

Simon looked at each of them in turn.

"Yes," he said. "We should."

The plane continued north, steady and indifferent, carrying them toward Massachusetts, and whatever came next.

Chapter Twenty-two

Toward What End

The house in Lexington held a silence that felt unnatural, too complete, too deliberate, as though even the walls understood they were waiting.

Outside, the afternoon rested in that quiet space that a warm summer day provides. Inside, it felt like anticipation before a storm that just wouldn't arrive.

Simon, Sabrina, Drew, and Lauren had gathered once again in the familiar comfort of Simon and Sabrina's home, though comfort had become something theoretical, something remembered rather than felt. Two days had passed since their trip to the Metropolitan Museum in New York. Two days had passed since they had followed the strange instructions, studied the paintings, taken the photographs, and left with nothing but a deeper sense of confusion.

And now, they waited.

The four of them occupied the living room in different states of unease, each carrying their own version of the same question: *What comes next?*

Drew had long since abandoned any pretense of sitting still. He paced the length of the room in restless, measured strides, turning sharply at each end as though the walls themselves had offended him. His hands occasionally ran through his hair, then dropped to his sides, only to clench again a moment later. The rhythm of his pacing had become a metronome for their anxiety.

"This doesn't make any sense," he muttered, not for the first time.

“Last time, she wasted no time. The demand came the very next day.”

Simon sat in a chair near the window, angled slightly toward the others. His posture was relaxed, deliberately so, but not careless. One leg crossed over the other, his hands loosely clasped in his lap, he watched Drew’s movement with quiet attentiveness. If there was tension in him, it was buried beneath a practiced calm.

“Perhaps that’s the point,” Simon said evenly. “To make us wait.”

Drew stopped mid-stride and turned. “To what end? We already know she’s capable of anything. What does she gain by dragging it out?”

Simon didn’t answer immediately. His gaze shifted briefly to Sabrina, then to Lauren, before returning to Drew.

“Control,” he said at last. “She gains control.”

The word seemed to settle over the room like a weight.

Lauren sat on the edge of the sofa, her hands clasped tightly together in her lap. Her shoulders were drawn inward, as though she were trying to make herself smaller, to contain something that threatened to spill out of her. Her eyes were red, not from fresh tears, but from the constant threat of them.

“She already has control,” Lauren said softly, her voice trembling despite her effort to steady it. “Doesn’t she?”

No one answered.

Sabrina sat close beside her, one arm gently around Lauren’s shoulders. She had taken on the role of comforter without hesitation, though there was a quiet strain in her own expression that betrayed how much effort it required. Her voice, when she spoke, was warm, steady, and deliberate.

“We don’t know that,” Sabrina said. “We don’t know anything yet. That’s what’s so difficult about this.”

Lauren let out a shaky breath. “Sabina…” she whispered, barely able to say the name. “We still don’t know where she is. What she’s doing to her…”

Her voice broke.

Sabrina tightened her arm around her and drew her slightly

closer. "We will find her," she said softly. "We will. Catherine wants something. That's the only reason Sabina is still alive. As long as she wants something from us, Sabina matters."

Lauren shook her head, tears finally slipping free. "That's supposed to make me feel better?"

Sabrina didn't respond immediately. She simply held her, letting the silence do what words could not.

Drew resumed pacing, though slower now, more deliberate. "The first demand was obvious," he said, almost to himself. "Make Simon quit his job. Take away his stability, his identity, fine. That's classic. Predictable, even."

He stopped again, looking around the room.

"But the museums?" he continued. "What is that? A field trip? We looked at paintings. Famous ones, sure, but what were we supposed to learn? What was the message?"

Simon leaned back slightly in his chair, his expression thoughtful. "If it was a message," he said, "it wasn't meant to be obvious."

"That's comforting," Drew replied dryly.

"It's intentional," Simon said. "Catherine doesn't deal in clarity. She deals in unease. Confusion. She wants us questioning everything, what we saw, what we think we understand, even each other."

Lauren looked up at that, her eyes searching Simon's face. "Then what if we're missing something?" she asked. "What if there was something in those paintings we were supposed to notice?"

"There probably was," Simon said calmly.

Drew threw up his hands. "And we're just… what? Waiting for her to explain it to us?"

"No," Simon replied. "We're waiting because we don't have a choice."

The bluntness of it cut through the room.

For a moment, no one spoke. The ticking of a clock somewhere in the house became suddenly audible, marking each second with quiet indifference.

Lauren wiped at her cheeks, trying to regain some composure, though her hands still trembled. Sabrina reached for a tissue from the table and handed it to her without a word.

Drew exhaled sharply and sank into a chair at last, though his restlessness remained in the tension of his shoulders.

"I don't like this," he said. "I don't like not knowing. I don't like sitting here waiting for her to decide how she's going to hurt us next."

"No one does," Sabrina said gently.

All eyes turned, almost unconsciously, to Simon.

He had not moved much throughout the conversation. His calm remained intact, though now there was something deeper in his expression, something harder to read.

"You're taking this remarkably well," Drew said, narrowing his eyes slightly. "Considering you're the primary target."

Simon gave a faint, almost humorless smile.

"I've already accepted something the rest of you are still resisting," he said.

"And what's that?" Drew asked.

Simon looked at each of them in turn before answering.

"That whatever comes next," he said quietly, "is going to cost me something."

The room fell silent again.

And still, there was no message.

ϒ ϒ ϒ

Night came quietly to the island, as though it, too, understood the value of secrecy.

The last of the light drained from the horizon in a slow surrender, leaving behind a sky washed in deep indigo. The sea followed suit, its surface darkening into an almost seamless expanse of shadow, broken only by the occasional glint of reflected starlight. There were no city lights here, no distant hum of civilization, only the steady rhythm of the tide and the whisper of wind across low scrub.

And then, cutting through that stillness, came the sound.

Low at first. Almost indistinguishable from the natural cadence of the ocean. But growing, deliberate, mechanical, controlled.

A boat.

It appeared without announcement, gliding across the dark water like something conjured rather than constructed. Long and narrow, its profile hugged the surface, sleek and predatory. Even in the dim light, its design was unmistakable, a cigarette boat, the kind built for speed, for pursuit, or more often, for escape. The kind that had made its reputation outrunning coast guards along the coasts of Florida and the Caribbean, engines screaming as it danced across the water at impossible speeds.

Tonight, however, it moved with quiet restraint.

Its engines were throttled low, a quiet purr rather than a roar, as it approached the small concrete pier extending from the island's shore. There was no need for spectacle. Speed had delivered them here; discretion would see them the rest of the way.

The pilot stood at the helm, his posture relaxed but his eyes alert. He scanned the shoreline not out of fear, but out of habit. Men like him did not rely on assurances, no matter how confidently they were delivered.

Still, Catherine had been… persuasive, or at least her money had.

She had told the local authorities that she was expecting the vessel, a new pleasure craft, she had said, something to be admired rather than questioned. Even so, the men on the boat had taken precautions.

All three men aboard bore no resemblance to who they had been just days before. Their faces were clean-shaven, stripped of the stubble and beards that had once marked them as something rougher, less refined. Their hair was neatly trimmed. Their clothing, black slacks, clean black shirts, and canvas shoes, spoke of normality and professionalism. They looked, at a glance, like men who sold luxury, not men who dealt in its darker counterparts.

It was a costume, nothing more. But it was convincing.

The boat eased alongside the pier with practiced precision. Lines were secured quickly, efficiently, without wasted motion. No one spoke until the engines were cut off, and even then, their voices were low and measured.

"Strange place," one of the men muttered, glancing toward the dark outline of the house beyond the rise.

The captain gave a faint shrug. "Doesn't matter what it looks like."

No, it didn't.

What mattered was why they were here.

Headlights appeared in the distance, cresting the slight incline that separated the shoreline from the main approach to the house. A vehicle, a new white jeep, bounced lightly over the uneven ground, its beams cutting through the darkness in wide arcs before settling on the pier.

The jeep came to a stop a few yards away.

The driver stepped out.

Catherine's butler was a man who moved with quiet efficiency, his posture upright, his demeanor composed to the point of invisibility. He wore dark clothing appropriate for the hour, though there was nothing hurried or anxious in his manner. If anything, he seemed mildly inconvenienced, as though this late-night errand were simply another item on a well-managed schedule.

"Gentlemen," he said, his voice smooth, controlled. "You are expected."

The men exchanged brief glances, confirmation, nothing more, before stepping onto the pier.

Up close, the illusion of their attire held firm. They looked every bit the part Catherine had described: polished, professional, men accustomed to dealing in expensive boats. If the butler noticed anything incongruous beneath the surface, he gave no sign.

"This way," he said, already turning back toward the jeep.

There was no small talk, no attempt at pleasantries. Whatever transaction had brought them here did not require conversation.

The ride to the house was brief but jarring, the jeep navigating through the small labyrinthine town with ease born of familiarity. Outside of town, the island revealed little of itself in the darkness, only glimpses of low vegetation, the suggestion of rocky outcroppings, the faint outline of the sea to one side.

Then the house emerged.

It stood alone against the night, its structure both elegant and severe, illuminated just enough to assert its presence without inviting scrutiny. Light glowed from within, warm, steady, intentional.

She was waiting.

The jeep came to a stop near the entrance. The butler stepped out first, opening the door with practiced courtesy, though the gesture carried no warmth.

"Inside," he said simply.

The men complied.

The front door opened without hesitation, as though their arrival had been timed to the second. They stepped into a space that contrasted sharply with the darkness outside, polished floors, carefully chosen furnishings, the quiet luxury of someone who not only possessed wealth but also understood how to wield it.

And there, at the far end of the room they were led to, stood Catherine.

She did not immediately move to greet them. She stood with a composure that bordered on theatrical, her posture perfect, her expression calm, almost pleased. The light caught her features in a way that made her seem both inviting and distant, a contradiction she carried effortlessly.

"Welcome," she said, her voice smooth as silk.

The men inclined their heads slightly in acknowledgment. No one offered a hand. No one asked unnecessary questions.

Catherine's gaze moved over them, assessing, approving.

"You've done well," she said. "Appearances matter."

"They usually do," the captain replied evenly.

A faint smile touched her lips.

"Yes," she said. "But tonight, substance matters more."

She turned slightly, gesturing deeper into the house.

"Come," she said. "We have plans to make."

There was no hesitation.

The men followed.

Whatever curiosity they might have felt about the nature of that work did not manifest in their expressions. They were professionals, accustomed to tasks that others preferred not to name. Payment had been agreed upon. Instructions had been given.

The rest was irrelevant.

As they moved farther into the house, the door closed softly behind them, sealing the night outside.

Catherine walked ahead of them, her steps unhurried, her confidence absolute. She did not look back to see if they followed. She didn't need to.

Their task would be difficult for most.

Gruesome, even.

But for these men, it was simply another assignment.

And whatever awaited them in the depths of Catherine's design… it did not trouble them in the slightest.

ϒ ϒ ϒ

The Massachusetts afternoon stretched longer than it should have, as though time itself had slowed in quiet complicity with Catherine's design.

By late day, the light had shifted from bright and hopeful to something softer, more uncertain. It filtered through the tall windows in muted gold, casting long shadows across the living room floor.

The clock had long since ceased to matter. Each passing minute felt indistinguishable from the last.

Still, nothing had come.

The four of them remained where they had settled hours before, unwilling to stray too far from one another, as though proximity alone offered some measure of protection.

Sabrina had made an effort, quietly, without announcement, to soften the edges of the tension. A chilled bottle of Chablis now rested on the table, its pale gold contents poured generously into slender glasses. She and Lauren each held one, though neither had truly been drinking so much as holding something to steady their hands.

Lauren sat back now, though not fully at ease. Her posture suggested an attempt at relaxation, but her eyes betrayed her. They drifted repeatedly toward the front door, then back to Simon, then down again, as though she were trying to anchor herself to something that refused to hold.

Sabrina remained close to her, her own composure intact, though thinner now. She lifted her glass occasionally, taking measured sips, her gaze thoughtful, distant, always listening.

Across from them, Drew sat forward in his chair, elbows on his knees, a glass of orange juice resting loosely in one hand. It was an oddly ordinary choice in an increasingly extraordinary situation, but Drew had clung to it with quiet defiance. If the world insisted on unraveling, he would at least maintain the small constants.

Simon sat slightly apart, his chair angled as it had been all afternoon. In his hand, a glass of bourbon, deep amber, catching the fading light, moved only occasionally to his lips. He drank slowly, deliberately, as though each sip were part of a larger calculation.

The air conditioning hummed steadily, filling the silence with a low, mechanical reassurance. Outside, the day had turned unseasonably warm for Massachusetts, the kind of heat that felt misplaced, almost intrusive. It pressed against the windows, held at bay only by the steady artificial cool inside.

Lauren broke the silence.

“Simon…”

Her voice was soft, but it carried through the room with quiet insistence.

He looked at her immediately. "Yes?"

She hesitated, her fingers tightening slightly around the stem of her glass.

"Do you still believe…" she began, then stopped, gathering herself. "Do you still believe she won't harm Sabina?"

The question settled heavily between them.

Drew's head lifted slightly. Sabrina turned her eyes to Simon. Even the soft hum of the air conditioning seemed to recede.

Simon did not answer right away.

He lowered his glass, resting it lightly against his knee, and considered her. There was no irritation in his expression, no impatience, only a careful weighing of something that had once seemed certain.

"I believe," he said slowly, "that Sabina is valuable to her."

Lauren's eyes searched his face. "That's not the same thing."

"No," Simon admitted.

The honesty of it landed harder than reassurance ever could.

Lauren's composure faltered. "Then what does that mean?" she asked, her voice tightening. "That she'll keep her alive until she doesn't need her anymore?"

Sabrina reached for her hand, but Lauren barely seemed to notice.

Simon leaned forward slightly, his voice still calm, though there was something more measured now, less assured, more deliberate.

"It means," he said, "that Catherine operates with purpose. Everything she's done has been calculated. She hasn't acted impulsively. That hasn't changed."

"But people that are like her, " Lauren began.

"People like her," Simon interrupted gently, "don't destroy leverage unless they have something better to replace it."

Lauren shook her head, tears threatening again. "You're talking about her like she's predictable."

"In some ways, she is," Simon replied.

"And in others?" Drew asked quietly.

Simon glanced at him.

"In others," he said, "she's not bound by anything we would recognize as restraint."

That was as close to uncertainty as he had allowed himself.

Lauren closed her eyes briefly, her breath unsteady. Sabrina squeezed her hand more firmly now, grounding her.

"We'll get her back," Sabrina said softly. "We will."

Lauren nodded faintly, though it was more an act of will than belief.

The silence returned, heavier now.

And then,

The doorbell rang.

The sharp, sudden sound cut through the room like a crack of thunder.

All four of them startled.

Even Simon.

Drew was on his feet instantly. Lauren's glass rattled slightly against the table as she set it down too quickly. Sabrina rose without thinking, already moving.

For a brief moment, no one spoke. The sound seemed to echo, lingering in the air long after it had stopped.

Sabrina reached the door first.

The same DHL courier stood on the step, composed, neutral, holding a small envelope with professional indifference. He offered no greeting beyond a slight nod.

"Delivery," he said.

Sabrina didn't ask questions. None of them did anymore.

She took the envelope.

"Thank you," she said quietly.

He turned and left without another word.

By the time she closed the door, the others had already gathered behind her. There was no need to call them; they had moved instinctively, drawn by the inevitability of what had arrived.

For a moment, they all simply looked at the envelope.

Small. Elegant but almost absurd in its simplicity.

Sabrina turned and walked back toward the living room, the others following closely. The air seemed tighter now, more confined, as though the house itself had contracted around them.

Her hand trembled.

Just slightly, but enough.

She held the envelope out to Simon.

He took it without hesitation.

"Thank you," he said softly.

They did not sit.

No one suggested it.

Simon turned the envelope over once, examining it briefly, not for clues, but out of habit, before sliding a finger beneath the seal.

He opened it slowly.

Deliberately.

No one spoke.

The faint sound of paper against paper seemed unnaturally loud as he withdrew the single sheet inside.

He unfolded it.

And without reading it to himself, without pause or preparation, Simon lifted his eyes to the others and began to read aloud.

Simon's voice did not rise, but something in it sharpened as he read, each word laid out cleanly, without embellishment, without mercy.

"*Are we having fun yet?*" he began.

There was the faintest pause, not for effect, but because the tone of it, light, mocking, was so at odds with the weight it carried.

"*I am. But none of you are, probably.*"

Drew let out a quiet, incredulous breath through his nose. Sabrina's grip tightened unconsciously around the back of Lauren's chair.

Simon continued.

"*Least of all Simon... after he reads this.*"

A frown, just a flicker, crossed Simon's expression, but his voice remained even.

"*Have your visits to the museums caused you to remember me? What I used to be? Or have you already decided I was nothing more than an inconvenience... a footnote you could step over on your way to something better?*"

Lauren's eyes lifted slowly toward him.

"*Oh, how I do love the paintings,*" Simon read, the words almost gentle in their phrasing, though anything but in intent. "*Each one a masterpiece. Each one preserved, protected, revered... while I was discarded.*"

The room seemed to contract around them.

"*But don't mistake sentiment for weakness. There is far more purpose in these little excursions than your limited imaginations can grasp. Every step you take now has already been chosen for you.*"

Drew shifted, his jaw tightening.

Simon did not slow.

"*There are two requirements left. Only two. This is the next.*"

A faint, almost audible smile seemed to hang in the words that followed.

"*I suspect Sabrina will like this one. Or at the very least... she will appreciate its elegance.*"

Sabrina's eyes narrowed slightly, though she said nothing.

Simon read on.

"*It is time to retrieve the painting.*"

The sentence landed like a stone.

"*You know the one. The one that ruined my life. The one that cost me everything that mattered. The one that took my future and replaced it with... nothing.*"

Lauren's hand rose slowly to her mouth.

"*The invaluable treasure of my former employer, the Museum of Fine Arts. Yes... that one.*"

Simon's voice remained steady, but the weight of it pressed into every corner of the room.

"*It is long past time that it was returned to its rightful place. Or perhaps... to a more fitting one. I leave that to your imagination. Though I must say, I rather like the idea of it hanging somewhere appropriately humiliating. Your bathroom, perhaps? Somewhere it can be admired between far less dignified pursuits.*"

Drew muttered under his breath, but didn't interrupt.

Simon continued.

"*You will demand it back. Not a request. Do not negotiate. Demand. You will make it very clear that it belongs to you now. That its history is no longer their concern.*"

He turned the page slightly, though there was no need, just a reflex, something to do with his hands.

"*I imagine this will make for a delightful piece in the good old Boston Globe. Think of it, your names, your faces, your audacity. A theft not of shadows, but of declaration. I wonder how they will frame you... heroes? Madmen? Criminals?*"

A faint tremor passed through Lauren's shoulders.

"*I'll be watching,*" Simon read, quieter now. "*You have already seen what I am willing to take from you. Do not force me to become... more creative.*"

Lauren closed her eyes.

Sabrina's hand moved to her shoulder.

Simon finished.

"*I would hate to think of what I might do... if you disappoint me.*"

A final pause.

Then, almost playfully,

"*Ta ta.*"

Simon lowered the page slightly.

"*Catherine.*"

Silence.

No one spoke immediately.

The air conditioning continued its steady hum, indifferent to the shift that had just taken place. Outside, the light had faded further, and the room now caught between day and night.

Drew was the first to move.

"You've got to be kidding me," he said, though there was no humor in it. He turned away, running a hand over his face. "She wants us to *steal a painting* from the MFA? Not sneak it out, *demand* it? Publicly?"

Lauren looked at Simon, her fear now mixed with something else: confusion and disbelief.

"She's not asking for theft," he said at last.

Simon looked up.

"She's asking for a spectacle," he said quietly. "A public confrontation. One that forces the museum, and us, into a result we can't avoid."

Lauren's voice trembled. "And if we don't?"

Simon folded the letter once, carefully.

"We don't have that option," he said.

No one argued.

Chapter Twenty-three

A Convenient Lie

The interior of the Foreign Office in London is one of the great, hidden masterpieces of British state architecture: a setting where diplomacy unfolds amid almost theatrical grandeur. Upon entering, one is immediately struck by a sense of imperial confidence. The Grand Staircase rises in sweeping arcs of polished marble, its curves framed by stately columns and ornate balustrades that evoke a palace more than a place of work. Light spills downward from tall windows and glittering chandeliers, bathing the space in a soft, golden glow.

The State Rooms form the true heart of the building's splendor. Spaces such as the Durbar Court open into vast, resonant halls crowned with gilded ceilings, allegorical murals, and towering columns. These rooms were designed for function, for receptions, treaty signings, and gatherings of ambassadors, where symbolism carries as much weight as substance.

Chester and Harold had been shown into the Deputy Minister of Foreign Affairs' private office. The room retained its nineteenth-century character, dark wood paneling, a wide desk worn smooth with years of use, and tall windows that admitted a restrained London light.

The Deputy Minister rose as they entered, a faint smile already forming.

"Nigel, thank you for seeing us on such short notice," Harold said.

Nigel extended his hand warmly. "Harold, I owe you far more than this. Your assistance during the Falkland affair is not something I've forgotten."

Harold waved the comment aside with practiced modesty before replying. “I’m not certain this falls within your purview.”

Nigel’s expression sharpened slightly, curiosity replacing courtesy. He gestured toward the chairs. “Perhaps not. But do sit, and tell me everything.”

Harold took the chair nearest the desk, settling into it with the ease of a man long accustomed to rooms where decisions carried weight. He was in his late fifties, tall, spare, his silver hair combed with disciplined precision. There was nothing flamboyant about him; his authority came not from presence alone, but from the quiet certainty with which he spoke. Years in intelligence had refined him into something measured and exacting; he wasted neither words nor motion.

Chester, by contrast, carried a different energy. Younger by at least a decade, broader in the shoulders, with a face that seemed perpetually on the verge of impatience, he leaned forward slightly even as he sat, as though already prepared to rise and act. His eyes moved constantly, across the room, over Nigel, to the windows, as if mapping exits, contingencies, possibilities. Where Harold was restrained, Chester was ready.

Nigel observed them both before taking his seat.

“Well,” he said lightly, “this already feels less like a social call and more like trouble.”

Harold allowed himself the faintest smile. “I’m afraid that’s accurate.”

Chester did not bother with a preamble. “We’re dealing with a woman named Catherine Lodge.”

Nigel’s brow lifted slightly. “Should I know the name?”

“No,” Harold replied. “But you may, before this is finished.”

He folded his hands loosely in front of him.

“She orchestrated the abduction of a young girl. Nigel glanced at Chet. “Here or in the U.S.?

“In Washington, D.C.,” Harold said.

“There’s been no ransom. Her demands are personal. Instead, she’s issuing… ultimatums. She wants to ruin the reputation of a highly regarded scholar."

Nigel leaned back, the levity draining from his expression. "That suggests deep animosity."

"Oh yes," Chester said flatly. "Painfully so."

Harold nodded. "We've been following her trail across multiple locations, New York, Boston… and now, abroad."

Nigel steepled his fingers. "I see. And you're here because…?"

Harold met his eyes directly. "Not to ask you to find her."

That drew a faint, curious smile. "Okay."

"We'll locate her," Chester said, his tone leaving no room for doubt. "One way or another."

Harold continued. "But when we do, there is a strong likelihood she will be in a remote location, with an equally remote possibility that it is within British territory. A protected holding. Somewhere jurisdiction becomes… inconvenient."

Nigel's gaze sharpened. "Ah."

"We're here," Harold said evenly, "to ensure that when that moment comes, we are not delayed by procedure."

Chester leaned forward, resting his forearms on his knees. "We don't want her slipping away because someone needs three signatures and a committee review."

Nigel allowed himself a quiet chuckle. "You wound me. We're not quite that inefficient."

Harold's voice softened, but only slightly. "Nigel, this woman is calculating, patient, and increasingly emboldened. If we hesitate when we finally have her location, we may lose her again…and the child. We may not get another chance."

Nigel rose from his chair and crossed slowly to the window, looking out over Whitehall for a moment before turning back.

"And what, precisely, are you asking of me?"

Harold stood as well, meeting him halfway.

"If Catherine Lodge is found on British soil, probably not, but possibly, we ask for your help in facilitating immediate apprehension. Quietly. Efficiently. Without delay."

Nigel studied him, the old familiarity between them evident now, layered with the understanding of past shared risks.

"And you're certain," Nigel said, "that when you find her, you'll be able to tell us precisely where she is?"

Chester answered before Harold could.

"We will; I assure you."

A long pause followed.

Then Nigel nodded once.

"Very well," he said. "If she sets foot within my reach, you will have our immediate assistance."

Harold inclined his head. "That's all we need."

Nigel's expression hardened just slightly. "For your sake, and hers, I suggest you find her quickly."

Chester stood, already halfway to the door in his mind.

"We intend to."

ϒ ϒ ϒ

The Vintage Tea and Cake Company in Lexington was a vision in white, so thoroughly and deliberately composed that it felt more like a carefully curated dream than a café. The walls gleamed in a soft ivory sheen, the polished floors reflected the light like still water, and the chairs, painted in varying shades of cream and pearl, stood in quiet symmetry around the room. Even the waitstaff moved through the space in crisp white uniforms, their presence almost ghostlike, as though they were part of the design rather than separate from it.

Framing its floor-to-ceiling windows were long sage-green drapes, their color chosen with deliberate restraint. They fell in soft, elegant folds, breaking the whiteness just enough to give the eye a place to rest. When stirred by the faintest breeze, they moved like slow water, adding a quiet sense of life to the otherwise composed stillness.

The café had taken on that peculiar stillness that settles over a place when conversation exists, but no one is truly present for it.

Drew sat angled slightly toward the window, though he had not once looked outside with any real intention of seeing. His fingers drummed softly against the side of his untouched coffee cup. He had always been the practical one, the one who measured problems, broke them apart, and found angles. But this was something else entirely. There was no strategy for dealing with a woman like Catherine. No precedent for negotiating with someone who seemed to treat human lives as pieces on a board.

Across from him, Lauren held her teacup with both hands, as though it offered warmth beyond its temperature. She had taken only a single sip since it arrived. Her eyes moved often, door, window, then Drew and Sabrina. Each glance carried a quiet hope that Simon would suddenly appear and end this suspended moment. There was deep concern in her face. Catherine's demands were no longer abstract puzzles; they were violations. Personal now. Dangerous.

Sabrina, by contrast, made no attempt to disguise her agitation. She sat forward, elbows on the table, her cappuccino forgotten entirely. One leg bounced beneath the table in a rapid, relentless cadence. Every few seconds, she checked her phone, not because she expected a message, but because doing nothing felt intolerable.

"This is insane," she muttered, not for the first time.

Drew didn't respond immediately. He let the words sit between them, as though acknowledging them might give them weight he wasn't ready to accept.

Sabrina leaned back just enough to look at him directly. "She's demanding that the Museum of Fine Arts just… hand over a painting…an invaluable work of art."

They all knew which one.

The painting that had cost Catherine everything. The one she claimed had ruined her life. The one she now wanted back, not as a thief, but as if the world owed it to her.

Sabrina exhaled sharply. "And Simon is supposed to walk in there and what? Ask nicely?"

"He won't ask," Drew replied. "He'll explain."

"And they'll laugh him out of the building."

"No," Lauren said, her gaze steady now. "They won't."

Drew turned slightly toward her. There was something in her tone, certainty, or perhaps intuition.

"They'll hear him," she continued. "Maybe not believe him. But they'll hear him."

Sabrina shook her head. "And if they don't?"

No one answered.

The question lingered, heavy and unwelcome.

Outside, a car passed. Somewhere behind them, a barista called out an order. The world continued with its ordinary rhythms, indifferent to the quiet crisis unfolding at their table.

And the three of them sat there, suspended between action and consequence, waiting for a single conversation, in a distant office, to determine what came next.

The bell above the café door gave a soft, welcoming chime, but all three of them reacted as if it had been struck like a gong.

Simon stepped inside.

For a moment, he simply stood there, letting his eyes adjust, his shoulders still carrying the weight of where he had just been. His coat hung open, one side slightly askew, as though he had put it on without thinking. There was something different in his expression, not relief, not exactly, but resolution.

Drew was on his feet first, but waited.

Simon crossed the room without hurry, though there was purpose in every step. He reached the table, pulled out the chair, and sat.

"It's done."

The words landed with a quiet finality.

Sabrina leaned forward immediately. "What do you mean, 'done'?"

Simon exhaled once, then looked at each of them in turn. “I told her everything. The entire affair. Catherine, the demands, the paintings, all of it.”

Lauren’s brow furrowed. “You told the director? Everything?”

“Yes.” He gave a slight nod. “Her name is Lydia Gardner.”

Drew folded his arms. “And?”

Simon allowed the faintest trace of a smile. “She didn’t throw me out, if that’s what you’re asking.”

Sabrina narrowed her eyes. “That’s not reassuring.”

“It should be,” Simon replied calmly. “Because she wasn’t angry in the least.”

Simon continued. “She was livid. Not controlled irritation, not institutional concern, furious. She was still angry that Catherine had betrayed the institution so egregiously. And now this…” He shook his head slightly. “I think she took it personally.”

Lauren leaned in. “So what happens now?”

Simon rested his hands on the table. “We made a plan.”

That got all of their attention.

“The museum will remove the painting from display immediately. It will be placed into protected storage, completely inaccessible, even to museum officials.”

Drew nodded slowly. “And?”

“And then,” Simon said, “they will issue a press release.”

Sabrina blinked. “A press release?”

“Yes. Public statement. It will say that I demanded the return of the painting.”

There was a beat of silence.

“They’ll send it directly to the *Globe*,” Simon added.

Drew stared at him. “You’re going to let them paint you as the villain?”

Simon didn't flinch. "It's what Catherine wants, isn't it? Visibility. Consequence."

Lauren's voice was quieter, but sharper. "But the truth, "

"Will not be told," Simon said. "Not yet."

He let that sit for a moment before continuing.

"Dr. Gardner and I agreed that revealing the full story now would jeopardize everything. Catherine is watching. If she senses anything off, anything at all, she could escalate."

Sabrina leaned back, folding her arms. "So we play along."

"We give Catherine exactly what she expects to see," Simon said. "Nothing more."

"And later?" Drew asked.

Simon nodded. "Once Catherine is found, once this is over, Gardner will go public. She'll explain everything. The coercion, the demands, all of it."

Lauren studied him carefully. "You trust her?"

"Yes. Her anger assures it."

There was no hesitation in his answer.

The table fell quiet again, but this time the silence was different. Not empty, charged.

Sabrina shook her head slowly. "This is insane."

Drew gave a faint, humorless smile. "No. This is a strategy."

Simon leaned back slightly in his chair, some of the tension finally leaving his shoulders.

"It's a start," he said.

Outside, the world continued as it always did, cars passing, people moving, headlines yet to be written.

Chapter Twenty-four

Signs in the Dark

Catherine's study gleamed with a cold, immaculate brilliance. Sunlight poured through the tall, uncurtained windows in great sheets of white-gold light, illuminating every polished surface, every carefully chosen object. Beyond the glass, winter held the landscape in its grip. frost clung to the bare branches, and the ocean lay flat and metallic beneath a pale sky. It was the sort of cold that hollowed the air, that made the world feel distant and untouchable.

Inside, however, Catherine had created her own climate.

A fire burned low in the hearth, not for necessity, but for atmosphere. The room smelled faintly of cedar and citrus polish. Books lined the walls, arranged not merely for reading but for effect. Everything was curated, intentional.

And yet, today, Catherine herself was anything but composed.

She sat forward in her chair, elbows resting lightly on her knees, her tablet held in both hands. Her usual poise, cool, measured, impenetrable, had given way to something far more animated. Her lips curved in a smile she did not attempt to suppress, and her eyes moved quickly, hungrily, across the screen as she read the article for the fourth time.

Each reading seemed to delight her more.

Boston Globe (Arts & Culture Section)
Sterling's Demand Raises Alarms at MFA

Boston. A growing controversy has erupted at the Museum of Fine Arts following an unexpected request from private collector

Simon Sterling, who has formally asked for the return of a painting currently in the museum's collection. The highly discussed work, "The Soulfast," was the infamous subject of the scandal that rocked the institution five years ago.

Sterling's claim, delivered through private channels and confirmed by individuals familiar with the matter, appears to rest on what he has described only as "deeply personal grounds." The lack of transparency surrounding both the request and the painting itself has fueled speculation among art historians and institutional critics alike.

While the MFA has declined to comment publicly, sources suggest the situation has placed Director Lydia Gardner in an increasingly precarious position. Known for her emphasis on academic rigor and ethical stewardship, Gardner now faces mounting questions regarding the provenance of the work and the circumstances under which it came into the museum's possession.

"The troubling aspect here is not merely the claim," said one observer within the Boston arts community, "but the possibility that the museum may have accepted, or continues to hold, a piece whose ownership is not as clear as it should be."

Others have been more pointed. "If a private individual can compel the removal of a work from a major public institution," another critic noted, "then we are looking at a failure not just of process, but of principle."

The painting itself. its origins, its significance, even its true name. remains shrouded in ambiguity. Yet its sudden prominence raises broader concerns about curatorial oversight, institutional accountability, and the uneasy intersection of private claims and public trust.

For now, neither Sterling nor the MFA has offered further clarification. But as the story gains traction, the pressure on the museum increases. and on its leadership. continues to build.

Catherine let the tablet lower slowly into her lap.

For a moment, she said nothing.

Then she laughed.

It began as a soft, contained sound, but grew into something richer, full of satisfaction, of vindication, of something almost celebratory. Not hysteria, not madness, but something far more dangerous, controlled.

"Oh, Simon, how beautifully you've played your part," she murmured.

She rose gracefully, crossing to the small table beside her chair where a bottle of champagne rested in a silver bucket, beads of condensation sliding down its neck. Her fingers lingered on the glass for a moment, as though savoring the anticipation.

With a deft twist, the cork released with a sharp, elegant pop. an exclamation point in the stillness of the room.

She poured slowly, watching the bubbles rise, catching the sunlight like fragments of something precious. Then she lifted the flute, studying it briefly before taking a long, deliberate sip.

"Revenge," she said, her voice low and thoughtful, "is oh, so sweet."

She turned, drifting back toward her lounge chair, and reclined with practiced ease, one arm draped loosely along its edge. The sunlight touched her face, illuminating the faintest trace of color in her cheeks, the gleam in her eyes.

"But this…" she continued, glancing again at the tablet. "This is artistry."

Another sip.

"Simon humiliated. Publicly. And without even understanding how thoroughly he's been used."

Her smile deepened.

"And Lydia…" She gave a soft, almost sympathetic sigh. "Dear Lydia Gardner. So careful. So precise. So proud of her institution. Of her reputation."

She lifted her glass slightly, as though addressing an unseen audience.

"A reputation built over decades," she said. "Carefully tended. Protected. Polished."

Her gaze returned to the article, her tone sharpening just slightly.

“And now...questions...doubt...whispers.”

She let the words hang, then took another drink.

“All it takes,” she added quietly, “is a single crack.”

Her eyes drifted across the room.

On the couch, Sabina lay curled beneath a blanket, her dark hair spilling across the cushion, her breathing slow and steady. The stillness of her form contrasted sharply with the electric energy that filled the rest of the room.

Catherine watched her for a moment, her expression unreadable.

Then, gently, almost callously, she smiled.

“Yes,” she said softly. “The drugs are working better each day.”

She tilted her head, studying Sabina as one might observe a finished piece of work.

“You were always going to be the difficult one,” she went on. “Too perceptive. Too… intelligent. And a much too reliable memory.”

A faint shrug.

“We can’t have that.”

She turned back toward the windows, lifting her glass again, letting the sunlight refract through the champagne.

“Everything is aligning,” she murmured.

Her voice softened, becoming almost reflective.

“The painting… the museum… Simon… Lydia…”

Each word felt placed, deliberate.

“And you,” she added, glancing once more toward Sabina.

She leaned back fully now, settling into the chair, utterly at ease.

Outside, the cold world remained frozen, distant, irrelevant.

Inside, Catherine closed her eyes briefly, a smile lingering on her lips.

“And the best…”

Her eyes opened, gleaming.

"…is still to come."

ϒ ϒ ϒ

Sir Roger's rooms carried the same quiet authority they always had, high ceilings, paneled walls the color of aged walnut, and a fire that burned with disciplined restraint in the grate. Evening had settled outside, pressing softly against the tall windows, leaving the room suspended in lamplight and shadow.

Roger stood near the hearth, one hand resting on the mantel, his posture erect but tense. Fairfax occupied his usual chair, though tonight he did not sit comfortably in it. He leaned forward, elbows on his knees, fingers loosely clasped, his eyes fixed on the young woman standing before them. Chelsea.

She seemed entirely at ease in a room that unsettled most people. Dressed in her school uniform, she held herself with a quiet confidence that neither Roger nor Fairfax could quite decipher. There was no arrogance in her manner, only silent certainty.

"He's responded," Chelsea said, her voice even.

Roger turned slightly, his expression sharpening. "And?"

Chelsea folded her hands loosely in front of her. "Loki is… intrigued. More than that, actually. He's fascinated by what you're doing."

Fairfax exchanged a quick glance with Roger. "Fascinated," he repeated. "That's encouraging, but not especially helpful."

Chelsea's lips curved faintly, though not quite into a smile. "It is helpful. He doesn't use that word lightly."

Roger stepped away from the fire, crossing the room with measured steps. "What has he seen?" he asked. "What have we missed?"

Chelsea hesitated, not uncertainly, but deliberately.

"He says there is a possible pattern," she replied. "But it is far too early to interpret it."

Fairfax straightened. “What pattern?”

Chelsea shook her head. “He’s not ready to say.”

The silence that followed was brief but heavy.

Roger’s brow tightened. “Not ready,” he repeated, his tone controlled but edged. “We’ve given him everything we have. Every image, every note, every observation. And he chooses to withhold?”

“He’s not withholding,” Chelsea said calmly. “He’s waiting.”

“For what?” Fairfax asked, the frustration now clear in his voice.

“For confirmation,” Chelsea answered. “He believes there is at least one more piece to this…possibly more. Other paintings. Other visits.”

Roger exhaled slowly, turning away as if to consider the implications. “Another museum,” he murmured. “Of course.”

“He’s quite certain of it,” Chelsea continued. “And he’s equally certain that when it happens, the information must reach him immediately. Not hours later. Not after discussion. Immediately.”

Fairfax leaned back now, though his gaze remained fixed on her. “And until then, he tells us nothing.”

Chelsea met his eyes without flinching. “Until then, he cannot decipher it.”

Roger turned back sharply. “Chelsea,” he said, his voice firm but not unkind, “you must understand how this sounds. We are operating in the dark. If Loki sees something, anything, we need to know.”

Chelsea held his gaze for a moment, then shook her head.

“You’re asking the wrong person,” she said.

Fairfax frowned. “You speak to him.”

“I listen to him,” Chelsea corrected. “There’s a difference.”

Roger studied her carefully. “You mean to tell me you have no idea what he’s seeing?”

Chelsea’s answer came without hesitation. “None.”

It was too quick, too clean to be entirely satisfying.

Fairfax let out a quiet breath. “That strains belief.”

"It shouldn't," Chelsea replied. "Loki doesn't share conclusions prematurely. Not with me. Not with anyone."

Roger's expression softened slightly, though the tension remained. "Then why send you at all?"

Chelsea considered that, then said, "Because Loki trusts me."

The room fell quiet again.

After a moment, Roger inclined his head, conceding the point, at least partially.

"And what, precisely, does he want from us now?" he asked.

"Anything new," Chelsea said. "When the next paintings appear, and they will, he wants everything. Images, descriptions, context. Immediately."

Fairfax rose from his chair, pacing a few steps before stopping near the window. "We've seen the paintings," he said, more to himself than to the others. "Studied them. Photographed them. There's nothing obvious. No symbols. No markings that stand out."

"Not to us," Chelsea said quietly.

Fairfax turned back. "Then what? Style? Period? Geography? There's no consistency."

Chelsea gave a slight shrug. "There must be. You just haven't seen it yet."

Roger watched her closely. "And he has."

"Yes."

Another silence.

Then Chelsea stepped back slightly, signaling the end of the conversation before either man could press further.

"That's all I have," she said.

Fairfax opened his mouth to speak again, but Roger lifted a hand, just enough to stop him.

Chelsea inclined her head politely. "I'll let him know you're ready."

And with that, she turned and moved toward the door.

A moment later, she was gone.

The room seemed larger in her absence.

Fairfax exhaled sharply. “Infuriating.”

Roger did not respond immediately. He stood still, his eyes fixed on the door as though expecting it to open again.

“At least Loki is certain,” Fairfax continued. “Another museum. Another painting. As if this weren’t already maddening enough.”

“That’s supposed to reassure me?”

“It does,” Roger replied, sitting. “It seems clear that Loki does not indulge in guesswork.”

Fairfax crossed his arms. “Then what in God’s name are we missing?”

Roger didn’t answer.

He pulled a sheet of paper closer, then paused, reconsidered, and instead opened his laptop. The soft glow of the screen lit his face as his fingers moved across the keys.

“We’ve examined composition, subject, provenance,” Fairfax went on. “We’ve compared artists, schools, and time periods. There is no obvious connection.”

“Not obvious,” Roger said quietly.

Fairfax let out a short, humorless laugh. “Yes, well, that’s becoming something of a theme.”

Roger began to type.

Simon,

We have finally heard back from Loki.

He confirms that he is seeing a possible pattern in the materials we have provided. However, he is not yet prepared to reveal his inclinations. Additional information is required.

He anticipates more museum visits. When this occurs, it is critical that all information, images, notes, and any contextual observations be transmitted immediately.

We remain, as you might expect, somewhat in the dark. But for the first time, there is a sense that the darkness may not be impenetrable.

Roger

He read it once, made a minor adjustment, then sent it.

Fairfax watched him. "You sound more optimistic than you feel."

Roger closed the laptop slowly.

"I sound," he said, "as though we are making progress."

"And are we?"

Roger leaned back in his chair, his gaze drifting toward the fire.

After a moment, he answered.

"I don't know."

The fire cracked softly in the silence that followed, offering no insight at all.

ϒ ϒ ϒ

Simon's library seemed unchanged, and yet the atmosphere was.

The tall shelves still rose from floor to ceiling, heavy with leather-bound volumes whose spines bore the quiet dignity of centuries. Glass cases still displayed their carefully arranged antiquities, Roman coins, fragments of carved stone, a small Egyptian figure worn smooth by time, and many other curiosities. Each object carried its own story, its own permanence.

And now, all of them seemed to be watching.

Simon sat behind his desk, though not in the posture of a man at ease in his own domain. The email from Sir Roger glowed on his screen, its words read and reread, weighed and turned over like one of the artifacts surrounding them.

Across from him, Drew and Lauren sat side by side, their chairs angled slightly toward the desk. Sabrina occupied the far end of the seating arrangement, curled slightly into herself, though far more alert than she had been before. Her eyes moved between them, attentive, thoughtful.

For a moment, no one spoke.

Finally, Drew broke the silence. "So… that's it?"

Simon exhaled quietly, leaning back. "That's it."

Lauren shook her head faintly. "He sees a possible pattern," she said, as though testing the phrase. "But won't tell us what it is."

"Not yet," Simon corrected.

Drew let out a short breath. "Convenient."

Sabrina tilted her head slightly. "Or careful."

They all looked at her.

"He doesn't want to be wrong," Sabrina continued. "If Loki thinks there's another piece coming, another painting, then whatever he's seeing isn't complete yet."

Simon nodded slowly. "That would be consistent."

Drew stood, restless, and began to pace a short line between the desk and one of the display cases. "We've already seen two," he said. "Two different museums. Four different artists. Several completely different periods."

"And nothing ties them together," Lauren added.

"Nothing we can see," Sabrina said quietly.

Drew stopped, turning back toward them. "We've photographed everything and studied every detail: brushwork, subject, background, even the frames. There's no message. No symbol. No obvious link."

Simon's gaze drifted to the nearest case, where a small bronze figure stood frozen mid-stride.

"And yet," he said, "there is one."

The room settled again.

Lauren leaned forward slightly. "For the first time," she said, "we have someone saying that with certainty."

Drew nodded reluctantly. "That's… something."

"It's more than something," Simon replied. "It's the first real progress we've had."

Sabrina watched him carefully. “You believe him.”

“I do,” Simon said without hesitation. “Roger wouldn’t phrase it this way otherwise. And if Loki is as precise as he suggests…”

“He doesn’t guess,” Sabrina finished.

“No,” Simon said. “He doesn’t.”

Drew resumed pacing, though more slowly now. “So we’re waiting,” he said. “Again. Waiting for Catherine to send us to another museum.”

Lauren folded her arms lightly. “At least now we know it means something.”

“That’s the difference,” Sabrina said.

They all looked at her again.

“It is,” Simon said. “Which suggests that whatever this pattern is, the next piece could clarify it.”

“Or complete it,” Sabrina added.

Complete.

The word lingered.

He let the words settle.

“We’re moving,” he said quietly.

Sabrina looked at him. “Even if we can’t see how.”

Simon nodded.

“Yes,” he said.

Outside, the light had begun to fade, shadows lengthening across the windows. Inside, the antiquities stood silent as ever, but now, perhaps, not entirely indifferent.

Something was unfolding.

They could all feel it.

Even if none of them yet understood it.

Chapter Twenty-five

A Summons

Simon sat in the worn leather chair by the window in their bedroom. The room was dimmed save for the pale, flickering glow of his laptop. The light carved sharp lines across his face, hollowing his eyes with fatigue. Behind him, Sabrina slept restlessly, one arm folded beneath her head, her breathing uneven as though even in sleep she could not fully escape the strain of the past days.

Simon barely noticed.

The silence of the room was oppressive, broken only by the faint hum of the laptop and the occasional shift of the bedsheets behind him. He stared at the screen for a long moment before opening the email.

From: *Chester Morris*
Subject: *Update on Catherine Lodge*

Simon,

I regret to report that our efforts thus far have yielded no tangible results.

We have systematically contacted every known associate of Catherine Lodge, friends, colleagues, former acquaintances, and anyone with even the most remote connection to her past. Without exception, the response has been the same: no one has seen or spoken to her in years. In several cases, they were unaware she was even still alive. Whatever path she has taken, she has done so with considerable care to erase herself from those who once knew her.

That said, there has been one area of progress.

We have established direct communication with both the United States State Department and the British Foreign Office. In both instances, we have received firm assurances that should Catherine surface anywhere within their respective jurisdictions, we will be granted full cooperation. They are prepared to assist in her apprehension and to act with urgency should the situation require it.

I am fully aware that this falls short of what you need, and for that, I offer my sincere apologies. We are continuing to pursue every available lead, however faint, and will not abandon the search.

You have my word on that.

Chester Morris

Simon read the message twice, his jaw tightening slightly with each pass. No leads. No trace. Only promises, thin, bureaucratic assurances offered in place of answers.

Behind him, Sabrina shifted, murmuring softly in her sleep.

Simon closed his eyes for a moment, then opened them again, staring into the cold light of the screen as if willing it to offer something more.

ϒ ϒ ϒ

No sooner had the four friends gathered for breakfast than the doorbell rang.

The sound cut through the room with unnatural sharpness, as if it did not belong to the quiet domestic setting at all. The table had been set but barely touched, coffee poured but cooling, toast left uneaten, conversation hesitant and fragmented. The previous night's strain still lingered in the air like a storm that had passed but not yet released its grip.

This time, not one of them moved.

Lauren's hand froze midway to her cup. Drew glanced toward the door, then quickly away, as though refusing to acknowledge it might somehow make it disappear. Sabrina looked at Simon, her expression tightening, not fear exactly, but the weary recognition of a pattern they could no longer pretend was random.

Simon exhaled slowly, placing his napkin beside his untouched plate. The simple act carried the weight of resignation. He rose, each step toward the door deliberate, almost reluctant, as though he were walking toward something inevitable rather than unexpected.

The bell did not ring again.

When Simon opened the door, the early morning sun spilled across the threshold, momentarily blinding him. Standing there, framed in the soft gold light, was a teenage boy, no more than sixteen or seventeen, shifting his weight awkwardly from one foot to the other. He wore a wrinkled Redsox t-shirt and carried the faint impatience of someone who had already been up too early for reasons he didn't fully understand.

"Sir, are you someone called Simon?" the boy asked, squinting slightly against the light.

Simon blinked, still adjusting. "Yes, young man," he replied, his tone cautious, his brow furrowed. For a fleeting moment, he wondered if the boy was selling something, candy bars, school fundraiser tickets, the ordinary intrusions of suburban life. The thought felt almost absurdly out of place.

"Uh, this is for you, then."

The boy reached into his back pocket, pulled out an envelope, and extended it with casual indifference. But there was nothing casual about the object itself.

Simon's stomach tightened the instant he saw it.

The paper was unmistakable, thick, and cream-colored. It was expensive and elegant. Catherine's signature before he even touched it.

He took the envelope slowly, as though it might burn him.

"Young man," Simon said, his voice quieter now, more controlled, "where did you get this?"

The boy shrugged, glancing back toward the street as if already mentally done with the exchange. "Some guy gave it to a group of us after school yesterday. Said he'd pay a hundred bucks if one of us brought it here first thing this morning."

Simon's eyes flicked past the boy.

At the curb, a car idled. Another teenager sat behind the wheel, drumming his fingers against the steering wheel with visible impatience, glancing repeatedly at the house. There was nothing remarkable about the vehicle, intentionally so. Just another car on another quiet street.

"Did you…, " Simon began, then stopped himself.

It didn't matter. He wouldn't know anything.

It never mattered.

Simon forced a thin smile. "Thank you," he said.

The boy nodded, already turning away. "Yeah, sure."

He jogged back to the car, yanking open the passenger door and climbing in. The engine revved a little too eagerly, and within seconds they were gone, swallowed by the ordinary rhythm of the morning.

Simon stood in the doorway for a moment longer, the envelope in his hand suddenly feeling heavier than paper should allow.

Behind him, he could feel the others waiting.

He closed the door slowly and turned back toward the table, the elegant envelope now became the center of gravity in the room.

The coffee and breakfast sat untouched, slowly surrendering their warmth to the cool morning air, as Simon returned to the table with the envelope in his hand.

No one spoke.

Sabrina watched him with a quiet intensity, her eyes fixed not on his face, but on the paper itself, as though she could feel its contents before a single word was spoken. Simon remained standing.

For a moment, he simply looked at the envelope again, his thumb brushing the edge, as if confirming that it was real, that this was not some lingering nightmare from the night before.

Then, carefully, he broke the seal then removed and unfolded the letter.

His eyes moved slowly at first, then more quickly, scanning, absorbing, his expression tightening with each line "Simon…" Sabrina said softly.

He didn't answer immediately.

Instead, he lowered himself into his chair, the motion deliberate, controlled. But when he finally looked up, there was no hiding it.

"Yes, it's Catherine."

Drew exhaled sharply through his nose. "Of course."

"Read it," Lauren said, her voice steady but tight. "Don't summarize. Read it."

Simon nodded once.

He looked back down at the page and began.

"To: Simon and the three musketeers…"

As he read, Catherine's voice seemed to take shape in the room, not just in the words, but in the tone behind them. Playful. Mocking. Delighted.

"What an adventure! Don't you agree? I'm having the time of my life…"

Drew's hands curled into fists on the table.

Sabrina's expression hardened, her earlier quiet replaced by something colder, something sharper. The casual cruelty of it, the flippancy, struck deeper than any overt threat.

"…It is almost worth having my life ruined just to enable me this pleasure! Well, maybe not…"

Lauren let out a quiet, incredulous breath. "She's enjoying this," she murmured, more to herself than anyone else.

Simon continued.

"…The day after tomorrow, the ubiquitous man in the yellow hat awaits you in London…"

Drew sat up straighter. "London," he repeated. "We're back to London."

Simon nodded slightly as he read on.

"…Say hello to that old clock for me, Mr. Ben. Let's say eleven o'clock, at the Tate Museum, okay?"

A silence followed.

"…Oh, and give my best to those old coots in Oxford…ask them if they enjoy being outwitted by a gorgeous redhead."

Then Simon reached the final lines. And stopped.

"Simon?" Sabrina pressed.

He hesitated, just for a fraction of a second, but it was enough for all of them to feel it.

Then he read.

"Oh, Sabina is here. She's very sleepy. She gets sleepier each day. I wonder what's wrong with her? Ha ha."

The words hung in the air.

For a moment, no one reacted at all, as though their minds refused to process what had just been said.

Then,

"No." Sabrina's voice was immediate, sharp, almost instinctive. She pushed back from the table slightly, her chair scraping against the floor. "No, that's not, she's lying."

But there was no conviction in it.

Lauren's hand went to her mouth. "Sabina…" she whispered.

Drew stood abruptly, pacing once, twice, his agitation breaking through all restraint. "She's drugging her," he said, anger rising fast and hot.

Simon remained still.

The letter trembled slightly in his hand now, the only visible sign of what was happening beneath the surface. His mind was already moving, calculating, connecting, trying to impose order on chaos, but the emotional weight of it pressed in all the same.

"She wants us unsure," he said quietly. "Afraid."

"She's succeeding," Drew snapped.

Lauren lowered her hand slowly, her expression shifting from shock to something more focused. "Then we don't have a choice," she said. "We go to London."

Drew stopped pacing. "Of course, we go," he said.

"Yes, London, then Oxford," Simon said.

His voice was calm.

Decided.

But as he placed the letter on the table, the untouched breakfast between them now cold and forgotten, the room felt different.

Heavier.

More dangerous.

ϒ ϒ ϒ

Catherine carried Sabina with surprising ease, as though the weight of her was little more than an inconvenience. Sabina's head rested loosely against her shoulder, her arms hanging limp, her breathing slow and shallow in the unnatural rhythm of induced sleep.

Sugar padded along beside them, close to Catherine's legs, silent and attentive. The tiny dog's eyes moved constantly, watching Sabina, watching Catherine, as if aware that something in the room was not quite right, though unable to understand it.

The bedroom was dim, the curtains drawn just enough to soften the daylight into a muted gray glow. Catherine crossed the room and lowered Sabina onto the bed with careful precision, adjusting her gently, almost tenderly, as if tucking in a child.

For a moment, she simply stood there. Looking down. Sabina didn't stir.

Catherine tilted her head slightly, a faint smile forming, not warm, not kind, but contemplative. There was something clinical in her gaze now, detached, as though Sabina were less a person and more an experiment in progress.

"Well," she said softly, almost conversationally, "you have made this easier than I expected."

Sugar gave a small, uncertain whine and sat near the foot of the bed.

Catherine reached into her pocket and withdrew a small vial, holding it up between her fingers. The powder inside shifted lightly as she turned it, catching what little light filtered through the curtains.

Her smile deepened.

"Powdered methaqualone," she murmured. "Such an elegant solution."

She glanced back at Sabina, then at the vial again, almost admiring it.

"It works so well in milk. Dissolves perfectly. No bitterness if you're careful." A quiet, amused breath escaped her. "Quaaludes… surprisingly easy to come by, if one knows where to look."

She stepped closer to the bed, her shadow falling across Sabina's face.

"Just a little more each day," Catherine continued, her tone almost thoughtful now. "Not enough to harm, at least not immediately." Her eyes flickered with something darker. "Just enough to keep you exactly where I need you."

Sugar shifted again, uneasy.

Catherine lowered the vial, slipping it back into her pocket, her expression smoothing into something calm, almost serene.

"Rest," she said softly, brushing a strand of hair from Sabina's face. "We have much more to do."

Then she turned away, leaving Sabina motionless on the bed, the quiet of the room pressing in once more, thick, controlled, and deeply unsettling.

Chapter Twenty-six

The Price of Truth

Fairfax's rooms could not have presented a sharper contrast to those of Sir Roger.

Where Sir Roger's quarters embodied restraint and discipline, every paper aligned, every book precisely shelved, every surface curated with quiet authority, Fairfax's domain appeared to exist in a state of perpetual upheaval. It was not disorder in the careless sense, but something far more unsettling: a deliberate chaos, as though a brilliant mind had exploded outward and left its fragments suspended in the room.

Books were everywhere, stacked in leaning towers on chairs, splayed open across tables, wedged into corners as if abandoned mid-thought. Papers overlapped in layered drifts, some covered in neat handwriting, others in frantic marginalia that crawled up the edges like ivy. Maps, some ancient parchment, others crisp and modern, were pinned to the walls at odd angles or draped over furniture, their corners curling slightly as if they had been consulted too often to rest.

And yet, for all its disorder, the room was immaculate. Not a speck of dust, not a stain, not a single sign of neglect. It was chaos without decay.

Fairfax stood at the center of it like a man entirely at home in a storm of his own making.

"Before anyone so much as breathes too aggressively," he said, raising a long finger, "do not touch anything. I assure you, I know exactly where everything is."

Simon allowed himself a faint smile, unsurprised. Drew gave a small nod of recognition, as if the warning merely confirmed what he already suspected. But Sabrina and Lauren paused just inside the doorway, their discomfort immediate and unmistakable.

Lauren clasped her hands together in front of her, fingers interlaced tightly, as though physically restraining herself from brushing against anything. Her eyes darted from one precarious stack to another, calculating the probability of collapse. Sabrina took a careful step forward, then another, her movements deliberate, almost ceremonial, as though she were entering sacred ground, or a trap.

Sir Roger, seated comfortably in a deep armchair that seemed an island of calm within the room, watched the scene unfold with quiet amusement. His own presence brought a kind of balance, a counterweight to Fairfax's intellectual tempest. He smiled, reached out his hand, and knocked over a small stack of books.

Fairfax didn't even turn to look. With a tight voice, he said, "Someone seems to have forgotten the time his dress shoes somehow got stuck to the floor with superglue." He looked sideways at Sir Roger. He then looked at the rest of the group.

"So, the fellowship returns," Fairfax declared, sweeping an arm toward them with theatrical satisfaction. "Still entumbed in confusion, I trust."

"Confusion is putting it kindly," Simon replied, moving cautiously through the room, navigating its hazards with more ease than the others.

"Another pilgrimage, I understand," Fairfax said.

"A guided one," Drew corrected dryly. "Once again entirely without explanation."

Sabrina glanced toward Sir Roger. "We met him again. The man in the yellow hat."

That caught Fairfax's full attention. His pacing ceased, his posture sharpening.

"Ah," he said softly. "Your cartoon courier of mysteries."

"At the Tate," Lauren added. "Exactly as instructed. He was waiting for us, another stranger, calm as ever, as though this were all perfectly ordinary."

"And as unhelpful?" Fairfax asked.

"Entirely," Simon said. "He claims to know nothing. Paid to guide us, nothing more. If he knows anything beyond that, he guards it well."

Sir Roger leaned forward slightly, his fingers steepled beneath his chin. "And the paintings?"

There was a pause, one that spoke not of forgetfulness, but of frustration.

"Two, again," Drew said. "No explanation. No context."

Simon continued. "*Norham Castle, Sunrise* by Joseph Mallord William Turner… and *Autumn* by Giuseppe Ajmone."

The names settled into the room like pieces placed upon a chessboard.

Fairfax resumed moving, slower now, weaving between the clutter as though tracing invisible lines of thought. "Turner," he murmured. "Light. Atmosphere. Dissolution of form. And Ajmone…" He gestured vaguely. "Modern. Abstract. Emotional rather than representational."

Roger blinked. "How do you know these paintings, you old fossil?

Fairfax scowled. "Unlike you, I was a young idealist once."

Drew shrugged. "We've gone through every obvious contrast. Sunrise and autumn. Beginning and decline. Light and density. Romanticism and modern abstraction. We've tried to force a connection."

"And found none," Simon said.

"Or too many," Sabrina countered quietly. "Which may be worse."

Fairfax gestured broadly to the room, to the scattered notes, to the entire web of inquiry they had stepped into. "Not seeing," he said. "Or not recognizing? There is a difference."

Drew exhaled. "That's a comforting distinction."

"It should be," Fairfax said lightly. "It implies the answer exists."

Sir Roger shifted in his chair, his voice measured. "Catherine is not selecting these works at random. That much is certain. The question is whether the connection lies in the paintings themselves… or in something they reference."

"History?" Simon asked.

"Possibly," Sir Roger said. "Or geography. Or chronology. Or even something more personal."

"Personal?" Lauren said.

Sir Roger's gaze moved to her. "We must not forget, this is not merely a puzzle. It is her puzzle."

That reframed everything.

Sabrina looked down briefly, absorbing it. "Then the meaning may not be universal," she said. "It may only make sense through her perspective."

"Precisely," Sir Roger replied.

Fairfax's smile widened slightly, as though a piece had just shifted into place. "Now," he said, "we are beginning to ask the correct questions."

Drew shook his head. "That would be more reassuring if we had any answers."

Fairfax waved a hand dismissively. "Answers are sometimes overrated. Questions are the true currency of discovery."

Simon glanced between them, between Fairfax's restless intellect and Sir Roger's composed certainty. "We're being led somewhere," he said. "That much is clear."

"Yes," Sir Roger said quietly.

"But we have no idea where," Lauren added.

Fairfax chuckled softly. "Not yet. If you did, it would hardly be a game."

Sabrina shifted again, her eyes once more scanning the room, still uneasy, still out of place in its controlled disorder. "And until we understand it?"

Fairfax looked at each of them in turn.

"Until then," he said, "you remain exactly what I have called you, the fellowship."

Drew sighed. "Wandering blindly."

"Not blindly," Sir Roger corrected.

They all looked at him.

He held their gaze, calm and steady.

"Guided," he said.

The room gradually settled, the restless energy of speculation giving way to something more focused, if not resolution, then at least a shared understanding of what must come next.

Simon glanced at Drew, then to Sabrina and Lauren, each of them carrying the same quiet fatigue, the same lingering frustration. They had turned the paintings' pictures over from every angle they could manage, wrung them for meaning until nothing more would come. Whatever answer existed was beyond them, for now.

He turned back to Sir Roger and Fairfax. "Then we're at an impasse," he said. "At least on our own."

"Temporarily," Sir Roger replied, his tone calm but firm.

Fairfax, who had resumed a slow, thoughtful pacing, stopped and tapped a finger lightly against a stack of papers. "Which is precisely why you are not alone in this," he said. "We have Loki."

Drew nodded. "And he seems to see something we don't."

"Which makes him either very useful," Lauren said, "or very frustrating."

"Both," Fairfax said without hesitation.

Sabrina folded her arms, her earlier discomfort in the room now replaced by a more grounded resolve. "Then there's no reason to sit on this," she said. "We need to get everything to him, immediately."

Simon was already reaching for his phone. "Photos, descriptions, everything we observed," he said. "No interpretation left out, no matter how trivial it seems."

"Especially the trivial," Fairfax added. "Those are so often the keys."

Sir Roger inclined his head in agreement. "Send it all to Chelsea. She will see that Loki gets it immediately."

There was a quiet moment as that decision settled among them, not triumphant, not even hopeful in any grand sense, but purposeful.

Drew exhaled. "And then we wait."

"Yes," Sir Roger said.

Lauren gave a faint, uneasy smile. "We seem to be doing a lot of that."

Fairfax's expression sharpened slightly, though his tone remained light. "Waiting, my dear, is not inactivity. It is the space in which other minds go to work."

Sabrina glanced toward Simon as he began organizing the images and notes. "Do you think he'll respond quickly?"

Simon paused for just a moment before answering. "If he's as close as Chelsea believes… he won't take long."

Sir Roger leaned back once more, his composure returning to its familiar stillness. "Loki understands the stakes," he said. "And, I suspect, he relishes the challenge."

Drew gave a small, wry smile. "Then let's hope he enjoys it enough to explain it."

Simon finished compiling the message to Chelsea, his thumb hovering briefly before sending. For a second, the entire room seemed to hold its breath, Fairfax motionless, Sir Roger watchful, Sabrina and Lauren quietly tense.

Then he pressed send.

"That's it," he said.

Fairfax nodded once, decisively. "Good. Now we shall see whether our elusive friend can do what you cannot."

"And until then?" Lauren asked.

Sir Roger's eyes lifted, steady and assured.

"Until then," he said, " as you said, we wait."

ϒ ϒ ϒ

That night, the four of them sat in a quiet corner of the Randolph Hotel, their drinks resting untouched longer than any of them cared to admit.

The room itself carried an air of cultivated stillness, high ceilings adorned with ornate plasterwork, heavy drapes framing tall windows that looked out toward the dark Oxford streets, and chandeliers casting a warm, honeyed glow over polished wood and deep, upholstered chairs. There was something distinctly Victorian in its sensibility: not ostentatious, but quietly confident in its elegance.

Yet none of that comfort reached their table.

Simon sat slightly forward, a glass of whiskey in hand, though he had scarcely taken a sip. His eyes were unfocused, fixed somewhere beyond the room, as though replaying the images of Turner and Ajmone over and over again, searching for something that refused to be found.

Drew leaned back in his chair, one arm resting along its edge, his orange juice held loosely in the other hand. He looked relaxed at first glance, but the stillness in him was deceptive, his mind working steadily, turning possibilities over with quiet persistence.

Across from them, Sabrina cradled her glass of wine, her fingers tracing its stem absently. Her gaze drifted occasionally around the room, but never settled. The unease from Fairfax's rooms had not entirely left her, and now it had deepened into something more introspective, an awareness that they were moving through something far larger than they understood.

Lauren sat upright, composed but distant, her drink untouched on the table before her. She watched the others from time to time, as if searching for reassurance, but found none. The silence between them was not uncomfortable; it was simply heavy, filled with too many unanswered questions.

No one spoke.

The low murmur of other guests, the faint clink of glassware, the soft tread of footsteps across carpet, these sounds seemed to exist at a remove, as though the four of them occupied a different layer of the room entirely.

Time passed without measure.

Then, quietly, a figure approached.

A server, polished, discreet, moving with the practiced ease of someone accustomed to not intruding, stopped beside their table. None of them noticed at first.

"Pardon me," he said gently.

Simon looked up, pulled from his thoughts. The others followed.

"Yes?" Simon asked.

The server inclined his head slightly and extended a silver salver with a small envelope toward him. "This was left for you, sir."

A faint crease formed in Simon's brow. "Left? By whom?"

"I'm afraid I wasn't told," the server replied. "Only that it was to be delivered to your table."

For a brief moment, no one moved. Then Simon reached out and took the envelope.

Sabrina leaned forward slightly. "What is it?"

Simon turned it over in his hands, studying it. "I think we all know," he said quietly.

Drew straightened in his chair. Lauren's composure tightened. Simon opened the envelope. A single sheet of paper slid free.

He unfolded it. And as his eyes began to move across the page, the silence at the table deepened, not with uncertainty this time, but with recognition.

Catherine had found them again.

I knew you'd be here. Ah, the Randolph Hotel, haven for kings, presidents, poets, and dignitaries. How perfectly appropriate.

Only one clue remains. Do you want it? Of course you do.

Very well. Like Hercules, it is time to clean the Augean stables.

Do you remember that little trinket you received, the Wolfson Prize? It is time to give it back, and not graciously. Return it with prejudice. Confess to plagiarism. Publicly.

Oh, the London Times, how delicious that will be to read.

You may as well remain where you are, because once this charming little task is completed, you shall receive your final clue.

Goodness, though, if you still cannot decipher the puzzle after that, I fear poor Sabina may be introduced to Poseidon.

The last line had barely left Simon's lips when Lauren shot to her feet.

The movement was violent, sudden enough to send the table shuddering. Her wineglass tipped, teetered for the briefest second, and then toppled, spilling a dark red arc across the pristine white linen like a wound opening in slow motion.

"Oh, God… oh, God!" she gasped, her voice sharp, unraveling.

She began pacing immediately, as if sitting still had become impossible, long, rapid strides that carried her a few steps away, then back again, then off in another direction. Her hands dragged through her hair, then dropped, then clenched into fists. She looked like someone trying to outrun a thought that would not let her go.

The quiet dignity of the room crackled around her.

Heads turned. Conversations faltered. A few nearby guests stared openly now, their curiosity barely disguised beneath polite discomfort. The Randolph, with all its cultivated restraint, was not accustomed to scenes.

The server appeared almost instantly, materializing at the edge of the table with professional calm, though his eyes flicked nervously between the spreading stain and Lauren's agitation. He began blotting the cloth with quick, precise movements, as though restoring order to the linen might somehow restore it to the moment. He motioned across the room for a fresh cloth.

Sabrina was on her feet in an instant, crossing the space between them and catching Lauren by the arm, not forcefully, but firmly enough to interrupt the pacing.

"Lauren, hey, look at me," she said, her voice low, urgent, trying to anchor her.

Lauren barely seemed to hear her.

"Oh, God… she's going to kill her," she said, the words tumbling out, breathless, raw. "She's actually going to, "

Drew reached them at the same time, stepping in on Lauren's other side, his presence steady, grounding.

"Precious," he said quietly, using the name with deliberate softness, "we'll find her. We will. We'll figure this out."

Lauren stopped.

For a single, suspended second, she stood perfectly still between them.

Then she turned on him, fast, fierce, eyes blazing with something far beyond fear.

"We haven't got a goddamn clue!" she snapped, the words cutting through the room like glass.

A few more heads turned.

The server hesitated, then resumed his work with even greater focus, as though invisibility might be achieved through efficiency.

Lauren's chest rose and fell in sharp, uneven breaths. The fight was still in her, but it was cracking now, splintering under the weight of helplessness.

Sabrina tightened her grip slightly, her voice softening. "We will," she said. "We're closer than we were. We just need a moment. Come on. Sit down."

Drew nodded, his tone calmer now, but no less firm. "You're not wrong," he said. "We don't have it yet. But losing it won't help Sabina."

That landed.

Lauren's eyes flickered, anger giving way, just slightly, to something more fragile.

Between them, Drew and Sabrina guided her back toward the table. She resisted for half a step, then another… and then, finally, let herself be led.

They eased her into her chair.

The table had been straightened, and a new cloth was being laid.

Beneath a fresh cloth, the illusion of order was hastily restored. But the air around them was charged with anxiety.

Lauren leaned forward, elbows on her knees, her hands covering her face now.

No one spoke.

Across from her, Simon still held the letter. It was no longer a message; it was a threat.

Chapter Twenty-seven

The Refusal

The offices of the Wolfson Foundation did not announce themselves with grandeur. There were no marble staircases, no theatrical domes, no sweeping gestures toward immortality. Instead, the building stood with a quiet, deliberate confidence, glass, stone, and clean lines, its restraint suggesting something far more formidable than display: permanence.

Inside, the air carried that peculiar stillness found only in institutions accustomed to making decisions that outlast reputations.

Simon paused just inside the entrance.

For a fleeting moment, he considered turning back.

Sir Roger Abelard, standing beside him in his dark, impeccably cut coat, glanced over with mild curiosity.

"Steady, my boy," Roger murmured. "One does not retreat from a room simply because it contains intelligent people."

Professor Eustace Fairfax, already halfway to the reception desk, snorted without turning.

"There are no intelligent people."

Simon managed a thin smile, though it faded almost immediately. His hand brushed unconsciously against his coat pocket, an old habit when under pressure, before he forced it still.

"I'm not concerned about intelligence," Simon said quietly. "I'm concerned about falsehood."

Fairfax turned then, his sharp eyes fixing on him.

"Yes," he said. "As you should be. Falsehood is the most dangerous thing in this building."

They were shown into a conference room on the upper floor.

It was understated but exacting, an oak table, high-backed chairs, a long wall of glass that looked out over London in summer light. No ornament. No indulgence. Everything here served a purpose.

Three officials were already seated.

At the center sat a woman in her early sixties, composed, silver-haired, with the unmistakable bearing of someone accustomed to authority that did not need to be asserted. To her right, a younger man with a tablet already open, fingers poised. To her left, an older gentleman with rimless glasses, hands folded as though in quiet judgment.

They did not rise.

The woman inclined her head slightly.

"Simon, Sir Roger. Professor Fairfax. This is Mr. Harrington; he is the foundation's solicitor."

Her tone was polite.

Not warm.

Simon felt it immediately, the shift in the air, as though they had stepped into a courtroom where the verdict had already been reached.

They took their seats.

The woman folded her hands.

"I am Eleanor Whitcombe," she said. "Chair of the Historical Awards Committee. We understand you have requested this meeting to discuss the return of the Wolfson History Prize."

Simon did not hesitate.

"Yes."

The word landed harder than he intended.

A faint pause followed.

Whitcombe exchanged the briefest glance with her colleagues, something already understood passing silently between them.

"I see," she said. "Then I think it best that we proceed directly."

She leaned forward slightly.

"The Wolfson History Prize is not awarded lightly. As you are aware, it is the result of a rigorous and multi-layered evaluation process. Your work was reviewed by subject-matter experts, assessed by advisory panels, and scrutinized for both originality and scholarly integrity."

The man to her right tapped his tablet once, almost reflexively.

Whitcombe continued.

"The Foundation itself," she said, "has, since its establishment in 1955, distributed over one billion pounds in grants, two billion in real terms, to more than fourteen thousand projects. Our endowment, as of last year, stands just under one billion pounds. We do not arrive at decisions casually."

Her gaze fixed on Simon.

"And we do not make mistakes of this nature," Harrington added.

Simon held her eyes.

"I plagiarized."

The word hung there.

Flat. Final.

Sir Roger shifted slightly beside him but said nothing.

Fairfax, by contrast, leaned back in his chair, watching with open interest, as though attending a particularly promising duel.

Whitcombe did not react immediately.

When she spoke, her voice had cooled.

"No," she said.

Not loudly. But with absolute certainty.

Simon blinked.

"I'm afraid…, " He began.

"No," she repeated, this time with the faintest edge. "You did not."

A silence followed, long enough to become uncomfortable.

Harrington finally spoke, his voice dry and precise.

"We have re-examined your work, Dr. Sterling. Thoroughly. Every citation. Every argument. Every source."

He adjusted his glasses.

"There is no evidence of plagiarism. None."

Simon leaned forward, his composure beginning to crack.

"You're wrong."

The younger man looked up for the first time, studying Simon with something bordering on curiosity.

Whitcombe's expression did not change.

"We are not," she said. "And I believe you know that."

That landed.

Harder than anything so far.

Simon's jaw tightened.

Sir Roger finally spoke, his tone measured, almost diplomatic.

"Ms. Whitcombe," he said, "surely you can appreciate that Dr. Sterling would not make such a claim without cause."

Whitcombe turned her gaze to him.

"I appreciate many things, Sir Roger," she replied. "Among them, the distinction between truth and coercion."

The word settled into the room like a shadow.

Coercion.

Fairfax's eyes flickered, just briefly, but enough to register interest.

Whitcombe continued, now addressing all three of them.

"We believe," she said, "that Dr. Sterling is acting under duress."

Simon said nothing.

"That," she went on, "is not our affair. We are not an investigative body, nor are we an instrument of law enforcement."

A slight pause.

"But we will not," she said, her voice sharpening for the first time, "be made party to a falsehood."

Harrington nodded once, as if sealing the statement.

Whitcombe leaned back.

"If Dr. Sterling attempts to return the prize on the basis of plagiarism," she said, "we will reject it formally. And should he choose to publicize such a claim, "

She stopped.

Not out of hesitation.

But precision.

"We will respond," she said, "vociferously."

The word carried weight.

Measured. Deliberate. Final.

Simon felt the ground shifting beneath him.

The younger man closed his tablet with a soft click.

"We would be compelled," he added, almost apologetically, "to defend both the integrity of the Prize and the Foundation itself. Publicly."

Sir Roger exhaled slowly.

Fairfax, on the other hand, allowed himself the faintest smile.

Whitcombe's gaze softened, not with sympathy, but with something closer to resolve.

"Dr. Sterling," she said, "whatever is driving this… it is not scholarship."

She leaned forward one final time.

She held his eyes.

"If you are being pressured, threatened, or manipulated into making this claim," she said, "then understand this: we consider that an attack. Not merely on you, but on this institution."

"And we will not stand idly by."

Silence settled over the room.

Outside, London moved on, indifferent, unaware.

Inside, something had shifted.

Simon sat very still, the weight of Catherine's demand pressing harder than ever.

Because for the first time, he must deny her ultimatum…and suffer the consequences.

ϒ ϒ ϒ

Sir Roger's rooms at Balliol seemed, that afternoon, to lean inward, as though the centuries themselves had gathered to listen.

The shallow light shone through the windows, casting a restless amber light across the Oriental rugs and the long walls of books that climbed toward the ornate ceiling. Outside, Oxford moved in its usual quiet rhythm, bicycles whispering past ancient stone, students arguing across quadrangles that had hosted arguments for nearly a millennium.

Inside, the Fellowship sat in uneasy stillness.

Simon stood near the dormant fireplace, one hand resting on the mantel, his posture rigid, not from formality, but from the effort of holding himself together. Sir Roger occupied his usual chair, composed but watchful. Fairfax had claimed the opposite side of the room, angled slightly away, as though refusing to grant the moment full legitimacy.

Sabrina sat closest to Simon.

Drew and Lauren sat together on the settee.

For a moment, no one spoke.

Then Simon did.

"They refused," he said.

The words were simple, but they carried the residue of the meeting, the weight of certainty he had not been able to dislodge.

"They wouldn't accept the return of the prize. Not under any circumstances."

Sabrina leaned forward slightly, her eyes searching his face.

"What did they say?"

Simon let out a slow breath.

"That their process is too thorough for a mistake like this. That they've reviewed everything again." A faint, humorless smile touched his mouth. "They're quite certain I didn't plagiarize anything."

Fairfax gave a quiet grunt of approval.

"Well, there's a novelty," he muttered. "Competence."

Roger shot him a glance but said nothing.

Simon continued.

"They believe I'm acting under duress."

That landed.

Drew straightened.

"And?"

Simon looked at him.

"And they refuse to be part of it."

A pause.

"They made it very clear that if I try to return the prize publicly, they will oppose it. Forcefully."

Roger nodded, almost to himself.

"As, I guess, we should have anticipated."

Simon turned slightly, his voice tightening.

"They also said…" He hesitated, choosing the words. "They would defend me. That they consider this an attack on both the Foundation and me."

Sabrina exhaled with the unmistakable release of someone who had been holding something in for far too long.

"They believe in you," she said softly. "They *know* you."

Her voice carried something more than relief.

Gratitude.

Simon looked at her, and for the first time since entering the Foundation's office, something in his expression eased.

"Yes," he said quietly. "They do."

Lauren had gone very still.

Sabrina noticed first.

"Elle?"

Lauren's gaze was fixed, not on Simon, but somewhere just beyond him, as though she were seeing something none of the others could.

"That's not good," don't you see?" Her voice rose, edged with urgency. "Catherine wanted him to return the prize. Publicly. That was the point."

Lauren stood, pacing once, twice, her movements tight, controlled, but charged.

"If he can't do it, if they won't allow it, then the whole… performance collapses." She turned back to them. "And she won't like that. Not at all."

Sabrina's grip on Simon's hand tightened.

"And what will she do? She's been threatening from the beginning."

Drew rose now, stepping toward her.

"Hey, hey, this might, this might slow things down. Force her to change tactics."

Lauren shook her head immediately.

"No. No, Drew. People like her don't slow down. They adjust. And when they adjust, "

She didn't finish.

She didn't need to.

Simon stepped away from the mantel.

"Lauren," he said, his tone steady despite the tension threading through it, "we don't have a choice."

She looked at him.

That quieted her for a moment.

Roger rose then, smoothing his coat as he did, the movement deliberate, grounding.

"Let's not panic," he said calmly. "Catherine's methods, however diabolical, are not without pattern."

Fairfax snorted.

"She sets the stage. She allows anticipation to build. Then she delivers the next act."

"But how long do we have before she acts?" Drew asked

"Not long," Simon said at last. "She enjoys the interval, but only to a point. Too much delay and she risks losing control of the narrative."

"A few days," he said. "A week at most."

Sabrina looked between them.

"And until then?"

No one answered immediately.

The fire shifted in the grate, a soft collapse of embers.

At last, Drew spoke.

"We wait."

The word felt insufficient.

But there was nothing else.

Simon nodded.

"We wait…for Loki," he echoed.

At that, Roger allowed himself the faintest smile.

"Ah, yes. Our unseen oracle."

Fairfax folded his arms.

"If anyone can find a way out of this madness, it will be him."

Simon exhaled slowly.

"All we can do," he said, "is trust that he will find a way in the next few days."

The room fell quiet.

Chapter Twenty-eight

The Moment of Knowing

Catherine Lodge did not throw things.

She had long ago trained herself out of such vulgar displays, no shattered porcelain, no overturned chairs, no broken glass to betray a loss of control. Rage, in her world, was to be contained, curated, and expressed with precision. It was to be *directed.*

Still, the urge lingered.

She paced the length of the Emerald Room, her heels striking the marble with sharp, staccato authority. The fire in the jade-carved hearth flickered and snapped, its glow dancing across the pale green walls, casting her shadow in restless motion, long, distorted, predatory.

Outside, the rain lashed against the tall windows in cold, wind-driven sheets. The South Atlantic, usually a deep and mesmerizing green, had turned violent, whitecaps thrashing like the temper she refused to unleash.

Her hands curled.

Uncurled.

Curled again.

"He *refused,*" she muttered, her voice low, disbelieving, poisonous.

Even now, cornered, exposed, humiliated, he found a way to deny her. To rob her of the one moment she had engineered with such exquisite care: his public capitulation. His confession. His disgrace laid bare before the world that had once praised him.

The Wolfson Prize.

Her masterpiece of humiliation.

And he had dared to *refuse*.

She stopped before the window, staring out into the storm, her reflection faintly superimposed over the chaos beyond. For a moment, she saw herself not as she was, but as she imagined they saw her, beautiful, composed, untouchable.

They had no idea.

Her lips curved into a tight, humorless smile.

"Oh, Simon," she whispered. "You do make this so much worse for yourself."

Her gaze shifted, unfocused now, calculating.

The knock came, soft, deliberate, controlled.

She did not turn immediately. She let it linger, let the silence stretch, a small assertion of dominance. Only then did she speak.

"Come in."

The door opened with quiet efficiency.

The man stepped inside without hesitation. He had been on the boat and carried with him the faint scent of salt and diesel, of wet canvas and machinery, out of place amid the polished elegance of the room. His coat was damp, his boots heavy, but he made no apology for it. Men like him did not belong in rooms like this.

They were tools.

Necessary, crude tools.

"Ms. Lodge," he said, his voice even.

Catherine turned at last, her expression already composed, the storm within her sealed behind a veneer of cool command.

"You're prepared?" she asked.

"We've been prepared," he replied. "Since you hired us."

She studied him for a moment, measuring, as she always did. Competence mattered. Reliability mattered more.

"Good," she said. "Then get the boat ready."

A flicker of something, interest, perhaps, passed through his eyes.

"Timeline?"

Catherine walked past him slowly, trailing her fingers along the back of a chair, feeling the smooth, expensive fabric beneath her touch.

"If nothing happens in the next two days," she said, "it will be time."

The man nodded once, accepting the unspoken.

"The girl will need to be under," he said. "Completely. No risks."

Catherine's expression did not change.

"Of course," she said. "She'll be unconscious."

He shifted his weight slightly, then added, "And I'll need confirmation on the remaining funds. Electronically. Before we move."

There it was, the true anchor of his loyalty.

Money.

Catherine turned her head just enough to meet his gaze, her eyes sharp, assessing.

"You'll have it," she said. "Every cent."

Then, almost as an afterthought, though it was anything but,

"And the dog goes too."

The man frowned, just slightly.

"The dog?"

"Yes," Catherine snapped, the first crack in her composure. "The *damn* dog. I will not have it left behind to deal with."

He held her gaze for a moment longer, then gave a short nod.

"Understood."

He turned to leave, already dismissing the conversation, the task settling into place in his mind as logistics, weight, timing, tides.

The door closed softly behind him.

She exhaled sharply, the sound almost a hiss, and resumed her pacing.

Two days.

She could almost feel the clock ticking, not in seconds, but in consequences.

Her plan had been elegant. Laycred. Inevitable.

And yet, Simon had introduced uncertainty.

That would not stand.

She crossed to a small table and placed her hands flat against it, leaning forward slightly, her head bowed for just a moment.

Then she lifted it again, her eyes hard, glittering.

"No," she said aloud, her voice steady now, resolved.

"If you won't give it to me…"

A faint smile crept across her lips, cold, precise, merciless.

"…I'll take something far more valuable."

Outside, the storm intensified, rain hammering against the glass like impatient fingers.

Inside, Catherine Lodge finally stopped pacing.

Not because her anger had subsided,

But because it had found its direction.

ϒ ϒ ϒ

Sir Roger's rooms at Balliol, usually a sanctuary of civilized thought and gently combative scholarship, now felt close, almost oppressive, despite the open windows and the unseasonably warm Oxford afternoon.

They were all there except Fairfax, who was conspicuously absent.

No one could be.

Lauren stood near the window, her back half-turned to the others, her arms wrapped tightly around herself as if she could physically hold together something that was coming apart. She had not slept, of that there was no doubt. Her hair, usually so carefully composed, had loosened into disarray, and her face carried the pale, strained look of someone being consumed from within.

"She's not waiting," Lauren said suddenly, her voice thin but edged with rising panic. "You all know she's not waiting."

Drew rose immediately from his chair, crossing the room to her.

"Lauren, "

"No," she snapped, turning on him, her eyes bright and unsteady. "Don't tell me to calm down. Don't, " Her voice broke, and she pressed a hand to her mouth, forcing herself to continue. "Every hour that passes… every hour…"

Her composure was shattered for a moment. She turned away again, staring out into the quiet Oxford quad as if the answer might appear there among the trimmed lawns and ancient stone.

Sabrina rose more slowly, her movements deliberate, controlled. If Lauren was unraveling, Sabrina was doing the opposite, pulling herself inward, tightening every emotion into something contained, something usable.

She stepped beside Lauren and placed a steady hand on her arm.

"We don't know that," Sabrina said softly.

Lauren gave a hollow, disbelieving laugh.

"We're killing my daughter," she replied.

That silenced the room.

Because it was true.

Simon stood near Roger's desk, one hand resting on its edge, his posture rigid. The Wolfson Foundation's refusal still echoed in his mind, not as a victory but as a trigger. Catherine had wanted humiliation. Public, irrevocable humiliation. And she had been denied it.

Denied by him.

"We've had nothing from her," Drew said, more to fill the silence than because it needed saying. "No message. No instructions.

Nothing."

"She is not a creature of hesitation," Roger said. "Her pattern thus far has been one of… sequencing. Each act is carefully staged. Each demand escalating the last."

He glanced toward Simon.

"And now she has been thwarted."

Simon met his gaze.

"Yes."

"So what does that mean?" Sabrina asked.

Roger exhaled slowly.

"It means," he said, "that we must assume her next move will be… disproportionate."

Lauren turned sharply at that.

"Disproportionate?" she repeated, her voice rising. "You mean she's going to *kill her*."

Drew stepped in again, more firmly this time.

"Lauren, listen to me, "

"No, you listen!" she shot back, tears now spilling freely. "We have done *nothing*. We sit here, thinking, analyzing, waiting for clues like this is some kind of puzzle, and she has my daughter!"

The word *daughter* cracked through the room like a gunshot.

Silence followed.

Heavy. Absolute.

Simon stepped forward then, his voice low but steady.

"We are not doing nothing," he said.

Lauren turned on him, raw and unfiltered.

"Then what are we doing, Simon?" she demanded. "Because from where I'm standing, we are losing."

He did not flinch.

"We are waiting for the only advantage we have," he said.

“Loki?” she said, almost spitting the name.

“Yes.”

Lauren shook her head, despair overtaking anger.

“False hope,” she whispered. “That’s all that is.”

Sabrina tightened her grip on Lauren’s arm.

“It’s not nothing,” she said firmly. “It’s the *only* thing.”

Drew nodded, though his expression betrayed how fragile that belief had become.

Roger leaned forward slightly.

“Chelsea would not have sent word unless it mattered,” he said. “She is not prone to dramatics. If she says she must see us immediately, then Loki has found something.”

Simon turned to Roger. “Is Eustace getting her?”

“Not exactly,” Roger replied. “he’s doing something else. Something that could be important to us.

A flicker of hope.

Or perhaps simply the refusal to surrender to despair.

Time passed.

Every small sound, the distant echo of footsteps in the quad, the murmur of voices outside, the ticking of a clock somewhere unseen, seemed amplified, each one tightening the tension further.

Lauren sank at last into a chair, her energy spent, though her eyes remained fixed on the door.

“Please,” she whispered, barely audible. “Please let there be something.”

No one answered.

ϒ ϒ ϒ

The knock came sharp and urgent, three quick raps that seemed to echo more loudly than they should have in the stillness of Roger’s rooms.

Every head turned at once.

Roger rose halfway from his chair, but before he could speak, the door opened, and Chelsea stepped inside.

She looked as she always did, composed, self-contained, almost spectral in her restraint. Yet today there was something else. Not excitement. Not quite urgency. But a gravity that pulled the air tight around her.

She closed the door softly behind her.

“I have something,” she said.

No greeting. No smile. Only that. The room seemed to contract.

Simon leaned toward Roger immediately. “Where is Fairfax?”

Roger did not look at him. “Occupied,” he said. “On something… essential.”

Simon frowned. “Essential to *this*?”

Roger finally met his eyes. “Yes. But not something I can yet share.”

There was a brief, uneasy silence. No one pressed further. They had all learned, by now, that Roger did not speak lightly.

Chelsea stepped closer to the table, setting her tablet down with deliberate care.

“Loki has made progress.”

The words landed heavily.

Lauren inhaled sharply. Drew reached for her hand without looking at her. Sabrina leaned forward, her eyes fixed on Chelsea as if afraid the moment might vanish if she blinked.

Simon spoke quietly, but there was an edge beneath it. “Then please, tell us. We are… well past the point of needing good news.”

Chelsea nodded once.

“I am aware of the stakes.”

Her voice, as always, was flat, measured, almost mechanical. But today, beneath it, there was something else. Not emotion, exactly. But recognition.

She began.

"From the beginning, Loki accepted your premise that the destination would be remote. Difficult to access. Symbolically aligned with Catherine's… clandestine inclinations."

Roger gave a faint, approving murmur.

Chelsea continued.

"The puzzle presented a contradiction. The paintings appeared meaningful, carefully constructed, culturally rich, and intellectually demanding. Yet, when analyzed conventionally, they yielded nothing."

Drew frowned. "Nothing?"

"Nothing," Chelsea repeated. "No geographic commonality. No thematic continuity. No chronological logic."

Sabrina shook her head slightly. "But the paintings…there had to be something."

"Yes," Chelsea said. "That was the assumption."

She tapped her tablet.

"One by one, Loki catalogued the works."

Her voice became almost rhythmic, like a recital.

"*The Entombment of Christ. Bal du Moulin de la Galette. Still Life with a Brass Candlestick. A Sunday on La Grande Jatte. Norham Castle, Sunrise. Autumn.*"

She paused.

"Each is significant. Each is celebrated. Each, in isolation, offers depth. But together…"

She looked up. "They offer nothing."

The words hit the room like a quiet detonation.

Lauren's shoulders sagged. "Nothing?" she whispered.

Drew exhaled slowly. "You're telling us we've been chasing ghosts."

Sabrina looked stricken. "Then we have no direction at all?"

Chelsea almost smiled. It was subtle. Brief. But unmistakable.

"There is no pattern *to the paintings*," she said.

A pause.

"That doesn't mean there is no pattern, however."

The room stilled again, this time sharper, more focused.

Chelsea turned the tablet toward them. On the screen was a simple list.

Names.

"Titian. Renoir. Ingres. Seurat. Turner. Ajmone."

Roger's eyes narrowed.

Drew blinked. "The artists?"

"Yes."

Chelsea picked up the stylus.

"Loki shifted the frame of reference."

Slowly, deliberately, she wrote a single letter beside each name.

T R I S T A

They stared.

Uncomprehending at first.

Then, Simon's breath caught.

"Tristan."

The word seemed to ripple through the room.

He rose to his feet, energy surging back into him. "Tristan d'Argent," he said, his voice gaining strength. "From the first Soulfast ceremony."

Sabrina's eyes widened. "Of course…"

Roger leaned back, a low chuckle escaping him. "Elegant," he murmured. "Infuriatingly elegant. There is no 'N,' but Catherine planned to give one more clue. "

Lauren looked from one to the other. "But what does it mean?" she demanded. "It's a name, an important name to us, but where does that take us?"

Chelsea's gaze shifted to her.

And now she smiled fully. For the first time since any of them had known her.

She tapped the screen again. The image changed.

A jagged island rose out of a vast, endless ocean. Dark volcanic slopes. A small settlement clinging to its edge. Nothing else but water, mile after mile after mile.

Text appeared beneath it.

Tristan da Cunha, the most remote inhabited island in the world.

For a moment, no one spoke.

The realization settled slowly, then all at once.

“Remote,” Simone whispered.

Roger sat forward, eyes alight. “Practically unreachable.”

Drew stared at the image. “My God…”

Sabrina covered her mouth. Lauren broke.

A sound escaped her, half sob, half laugh, as tears spilled down her face.

“That’s where she is,” she said, her voice trembling. “That’s where Sabina is.”

The room erupted.

Voices overlapping. Questions. Exclamations. Relief colliding with urgency.

Roger stood, suddenly animated. “We’ve found her,” he declared. “We’ve actually found her!”

Simon turned to Chelsea, his voice steady now, resolved. “Are we certain?”

Chelsea met his gaze.

“Loki is.”

“And you?” Simon asked.

Chelsea reverted to a smile that almost wasn’t there. “I’m Loki. I’m certain.

The excitement of the room paused for a moment, as they realized they had been talking to Loki the whole time.

Chapter Twenty-nine

The Ringbearer

Nigel Forester, Deputy Foreign Service Secretary, remained seated long after the call had technically ended, the receiver still resting lightly against his ear as if reluctant to release the weight of what had just been set in motion.

His office in the British Foreign Service was a study in restraint and authority, dark wood paneling, a broad mahogany desk polished to a muted sheen. He finally replaced the receiver with deliberate care.

Across the line, Admiral Geoffrey Halstead had been precise, efficient, naval certainty distilled into a few clipped sentences.

"They're fortunate," Nigel had said, his tone measured but edged with urgency. "Quite fortunate that *HMS Sutherland* is in the southern Atlantic."

A pause. Papers shuffled faintly on the admiral's end.

Nigel leaned forward slightly, fingers steepled. "And you are certain of the timing, Admiral? I want no ambiguity here. How long to Tristan da Cunha?"

The answer came without hesitation.

"About 36 hours, Mr. Forester. She's already been ordered to flank speed."

Nigel had closed his eyes briefly at that, *flank speed*. There was something both reassuring and ominous about it. Warships did not often run at maximum speed unless something had gone decidedly wrong.

"Very good," Nigel replied. "Proceed."

Now, alone again, he stared at the silent telephone.

Out there, in one of the most remote places on earth, events were already unfolding without them.

ϒ ϒ ϒ

Morning light filtered through the tall windows of Roger's rooms in Oxford, carrying with it the faint promise of warmth that had not yet arrived. The air inside, however, was charged, restless, electric, stretched thin by urgency.

Simon stood near the center of the room, an open laptop in his hands. The others gathered around him in varying states of agitation.

Roger leaned against the mantel, composed but alert, his eyes sharp beneath a furrowed brow. The absence of Fairfax hung in the room like an unanswered question.

Sabrina sat forward on the edge of her chair, hands clasped tightly, her gaze fixed on Simon. Drew paced once, then stopped, forcing himself still. Lauren stood apart, phone pressed to her ear, her voice cutting and relentless.

Simon cleared his throat slightly.

"I've just received an email from Chester Morris."

The room stilled.

He glanced down briefly, then began to read.

"Arrangements have been completed. A British warship currently in the South Atlantic, *HMS Sutherland*, has been redirected and is proceeding at maximum speed to Tristan da Cunha. Estimated arrival: 36 hours."

A flicker of relief passed through the group, but it was thin, fragile.

Simon continued.

"American authorities have been notified. The FBI has assigned top priority. The State Department is coordinating with the British Foreign Service."

Roger gave a small, approving nod. "Good. That escalated nicely."

Simon's expression tightened.

"There's more."

The room seemed to contract.

"There is a major storm over Tristan da Cunha. Communications are down, phone and internet, indefinitely."

Silence.

Not the quiet of calm, but the suffocating kind that follows bad news.

Lauren turned sharply away, her voice rising again into the phone.

"I don't care what your schedule looks like! We will pay double, no, triple if necessary, but I need your fastest vessel ready to depart Cape Town within twelve hours! This is not a negotiation, it's a requirement!"

She listened, her jaw tightening.

"Then make it happen."

She ended the call with a sharp motion.

Across the room, Drew stepped aside, speaking low into his phone.

"Yes… wheels up in two hours. No delays. Full fuel, full crew. We're not stopping."

A pause.

"No, this isn't flexible."

He hung up and exhaled slowly.

Roger had moved toward the window, his back partially turned as he spoke quietly into his phone.

"Yes… Yes, Eustance, I understand." He stopped himself, glancing briefly toward the others.

He ended the call.

One by one, the room settled as conversations concluded, phones lowered, and the immediacy of action gave way to the weight of what remained unknown.

Simon stepped forward, his voice steady, controlled, anchoring.

"Alright."

They turned to him instinctively.

"Let's bring this together."

He looked at each of them in turn.

"We now know three things. First, the British are moving. A day and a half until *Sutherland* reaches the island."

A nod toward Roger.

"Second, American law enforcement is fully engaged."

Then, more gravely:

"And third, we are completely blind; there is no way to communicate with the island authorities before the Sutherland arrives."

Lauren crossed her arms tightly.

"Then we don't wait."

Simon met her gaze.

"No. We don't."

"Our planet is ready. We leave in two hours. Direct route as far as possible, Cape Town first. From there, we coordinate with whatever transport Lauren secures."

Simon nodded.

"Good."

His eyes shifted.

"Lauren."

She lifted her chin, still simmering.

"I've got a yacht company in Cape Town scrambling. Fastest vessel they have. Crew on twelve-hour notice. They're resisting, but they'll fold. Money talks."

Simon inclined his head.

"Make sure they understand, speed over comfort."

"They already do. But it's so frustrating. The only way to get there is by boat, and it will take five days. Five days!"

Simon turned. "Damn! My God, you practically can't get to this place!"

"Roger, how about Fairfax? What's he doing?"

Roger held his gaze for a fraction too long.

"He'll be here in half an hour."

Simon didn't press, "Then we are as prepared as we can be."

He stepped closer to the center of the room, his voice gaining quiet intensity.

"We are going to one of the most isolated places on earth. In the middle of a storm. With no communication. And a 36 hour delay on the only official help we have coming."

He let that settle.

"No assumptions. No hesitation. We move fast, and we try to stay ahead of whatever Catherine has planned."

Lauren's expression hardened.

"Because she won't wait much longer."

Simon met her eyes.

And somewhere, far out in the South Atlantic, beyond the reach of signals and certainty, the storm was smashing against the tiny island.

ϒ ϒ ϒ

Catherine stood at the tall window, her fingers resting lightly against the glass as rain lashed against it in relentless sheets. The storm had deepened overnight, not merely rain now, but a full tropical fury. The wind howled like a living thing, bending the sparse vegetation of Tristan da Cunha nearly to the ground, hurling spray and debris through the air with indiscriminate force.

She did not flinch. Anger had passed. What remained was far more dangerous. Determination.

Her reflection hovered faintly in the glass, composed, elegant, entirely in control. There was no trace of the woman who had once lashed out in rage or surrendered to emotion. That woman had been inefficient. This version of Catherine was not.

She turned slowly from the window and crossed the room, her movements deliberate, economical. Three large leather valises lay open on the bed, already half-packed with carefully folded clothing, practical, understated, chosen not for beauty but for utility. Everything had a purpose now.

She did not concern herself with her own safety. That was almost an afterthought, an irrelevant variable in a much larger equation. Simon had not solved her puzzle. Of that, she was certain. The clues had been too elegant, too deliberately meaningless.

A puzzle without a pattern. A trail that led nowhere. No, he was still searching museums, still chasing shadows, still trying to impose logic where none existed.

Which meant she remained ahead. And yet…

Her jaw tightened almost imperceptibly. The storm had taken something from her.

Control.

She crossed to the small table where her laptop sat open, its screen dark, useless. No signal. No connection. No confirmation.

That was the irritation. Not fear, never fear. Uncertainty, yes.

There was still hope. Had Simon finally complied? Had he surrendered the Wolfson Prize? Had he publicly humiliated himself as she demanded? Or had he defied her?

Her fingers tapped once against the table, sharp and impatient.

Without the internet, without communication, she could not know. And worse, she could not act.

She could send no messages, no threats. No carefully timed

provocations. The game had paused, not by her choosing, but by the blind indifference of nature. She despised that.

Behind a closed door down the hall, silence reigned. Sabina slept.

Catherine's lips curved faintly, not quite a smile.

The medication had worked well.

Methaqualone, so unfashionable, so forgotten, and therefore so very easy to acquire. Dissolved in milk, it was nearly undetectable. A little more each day, carefully measured. Enough to keep the girl docile. Enough to ensure compliance.

Not enough to cause harm. Harm was yet to come.

She moved toward the door, pausing just outside Sabina's room. For a moment, she simply listened. Nothing. She opened the door softly.

The room was dim, the curtains drawn against the storm. Sabina lay small against the wide bed, her breathing slow and even, her face pale but peaceful in its artificial sleep. Sugar lay tucked under her arm, held loosely, as though even in unconsciousness she clung to something familiar.

Catherine stepped inside, closing the door quietly behind her.

She stood over the bed, looking down.

"So much trouble," she murmured softly. "For someone so small."

No response.

She reached into her pocket, withdrawing the small vial. The powder inside shifted faintly as she tilted it, catching what little light filtered through the room.

"Just a little longer," she said, almost absently. "Then this will all be over."

She returned the vial to her pocket. No need, yet.

Turning, she left the room, locking the door behind her with a soft, definitive click.

In the main room, the captain stood near the doorway, watching the storm through a narrow gap in the shutters. He was a broad-shouldered man, weathered, practical, less a villain than a tool, and Catherine preferred him that way.

He turned as she entered.

"Storm's worse," he said. "Island's taking a beating. But the boat will hold."

"The boat?" Catherine asked.

"Aye. Secured proper. As soon as this passes, we can move."

"How long?"

He shrugged slightly. "Day… maybe two. Hard to say. Island like this, weather does what it wants."

Catherine considered that. Forty-eight hours. An eternity.

"And no communication?" she asked, though she already knew the answer.

He shook his head. "Lines are down. Satellite responders are useless in this. We're cut off."

Cut off.

The words settled into her mind, not as a problem, but as a condition. Very well. Then the game would resume when the storm allowed it.

Until then, she would prepare.

"Everything will be ready," she said, more to herself than to him. "The moment this ends, you leave."

He nodded.

"And the girl?"

Catherine's gaze flicked toward the hallway, then back.

"Unconscious," she said coolly. "She will remain so."

The man shifted slightly but said nothing.

Catherine turned away, returning to her packing.

Dresses folded. Documents secured. Jewelry selected with care, not sentiment, but value. Portable wealth. Insurance against uncertainty.

Every movement precise. Every decision final.

Outside, the storm intensified, wind screaming against the structure, rain hammering the roof with unrelenting force.

Nature raged. But inside, Catherine waited. But like a coiled spring, held in perfect tension.

But somewhere far across the ocean, forces were already moving toward her, unseen, unknown, and very much not part of her design.

ϒ ϒ ϒ

Coats had been gathered. The long, anxious hours had drained them all, and what remained was that hollow, brittle exhaustion that comes when hope has been stretched too thin.

Simon stood near the window, staring out but seeing nothing. Sabrina lingered close to Lauren, unwilling to let her drift too far into herself. Drew hovered between them, restless, his hands opening and closing as though he needed something, anything, to *do*.

Roger moved toward the door, prepared to say something measured and reassuring, when,

The door burst open.

Professor Eustace Fairfax stormed in.

He looked as though he had been assembled hastily from irritation itself, coat half-buttoned, hair slightly disordered, spectacles crooked on his nose. His cheeks were flushed, whether from travel or indignation was unclear.

Everyone froze.

Roger blinked. "Eustace, "

Fairfax waved a hand dismissively as he pushed past them into the room, "If I never set foot in that god-forsaken place again, it will be too soon. A damp, obstinate, thoroughly irascible country. The roads alone try to kill you. I'm serious; they do!"

Despite everything, there was the faintest flicker of humor in the room.

Fairfax dropped heavily into a chair, adjusting himself with irritated precision, as though the furniture itself had wronged him.

Only then did the room exhale.

They gathered around him, drawn by the urgency beneath his bluster.

Simon stepped forward first, his voice tight with something between hope and disbelief.

"You've been to see Emryn, haven't you?"

Fairfax looked at him as if he'd just asked whether the sun had risen.

"Yes, Simon, I have been to see Emryn. Who else, pray tell, would compel me to travel to that prehistoric corner of the world? A sightseeing tour?"

Simon almost smiled, but it vanished quickly.

"What did he say?"

Fairfax didn't answer immediately. Instead, he turned. Slowly. Deliberately. His sharp, impatient eyes fixed on Lauren. The room shifted. Something in his expression, something newly serious, cut through the lingering tension like a blade.

"Lauren," he said, his voice suddenly stripped of all irritation, "I need you to think very carefully."

She stiffened.

"Yes?"

"When Sabina was taken… did she have the ring with her?"

The question landed like a stone dropped into still water. Everyone turned to Lauren. Her breath caught. For a moment, it seemed she might not be able to answer.

"The ring," she whispered.

Fairfax didn't blink. "The Soulfast ring. The one Sabrina gave her."

Lauren's eyes flickered to Sabrina, then back to Fairfax. Her hands trembled slightly as she clasped them together.

"Yes," she said, her voice fragile but certain. "She wore it on a chain. Around her neck. Like a necklace."

She swallowed.

"She never took it off. Not for anything."

Silence. Fairfax closed his eyes. Just for a moment. And in that brief, unguarded instant, something extraordinary happened. Relief.

Not subtle. Not concealed. Relief washed over his face like a man reprieved from a sentence he had already begun to accept.

Drew leaned forward sharply. "Why does that matter? What did Emryn say?"

Fairfax opened his eyes again, and the irritation returned, but thinner now, less certain.

"Oh, for heaven's sake," he muttered. "You all know perfectly well that Emryn never says anything plainly. The man communicates as though clarity were a personal failing."

Roger allowed himself a faint smile. "And yet?"

Fairfax exhaled, leaning back in his chair.

"And yet," he said, "on this occasion, he was, miraculously, concise."

The room tightened again. Fairfax looked once more at Lauren, but this time his gaze was steadier. Reassuring, even.

"He said only this."

A pause. Long enough for every heartbeat in the room to become audible.

"Mother Nature always protects the ringbearer."

The words hung there.

Lauren's breath hitched. Sabrina reached for her hand and held it tightly.

Drew frowned, trying to force logic into something that clearly refused to be logical. "That's it? That's all he said?"

"Yes," Fairfax replied, with a trace of impatience. "That is all he *needed* to say."

Simon hadn't moved. Something had shifted in him. Not certainty, no, not that, but something close to it. A thread of belief where there had been only darkness before.

"Protected…" he murmured.

Fairfax nodded once. "Emryn does not deal in guarantees. But when he speaks in absolutes, one would be wise to listen."

Lauren closed her eyes, tears slipping free at last, but they were different now. Not despair. Something else. Something fragile. Something dangerous.

Hope.

Chapter Thirty

The Final Measure

The storm did not end so much as withdraw.

For two days, it had ruled the island, howling through the palms, flattening the grasses, tearing at roofs and shutters as though determined to strip the place down to its bones. Rain had fallen in blinding sheets, turning paths to rivers and sky to a single, roaring presence.

And then, without ceremony, it was gone. What remained was silence.

Not the gentle quiet of a calm evening, but something deeper, emptier. The air felt newly made, rinsed of heat and dust, carrying the sharp scent of salt, wet wood, and torn vegetation. Water still dripped from the eaves of the buildings and ran in thin rivulets down toward the shore, but even those sounds seemed tentative, as if unsure they were permitted to exist again.

Above, the stars returned in force.

They appeared not gradually but all at once, thousands upon thousands scattered across the black vault of sky, cold and distant and utterly unconcerned with what had just taken place below. The moon had already slipped beneath the horizon, leaving the island in a darkness that was clean and absolute.

It was the kind of night in which things could be done. Unseen. Unrecorded. Forgotten.

Out along the narrow wooden pier, three men dressed entirely in black moved with deliberate purpose. They spoke little. Each knew his role. Each understood the urgency.

The pier itself creaked softly under their weight, its planks still damp from the storm, glistening faintly in the starlight. Small waves lapped against its supports with a hollow, rhythmic sound, as though the sea itself were breathing again after its exertion.

Moored at the far end was the boat. It did not belong to the island. It did not belong anywhere, really.

Low and elongated, its lines were sleek and aggressive, a fusion of a high-performance cigarette boat and a luxury yacht stripped of anything that might slow it down. Its hull was finished in a deep, light-absorbing black that rendered it almost invisible except where the faintest reflections traced its edges. Even at rest, it suggested motion. Escape.

Beneath its long, tapering bow was a narrow sleeping compartment, accessible through a low hatch. Inside, a series of thin mattresses had been laid side by side, covered in rough fabric already damp with humidity. There were no comforts, no proper bunks, no lighting beyond a single battery lamp, no space for anything beyond bodies laid down out of necessity.

It was not a place for sleep. It was a place to endure.

On the deck, the men worked. Large, dented, and heavy fuel cans were lifted from a small cart and carried aboard one by one. Each was handled carefully, though without hesitation. Metal scraped against wood. Caps were checked, tightened, checked again.

The smell of gasoline spread quickly, sharp and invasive, cutting through the cleaner scents left behind by the storm.

One man secured the cans beneath a hidden compartment along the midsection of the boat, lifting a panel that revealed a space clearly designed for cargo, meant to remain unseen. He stacked them tightly, maximizing every inch, then sealed the compartment with practiced efficiency. Another man moved between the cart and the deck, his pace steady but his shoulders tense.

The third man, the captain, stood slightly apart. He did not carry anything. He observed. His gaze moved from the boat to the horizon, then back again, as though measuring time not by a watch but by instinct.

"We leave in thirty minutes," he said at last, his breath frosted by the cold.

His voice was calm, controlled, and entirely without doubt. The older of the two working men grunted in acknowledgment without pausing. The younger one did stop.

He straightened slowly, one hand still resting on the rim of a fuel can, his breathing just a fraction too quick.

"Thirty?" he repeated. "That's… soon."

The captain did not look at him immediately.

"It is exactly as planned."

The younger man hesitated, then forced himself to continue working, lifting the can and carrying it toward the boat. But his movements had changed, less fluid now, more deliberate, as if each action required conscious effort.

When he returned for the next container, he spoke again.

"You're certain about the route?"

The captain turned his head slightly.

"We go south."

"To Cape Town."

"Yes."

The younger man set the can down a little too hard. The dull clang echoed across the water.

"That's a long run," he said. "With this weight, "

"We have calculated the fuel."

"And if something goes wrong?"

The captain's eyes settled on him fully now.

"What do you propose we do instead?"

The question hung in the air.

The younger man opened his mouth, then closed it again.

There was no answer.

Behind him, the older man exhaled sharply through his nose.

“Stop asking,” he muttered. “It’s done.”

But the younger man could not stop.

His gaze drifted, almost involuntarily, toward the stern of the boat.

Partially concealed beneath a heavy tarp was something that did not belong with the rest of the equipment. A length of chain. Thick. Industrial. Its dark metal links caught what little starlight there was, giving off a dull, cold sheen.

At its end lay an iron anchor, far larger than anything the boat would require to secure itself. It was old, its surface pitted and scarred, as though it had already served its purpose many times before.

The younger man stared at it.

“That,” he said quietly, “wasn’t part of the original plan.”

The captain followed his gaze.

“It is now.”

The man swallowed.

“You’re sure… it will work?”

The captain stepped closer, his boots sounding softly against the damp wood of the pier.

“It will not fail.”

“But, ”

“There will be no trace,” the captain said, his voice dropping just enough to remove any possibility of argument. “Not for them. Not for anyone.”

A long silence followed. The sea lapped gently beneath them. The younger man nodded. Not because he was convinced. But because he understood.

He turned back to the task. The final cans were loaded. The compartments were sealed. The deck cleared. Everything was in place.

The captain looked once more at the boat, taking in every detail, the lines of the hull, the distribution of weight, the position of the equipment. Satisfied, he stepped back.

"Finish here," he said. "I'll return shortly."

Neither man responded. It was not required.

He turned and walked the length of the pier, his pace unhurried, his posture relaxed. There was no sense of urgency in him now. Everything that needed to be done was already set in motion.

At the shore, the ground shifted from wood to gravel. The sound of his boots changed, soft creaks giving way to the crisp crunch of stone.

Ahead stood the tiny port authority building. A shack. It was functional and unremarkable, its paint faded by sun and salt. A single flagpole stood beside it, the flag hanging limp and dark in the still air. No light showed in the windows. No movement stirred inside. The storm had emptied the place for days. And it was not manned at night anyway. The captain passed it without slowing. He did not look at it. He did not need to.

Beyond, partially concealed by a stand of wind-bent trees, a white jeep waited. Its engine idled quietly, the low vibration barely audible but somehow intrusive in the otherwise perfect stillness.

The driver sat behind the wheel, a shadow within a shadow. The captain opened the door and climbed in.

"Half an hour," he said.

The driver nodded once. Nothing more was required. The jeep turned slowly, its tires pressing into the damp earth, then began the gradual climb back toward the house. As they moved, the captain glanced back. The pier stretched out into the darkness. At its end, the boat sat low in the water, ready.

Prepared. Silent. Fuel loaded. Course set.

And beneath the tarp, the chain and anchor. The final certainty that what would be placed in the water would not remain long enough to be discovered.

By the time the sun rose, the island would look untouched, as though nothing had ever happened there. As though no one had ever been there at all.

ϒ ϒ ϒ

Catherine moved quickly from room to room, her pace sharp, purposeful, almost frantic, though she would never have admitted it. Drawers opened and shut with crisp finality. Cases lay open across the bed, garments folded with mechanical precision and placed inside as though they were pieces on a board rather than possessions accumulated over a life.

She packed only what mattered. Which, in her estimation, was very little.

The house, once a place of calculated elegance, now felt hollow, stripped of warmth and meaning. Only a few lights burned, leaving large portions of each room swallowed in shadow. The result was unsettling. Corners seemed deeper than they should be. Hallways stretched longer. Familiar furnishings took on unfamiliar shapes.

It no longer felt like a refuge. It felt like something abandoned. She snapped a case shut and stood still for a moment, listening.

Nothing. No wind now. No rain. Only the faint, distant hush of the sea. It was time.

Catherine turned and moved down the hall, her heels striking softly against the polished floor, the sound echoing just enough to remind her how empty the house had become.

She reached the door to Sabina's room and paused, only for a second. Then she opened it. The room was dim, lit by a single lamp that cast a warm but insufficient glow. Shadows gathered along the walls, creeping up the corners like something alive. On the bed, the child lay exactly as she should. Still. Peaceful. Unaware.

Sabina's small chest rose and fell in a slow, steady rhythm, the faintest whisper of breath marking the passage of time. One arm was curled beneath her cheek, the other resting loosely at her side. Beside her, Sugar, the tiny white fluff of a dog, was nestled against the child's shoulder, its small body rising and falling in synchrony, as though guarding her even in sleep.

Catherine stood in the doorway. Watching. Her expression did not change, but something, some fleeting, unwelcome flicker, passed behind her eyes. She frowned. Then, with a slight shake of her head, she dismissed it entirely.

"Sentiment," she murmured under her breath, almost with contempt.

She turned away and closed the door quietly behind her. The moment was over. It had never existed.

Down the hall, movement approached. The captain. He was a large man, his presence filling the space before him as he walked. Water still clung faintly to his coat from the earlier storm, and his boots left subtle marks along the floor, small intrusions into Catherine's carefully maintained order. He did not apologize for them. He stopped a few paces from her.

"Everything is ready," he said.

Catherine did not look at him immediately. She adjusted the clasp on one of her cases, ensuring it was perfectly aligned, before finally turning her gaze toward him.

"We leave in half an hour."

"I'm aware of the schedule," she replied coolly.

The captain inclined his head slightly.

"I've confirmed the money transfer," he continued. "Funds are in place."

That earned him her attention.

"Good."

The word was clipped, efficient.

Satisfied. Silence followed. The kind that did not invite conversation.

But the captain did not leave. He remained where he stood, his posture steady, his expression unchanged.

After a moment, Catherine's eyes narrowed slightly.

"Yes?" she said.

There was the faintest hesitation, so slight it might have been imagined.

"How would you like the task handled?"

The question hung between them.

Catherine did not hesitate.

“I don’t care.”

Her voice was immediate, dismissive.

“I don’t want to know the details. I don’t want to hear about it before, during, or after.”

She stepped closer, her gaze hardening.

“And I never want to see you again.”

The captain held her stare. There was no offense in his expression. No reaction at all. Only acknowledgment.

“Nor I you.”

He turned slightly, as though to go, when another presence entered the space. The butler. He had been with Catherine long enough to understand the rhythms of her moods, the cadence of her decisions. He moved quietly, respectfully, but not without purpose. His posture was impeccable, his expression composed, though there was something in his eyes, something searching.

He came to stand beside them.

“Madam,” he said.

Catherine did not turn.

“Yes?”

“The child,” he said carefully. “Is she ready?”

The question was simple. Too simple. For the first time that night,

Catherine paused. Not outwardly. Not in any way that would be obvious to anyone who did not know her. But it was there.

A fraction of a second. A flicker. Something uninvited was pressing against the walls she had so carefully constructed. Her mind, so quick and decisive in all things, offered her, unbidden, a single image:

The child, asleep. The small rise and fall of her breath. The absurd little dog pressed protectively against her.

Catherine’s jaw tightened. The moment passed. Her face hardened, every line returning to its proper place.

"Yes," she said.

The word was firm. Final.

The butler inclined his head.

"Very good, madam."

He stepped back.

The captain said nothing.

Neither did Catherine.

For a moment, the three of them stood in the dimly lit hallway, suspended in a silence that felt heavier than the storm that had come before.

Then Catherine turned away.

"See that everything is brought down," she said, already moving toward the stairs. "We are not delaying for anything."

"Yes, madam," the butler replied.

Behind her, the captain watched. Then, without another word, he turned and walked back down the hall, toward the closed door.

The butler moved to pick up the sleeping child. And toward the task Catherine had chosen not to see.

Minutes later, Catherine stood at a window. She could see the pier clearly, just by the light of the stars. She cracked the window and heard the boat leave, slowly and quietly.

Chapter Thirty-one

Nature's Choice

Outside in the city of Cape Town, the light shifted, clouds breaking just enough to give hope that their boat could finally leave. The storm in the Atlantic had kept them from leaving for Tristan da Cunha for two days. It had been barely possible to remain sane.

Inside their hotel, for the first time in days, the air felt different for everyone.

At that moment, Simon's phone pinged, sharp, insistent, unmistakably urgent.

Every head turned.

He snatched it up, already feeling the weight of what it might contain, and opened the message. His eyes moved quickly, then slowed… then fixed.

"It's from Chester," he said, his voice tightening.

"Read it," Roger urged.

Simon swallowed and began:

"*Urgent. Simon, the* Sutherland *is on scene at Tristan da Cunha. The captain reports that two boats left the island six hours ago. After intense questioning of a butler at the house Catherine occupied, they learned that one vessel carried the girl and headed for Cape Town, South Africa.*"

Lauren's hand flew to her mouth.

Simon pressed on.

"The men on that boat had been paid to dispose of the girl."

The words seemed to drain the air from the room.

"The second vessel, a yacht, headed west to an unknown port. The Sutherland is currently pursuing the boat carrying the child. They suggest you stay in Cape Town and wait there. I'll send updates as I receive them."

Silence followed, stunned, suffocating.

Then Lauren collapsed into a chair as though her legs had given way. A raw, broken sound escaped her, and she buried her face in her hands, sobbing uncontrollably.

"No… no… no…"

Drew was beside her instantly, dropping to one knee, pulling her into him.

"We're too late," she said, though her voice trembled. "We are too late."

The room teetered on the edge of collapse until Simon spoke. Not loudly. Not forcefully. But with a quiet authority that cut clean through the chaos.

"Mother Nature always protects the ringbearer."

The words fell into the room like a stone into still water.

Everything stopped. Lauren's sobbing faltered. Drew looked up. Sabrina went still. Even Simon turned. And slowly, very slowly, something shifted. Lauren lowered her hands. Her breathing steadied. The tears did not stop, but they changed. They were no longer caused only by despair. Hope, fragile, improbable, but undeniable, found its way back into her eyes.

ϒ ϒ ϒ

Far out in the deep ocean, where no land offers protection, and no human eye can fully grasp the scale of things, there exists a phenomenon long dismissed as myth.

Rogue waves.

They are not storms, nor are they tsunamis born of seismic upheaval. They rise from the sea itself, sudden, unannounced, and terrifyingly real.

A rogue wave can tower to heights of eighty, even one hundred feet, often twice as tall as the surrounding swells. Sailors who survive them speak of a vertical wall of water, steep-sided and dark, as though the ocean had momentarily decided to stand upright.

It simply strikes. No warning. No pattern. No mercy.

ϒ ϒ ϒ

The sleek craft tore across the open water, its engines screaming as it left the last faint suggestion of land far behind. The horizon had long since dissolved into an unbroken circle of gray-blue emptiness.

On deck, the older man braced himself against the rail, his coat snapping violently in the wind. He turned toward the captain, his voice raised over the roar.

“When do you want to take care of the business?”

The captain didn’t look at him. His eyes remained fixed ahead, hard and calculating.

“When we’re far enough out,” he said. “Far enough that nothing comes back.”

The older man frowned. “You think it could?”

The captain gave a short, humorless laugh. “Weighted or not, the sea has its own ideas. Currents shift. Things rise. Things travel.” He finally glanced over. “I don’t take chances. One more day, I think.”

Below deck, the world was different. Muted. Contained.

The young sailor sat on the floor beside the narrow berth where the child lay, her breathing slow, unnaturally deep. The small white pup nestled against her side, occasionally lifting its head to nuzzle her hand before settling again.

The sailor smiled faintly, scratching the dog behind its ears.

“You’re a loyal one, aren’t you?” he murmured.

The engines hummed above them, a constant, reassuring vibration.

The sea was choppy, waves rising to six feet, their crests snapping white in the sunlight. But the boat was built for this, its hull slicing cleanly through the water, engines steady, confident.

Above them, the sky was flawless—a hard, perfect blue. The storm had scoured it clean, leaving no trace of what had come before.

On deck, the men had begun to relax. Laughter returned in fragments. Muscles loosened. The long days ahead felt manageable.

Then,

Something changed.

It did not happen all at once. It crept in. The air thickened. Not warmer. Not colder.

Just… heavier.

The wind died. Not faded, died.

The sails slackened. The engine noise seemed suddenly too loud, intrusive, unnatural. The sea, which had moments ago been alive with motion, seemed to hesitate.

And yet, the waves began to grow. Slowly at first. Then unmistakably.

On deck, the captain froze. Every instinct he had, every mile he had ever sailed, rose at once.

This was wrong. Violently wrong. The ocean did not behave like this.

The air pressed in around them, dense and breathless. Sound dulled. The world felt… suspended.

"What the hell, " the older man began.

Then he saw it. To starboard. At first, his mind refused it.

It was not a wave. It could not be. It looked like the sea itself was standing up.

A vast, black mass lifting from the water, sheer, smooth, vertical. Not rising like a wave, but *forming*, as if something beneath the ocean were pushing upward, shaping it, forcing it into being. A wall. A cliff.

And it kept rising. Higher. It blotted out the horizon, then the sky.

The captain moved before he thought.

"Turn her!" he roared, already wrenching the wheel with a violence that tore the spokes beneath his grip. "Head into it! Now! NOW!"

The engines screamed, pushed beyond reason. The bow swung, too slow. Far too slow.

The sea surged beneath them, lifting the boat as if it weighed nothing. The incline rose sharply, unnaturally sharply, until the deck pitched at an impossible angle. The men dropped to their hands and knees. Fingers clawed for purchase.

Boots slipped. The sky vanished. There was only water.

The boat climbed. And climbed.

The engine howled in protest. The hull shuddered violently, every joint groaning, every bolt straining as if the vessel itself understood it had gone somewhere it did not belong.

For one impossible moment, they neared the top—a suspended instant.

Then there was silence as though the ocean were deciding.

Then gravity returned.

Brutal. Immediate. Absolute.

The boat shuddered. And began to slide backward.

"No!" the captain screamed, fighting the wheel, fighting the laws of the world itself.

The stern lifted high into the air.

The vessel twisted sideways. The water mountain broke.

Like a collapse.

It came down with annihilating force, a crushing, roaring mass that obliterated sound, light, direction, everything.

The impact was beyond noise. It was a physical blow to the world.

Wood cracked. Metal shrieked. The air vanished from the lungs.

The two men on deck were torn away instantly, snatched, erased, flung into the boiling blackness as if they had never been there at all.

The sea swallowed them without acknowledgment.

The boat disappeared beneath the collapse, hurled downward into a churning void of white and black, spinning, tumbling, direction meaningless.

Below deck, the young sailor was thrown violently across the cabin, his body slamming into the bulkhead with a sickening crack. Pain exploded through him, but he could not even cry out; the air had been driven from his chest.

The pup shrieked, scrambling wildly, claws scraping uselessly against the slick floor.

The lantern shattered. Darkness surged in. And the child, the child did not move.

She lay still. Wrapped in her blanket

As if untouched. As if held.

The boat flipped. Once. Twice. Again.

End over end, swallowed in a chaos so complete it erased all sense of up or down, life or death.

Time stretched. Or vanished. Then, finally, released.

As sudden as the violence had come, it let go.

The boat surged upward, bursting through the surface in a violent gasp of air and spray. It rolled hard, water pouring from every seam, every edge,

And impossibly, it righted itself.

The hull groaned, a long, wounded sound. But it floated. It lived.

Around it, the ocean lay flat. Still.

The sky shone, blue and endless, as if the world had never been broken.

No sign of the wave. No sign of the men.

No sign that anything had happened at all.

Only the faint, unnatural silence remained.

Below deck, the young sailor dragged in a ragged breath, trembling, barely conscious. The small white pup pressed against him, whining softly.

And the child still slept. Untroubled. Untouched.

As if whatever had risen from the deep had seen her,

And chosen to protect her.

Chapter Thirty-two

That Which Was Lost

South Africa's primary naval base lay some forty kilometers south of Cape Town on the curve of False Bay, a place where history and strategy had long ago learned to inhabit the same shore. It was the largest facility of the South African Navy, home to its frigate and submarine flotillas, with its dockyard, fortified harbor, and sprawling infrastructure of piers. Uniformed officers moved with clipped efficiency across the tarmac and along the quays, while beyond them the waters of False Bay shone in hard, glittering bands of blue and silver.

But Simon, Sabrina, Drew, and Lauren saw almost none of it.

They stood together near the harbor's edge on the broad expanse of sun-struck tarmac, every nerve turned toward the open water. Behind them, a South African admiral in immaculate white stood in courteous attendance with several senior officers, all of them grave, respectful, and wisely silent. They understood that what was about to happen transcended protocol. Somewhere not far off, beyond the sweep of the bay and beyond the last formal stages of naval coordination, a child was coming home.

HMS *Sutherland* had located the boat with young Sabina a day earlier. Ever since, time had seemed to move with unbearable slowness. A seaplane had been dispatched to rendezvous with the ship. Those practicalities had been necessary, but for Lauren, they had been agony. She stood slightly ahead of the others, her hands clenched and unclenched at her sides, her eyes fixed on the mouth of the bay with such intensity that she seemed afraid that if she blinked, the vision she longed for might disappear.

Drew remained close beside her, though he knew better than to speak too much. Every so often, he glanced toward her, as though checking that she was still standing, still breathing. Simon and Sabrina stood just behind them. Sabrina's face was taut with emotion, her hands pressed together before her as though in unconscious prayer. Simon, normally the one most capable of turning thought into action, wore now the fragile expression of a man who had passed through fear into gratitude and had not yet found the language for either.

At first, the approaching craft was only a bright disturbance in the distance, a white fleck flashing in the sunlight. Then its form sharpened: a boat plane skimming low across the bay, its pontoons hissing over the surface, throwing up twin fans of water in its wake. It came on fast and beautifully, riding the bright skin of the harbor. As it angled toward the dock area, the sunlight struck its windows, briefly turning them into mirrors. The engine noise rolled over the water in a hard metallic swell.

The aircraft slowed as it neared the pier, its wake fanning outward in broken ripples that slapped against the pilings and sent gulls wheeling noisily into the air. The pilot handled the final approach with expert care, bringing the craft alongside the dock with a series of measured corrections. Before it had fully settled, three sailors in working rig came running down the pier with lines in hand. Their movements were swift and practiced. One leaped lightly to a mooring point, another crouched to secure the forward line, and the third called something sharp and technical that was lost beneath the engine's dying roar. Within moments, the boat plane was fast to the pier, rocking gently as though relieved to have reached stillness.

Lauren could bear no more.

She bolted toward the plane's hatch before it had even opened. Drew went after her at once, and Simon and Sabrina followed a few paces behind, not wanting to restrain her, not wanting to crowd the instant, but needing to be there. The cabin door swung open.

Two airmen emerged first, descending carefully and efficiently, one stepping onto the gangplank while the other checked the handrail and fastening points. Even in that moment of desperate emotion, procedure held. One gave a brief nod to the officers on the dock, then turned back toward the craft's interior. For a heartbeat, no one else appeared.

Lauren stopped dead at the foot of the gangplank, her whole body rigid with suspense.

Then two more airmen came into view, escorting a small figure between them.

Sabina.

The little girl stepped out into the light, dark hair tumbling about her face, her expression dazed for the merest instant by the brightness and the crowd. Then she saw them.

Her smile broke over her face like sunrise.

It was gloriously bright, pure, and immediate. Any remaining distance between certainty and hope vanished at once. She was alive. She was smiling. She was here.

Lauren let out a half-sob, half-laugh and surged forward. All restraint vanished. She snatched Sabina up into her arms with such desperate gratitude that the child emitted a tiny surprised frown, squeezed by the sheer force of her mother's embrace. Lauren held her as if she would never, ever release her again, burying her face in her daughter's hair. Tears streamed down Lauren's face unchecked, but she was smiling through the tears with the bright radiance of someone who had been handed back her own life.

Caught between them, poor Sugar gave a faint protesting squeak.

Lauren jerked back in alarm and then laughed, a breathless, shattered laugh, and loosened her hold just enough to rescue the tiny white fluff of a dog from the crush. Sugar, somewhat flattened in dignity though not in spirit, wriggled free into the crook of Sabina's arm and blinked indignantly at the assembled world. That tiny comic note, so absurd and so ordinary, broke the last of the tension. Drew wrapped his arms around Lauren, Sabina, and even Sugar.

Lauren looked at Sabina again as though she could not stop looking, as though each second required fresh proof. "Oh, my darling," she whispered. "Oh, my darling girl."

Sabina, puzzled by so much emotion yet happy to be the center of it, reached up and patted Lauren's face with one small hand. "Mama," she said, as though that word were explanation enough for everything. "This is Sugar," she said with a big grin.

"Oh my," Drew said softly, "Such a sweet puppy!"

Once again, he gathered both child and mother into his embrace. Lauren leaned into him without taking her eyes from Sabina. For a moment, the three of them stood as a single figure against the bright harbor, bound together by relief so profound it seemed to hush even the gulls and the wind.

Simon and Sabrina approached next. Sabrina was openly weeping now, though her smile was luminous. She touched Sabina's shoulder, then Lauren's arm, then Drew's, as if assuring herself that all of them were truly here. Simon, usually so self-possessed, bent and kissed Sabina lightly on the top of her head. The child grinned at him, and he laughed under his breath, the sound edged with disbelief and gratitude.

Behind them, the admiral and his officers kept a respectful distance. They understood that the reunion belonged not to the state but to the heart. Still, the admiral's stern face softened at the sight, and one of the younger officers looked discreetly away, granting the family the privacy of not being watched too closely in their joy.

Lauren at last drew back enough to look at Sabina truly. "Are you all right, sweetheart?" she asked, though her voice trembled so badly the words nearly fell apart.

Sabina nodded contentedly, then lifted Sugar a little as if in evidence. "Sugar is too."

A medical officer approached quietly then, pausing a few feet away until Simon acknowledged him. He spoke with tact, explaining that the child had already been examined aboard the transfer craft and appeared in good condition. However, they recommended a fuller assessment once everyone was settled.

There would be time soon for procedures, statements, debriefings, official gratitude, and even planning. Time, too, for consequences. Time to reckon with Catherine, with those who had aided her, with the damage done and the justice still required.

And so they stood together on the tarmac of the great naval harbor, beneath the South African sun and before the patient witness of sea and ships, holding the child who had been lost and was now found. Around them, the officers gave space, the sailors went about their duties in softened silence, and Cape of Good Hope glittered like beaten silver beyond the pier. In Lauren's arms, Sabina rested secure at last, Sugar tucked between them like a ridiculous and beloved scrap of white cloud. Lauren's tears still fell, but they fell now from relief, not despair.

Luaren gently lifted the gold chain around Sabina's neck. The ring popped out. The silvery writing that laced its surface was now glowing brightly.

Quod non erat, fit

That which wasn't, becomes.

Epilogue

Six Months Later

An antiquated Argentine fishing boat chugged steadily through the gray-blue water about five miles off Mar del Plata. The *Sirena del Sur*, a weathered *lancha amarilla*, bore the unmistakable yellow-orange paint that had long defined the working boats of the port. Her hull creaked with age, her engine coughed and settled, and her crew, five men hardened by salt and years, worked the nets with the rhythm of habit.

The morning was still young. The catch, so far, was disappointing.

Still, the men talked.

Always, they talked.

"Eh, Ramón," one called, laughing as he hauled at the line, "if this keeps up, we go home with empty pockets, sí?"

Ramón grinned, shaking his head. "No, no… we stay, hermano. The fish, they come. Always they come when you no expect, eh?"

Another chimed in, voice thick with accent and humor. "You say that yesterday too. And what we get? Fifteen sad fish and one boot!"

Laughter broke across the deck, easy and familiar.

At the winch, the youngest of them wiped his hands on his trousers and shouted back, "And the boot not fit, eh?"

More laughter.

Then, the crane jerked. The grinding metallic groan cut through the air as the net strained mid-lift. The winch shuddered, halted for a heartbeat… then resumed, slower now, laboring under a sudden, unexpected weight.

The laughter died instantly.

"Eh… what is this?" the young man at the winch muttered, tightening his grip. "Is stuck… or something heavy, muy pesado."

The others turned, their expressions sharpening.

From the ragged wheelhouse, the captain stepped out, pulling his coat tighter against the wind. His face was lined, eyes narrowed from years of sun and suspicion.

"What happen here?" he called, his voice calm but edged. "Why we stop?"

One of the crew looked up at him, shrugging uneasily. "Capitán… the net, she catch something. Not fish… something else."

The captain frowned, stepping closer. "Then bring it up. Slowly. We see what the sea give us today."

The men gathered at the stern, instinctively forming a half-circle around the rising net. Only the winch operator remained at his post, jaw set, coaxing the mechanism along as it strained and groaned.

The net broke the surface.

Water streamed off it in sheets.

For a moment, nothing was clear, just tangled rope and dripping shapes, then something solid emerged.

"Madre de Dios…" one man whispered.

It was not a fish.

An eight-foot slab of fiberglass came into view, pale and unnatural against the sea. Jagged edges. Torn clean from something much larger.

"A boat…" another said softly. "Piece of a boat."

"Más grande que this," Ramón added, stepping forward. "Much bigger."

With effort, they dragged it over the rail and onto the deck. It landed with a hollow thud, slick with seawater, its surface scarred and splintered.

They circled it, studying.

"Look," one said, crouching. "This… from a yacht, no? You see, finish?"

"Sí… not fishing boat," another agreed. "Too clean. Too… rich."

One of the older men crossed himself slowly. "Que Dios tenga misericordia… God have mercy on whoever is on this boat."

The others fell quiet for a moment.

The sea stretched endlessly around them. Indifferent.

Another man ran his hand along the surface, frowning. "Strange color, no? Not white… not blue…"

He leaned closer.

"Verde… like mist. Like sea ghost."

"Sí," Ramón nodded. "…green mist. Nunca see boat with this color before."

The captain stepped forward, placing a hand on the wreckage as though feeling for some story it might tell. His eyes moved over it, thoughtful, unsurprised.

"Many boats go down here," he said quietly, his accent thick, his tone steady. "South Atlantic… she is not kind. She takes what she wants."

He looked out over the water for a long moment.

Then back to the men.

"Madre Naturalezla… she is cruel," he said. "Especially to those who do not respect her."

The men nodded. No one argued.

There was nothing more to say.

With a grunt, two of them lifted the fragment and carried it to the rail.

"One, two, "

They heaved it back into the indifferent depths of the sea.

Terrance Glasscock is a passionate student of ancient history and an ardent admirer of romantic historical fiction. His academic background and lifelong personal studies reflect a deep and continuing exploration of world history, with particular focus on medieval Europe, ancient Egypt, Greece, and the Roman Empire.

His novels weave together romance, adventure, global travel, and mystical connections to the past. His stories provide a tapestry where history and imagination intersect.

Terrance lives with his wife in historic Charleston, South Carolina, and welcomes hearing from his readers.

website: www.terranceglasscockbooks.com

email: terranceglass@aol.com

Terrance Glasscock

www.ingramcontent.com/pod-product-compliance
Lightning Source LLC
LaVergne TN
LVHW030908080826
845145LV00010B/2811

* 9 7 8 1 6 0 7 8 9 3 8 3 7 *